Just trying to do the right thing, he never could have predicted what would happen…

He got the nine-one-one operator immediately.

"This is Sandra. Who am I speaking with?"

The crisp, friendly voice reached out to him in this desolate place like a lifeline. He gave his name, described the van and the injured girl.

"And what is your location, sir?"

"Off the Interstate just before…" He couldn't remember the town. "At the intersection of County Highway…" Cursing his nearsightedness, he told her he couldn't see the sign without his glasses.

She was patient. "How about a landmark? Any buildings you can see?" There weren't any buildings.

In the distance, the whine of a truck engine was carried through the still air. "Hold on, I think someone's coming." He had sprinted into the road waving both arms like a wild man.

The truck had slowed as it approached him but, instead of stopping, kept moving past him. "Stop! Help! Please help!" The driver, an old man in a battered Stetson, stared at him with hostile eyes through the dusty window. "Emergency! Damn it, stop!"

But the truck crossed the intersection and rattled away down the road as if the driver were afraid of a holdup.

"Bastard!" Then he had realized he still had nine-one-one on the phone. "He just went right past me. God, this is unreal!"

"Okay," the calm voice had said, "do this for me, Mr. Carreras. Walk back up to the exit ramp and give me the exit number."

"But the girl. I thought I detected a weak pulse and—"

Sandra was the soul of patience. "I've got the paramedics on board and ready to go. The faster they get there, the faster they can help her. I just need your exact location, Mr. Carreras."

"Wait! I hear sirens! They're here!"

Two patrol cars, sirens blasting, came racing down the ramp from the Interstate.

"They are?" The question hung in the air like the tornado of yellow dust as the patrol cars pulled to a screeching stop beside the van.

It all went south from there.

Los Angeles attorney, Alex Carreras, has it all—a position with a prestigious law firm, an engagement to the boss's daughter, and a budding political career—until the night he stops to help a murdered girl in a battered Chevy van. Now he's a suspect. The cops are saying he knew her. He didn't, but, in order to clear his name, he must get to know the victim—and everyone *she* knew—very well.

Alex is clearly being set up, but by whom and for what reason? Most of the investigators on the case just want to close it and move on, but Detective Murray Schmitz believes there's more to story than meets the eye. And she not only has the ability to track down the real killer, she has the desire. Both Alex and Murray want to find the truth, no matter the consequences. But while it can clear Alex's name and cement Murray's reputation in her department, it can also lead them both to the same end as the girl in the van…

KUDOS for *Poseidon's Eye*

In *Poseidon's Eye* by Trisha O'Keefe, Alex Carreras is an attorney on the run. Falsely accused of a murder he didn't commit, he decides he has a better chance of clearing his name if he is not in jail. One of the cops on the case, Murray Schmitz, isn't convinced he's guilty, and she decides to go undercover to see if she can both find Alex and prove his innocence or guilt, one way or the other. But the forces at work are more than either Alex or Murray is prepared to take on, and they will both be lucky to walk away with their lives. A chilling mystery, filled with intriguing characters and numerous twists and turns, this one will be hard to put down. ~ *Taylor Jones, The Review Team of Taylor Jones & Regan Murphy*

Poseidon's Eye is the story of racial prejudice, greed, and corruption. Alex Carreras is an LA attorney. A Hispanic, he doesn't know that he is the token minority in his law firm and his engagement to the boss's daughter is a sham. Until, that is, the night he stops to help an injured motorist on the highway. But the girl is beyond help, and Alex is soon charged with her murder. He knows it's a setup, but to prove it, he has to stay out of jail. Most of the cops on the case are convinced they have their man, if they can just find him. But Detective Murray Schmitz isn't so sure. Things just don't add up for her, and she decides to go undercover for more information and evidence. But neither Alex or Murray is aware of just how high up this conspiracy goes, and how much is on the line. From bigots to terrorists, Alex and Murray dodge one danger after another, only to run into a worse one each time. It is hard to imagine how they can possibly get out alive. O'Keefe tells a chilling tale, with a solid plot full of surprises. The story caught and held my interest from the very first paragraph. This one is a page turner and you won't want to stop until you've read the very last one. ~ *Regan Murphy, The Review Team of Taylor Jones & Regan Murphy*

OTHER BOOKS BY
TRISHA O'KEEFE

Hanahatchee
Love Song of the Chinaberry Man
The Magi's Well
The Mama Tree
Of Unknown Origin.

POSEIDON'S EYE

TRISHA O'KEEFE

A Black Opal Books Publication

GENRE: MYSTERY-DETECTIVE/CRIME THRILLER

POSEIDON'S EYE
Copyright © 2016 by Trisha O'Keefe
Cover Design by Jackson's Cover Design
All cover art copyright © 2017
All Rights Reserved
Print ISBN: 978-1-626947-43-6

First Publication: JUNE 2016

Published by Black Opal Books **http://www.blackopalbooks.com**

*To Reg, and all those gentle people
who loved the Earth, but left it too soon.
This one's for you.*

CHAPTER 1

"What's her name again?"

"Driver's license says Shelby Turner," Jonesy said around his toothpick. "Diamondback City. Age seventeen. Birthday November something. If you're going to be a detective, Schmitz, you have to carry your file with you at all times."

If you're going to be a detective. If. Murray Schmitz took a breath, held it for a count of three, and exhaled without a trace of rancor. The jab was only the first of many she would have to take as the only female detective in the county. It went with the all-male territory she was invading. On the other hand, it had been a long day and her patience was running thin. "In that case, can I take a look at yours?"

Detective Jones was equally fast on the defensive. "I was off-duty at my three-year-old-daughter's birthday party when I got called in. But they filled me in on the vitals."

"I was in the middle of a drug bust when I got the call to come straight down here to the hospital." As they headed down the long haul to the hospital's temporary morgue, their voices echoed off the white tiled walls which always reminded her of the corridor between life and death described by the dying. Only in Kern County Hospital, the corridor smelled of formaldehyde. "Where, I was told, a senior officer would be there to assist me. I am, remember, still attached to the Juvenile Crime Division."

"Just filling you in on standard op." Excuses were wasted on Ronnie Jones. Taking the lead, he pushed open the outside door to the lab and went in, leaving it to swing back on her. Chivalry was a dusty word around Bakersfield. It matched the scenery. "I understand it's a long learning curve, Detective. But it's also Sunday at seven-thirty in the evening, and I should be home with my kid. Didn't mean to get in your face."

"No problem." But it was definitely going to be if they had to work together any longer.

The hospital's morgue technician clapped Detective Jones on the shoulder with a gloved hand. "Hey, Jonesy, what's up? Two guesses it's the DOA we just got in. Nothing else would bring you out on a Sunday night, am I right?"

Murray couldn't imagine how anyone who worked in such a grim setting could be so cheerful. But Jones was equally breezy, as if the two of them were in a sports bar together having a beer.

"You got that right, Darrel. Hey, watch the meat mitts." Jones faked a cringe at the sight of the tech's gloved hand on his shoulder. "This is my good suit I got on. No telling what those gloves have been into or *who* they've been into." The two men carried on the guy-thing until Jones remembered she was standing there. "Hey, meet Murray Schmitz from Juvie. Murray, meet Darrel the Barrel. Master of the Morgue, right hand man to Doctor Death."

Murray corrected the introduction as she offered her hand. "It's Detective Murray Schmitz. Murray to you."

Jonesy traded conspiratorial grins with the lab tech whose nickname was an obvious reference to his significant paunch. "Sorry, Detective Schmitz. Can we take a look at the girl? You up for that, Schmitz?"

"I am if you are." At first, Murray's annoyance with Jones superseded the impact of seeing the girl. In the course of four years as a detective, she had seen many dead people. This one was one too many. Drug wars casualties, teen suicides, robbery victims—stabbed, shot, strangled, bludgeoned. None of them were easy to look at, but some were harder to mourn than others. This one, lying in her chilled innocence, brought sudden tears to Murray's eyes which she tried to hide from the two men.

The girl in her icy tomb was as indifferent to life as a stone effigy. The only indications of violence were two shaved areas on her left temple, daubed with red disinfectant. Murray steeled herself for what might lie beneath the sheet pulled down to her waist. That was the worst part for her, having to remain standing through discussions of sexual crimes.

Murray found herself standing with clenched fists, wanting to wring somebody's neck. Her stiffened posture didn't go unnoticed. Clearing his throat ceremoniously, Darrel began the initial exam. "Shot twice at close range with small caliber pistol." His tone as blank as the concrete walls, he went on pointing at the girl's body with a ballpoint pen as if she were a lab specimen. "Silencer. No powder burns. Wounds just above right ear and temple. Didn't see any other signs of violence on the body, but the medical examiner hasn't seen her yet. Doesn't look like a sexual assault, though. Clothes were intact. Cause of death pretty clear."

Something like writing on a concrete wall flickered across Murray's mind. "Did she die instantly?"

Darrel shrugged. "Maybe. If not, she was brain-dead. One shot entered the frontal lobe. The other shattered the cerebral cortex."

"So she wouldn't have been able to grasp anything?" The two men regarded her as if she had made a bad joke. "Just something's in the suspect's statement about holding a handkerchief in her hand. And the fingers of her left hand are curled. So she must have been holding something when rigor mortis set in, am I right?"

Darrel was the kinder of the two. "Oh, yeah, I remember now. I already put it in the bag with her other personal effects. Some kind of linen thing you don't see any more. Embroidered hanky. I'd show it to you, but CSI don't like anybody touching evidence until they check for fibers and prints and stuff." He started to proceed, but Murray was at it again.

"You said embroidered? What with?"

"Initials. I've forgotten what." Darrel was just plain annoyed now and Detective Jones was doing a bad job of being indulgent.

"Is this relevant, Detective?" Jonesy said, sending all kinds of back-off signals with his eyes. "I mean, he just said CSI hasn't looked at the stuff yet. And we need to get on upstairs to meet the parents."

What they didn't know was Murray hadn't gotten where she was without persistence. "Just asking," she said. "Linen hankies are kind of..." She shrugged. "...I don't know, obsolete in the age of disposable tissues."

Cornered, the tech threw her a crumb of information. "The blood had soaked through them, but they were something like AC something. I've got it written down." He consulted a clipboard. "That's right. AAC. Anyway, like I said, CSI will take a look and give you a better picture." After a heavy sigh, indicating their welcome was wearing thin, Darrel the Barrel went on. "There were some other personal effects, like a friendship ring on her left hand, engraved on the inside. Birthstone ring, right hand. Small tattoo of a winged heart on right shoulder blade, and ears pierced with nice little diamonds."

"So, was she right-handed or left-handed? Can you tell?"

"Right-handed. I'll bet you anything, right-handed."

"Why? How do you know?" She beat Jones to the question.

Darrel was on a roll now. "The pretty birthstone ring was on her right hand. Probably a gift from her parents or grandma. And there's a faint ballpoint pen mark on her right thumb where she had been writing earlier in the day. And the bottom of the right thumb and forefinger are slightly calloused where she gripped her pen."

Jonesy looked restless. "Any questions, Schmitzy?" His eyes said get this over with fast.

"Just one. Can I see her hands?"

Darrel had to pull down the sheet to let her look. The girl was naked and Jonesy glanced away.

Murray touched the girl's cold fingers. They were calloused, especially the right ones. Left hand was smoother. Was she a migrant's daughter that she worked with her hands? "You didn't find anything else on the body? Which hand was she holding the handkerchief in? The left or the right?"

Darrel gave an offended look and consulted his chart. "The left."

"But the first bullet killed her instantly, you said. So how could she be holding a hanky with her own blood on it in her left hand?"

Darrel shrugged. "That's for you to find out, I guess. Maybe the killer put it there for some weird reason. I've seen weirder things."

The buzzer on Darrel's cluttered desk rang, causing the two detectives to jump nervously. Darrel glanced back at the flashing light. "That's reception. Time to bring the parents down."

"I want a piece of this guy when we get him," Jonesy said as they waited for the elevator. "A big piece. Anybody who'd kill Miss Angel Wings back there's got it coming. And more."

It took a moment to sink in. "That's Duncan's job. I'm with Juvie and I've got a bunch of teenagers about to pick up five kilos of crack down in the Valley."

Detective Jones suppressed a smile. "According to her driver's license, Miss Turner wouldn't have been eighteen until November, remember? Don't worry, Officer Duncan's going to be there and let him do the talking, okay? He does this stuff for a living as a funeral director on the side. You just offer support, stuff like that. Don't say anything about what you think happened, don't ask no questions, got it?

Duncan's the master at this. This is for training purposes only."

His condescending tone drew fire. "It's not like I'm a rookie, Detective. I know what to do. I've earned my stripes just like everybody else."

It didn't pay to get smart with Detective Sergeant Jones. His six-foot-four-inch-something frame straightened to an even six-five. "Then tell you what, Detective Schmitz. We'll just let you handle this whole thing by yourself, how's that?" He signaled to the technician to close the drawer and Sleeping Beauty slid away into the darkness. "Let's go."

Jonesy's footsteps across the tiled floor were beating a final tattoo, but Murray couldn't just leave without a good-bye. She stood before the wall of steel vaults and addressed the one labeled Turner, S.

"I'm going to find out who did this, honey," she whispered. "Whoever they are, they're going to pay." The cold room magnified the echoes of rage in her soft voice meant only for the girl and her.

At the sink, Darrell pretended not to hear as he washed up. But as she followed Jones to the door, he said, "Keep that fire in your heart, Detective. But know you've got to be cool to catch a killer. They have hearts as cold as the bodies they leave behind them. Good hunting."

Outside in the hall, Jones gave her a hard look, the kind that said you weren't coming up to the mark. "You okay, Schmitz? Look, I know homicides are tough but—"

"Any suspects?" Murray cut him off, all business now. Utter determination took the rose out of her tan skin, leaving her golden from her hair to long legs in her khaki shorts. With her blonde ponytail pulled through her Kern County Law cap, she didn't look long out of high school herself.

"One." Jones pressed the elevator button, watching the down arrow as if it would rescue him from further situations in which he said the wrong thing. "Some LA lawyer. His stuff's all over the scene. Claims he just stopped for directions to a gas station and found the girl dead. Says somebody in a car like his drove away just as he got to the murder scene. Even I could think of a better story than that. Guy must be strung out on coke. Only LA lawyers can afford it nowadays." His cell phone rang, relieving him of having to be jovial.

"They're here," he said, after a two-word conversation. "Duncan's on his way. Been bowling or something. You're on your own until he gets here. Remember what I said. You don't know anything. Just listen. They're up in the Visitor's Lounge, first floor."

"You're leaving?" It dawned on her she would be alone with these stricken people. "Can't you just wait until Duncan gets here?"

Jonesy's glance softened. "Why do I get the feeling you can handle this, Schmitz? And I'm sorry if I put you down earlier this evening. You realize one of us minorities has got to get the edge. And being all male, it's my duty to my gender to be alpha dog."

He found out the cool blonde looked even prettier just before she cut you off at the knees. "Great. Have a good evening, Leader of the Pack. Remember, the pack always follows the bitch." While he was thinking of a reply, the elevator came.

The Turners were easy to spot in the crowded Visitors' Lounge. Other visitors were chatting or watching the blah television show with canned laughter. The girl's parents clung to each other like people in a windstorm. The man encircled the small, slender woman with an arm as strong as a tree branch. Parents were written all over them. "Mr. and Mrs. Turner?"

Turning in tandem, they faced Murray as if she were commanding a firing squad. "Yes, that's us. How's Shelby doing? Is she all right?"

Their eyes pleaded, begged her for good news, anything to relieve three hours of hell. And, like a dry well, she had nothing to give them. She had worked in Juvenile Crime for four years, first as a beat cop and recently, as a detective. Her own youth and gentle beauty had only earned her the unenviable task of giving parents the terrible news of their child's death.

But Murray had never mastered the words to assuage grief. Maybe because there just weren't any. Everything she thought of saying echoed with the platitudes of sympathy cards.

"Let's talk over here in this room. It's a little more private." She gestured toward a small alcove doubling as a chapel with a couple of candles flanking a cross. They followed her, still clinging together like drowning people.

As she led the way into the claustrophobic room, Murray silently begged Duncan to show up with all the right words. But deep down, she knew he wouldn't. They had assigned her this task because it was the one law enforcement hated most: to admit to a family that, with all their training and weapons, they had failed to stop a criminal from taking a loved one from them.

She stalled as long as she could, waiting for help to arrive, but there was no putting off Mr. Turner. A weathered, wiry version of Ronald Reagan, he took aim with a question. "Is our daughter dead or alive? We need to know."

Murray swallowed. "She's passed, I'm afraid." She used the colloquial form of the word for dying, bridging the gap between legaleeze and the language of the people.

Mrs. Turner shriveled down into a pew, but he stood tall and straight as a mountain pine, refusing to crack in a storm. "Did she suffer any?"

Softening the truth, she replied, "No, sir. I believe it was instantaneous. Death, I mean." As if they didn't realize all their fears had been validated.

"Mind telling us how it happened?" His gaze was relentless, trying to relive his child's last moments with her.

She ran out of the right words then. "Mr. Turner, I—I'm waiting for another officer, and I shouldn't—"

But their eyes, leaking wounded souls, wouldn't let her

beg rank. "Young lady, if you were us, you'd want to know, now wouldn't you? Please."

Murray nodded. "She was shot, point blank. Twice in the head."

"My God! By who? Who shot her?"

She knew now how interrogated prisoners felt. Trapped by barbed questions. Stepping over land mines. Dodging bullets.

"We're still investigating. She was found in her car—van, as if she had just pulled over for some reason. She had two dogs with her. Shepherds." Murray, in turn, pleaded to be let off the hook. "They were scared, but okay."

Mrs. Turner raised her tear-streaked face, and Murray was struck by how much she resembled her daughter.

"Rusty and Dustybutt. We'll take them home."

"They're at the animal shelter, just for the night. We thought it was the best place, considering."

"May we see her?" Here it came—the worst-case scenario, having to see a wounded child who was beyond their help, beyond their words of comfort.

Murray tried to stall them. "I have to wait for my superior, Detective Duncan. He does all the paperwork."

"Please." It wasn't the word, it was the look in Mrs. Turner's eyes. Like that of someone clinging to a cliff, begging to be rescued. "It isn't a question of paperwork. We just want to see our daughter. To tell her goodbye."

To hell with the regulations if they're going to leave me alone in this. "Are you sure? I mean, she looks as if nothing happened, but—"

"No matter what, we just want to say good-bye to our daughter, Shelby. Please." They were a tribunal of two. Regardless of what Detective Hansen said, they were judge and jury of the moment.

Asking them to wait, Murray went out into the hall and called Jonesy, getting his voice mail. Then she called Headquarters and asked them to find Duncan ASAP. No one returned her call.

Returning to the chapel where the parents sat like stone effigies, regarding nothing, she said, "Come with me, please." By this time, she didn't care if she would end up teaching CPR and First Aid for a living.

Darrel the Barrel had gone for the night and the night duty pathologist was in the lab, a young resident who knew as little about procedure as she did. They all went to the holding room where he did a text book job of being objective and technically proficient which was a little much for the lady, but Mr. Turner listened, nodding occasionally. He'd been a soldier, he said, and he could take it. What he didn't say was that listening to how his child had died was slowly killing him. When it was over, the parents kissed their daughter's marble face and Mrs. Turner prayed over the body, wrapping a crucifix through the lifeless fingers. The coroner would remove it later and Murray would have to explain how it got there, but she couldn't have cared less. Saying goodbye was the first step in letting go.

At that point, Duncan arrived and took over, giving her occasional dirty looks. But as she was leaving, the Turners hugged her as if they, through tragedy, had become a family. "You'll come to the funeral, won't you?"

She said sure, just give her a call, and surprised herself because she meant it. As they stood in a triangle, holding each other's hands as if they were in free fall, Murray blurted something she rarely mentioned to anyone, let alone strangers. "I just want you to know, I can relate to what you're going through. And will go through. My father was a policeman who died the same way your daughter did. His killer's in prison and your daughter's will be, too. I won't give up until I get him."

"Then I will pray you stay safe." Mrs. Turner dropped her hand and hugged the tall officer again. "*Vaya con Dios*, darling," she whispered.

As she stepped into the fresh spring night outside the hospital, Murray wondered when the turning point came when you didn't take it home with you.

That evening she put in a load of wash, heated up her TV dinner, and sat cross-legged in front of the TV. A person who rarely did fewer than two things at once, Murray combined eating, folding laundry and drying her hair while watching the evening news.

The news came and went without mention of Shelby Turner. Another roadside murder of a young girl was too common an occurrence to merit expensive air time, it seemed.

But this case differed from the all-too-frequent murders of young California women. There was the style, for one thing. The Turner girl was killed with two shots at close range. No signs of violence to the body. No sign of robbery. It was more like an execution by a paid-killer. Detached. Quick and clean. Efficient.

Except for the oddity of a handkerchief in her left hand, monogrammed with the initials AAC. Apparently, they matched those of the LA lawyer with the fancy Malibu address. Some Hispanic guy who claimed he'd never seen the Turner girl in his life. So if he shot her, why was he still standing there?

Her TV dinner tasted like toasted paper, but she ate it anyway, flanked by stacks of folded laundry. Feeling ignored, the cat brushed her legs and was still ignored. Finally, it jumped into her lap. Detective Murray Schmitz had fallen asleep, still searching for answers across the dreamscape while the cat finished her dinner.

CHAPTER 2

Alex Carreras was leaning back in his leather chair, staring out his office window at the tranquil Pacific when his office door seemed to explode. Before he could react, two wedge-shaped men in business suits walked in, followed by his alarmed secretary. They didn't have to display their badges to announce they were law enforcement. It was written all over them.

"Mr. Carreras?" The shorter one flashed his badge along with the question.

"Unless you've got the wrong office," he said, "that's me. What can I do for you, gentlemen?"

Sylvia, who ordinarily produced order out of chaos, regarded the intruders, hands on ample hips. "I'm sorry, Mr. Carreras. They just barged past me! I asked them to wait in the waiting room, but no, they just pushed me out of the way!"

"I didn't push you, ma'am," the short, bald one said. "You got right in front of me and I was trying not to step on your foot."

"You barged past me, don't try to hide it, young man!" Her outrage had the effect of tempering the officers' zeal. It seemed to dawn on them they were in an attorney's offices.

"It's okay, Sylvia."

She left with hostile stares at the two strangers while Carreras straightened his tie, and tried to look busy.

"What's the problem, gentlemen?"

It was their signal to appear official again. "Detective Joe Stockman," said the short one, "and this is Detective Ronnie Jones." The tall black man stopped looking around long enough for a brief nod. "We'd like to ask you a few questions, if you don't mind."

"Sure, sit down." Alex waved them to his only chairs in front of the desk. "What's it about?" He knew very well what they had come about—the girl whose body he had found the previous afternoon. But he also knew enough about the police to let them do all the talking.

But neither of the plainclothesmen sat. Instead, they stood at parade rest in front of him. They wanted him on their turf. "We'd like to talk to you up at the station."

"In Kern County?"

"Bakersfield, yes, sir." They didn't look like the types to take no for an answer.

"But if it's about that girl up in Kern County, I told them everything I know yesterday. I just stopped to help her and she was dead. That's all there is to it. I mean, I'd never seen her before or anything."

"If you'd just come along with us," the tall dark one repeated. "Just to answer a few more questions. You might want to bring someone with you," the detective added, keeping his expression bland as milk.

"I don't need someone with me to tell you exactly what happened, Detective." He punched the intercom. "Sylvia, hold my calls, will you? I'll be out for the rest of the morning."

At the other end, there was a pause full of unspoken questions. "But you have a meeting at ten with—"

"Just tell Mr. Crittenden it's about the incident yesterday up in Kern County. Just Parker, not Chelsea. She's already had a meltdown about it."

"Will do, Mr. Carreras. I hope everything is all right."

"Me, too."

They left the office in a cozy group, chatting about the real estate prices in Southern California as if they were going to coffee. Only, Sylvia knew Carreras would never cancel a meeting with an important client just to accommodate a pair of cops from the sticks. Before they were in the elevator, she would be on the phone to the firm's director and Alex's future father-in-law, Parker Crittenden.

The *LA Times* was lying on the back seat of the detective's car, folded to a small article under *REGIONAL NEWS*. In smaller bold type, it read *YOUNG WOMAN FOUND IN VAN*. Her identity was withheld pending notification of relatives. He picked it up, reading on. Two shepherd dogs found with her had been taken to the local shelter. A suspect in the murder was questioned and released, pending further investigation. That was it. A few perfunctory lines. The amount of attention your death received in Southern California depended on who you were. This one was on the back page of the second section, buried in a larger column called *AROUND THE STATE*.

As they skirted the inland traffic, taking the coastal road, the dead girl's face kept returning to him like the sad melody of a country song. In fact, the tune was so clear, he almost started to hum it. "There's a young boy that I know, his age is twenty-one."

Although Alex was ready to swear he had never seen her before, the song somehow linked him to this girl some time before her lonely, violent death.

But where? When? Her image eluded him, wandering through his memory as if he were following her through a medieval maze to try the soul. Had he slept with this girl and been so drunk and out of it, he didn't remember? And Saturday night, he had tied one on at Sunrise Resort since that was what one did at bachelor parties. In the morning, he couldn't even remember how he got home from the bar. The night before was a total blank.

Staring out the car window at the sea, Alex tried to visualize the face of the girl in the van, her face crystallized in death. Her hair, brown like the darkest chocolate, beckoned his touch when he had leaned forward to find a pulse. The van smelled of orange blossoms and dogs. A bumper sticker said she liked rodeos and country music. Like a puzzle with a million pieces, he couldn't put it together for a complete picture.

Yesterday afternoon, he had been heading down the Interstate from Sunrise Resort with a hangover big enough to stop a train when he had a flat. Almost simultaneously, his oil gauge light went on and he had pulled off on the shoulder, cursing in two languages. Chelsea was supposed to have taken the Jeep to get the oil changed before he left. Probably an appoint with her personal trainer had interfered. To complicate the situation, when he opened the tire kit, the jack wasn't there. He was searching for his cell phone when flashing blue lights behind him announced help had arrived.

A highway patrol officer joined him on the shoulder. "Got car trouble, buddy?" After giving him a can of flat fixer, the patrolman directed him to the next exit. "Turn right and there's a filling station a few miles down," he said. "Should be open. If you're not in a big hurry, you could wait here and I'll call road service for you, but it'll take up to forty-five minutes to get here. You're about twenty miles from anywhere."

"I'll take my chances, thanks." Alex was already late to his own engagement party hosted by his future-in-laws who were less than impressed with him in the first place. Coupled with their well-bred disapproval, the thought of facing one of Chelsea's ice storms that took a week to defrost gave him no choice. He used the flat fixer and limped to the next off ramp, his oil light glaring cyclops eye on the dashboard.

The view at the bottom of the ramp was a panorama of vast brown field stretching unobstructed to the horizon. The only signs of human life were two vehicles pulled over to the right shoulder, a few yards past the stop sign. One was a battered blue van, parked at a sharp angle as if it had stopped abruptly. In sharp contrast, a red Cherokee similar to his own had pulled over within a door's width of it.

Alex's hopes had lifted. The red Cherokee, smartly trimmed in chrome with wire wheels that must have set somebody back a few rounds of beer, was a better prospect for a tire jack than the van. But the tail lights were lit, indicating the driver had a foot on the brakes and was in a big hurry to leave. As he made the turn, Alex caught a glimpse of someone closing the passenger door even as the driver put the car in gear. With a lack of cordiality not typical of the country, the jeep had spun off the shoulder just as he pulled up, spattering his windshield with mud.

"What the hell—" Alex had watched the jeep retreat, noting it had vanity plates beginning with MAC. *Weird.* Nearly same make, model and initials on the plates as his which had been an engagement gift from Chelsea.

But the van was another puzzle. Something in the way it had stopped astride the road and the shoulder shouted trouble. At the sight of the girl slumped over the steering wheel, the six-inch scar across his ribs began to tingle. Drive on, it said.

But reason had always played the role of temptress in his life. Even if she'd been sleeping in an exhausted stupor, the noise of the SUV's screeching departure would surely have roused the driver. Instead, she hadn't changed position, even when he slammed his car door deliberately. In fact, the only other sounds in the ensuing silence were the whine of the retreating SUV, the steady sizzle of tires on the nearby Interstate and the mournful howl of a dog from somewhere inside the van.

Then another howl joined the first in an elegy of profound loss. Yet, even the chorus of howls behind her did not disturb the sleeping girl.

As he approached the van, the howls abruptly became defensive barks and growls. Knowing there could be guard dogs inside, but seeing the driver's side window was down, he had called, "Miss, are you okay?"

She looked so peaceful, he was about to turn away when his second impression belied the first. The possibility that her stillness wasn't sleep but death now struck him with the force of a physical blow. Edging closer to the open window, he saw her eyes were frozen half-open staring into eternity. Disbelief rooted him to the ground as he had watched a bright red line slowly tracing the curve of her cheek. With an awful finality, the blood darkened as it glided to a stop just past her open lips. Following the red line back to a source hidden under the thick curtain of her hair, the truth became clear and terrible. She had been shot in the head.

Desperate for some way to help her, Alex fumbled in his shorts pocket for something to staunch the blood, but came up empty-handed. The handkerchief he always kept for allergy attacks was gone. *Had he left everything behind in Sunrise?* Something white in the girl's left hand snagged his skidding glance. Her lifeless fingers were curled around a piece of cloth with embroidered edges, soaked in bright red blood.

At the time, panic caused him to overlook that discrepancy, but something nagged at him now, recalling his own handkerchief embroidered with his initials, missing that morning. *It couldn't be his...how could it be? He'd never seen her before in his life. Or had he and just didn't remember?*

"Miss, do you hear me? Who did this?" A flock of crows gabbling in the muddy field and the anxious whine of the dogs cowering in the rear were the only reply. Otherwise, his absurd questions to the girl were met by the awful silence only dead things have. One of the dogs in the back of the van, a graying shepherd, changed its plaintive whine to a low growl. "Hey, take it easy, fellas. I need to find out what's going on with the lady, here."

Reaching through the driver's window, he had touched her shoulder, still talking to the dogs. There was no reflexive response. Her body was inert as if the steering wheel held it upright.

The two animals remained cautious, staring at him with alert almond eyes, growling softly as he felt for the girl's carotid pulse. His fingers touched something wet and warm and Alex had snatched them back, finding blood on his fingertips. Without thinking, he wiped them on his shorts and tried taking a pulse on her left wrist. "Hang in there, honey," he had whispered. "Don't go."

A sudden rush of wings came from the nearby field as the flock of crows rose skyward as if something had startled them. Hoping a worker there had disturbed them, he glanced at the birds. Among them flew a single white dove, caught up like a stolen soul amid the black wings.

Their abrupt flight had put the same instinct in his own mind. He could flee this hideous scene as well, even though he might be the only witness to this girl's death. On the other hand, no one had seen him standing here.

One late night four years ago, a situation similar to this one had nearly cost him his life. The scar across his ribs had begun to itch, as if the instinct for self-preservation had set off a subcutaneous alarm. *Don't be a hero, Superman. It ain't healthy.* His attacker's warning ticker-taped through his mind for the thousandth time. *Don't be a hero.*

But somewhere, there must be people who cared about this pretty, dark-haired girl who wouldn't see her twentieth birthday. Again, he had searched his pockets for the cell phone, keeping one hand on her wrist for any sign of a pulse.

Realizing he had left it in the car while trying to call Chelsea, he put her hand down and retrieved it. He got the nine-one-one operator immediately.

"This is Sandra. Who am I speaking with?"

The crisp, friendly voice reached out to him in this desolate place like a lifeline. He gave his name, described the van and the injured girl.

"And what is your location, sir?"

"Off the Interstate just before…" He couldn't remember the town. "At the intersection of County Highway…" Cursing his nearsightedness, he told her he couldn't see the sign without his glasses.

She was patient. "How about a landmark? Any buildings you can see?" There weren't any buildings.

In the distance, the whine of a truck engine was carried through the still air. "Hold on, I think someone's coming." He had sprinted into the road waving both arms like a wild man.

The truck had slowed as it approached him but, instead of stopping, kept moving past him. "Stop! Help! Please help!" The driver, an old man in a battered Stetson, stared at him with hostile eyes through the dusty window. "Emergency! Damn it, stop!"

But the truck crossed the intersection and rattled away down the road as if the driver were afraid of a holdup.

"Bastard!" Then he had realized he still had nine-one-one on the phone. "He just went right past me. God, this is unreal!"

"Okay," the calm voice had said, "do this for me, Mr. Carreras. Walk back up to the exit ramp and give me the exit number."

"But the girl. I thought I detected a weak pulse and—"

Sandra was the soul of patience. "I've got the paramedics on board and ready to go. The faster they get there, the faster they can help her. I just need your exact location, Mr. Carreras."

"Wait! I hear sirens! They're here!"

Two patrol cars, sirens blasting, came racing down the ramp from the Interstate.

"They are?" The question hung in the air like the tornado of yellow dust as the patrol cars pulled to a screeching stop beside the van.

It all went south from there.

CHAPTER 3

She started out so early that the mist still blanketed the low places between the bluffs and canyons. So early, her asthma kicked up a dry cough and Murray had to stop to use her inhaler. It wasn't a promising day. Monday never was in her experience. For one thing, she had to bring Darlene Santana in again.

And for another, her buddy Gilberto Sanchez who helped sponsor the department's Little League team had been gunned down the night before. That had been the news that greeted her on arriving at the office this morning. Gilberto who had a baby coming, his third child. Gilberto who had earned the nickname Gizmo because of his love for tinkering with gadgets.

This was when she hated her job. He was more than just a fellow officer—that was bad enough.

Gilberto Sanchez was a personal friend she had made when she volunteered for the sports program he ran for disadvantaged kids. Since she was with Juvie and loved sports, she fit right in. They were buddies after he got over the macho thing about women.

It was the worst possible start to a Monday and it was still only eight-thirty in the morning. Catching a couple of seventeen-year-olds buying weed from Darlene had been a piece of cake since the narcotics people were already there and scared the business right out of them.

Darlene, on the other hand, was giving the narcotics

boys the drama queen show and they looked relieved when she showed up.

"We'll take your kids into Juvie for you if you get Bride of Frankenstein to shut up so we can cuff her," the detective in charge said. "I haven't had enough coffee to listen to her bitch all the way in."

Darlene was a druggie who rarely left her neat, rusting trailer except to sell a new crop of marijuana and buy her meth fix. Tall, red haired, and skeleton-thin, she must have once been attractive, even beautiful. But after years of drug abuse, alcohol, and poverty, she looked like the dog's breakfast. Meth amphetamine had taken most of her front teeth, and she was covered with the mosquito-bite sores of crack users.

She recognized Murray immediately from her many court appearances. "Listen, honey, tell these Nazis I was only trying to make a little grocery money," she said in her characteristic nasal whine. "I don't know what you expect a person to do up here. There's no place to get a job and I can't move out 'cause I've got nowhere to go!" She kept up the outraged diatribe as they cleaned up her little grove of marijuana plants in neat window boxes. "It's almost legal anyway. I was growing in for medicinal consumption."

"I don't know, Darlene. Those boys looked pretty healthy to me."

"They have attention deficit disorder. It calms their nerves. And mine."

"It's still breaking the law." Murray waited patiently as she fed and watered the cat, blue jeans pale and tight on stork legs, long red hair pulled back in a ponytail. A photo of a little red haired girl sat on the window sill next to the daybed. Murray picked it up, figuring it must be Darlene as a child. "Is this you?" she asked. "You were a cute kid."

The woman's gaunt face softened from twisted rage to an expression of longing and tenderness. "No, that's not me. Now, give it here. It's personal."

"Sure, but she looks just like you. Your little girl?"

Somehow, in her wildest dreams, she would have never thought Darlene, an incurable addict, capable of having children. "You must have been very young."

Darlene pressed the frame against her flat chest. "Too young. I wasn't a good mother. I tried so hard, but he…" She shook her head in despair. "Let's go if we're going, okay? I need to get the hell out of here. Here," she said, relinquishing the picture. "Put it right back there."

Murray hesitated. "Listen, Darlene, you know they're going to tear up this trailer looking for more stuff. Let me keep the picture for you. I'll lock it in my desk drawer in an envelope with your name on it. It'll be safer there. And it may be awhile before you can come back." They both knew she was right. Selling drugs to minors meant hard time.

There was something like hope in Darlene's eyes. "Okay, thanks, honey. Hold on to it for me. I know how the narcs are. Take everything, give nothing back. I hope this is fried fish night," she added as they got in the car. "It's the only decent meal you get in there."

"Sorry. Monday's meatloaf."

After making sure Darlene had switched to complaining about the lockup's menu instead of narcotics agents, Murray put her into the back of the other cruiser and did a U turn back up Rt. 166. A cluster of spinning blue lights along the southbound shoulder told her the Crime Scene Investigation team was still sniffing around like khaki bloodhounds.

Knowing she was barging in on another team's operations, Murray Schmitz did it anyway. It sometimes took a week for them to grind out a report and even longer for it to trickle down to her. And this case had priority over anything else, including Darlene Santana's cottage industry and interviewing some pimply sixteen-year-olds with snotty attitudes.

She jogged smartly up the windy highway, aware of the smirk on the trooper directing looky-loo traffic. Murray wanted to kick herself for knowing what he was thinking and for knowing how she could use it. Prototype California blonde, hair tied behind her, slim as a diet Margarita, and just as salty.

Not even flashing her badge wiped the smirk of his clean-shaven face. The wind played with her long hair, and she brushed it impatiently away. "Detective Jones around?" The grinning trooper jerked his head toward the tight circle of investigators behind him. "Sure is, Detective. I'm sure he'll be glad to see you."

Jones of Homicide was squatting beside a pool of blood. "Hey, Jonesy. How's it going?"

He flicked a glance at her. "Schmitzy, watch where you're stepping, okay?"

She crouched beside him. "Any leads?"

"White sedan, could be a Honda Civic. He had stopped the driver to give a ticket and was calling it in." Jonesy looked grim. "We're doing tire tracks right now, so stay on the pavement." He glanced around at the highway patrol officers pushing the small gathering of onlookers away from the area. "Fat chance we're going to get anything, though. Man, where do all the vultures come from?"

"Kind of strange. That's the second homicide we've had in the last twenty-four hours. You think there might be a connection."

For once, Jones agreed with her. "At least, there's a suspect in the one yesterday. Killed that kid with the two dogs. I hear they're booking him this morning. Some fancy-ass lawyer from LA. Why does he have to drive up here to shoot somebody? Plenty of people to shoot in LA."

"Good point. And, according to station, he wasn't detained. But Sanchez would have been a good alibi for him."

Jones threw her a quizzical look. "Say what?"

Murray couldn't control the wide smile beneath her prescription sunglasses. "According to his statement, Sanchez made some important observations. One was the second set of tire tracks at the murder scene. Custom mountain treads which Sanchez took photos of. The other was the gun missing from the glove compartment that the lawyer said he always carried. And that the guy's tire was nearly flat."

"Meaning he could have pitched the gun somewhere and the tire tracks were made earlier in the day by some…I don't know, some farmer."

"So he just shot the girl knowing he wasn't going anywhere with a flat tire. Come on, Jonesy. Admit this is plain weird."

The detective stood up, brushing off his pants. "You're forgetting, California is the home of weird. So this guy is a hot-shot lawyer and he thinks he can make a case by playing the good Samaritan, calling nine-one-one and holding the girl's hand while she dies. It's nothing new, girl. Those guys get paid millions for defending criminals every day. You think they'd think of something more original than, 'Oh, gee, Officer. I just found her here with two bullets from my gun in her head.' What a twist of fate!"

Murray got to her feet, feeling as if she left her stomach on the pavement. "You found the gun?"

Jonesy was definitely back in control of the situation. "Right out there in the field, my girl. About a good javelin's toss away. No doubt we got this one nailed. They're booking him even as we speak. And we checked his alibi. He was in LA last night when Sanchez bought it."

"Hey, Jones, over here, will you?" The CSI people were giving them funny looks and she knew she wasn't invited.

Jonesy left her to join the huddle of forensics people, and she returned to her car where she sat for a long time, staring at nothing. Then she picked up Shelby Turner's file and read through Alex's statement for the tenth time.

Something about an old man driving an old Dodge truck with the words onions on the side snagged her eye.

Onions. Murray sat staring out at the spring fields. How many people around here grew onions? This was mainly garlic growing country, a product for which the area was famous. On an impulse, she dialed the station's dispatcher.

"Hey, Sandra, it's Murray. Got thirty seconds?"

The dispatcher's voice rarely moved faster than melting chocolate. "Try twenty-nine or hang on 'til I get the medics out to a pileup on the Interstate. Typical Monday fender-bender. Wish people wouldn't text and drive." She hung on and in exactly a minute, Sandra was back. "Sorry, the driver's English wasn't so hot."

"That's okay, I won't hold you up. Were you on duty yesterday morning?"

"Sure I was. You know my schedule. Four on, two off. Rotate night shifts. If you're asking if I spoke to the guys who called in the murdered girl out on 156, yeah, it was me. Hold on, Murray." While Sandra fielded another call, Murray played around with the word "guys." There was Carreras and the arresting officer, Jensen. He pulled Traffic. *What other guys would there be?*

Sandra came back on the line. "Three-year-old wanting Mommy. Why do they teach them to call nine-one-one at that age?"

"Listen, are you brown-bagging today?"

"Sure, rabbit-food." Sandra was on a permanent diet, something not helped by her nerve-shredding occupation.

"I'll grab a burger and eat with you, if it's okay."

There was a heavy sigh at the other end of the line. "Just you and your yogurt, no burger, please. Eddy asked me out and I've got nothing that fits anymore. See you at twelve."

Murray hung up and started the cruiser. Now there were two more pieces of the puzzle that didn't fit. Onions and Detective Jensen.

⌘

In the Kern County Sheriff's Department, he went over his story with at least five different people. Only one called Jones, the black detective who picked him up, seemed halfway inclined to believe him. At noon, when they told him he needed a lawyer, he called Parker Crittenden.

"Mr. Carreras?" His secretary Sylvia answered the phone. "Mr. Crittenden's not available." Her voice was hiding a chasm behind an icy edge. Not expanding on it, she seemed to want the conversation to end quickly.

"Okay, how about Mr. Lawley, then."

"Playing golf with Mr. Harris, Jr.," she added. "Is that all?"

Now what? It wasn't a good sign. Parker Crittenden was the head of Crittenden, Harris, and Lawley as well as his future-father-in-law. Glancing at the clear glass on the detectives' office door, he saw what the rest of the world saw—a tall man with close cropped dark hair in a suit he couldn't afford. What did he have to be nervous about? He hadn't done anything and still, he was feeling guilty.

Alex shook it off. "Okay, put me through to Hardaway, then."

Looking as if he were wasting her time, Sylvia connected him with another new hire, Tim Hardaway.

He and Hardaway had been in the same fraternity at UCLA and gone on to law school together. They were friends in the context of his present life—fellow surfers, frat brothers, and someone who had shared the agony and elation of graduate school.

If he could trust anyone, it was Tim whose feelings always registered on his face and made him the world's worst poker player.

Alex silently congratulated himself for inviting his old buddy to his bachelor party at Sunrise. Hardaway would make a very credible witness, even if he didn't open his mouth. Those hound dog eyes could convince anyone.

"Alex, where the hell are you?" The familiar voice brought a flood of relief he hadn't been prepared to handle.

"Bakersfield, baby. Where the surf meets the turf. Listen, Tim, can you come up and bail me out of a jam?"

"Hell, I heard about the thing with the girl yesterday. That's really bad news, man. Did you know this chick or something?"

Sometimes, Hardaway's surfer idioms were annoying. This was one of the times. "Never seen her before in my life. Listen, the girl was dead when I found her, Tim."

"God, no kidding. What a bummer! Did they book you?"

"Holding me on suspicion until tomorrow. Dock's full this afternoon. But I can get released on $10,000 bail. I just need representation. Can you do it?"

He pictured Tim running his hands through ear length brown curls. "Geez, you couldn't have struck at a worse moment, old dude. I've got to be in old Critterden's office in five minutes. And criminal law's not exactly my thing, anyway. I'd probably get you hanged. Geez! Let me think a minute. How about Quirky? Give him a call. Extension four-twenty-three. Listen, Alex, if you need me to act as a character witness or whatever, just count me in, okay?"

He started to say that's exactly why he called. Was he getting the runaround? "Thanks, Tim. This whole thing is weird. Talk to you later. By the way, how did you hear about it? Did they broadcast in between the Muzak?"

Nobody did vague the way Hardaway did. "Just water cooler talk, man. You know the drill. Office gossip is better than Channel Nine News."

It was no surprise he got Kent Kirkendall's answering machine. Leaving a message with his cell phone number, he called Tim back.

"Any more ideas? Quirky's out, leave a message."

Sounds of things falling off Hardaway's desk. "Shit! Sorry, Alex. Hey, I got it! Get Eli Feldman to spring you. He's just sitting around picking his nose, okay? I'll put you over. See you when you get back, okay? We'll get bombed together. And don't worry, I'll bring you a knife in a bottle if they lock you up."

Before he could say more, the phone clicked. Old buddy Tim was anxious to be rid of him. And why not? He knew the drill. He was a hot potato, being passed lawyer to lawyer.

A grumpy, nasal voice with a thick New York accent answered Feldman's number after four rings. "Yeah, what now, Laurie? I'm damned busy."

It wasn't a positive start. "Feldman, this is Carreras. Can you get up to San Luis Obispo? Maybe take the company plane?"

There was a pause. "Who the hell is this again? And why in hell should I know you, much less get on an airplane to San Luis Wherever?"

"Alex Carreras. In Corporate. I'm fairly new," he added, trying to inject some humility. "And I need some help."

"Corporate? Then what the hell are you calling me for? That stupid receptionist gave you the wrong extension. I'll send you back if you—"

"No, I asked for you. Crittenden said to contact you."

"Crittenden? Hell, this is Friday afternoon, Carreras. And it's almost Passover. That's like asking someone on their deathbed to go out and play basketball. Get somebody else."

Telling Feldman about the detainment hardly softened the man's heart if one existed. He wasn't coming up today if Alex was rotting in hell, but he would call the detectives and find out what was going on.

He was sitting there wondering what to do next when the phone rang and Feldman told him he would be there by two. Hearing at two-thirty. He had already talked to the judge and the bailiff. No problem.

Then he paused. The question came out of the blue. "Carreras, did you know this girl or what?"

"Never saw her in my life. Why?"

The pause at the other end was ominous. "I dunno, but they say they've got some evidence that proves you did know her. Listen, you'd better level with me or your little corporate ass is going to fry."

"What could they possibly have?" Alex ran his hands through his spiked black hair in frustration. This was like some Russian novel where everybody ends up with someone else's fate. "Look, Eli, I'm sure I never saw the girl in my life. At least, not that I remember."

"Not that you remember. What's that mean? You have convenient memory lapses?"

"Well, you know. There've been some times…you know in college, parties. That stuff. And, okay, I was drunk Saturday night. My bachelor party was at Critterden's place up there in the mountains at Sunrise. He has a condo up there."

"Oh, god. You're getting married in two weeks. I forgot. The wife's got the invitation. She takes care of all those things, you know." Feldman paused to belch in his ear. "Sorry. Go on."

At the mention of the head of the firm, his credibility must have automatically plummeted to zero. There could be no greater offense than creating scandal that touched the firm's platinum reputation in corporate law.

"Okay, I might have. You know, seen somebody like her in one of the bars we were in that night."

Feldman wasn't buying it. "How about sleeping with somebody like her? Would you remember that? God, you young people are like alley cats."

"No! Definitely not. I didn't sleep with her. Please believe me. I never saw her before."

There was a heavy sigh whistling through the receiver. "Okay, anybody with you that has a brain?"

"Kirk Kirkendall, Tim Hardaway, and my brother Ricky. He's a rookie cop with the LAPD. And three other guys, longtime friends from Santa Barbara. We were all drinking. Skiing naked, skinny dipping, and drinking."

Feldman belched again. "Jeezuz, only young people can ski naked and drink. Then what? Do you kids ever sleep?

"I think my brother Ricky drove me back to George's place."

"You think? You don't know?"

It wasn't time to panic. Yet. "I think so, but I'll double check with Rick, okay?"

"Great." Feldman's sigh whistled through the receiver.

"I get all the good ones nobody will touch. Why me? Okay, give me their names and phone numbers. I'll drum up some witnesses. Don't say anything else to the cops until I get there, understand?"

He was beginning to know the frustration of being a suspect. "I've got nothing to hide. I've already told them everything I know."

"That may be part of the problem. See you at two. Try to stay sober."

He called Chelsea. The answering machine told him in his own voice that no one was home and have a great day. He left a message telling her he would be back by five and he loved her. It was like talking to himself.

On the TV in the holding room, he had no trouble recognizing the dead girl's picture. She was alive and smiling. Bold, honest eyes with dark winged brows and a wide, smile showing straight white teeth. Shot by someone who didn't care how sweet or sincere she was. A killer who had just wanted her dead.

Cyclical panic spun his mind like a gyro wheel. She was from some place called Diamondback City, the announcer said, a small community outside of Bakersfield. Diamondback. Why did that ring a bell? His usually clear thoughts scrolled through an internal directory of names. It was there, somewhere. He jotted it down. Shelby Turner from Diamondback City.

He felt better just saying it. He'd never heard of the girl or the place.

But the television took care of his restored confidence in a matter of seconds.

The relentless newsman next flashed a picture of Sanchez, the cop who had taken his statement yesterday. There he was on the screen, broad Latino smile and all.

"A deputy with the Sheriff's Department was shot and seriously injured in a gun battle last night after he stopped to ticket a driver on Route 156. Deputy Gilberto Sanchez, thirty-two, is in the Intensive Care Unit at Kern County

Hospital after an unidentified motorist shot him and then drove away. Anyone with any information on either of these cases should call the Kern County Sheriff's Department, Investigative Division."

"What in the hell? Sanchez has been shot."

Then he realized he had said it out loud and his fellow detainees in the holding area were looking at him through the bloodshot eyes of night beings. "If he's a narc, he had it coming," one woman said. She was wearing stiletto heels and the briefest skirt he'd ever seen. Looking over at Carreras, she added, "But I'm sorry if he was your connection, honey. Sounds to me like a deal gone bad."

'I'm the token Chicano,' he had said. No, it had to be the patrolman from yesterday. The one who had taken the pictures of his flat tire and the set of tire tracks made by the Cherokee.

His next thought was that, by some erratic twist in the justice system, he could end up being blamed for shooting Sanchez as well as the girl.

"It's tough he's having a kid, though," the woman said to her companion, a short plump girl who appeared to have a bad hangover. "People who deal drugs shouldn't have kids."

The girl shifted to a corner of the bench and curled up against the wall. "Will you shut up and let me sleep, Mama?"

∽∾∽∾

"It's been kind of like the quiet after the storm this morning, gracias a Dios. What's up with you, Murray?" The lunchroom area was nearly empty and it felt good to get in some girl talk.

Sandra unwrapped her salad and Murray couldn't suppress a smile.

"That's rabbit food?" The miniscule pile of lettuce was

nearly hidden under a pile of cheese, chicken, and tortilla chips.

"Oh, be quiet, you skinny thing. You don't know what it's like, being fat." Sandra's dark eyes filled with quick tears and Murray was sorry she ever mentioned food. She felt guilty opening her fast-food burger after that and nibbled on French fries instead.

"Hey, Eddie asked you out on a second date. That's more than I've got going on in my love life."

Sandra beamed through her tears. "He sure did, didn't he? We're going to the movies and then to dinner. But I told him I'm on a diet, so guess what? We're going dancing after to work off the calories. Murray, as pretty as you are, I can't believe you haven't got something in skinny jeans and hot to trot, yet."

"Just nothing so hot I want to trot with yet. Listen, Sandra, I hate to bring up business at lunch but could you do a real favor for me?"

"If you promise to help me pick out a dress for this date, sure."

"Can you roll back the nine-one-one tape to Sunday afternoon, about four-twenty-five p.m.? What I want to hear is the call that came in from the witness in the Turner murder. Is that doable?"

"Sure, I'm off duty. When we finish, just come on in to the dispatch office and I'll cue it up for you."

❧❧❧

"It's kind of strange, you know?" Sandra wiggled into her leather swivel chair rounded to her curves.

"What's strange? Besides life in general?" Murray dropped down in the chair behind the nine-one-one operator's desk while they both savored a few minutes peace. Sandra said they wouldn't pick up again until six p.m. when people started driving home and killing themselves trying to get there.

"Well, listen and then tell me what you think. I've heard plenty of static, human and otherwise, but tell me if this doesn't sound like somebody crackling cellophane over the cell phone" Murray started to smile, but Sandra was serious. "Here it is, the guy calling about that poor little Turner girl." She pushed a button on her console and there was a garbled noise. Then Sandra's voice answered, "This is Sandra, nine-one-one. Can I help you?"

A male voice said, "Hey, nine-one-one, I'm calling to report something going on out on County Route 156."

"Exactly what's going on, sir?"

"Well, it looks like some girl's been hurt. Maybe even dead. And some guy's standing beside the van with a gun."

Sandra's matter-of-fact inquiry followed. "Where are you calling from, sir?"

"What's that?" There was a peculiar crackling sound. "Can't hear you! What?"

Sandra kept the same even tone. "I said, where are you now?"

"That's right. The van's just past the freeway exit just past the intersection with Maricopa Highway. Hey, my phone's breaking up."

Sandra's voice raised an octave. "What's your name, sir? Who is this calling?"

"Sorry, got to hang up. Can't hear." The call ended. They looked at each other for a moment.

"Caller ID?"

"None. Blocked. He never said his name or where he was."

Murray frowned, sitting forward in her chair. "Roll the tape back will you? What time did the call come in, exactly?"

The dispatcher checked the time. "Four-twenty."

Murray reacted as if someone had stuck her with a pin. "You're right about the noise. That isn't normal communication static. It's like somebody crumpling up a foil wrapper near the phone or even rubbing it over the receiver. And when did the trooper say he was responding?"

"Hold it. I'll look it up in the log." Sandra flipped through two days of calls. "Says Jensen responded at…huh? Now that is weird." She stared at Murray. "At four-fifteen p.m. Maybe I goofed. No, I always get the call time off the machine."

"Can we run that part of the recording? I'll tell you something else funny. I could swear that caller's voice is familiar. But muffled, like something's over the phone."

Sandra snapped her fingers. "Okay, here it is. I'll bet my bonus, which naturally we don't get any more, that I got it right. Here goes."

"This is Jensen, twenty-one, heading up 156 to check out a report of a guy with a weapon, I'll keep you posted, over."

"Time," Sandra looked at her victorious. "Four-thirteen p.m. See, I told you his call came in before the tipster."

"Did he ever say how he knew if you didn't tell him?"

Sandra gave her a saccharine smile. "I'd rather ask my boss what color his shorts are. That's your job, sweetie."

"And exactly when did Carreras call in?"

Sandra already had the answer to the question memorized. "Four-thirty-seven."

"He says in his statement he pulled off the freeway at four-twenty-two, give or take a few minutes." They stared at each other. "Unless he's lying, he wasn't even there at the crime scene when this tipster called in."

"And Jensen answered the call without me sending him."

This was going to be like pushing a bulldozer uphill with her nose. Murray got to her feet, feeling suddenly limp. Lack of sleep had caught up with her. "Thanks so much, Sandra. I owe you big time. I'll buy you a real lunch or maybe some tequila sours. Right now, I'm going over to the hospital to see how Gizmo's doing."

Sandra's large eyes softened with sudden tears. "Give him my love. Tell him we're praying for him. I'm glad it's you investigating this murder. While you're at it, get the bastard who shot Sanchez. And remember, we're going shopping for my dress some time before Saturday, okay?"

Murray tried a smile. "Sometimes one mystery begets another. Maybe Sergeant Jensen will clear them both up, you think?"

But Jensen merely stiff-armed her. "Since when did detectives from Juvie care what we do? Aren't you kind of out of your playpen, Detective Schmidt?"

"It's Schmitz and I happened to be temporarily assigned to the Homicide Division, Sergeant. And have you got something against sharing information, because if you do, we can take this up in Hansen's office?"

He folded his arms across his substantial beer gut. "Not at all. What d'ya want to know?"

"I was just curious why your response call came in before the tipster called in about the Turner girl's murder?"

Jensen's upper lip curled in a sneer. "I don't see why I should tell you. It's none of your damned business, little girl, so butt out. If Hansen wants to know, let him ask me."

"That answers my question," she said as he strutted away.

"Go to hell," he threw over his shoulder.

"At least I'll have company!" she called back.

Some of the traffic staff overheard the exchange. Somebody said, "Who's the babe?"

"Hell if I know," was the reply, "But if she gets busted to traffic for smart-mouthing, I'm up first for a partner."

"Hell, not even a police dog would partner you."

Returning to headquarters, she cornered Hansen in the lunchroom where he was trying to swallow scalding coffee. He looked pleased to see her for once.

"Murray, good work covering for Duncan last night. Real good, kid." He always called her kid, probably since he had a daughter about her age. "Nice to know I can count on you."

She wasted no time putting her request on the line.

"Thanks. I was wondering if you would assign me to the investigative unit."

The question took the department head by surprise. Hansen paused, mug half way to his mouth. "Why? You're happy where you are, aren't you? I thought Juvie was your thing? You're going great guns there, if you'll pardon the pun. You've put three local gang leaders behind bars, taken drug dealers off the street. You've got fifteen kids in rehab. Caught old Darlene Santana with the goods. It could hardly be boring. Why transfer?"

"Because I want to catch the perp who killed this Turner girl, that's why. Remember, you assigned me to the case?" She teetered on squeaking feet, anxious to be off and running down new leads. Here he was, quibbling over territory.

Hansen took a bite of his donut. "I assigned you temporarily to the Turner case, Murray. We've already got Carreras with enough evidence to put him away. We're bringing him in this morning a drugs charge and suspicion of murder. Don't waste your time and effort on that one. Game over."

"That's the point. I don't think Carreras did it, sir." She stood there as if waiting to get shot on the spot.

But the admission didn't rock any boats. "Can I ask why not?" Hansen said around a bite. She wondered if he ever thought about what he was eating.

Take another deep breath. "Someone else passed the murder scene before Carreras and called in to describe a man standing beside the vehicle. The person standing beside the Turner van might have been the driver of the red SUV Carreras says he saw leave as he pulled up. Or the call could have very well been made by the killer himself. It was made some twenty minutes before Carreras called in."

Chief Hansen put the stump of the donut down. "There must be a reasonable explanation for that. Carreras could have just been there that long. The material evidence still points to him. There is proof that he knew the girl and it was his gun found in the field at the murder scene. Everything points to a drug deal gone bad."

"With his prints?"

"What's that?"

She had to repeat the question to Hansen who temporarily seemed to have lost his hearing. "Prints?"

He brushed it off. "Naturally, he wiped the piece clean. There weren't any. It was registered to him, nonetheless."

"How about the drugs? Where were those?"

Hansen looked weary. "Inside the door of his car. High grade meth in a baggie. Drug dogs sniffed it out in the garage of his office building."

"Could have been put there after the fact, couldn't it? Besides, he told Sanchez the gun was in the glove compartment of his vehicle. "

The duel over, Hansen took another swallow of coffee. *No wonder we all die young in this profession. What a career choice.*

Then he pushed his chair back, scraping across the linoleum. "Okay, look. Murray, since you feel so strongly about it, I'm temporarily assigning you to the Investigative Unit. Under Detectives Jones and Figueroa. But there are plenty of unsolved cases out there beside this one. They take priority in terms of date, all right? And the Turner girl is the most recent."

"Therefore the most easily solved because the trail hasn't gone cold," she said, recognizing victory when she had it in hand.

Hansen realized it as well. "I know you know," he said. "You've been through it before."

That's why I'm here, she wanted to say but didn't. They both knew it already. Murray had a smooth, wide smile, like those pom-pom girls in the Rose Bowl.

"Thanks." Her perfect smile hid an absolute determination not to turn over anything to Forensics, yet. If they hadn't checked out Carreras's story, it was their loss.

Hansen read the look in her eyes, and retreated to sternness. "But you're going to have to do exactly what Jones and Figgy say, when they say it, and how they say it."

"Sure!" She nodded with the bright enthusiasm of a high school cheerleader. It was no good trying to appear cool. "You got it!"

He headed for his desk with her right behind him. "Why don't I believe you?" Hansen had turned around and pinned her down with small blue eyes like enamel map tacks. "Murray, why do you care so much about this guy?"

Her answer had come out cheerleader straight. "Because I believe him." To make it worse, she threw up her hands and looked female helpless. "I just do."

The director ran his hands through what was left of his pale hair. "Oh, god, I knew you were going to say that."

CHAPTER 4

At two-thirty, Carreras and Feldman saw the judge who released him on his own cognizance after posting a $10,000 bail. Apparently, there was a holdup with the coroner's inquiry and the jail was full. It didn't look good." The sheriff's department is sitting on a bunch of evidence," Feldman said. "Now, can we get back to the airport? I hate to mention this, but it's Passover."

"You did, already." Alex tried his argument out on the company attorney. "Look, Eli. They don't have a case. I just stopped to see if the girl was okay, that's all. They act like that's a federal offense or something. And I have no previous record of any kind. In fact, I have the Governor's Medal for Bravery for saving a girl being attacked on the freeway."

Feldman already looked tired. "Look, you want the truth, Carreras? Unless you get somebody to verify your whereabouts at the time of the murder, you're 'It' as far as suspects are concerned. The D.A.'s office has some witness that saw you two together prior to the crime and another one who saw you at the scene. Unless you've got a witness more credible than theirs, it's going to be one helluva legal battle."

"I know who these witnesses are and what they saw, but it wasn't me they saw with her. I never saw the girl before! Ever! And, anyway, I have a witness who can prove I was on the shoulder of the freeway when that girl was killed. A highway patrolman pulled me over and said I had a bad tire. He can back my story, okay? And another officer with the Kern County Sheriff's department witnessed the Sheriff making biased remarks about Mexicans and took pictures of my flat tire. I even remember his name. It was Sanchez. Deputy Sanchez."

"Sanchez." Feldman was only slightly impressed. "Did you get his patrol car number? Or his badge or anything?"

He felt like an idiot. "I hardly thought it necessary at the time. But I know where he is right now. He's in Kern County Hospital. I just saw it on TV."

Feldman rolled his eyes as if he were having seizure. "Oh, great. Your one witness at the murder scene is in the hospital?" The lawyer sighed and rubbed his stubbled jaw "Why me? Look, Carreras. Alex. You need more help than I can give you. I mean, bailing you out is one thing, but you need a real criminal attorney. The plane is waiting out at the airport for us so let's just get on it and get the hell out of here."

He knew he was floundering, grasping at loose facts. "I'd like to talk to him, is all. Sanchez. He's a good cop and straight. He'll give me an alibi, I know."

Feldman shifted behind the wheel and looked at his watch again. "Carreras. I got to get back to LA. And my Dramamine isn't working. Let me remind you that you're in my custody, young buck. Now, be a good lad and get in the car, will you?"

Alex kept talking as he slid in beside Feldman. "I have a cash register receipt putting me in Gorman at one-fifty-five p.m., Sunday." It was hard to keep the triumph out of his voice. "I couldn't possibly have been outside of San Luis Obispo when that girl was killed."

Feldman nodded, brightening slightly. "Better. Look, providing you can find this CP officer and we can use him as a witness as well as the other guy, Deputy Sanchez or whoever, to testify, maybe we have a defense. Like I said on the phone, they're saying they've got physical evidence you knew the girl, eye-witnesses up the ying-yang."

He stared at Feldman. Then it clicked in his mind, as he made a fast replay of opening the van door. "Fingerprints!" He snapped his fingers. "Fingerprints. Sure, I opened the door to help her. But when I saw she was dead. Oh, god. Fingerprints." He rubbed his burning eyes. "And there was somebody else who passed by. An old farmer came down the road and I tried to stop him for help, but he just went on by. I know he saw me by the car. He damn near ran me down."

"We'll find what they've really got tomorrow morning." Feldman yawned and looked at his watch again. "Just make sure you're leveling with me." Alex got the implication, but let it go. He was too tired to argue.

Feldman seemed to sense his growing despair. His long face softened to look even longer, like a bloodhound with glasses. "Look, the autopsy is going to set the exact time on death, give or take ten to fifteen minutes. If you can prove this CP patrolman saw you a few minutes before that, and you've got proof you stopped, like you said, up in Gorman, you may be in the clear. You say you had a gun with you, but who doesn't in LA? You've got a license I assume."

He was about to tell Feldman the deputies must have taken it when they searched the car, but the lawyer yawned again, showing a mouth full of metal fillings.

"Right now, the company pilot is getting a wedgie waiting to get the plane back to LA so let's get the rented wreck back to the airport or the guy will leave us here in the bergs."

In spite of his fatigue, his mind felt sharp again, fueled by coffee and facts. "I'll find the two cops who can vouch for me, Sanchez and the other highway patrolman and get them to testify. I know Sanchez, the deputy, will. And he probably took pictures of the tire tracks that prove there was another vehicle there before me."

"Let's hope." Feldman eased his large abdomen behind the wheel. "Don't they make these rental things with tilting steering wheels? But right now, let face it. They got no one else and you were at the murder scene. Are you coming or do you stay up here in Adobeville?"

Alex lingered on the sidewalk, leaning on the door. "Can't you see how ridiculous this is? I haven't done anything but stop to help somebody out. So that makes me a murder suspect? This is what I call real justice."

"Call it what you like." Feldman's long face grew even longer as he sat there. "I didn't make the laws. I just figure out how to get by them, that's my job. That's why they hired me. I've been on the wrong side of the law like you, boy. I know what it feels like. If George Crittenden had not come to my assistance, I'd probably still be serving time for obstructing justice. Trying to protect the firm I was working for and they wanted to dump me the minute the feds nailed me."

He turned his bloodshot eyes on Alex who recognized pain when he saw it. "I'll do my best for you. But you've got to help me out. Come up with somebody, anybody, a witness who can put you somewhere else besides on that county highway at the time of the murder, okay?"

"What am I going to do, go on TV asking for witnesses? Wait, I do have a receipt from the truck stop just before the Grapevine. It's got to be timed and dated."

Feldman's nod was grudging. "It's a start. Give it to me. I'll lock it up some place. You sure you never saw this girl before? One night stand? Anything?"

"Absolutely."

The lawyer shrugged again. "Whatever it takes to get a witness, that's what you're going to have to do. If it takes bungee-cord jumping off the Century City Towers at high noon. Now, are you coming or not?"

He hesitated, unwilling to let the situation slip out of his hands. "Listen, give me just half an hour, Eli. I've got to talk to Sanchez."

"The company pilot—"

"Screw the pilot. I've got to talk to Sanchez to see if he

got the pictures of the tire tracks. It'll take twenty minutes if we hurry."

"Hurry where? Where in hell are we going?"

He slid in beside Feldman and slammed the door. "Kern County Hospital."

Feldman sighed. "Why do I get involved in these things? My client's only positive witness is on death's door and it's Passover."

～

"Hey, Murray, you hear they caught the bastard that killed that girl yesterday?" Figueroa leaned around the wall of their adjoining cubicles. "I heard Jensen caught him red-handed at the murder scene, the story goes. Man, he'll get glory for that."

She had rolled her files on her favorite computer chair one door down from Juvie to Criminal Investigation. As she unstacked everything into the small cubicle, she saw the computer and printer took up all the desk space. "I heard. Some guy from LA, they said. A hot-shot lawyer. You hear about Sanchez?"

"Yeah, tough luck. Are we becoming the crime capital of California overnight or what?" Figgy dropped into his chair and put up his feet. "Is he gonna make it? Have you heard?"

She leafed through the stack of papers on her desk. "I've got a friend who works out in ICU. I'm going to go out and check on him as soon as I find some place to put this stuff. Darlene Santana's been selling to minors again. I can't believe she grows that much pot in her window sill. I can't even grow cactus. She must have a supplier."

"Old Darlene," Figgy said with a fond sigh. "I think I busted her a few times back in the eighties. She wasn't bad looking back then."

"You probably did. Never speaks of kids, but I saw the picture of a little girl, red-haired like her. She wouldn't tell me who it is, but I'll bet it's her daughter. Funny, she never spoke of having a daughter." She didn't tell him she had put the picture in a locked file after promising Darlene it would be safe.

Figueroa was following his own train of thought. "The weird thing was Sanchez was one of the ones who busted the girl's killer yesterday. Then somebody shoots him. Don't really seem like a coincidence. Does it?"

He had her attention now. Murray looked around the wall at the detective, a chubby, over-aged cherub her juvenile offenders. "I thought they released the suspect after questioning him today?"

"Yeah, on hefty bail." Figueroa's chair squeaked as he eased around to face her. "They found a bunch of stuff of his in her van." He passed some printouts around the divider on a spindle. "You can take a look, if you want."

The first picture on the spindle was a photograph of Carreras, the LA lawyer police were calling a significant person in the case. She took it off, turning it to the light. His dark eyes, honest and boyishly sincere, returned her gaze. Smile like a movie star.

The second picture came from the driver's license of the dead girl. Dark hair, dark eyes. Pretty smile. Alive, this was Shelby Turner. She took a deep breath. "I'm going out to see how Sanchez's doing, Figgy. Call me if anything comes up."

"Give him my best." She could tell Figgy was surfing the Net. "Tell him we're praying for him."

She wondered if people were just saying that or they really prayed. The thought never occurred to her to pray. "I will," she said, knowing she wouldn't. Prayers didn't help her father. He died with a punk's bullet in his chest. Almost perfect shot, the surgeon had told her mother.

There was only one ICU unit, and luckily, they were short-staffed. He arrived between shifts and the halls were quiet. Alex waited at the vending machine with his back to the nurses' station until the nurse at the desk went to answer a buzzer. Then he slipped down the hall and into Sanchez's room.

Sanchez looked like a neon sign on a *barrio* liquor store, full of tubes and blinking lights. In the half light from the overhead night light, he seemed to be sleeping and Alex hated to wake him. But he needed an alibi more than the deputy needed rest. "Sanchez, *compadre,* it's me, Carreras. How you doing, man? You look like the Las Vegas strip." Alex leaned down to speak in the deputy's ear.

Sanchez eyes opened heavily, and then focused in recognition. "Go away, Carreras, everybody wants your ass."

Alex nodded at the tubes. "I hope you nailed the bastard."

"Didn't even see them. I was giving this guy a ticket and somebody blasted me from a passing car. Never even got my gun out. Jeesuz. My wife's downstairs in early labor. Son of a bitch had to shoot me." Tears welled out of the deputy's eyes.

"What about the car? Did you get a look at it?"

"White. Something like Honda Civic. High beams on. Bastards."

"How about the guy you stopped or was it a girl?"

Sanchez squeezed his eyes closed. "Woman. Ugly blonde. I was just walking up to her and they got me."

"This is a bad time to ask, but did you get the pictures of the other set of tracks?"

Sanchez raspy reply was barely audible. "My brother-in-law got 'em. 1 hour-photo. Now get out. Whole world looking for your ass, man."

Alex closed his eyes. The pictures actually existed. "Listen, Sanchez. Gizmo. Will you speak up for me in court? I didn't try to run, did I?"

"Baby coming," Sanchez whispered back. "I need this job, but you didn't kill that girl."

Alex put his hand on Sanchez's head, the only part of him without wires. "Thanks. Got to go now."

Sanchez raised a finger. "No, something. Wait! Something funny."

"Somebody's coming." Alex straightened up to listen. The voices in the hall said something about Sanchez's room. Going to the door, he opened it a crack. A tall blonde young woman was talking to the nurse as they walked slowly down the hall…Going back to Sanchez, he said, "Looks like you've got a cute visitor. I'd better split. See you in court, okay?" Opening the door to the adjoining room, he looked back at the deputy with a thumbs up sign. Sanchez raised one thumb in response. "Be good. That's a pretty nurse out there. *Que heina*." He went out through the bathroom to the adjoining room.

Waiting behind the door until the hall was clear, he heard the tall blonde visitor say, "Detective Murray Schmitz, Homicide Division."

Ducking down the stairs and out into the late spring afterglow of a warm afternoon, Alex felt a surge of hope. There's a good chance he could beat the charge, if he could establish his whereabouts at the time of the Turner girl's murder. Sanchez had the pictures of the other SUV's tire tracks in the mud and he had the receipt from the Grapevine Cafe. With a little luck, he could locate the patrolman who spotted the flat tire on the Interstate. *With a little luck*

In the ICU, Murray walked into Gilberto Sanchez's room with a smile that quickly faded when she saw all the tubes and wires. The TV mumbled on about cooking pasta the perfect way. But his eyes were closed.

She had no idea why, but Murray had the distinct feeling someone had just left the room. The only indication was that the bathroom door was ajar, not unusual in a hospital room. Walking over to it, she saw the door to the adjoining room was open, but the room was empty.

As she returned to Sanchez's bed, Murray glanced down at the freshly mopped and waxed floor. The faint imprint of muddy sneakers told her someone else had been here just before her, someone who had left without being seen. The size of the sneakers indicated their wearer was a man. A tall man.

Going back to Sanchez, she saw his eyes were open, watching her. "It's okay, Giz. The nurses aren't going to like it, though. Having too many visitors coming and going."

Sanchez studied her face for a moment, weighing the odds this young, pretty cop might just be pulling a trick. But he knew Murray Schmitz. There was something about her that was as simple and uncomplicated as the valley she came from. "Okay, the pictures," he said finally. "He was looking for the pictures."

She leaned nearer, above him like an angel with her flawless skin and sky eyes. "Pictures of the tire tracts from the other SUV?"

Sanchez closed his eyes in agreement. "Tire tracks next to the van. Carreras parked ahead of it. Custom treads. Big D's special order mountain treads. Carreras's Jeep had regular treads. No match at all. And other driver had on boots. Carreras had sneakers."

"Who's got the pictures?"

"Brother-in-law. One hour photo."

"Gizmo, can I ask why you're holding them? I mean, they're evidence." Sanchez's silence gave him away. "Okay, I get it. You don't think he'll get a fair shake, do you? The Hispanic thing?"

Standing in the stark hospital room, listening to him fight for breath, Murray Schmitz had a feeling Sanchez wasn't telling her everything. His dark eyes peered out of the bandages like a raccoon stuck in a flour barrel.

"He was still asking them to call for an ambulance when I came up. He got mad at the chief for not calling the paramedics. Said she might still have a pulse. Jensen was a bastard."

Murray shuddered slightly. It was the kind of statement that would throw a scare into any county prosecutor. She wrote it on her notepad. "Anything else?"

His eyes closed. Maybe in defense, but she had to let up on him, even if he was hiding something. "He said he had a gun in his car, but there wasn't one."

Murray recalled the file. "They found out it the field. No prints."

"They won't find nothing."

"Why not?"

"Looked like a pro hit. Maybe drugs." Under the sheets, Sanchez shifted uncomfortably. "Whole thing's whacked. His handkerchief's in her hand. Why? He felt bad after he shot her or what? Don't make sense. Killers run. They don't give hankies. Killer was stupid. Carreras, no."

Murray had to smile. She had always liked the way Sanchez stated the obvious no one else dared mention. "Get well, Gizmo. You've got to help me out with the boys' team this year. You know I can't handle them by myself."

He struggled to smile. "Yeah, you could, Schmitzy. You can handle this, too. I'm counting on you."

She was glad when the nurse came in and drew the curtain. "Sorry, Detective. We have to have our bath."

Sanchez held up his hand. "Schmitzy, one more thing."

The nurse started to protest. "Really, miss. He's had enough for one day."

Sanchez beckoned Murray back to the bedside. "I wrote it all down but Jensen said to strike it."

The nurse pulling the curtain around her gave her a chance to hide her tears from him. '*Cops cry,*' her father had said. '*They just don't let anybody see.*'

Murray left the hospital and went to find Sanchez's brother-in-law.

He looked slightly alarmed when she showed her badge. "Gilberto said it was okay."

"Yes, Miss, I know, but I already gave them to somebody. He just left about ten minutes ago."

"What did he look like?" Without having to hear the description, she knew it had been Carreras. "You gave him the negatives, too?"

The man shrugged. "Don't I always?"

Murray started to leave. "Wait, miss. You didn't ask if I made copies. I always do that, too. Especially for Gilberto, I make copies. You want?"

Her knees actually felt weak. "You'll never know how much."

∾∾

At the private airport outside the city, the company pilot was waiting to fly them back to LA. As soon as they were on board, Feldman got a drink from the bar and popped a few airsickness pills before opening his briefcase.

"I'm warning you, Carreras. This guy flies like a Kamikaze pilot so fasten your seatbelt." Those were his last words before he settled back in his seat and began to snore.

As they flew down the coast toward Los Angeles, Alex tried to sort the whole thing out in spite of Eli's constant snoring. This was the man he would be trusting his life to, drink in hand, mouth wide open, making sounds like a mating walrus.

On the positive side, Officer Sanchez seemed a good bet as a witness to the Sheriff's obvious prejudice and to his resistance to getting immediate aid for the girl. He had the photos of the tire tracks and the clean imprint of a boot in his briefcase. He would copy them to a disk and set up a file of his own evidence, independent of Feldman who might turn out to be in Crittenden's pocket.

Relieved that he had found something to go on, he closed his eyes and recreated the scene for the millionth time. What was he missing? For one thing, the motive. Who would want to kill a pretty young girl who liked big dogs? Best bet was a jilted boyfriend or at worst, she was the victim of a robbery. And what were the items the police said were in the van?

Whatever it was, Sanchez's pictures proved there was

someone else there at the scene besides him. If he could find the old man in the truck, he could substantiate the presence of the real killer even further. The farmer had to have passed the red jeep on the road before he got to her van. That should be enough evidence to lift the suspicion from him and widen the search for the real killer.

He looked out the window of the company jet as it passed over Santa Barbara's peerless harbor. It was a beautiful sunny day, in the '70s, the kind Southern California was famous for. Relaxing a little, he turned on his laptop as they flowed smoothly over Camarillo where the foothills rose and fell in rhythm with the sea.

For a moment, the beauty of the scene spread below healed his immediate injuries to self-pride. Chelsea would probably get over it, cry a lot, spend hours with her friends asking for advice, only to follow none of it. She would then beg him to forgive her for not trusting him, and they would go on with their make-believe lives as the couple who lived happily ever after.

But the fact was, it came to him that he needed some space from her, anyway. She was the most demanding human being he had ever dealt with, jealous of every woman she thought was more beautiful, or taller, thinner, or smarter than she was. She had to have reassurance on the hour, sometime on the half hour, that she, Chelsea Leila Crittenden, was the apex of feminine beauty and charm just like the reporters had described her when she was named Miss Teen Los Angeles.

Los Angeles, being Mecca for beautiful people, was full of ex-Miss Teens to the point the competition was driving Chelsea into a frenzy of minor cosmetic surgeries, beauty treatments, and shopping sprees.

She was so absorbed with erasing every imperfection, there wasn't room for anyone else in her life except those who adored her.

The events of the last twenty-four hours at least provided a convenient hiatus for him to rethink their relationship.

❦

He glanced again at his laptop. There it was, his smiling face and all splashed all over the computer screen. "Alex Carreras, local attorney, is being held on suspicion of murdering a young Diamondback City woman after a weekend of heavy partying in a Sunrise ski resort."

"What the hell?" he burst out, but Feldman was somewhere in Never-Never land. Stunned, Alex followed the story. "No, you're crazy!" He slammed the keyboard with his fist. "That's a lie!" But the laptop chatted his life away, in one neatly tailored phrase after another.

"…Diamondback City near Bakersfield." He wanted to turn it off but his hand wouldn't obey him. "…girl found shot to death on a county highway outside San Luis Obispo. Carreras was questioned at the scene, and released. Later, he was arrested at his girlfriend's apartment in…"

"My god! They can't get anything straight!" Then it occurred to him to listen to every word. Reality wasn't jiving with the news report. No other suspects in custody. How could they have the information this fast and incorrectly unless…Unless it was a planted news story.

Now, he was really becoming paranoid.

His mind flitted back to his brother Ricky' question. '*Do you know anybody who has it in for you? You know, whose toes did you step on?*' That was open territory as vast as the ocean below. He was a careful lawyer and good one. He had found loopholes and tidbits where none had existed before, saving Crittenden's clients millions in one case.

If fact, Crittenden had been referring to the Synotech incident again the other day. Synotech, a huge chemical conglomerate with international branches, topped the list of one of California most profitable industries, a fact which also gave it substantial political clout in the state government. However, the feds had been hounding it for not paying appropriate taxes on thousands of international transactions.

They were getting hot for the lost revenue and the case was getting a lot of unpleasant publicity.

While he had found enough loopholes in international trade laws to get them off with a light fine and a don't-let-it-happen-again warning from the state appellate court, he had uncovered plenty of evidence that Synotech was indeed trafficking in something else even more lucrative than diet pills and heart medication.

On an official visit for the law firm, he had only been given a tour of offices and control room as well as a fancy lunch. Slipping away during one of their interminable meetings on efficiency, he had gone in the back door with a clipboard and a swiped hardhat. No one had ever called him on it, but he had discovered Synotech was shipping something out of their docks that wasn't listed on the official bill of lading. Even the crates themselves were stamped Hazardous Materials, and Highly Flammable Contents. He had told Crittenden about it and asked what the firm wanted to do about it, since Synotech was a deep pockets client. The head of the firm's reaction was one of absolute stark horror.

"What in the world inspired you to do that?" He re-framed Crittenden, tall, well-tailored, and urbane, martini in hand against the expensive view of his Pacific. "Why not just ask MacPherson in shipping to visit the plant and look around, if you're representing the company in court?"

Play it cool and dumb. Alarm bells went off all over his head. "I did that earlier, but he only showed me the executive gym, the lunchroom, and shipping control room."

Crittenden's expression was suddenly suspicious. "You said Shipping? Why? Why on earth did he take you through Shipping?""

"I don't know, we kind of just walked through it." He groped for the right posture enthusiastic but not snoopy. He decided on fresh-out-of-college, dazzled-by-corporate-spending. "But I loved the computer room. Now that's real-ly awesome equipment. Especially the satellite hookup with Europe and Asia. Must really speed things up." *Error mes-*

sage, he thought. *There was that odd stiffening again.*

"Yes, it does. It certainly does. Anything else? Impress you, I mean."

It was time to lighten up and Alex took his best shot. "They have one helluva a lunchroom. Things cooked to order. Salad mixed at your table. Unbelievable. And a full gym with an Olympic sized pool and a spa. Thought I'd died and gone to heaven."

It worked. Crittenden had smiled slightly and the edge in his voice softened. "So you liked the health club? Actually, it comes with the building but we did hire the trainer. Figured we wouldn't pay it out in health insurance claims. Kind of a humanitarian touch, I thought."

Alex took advantage to segue into a less controversial area. Firm loyalty. "Sometimes, it's just so hard to believe, Parker—" He used Crittenden's first name to remind him he was going to be his future son-in-law. "—that I could work for a firm like yours right out of law school. It's like a dream, you know. I'll wake up some morning and it will disappear."

It hadn't worked. Crittenden had stayed on the scent of trouble with bloodhound dedication. "Not if you don't play your cards right and don't go off on a tangent. If you suspected something wasn't on the up-and-up, you should have asked me, not gone on some undercover operation. What if you had been found out, Alex? Can you imagine how embarrassing for the firm that could have been? We could have lost one of our most influential clients!"

Thinking back on it now, it had become less of a conversation and more of an interrogation as Crittenden worked himself up into a lather. As he reiterated all the reasons for not annoying powerful clients, Alex recognized the old double standard so eulogized in a parody of John F. Kennedy's words, 'Ask not what the law can do for you. Ask what you can do to the law'.

Finally, he'd had enough. "Listen, Parker, imagine how embarrassing it would be to be identified as the law firm that helped them cover up an illegal operation? We could lose our licenses as well as the rest of our clients."

"That's precisely why I wish you'd cleared it with me first, Alex." Crittenden's ice rattled again as he studied the bottom of his glass. "Now, let's just pretend this didn't happen. I'm sure they've got all the proper licenses for shipping arms to any customer they choose, as long as the buyers aren't on the black list. But let me tell you, that list is getting shorter every day. Plus, even those countries like Libya and Iran can buy through brokers. It's not even worth the trouble to pursue."

"But…"

"Enough. I'm playing golf with Synotech's regional manager this afternoon as a matter of fact. I'll mention it to him and I promise he'll adjust things to pass inspection."

"In other words, cook the books. Is that it?" *Wrong move.*

"This is a big boy's game," Parker Crittenden said with that slight edge to his voice. "If you want the life you worked so hard to earn, you have to play by their rules, all right?"

The discussion was over. It had been the wrong thing to say and he sensed he had struck a nerve. There was something about Crittenden's frozen urbanity that made him increasingly uneasy. "You just don't mention it, that's all."

He waited a moment for the 'all clear'. It didn't come. "Hope I didn't step on anybody's toes."

He might as well have said he hoped he hadn't fallen flat on his ass. Crittenden's response was an unequivocal, "I hope you didn't either."

In the end, weeks of ground work had paid off. Synotech's accounting office had been notified of the discrepancies in the bills of lading. Having been caught, Synotech quickly anteed up not only the back taxes due the government, but the interest as well.

But hackles were raised as the settlement reached the business page of the papers. He became the firm's latest golden boy, with a tidy bonus which was gobbled up by student loans and so many executive lunches, he had to get the waistband on his best slacks let out.

Still, no one had raised the burning question in his mind. What exactly was Synotech shipping? Whatever it was, it was highly flammable, and dangerous enough to pretend it was diet pills. Diet pills in the Middle East Africa where adipose tissue is indicative of wealth? He hardly thought so.

However, keeping an eye on Synotech's operations had become an integral part of his duties at the firm with a strange twist. At the same time he was assigned to the account, someone had put a stop to the secretaries giving him access to Synotech's shipping files. All he got were the monthly balance sheets. He could never tell exactly where the order to limit the access to Synotech's records had originated, but when he asked Crittenden, the senior partner seemed mildly perplexed.

"I'll look into it" was all he got and that was the end of it. A girl he had flirted with in Filing had got them for him, anyway. As he had suspected, Synotech was still doing a cover-up, only it was nearly impossible for an outsider to follow, so the nebulous was the description of the shipment's contents.

Across the narrow aisle, Feldman was snoring like a bulldozer. He looked around, his eyes red and clouded. "We here already?"

"You slept the whole way."

"Thank God," Feldman said.

It took about twenty minutes to get to the scene of the murder. It had been picked pretty clean and the emergency vehicles had made mincemeat of any tire tracks where the girl's van had been parked.

Murray glanced at her file again, lying on the front seat. Shelby Turner, a kid from Diamondback City, a wide place in the road if there ever was one. She had been up that way to the county fair once. What had Shelby, a girl from the boonies, been doing way down here, almost one hundred miles from home on the side of the road? Was she really following Alex Carreras, the way everyone thought? Or did something else bring her so far from home?

The autopsy would prove whether she'd been pregnant or recently had sex with him. Or anybody else. The official autopsy was put on hold until Friday. Another bad break. Hard evidence was what she needed. And it was sadly lacking.

Murray climbed out into the sharp wind that struck her chest with a blow like a fist. She zipped up her windbreaker since she was just getting over a bout of bronchitis. It never rains in sunny California, it just mildews.

There were weeds beside the road, yellow scrub from the previous season, not yet turned to green. Forensics had made a list of items found at the scene. Geez, pretty bad for Carreras. Carreras's bloody handkerchief clutched in the girl's hand—that was damning. Car keys and his business card in the glove compartment.

All circumstantial evidence. No murder weapon, though, and no credible witness.

Then she wondered why she even wanted to prove this man's innocence in the first place? What was he to her? A spoiled rich boy who was probably playing mattress polo and got burned.

It was just a feeling. Then she remembered her father saying, "If you think they're innocent, you're probably right. It's kind of a gut thing." This was a gut thing, not a heart thing. She had to keep telling herself that as she went back to tell Hansen she wanted the case.

Fifteen minutes in the cold wind didn't improve things much. Murray got back in the car and studied the pictures Deputy Gilberto Sanchez had taken Sunday. The same Sanchez who had been shot by an irate motorist and now was in the ICU.

What was he hiding and why was he protecting Carreras? Was it an ethnic bond or did he genuinely feel Carreras was being set up?

Rotten luck all the way around. With guns available to every smalltime punk who had fifty dollars, all of their lives were in danger. Sanchez was a three-year man with a wife about to have a baby.

Her own father's story all over again. She had grown up fatherless because of just such a punk. Her father, a fifteen-year veteran, had been killed intervening in a domestic dispute. His killer had been paroled after just ten years because of his youth. He then killed the mother of his three-year-old daughter.

Murray studied the digital pictures again. Swinging in a wide arc from one side of the road to the other, were muddy tire tracks with a distinctive tread pattern. It hadn't rained since the Turner girl was found, but the emergency and law enforcement vehicles had made hash of any tracks around.

Putting her car in gear, she rolled slowly forward away from the intersection. About a half a mile north, something caught her eye. Another set of tire tracks had made a rut in the shoulder, tearing up the grass in a distinct arc. Pulling over, she studied the tracks for a minute, comparing them to the pictures in her hand. They were identical. In Sanchez's photos, Carreras's car was parked on the shoulder directly in front of the van. What was left of the mountain treads tracks had pulled right beside it, then moved up the road and stopped, but why?

Murray got out and studied the field on the other side of the barbed wire fence. Getting out on the muddy shoulder, she roamed around looking for God-knows-what. Anything Forensics missed. A tire track. A piece of paper. They were pretty thorough.

Squatting, she took out her ballpoint pen and poked through the long grass at the edge of the road. She swore and cursed her idiocy as she worked her way through itchy weeds looking for something she only half believed existed.

She climbed over the barbed wire fence, and dropped down on the other side. She hadn't done that since she used to steal rides on other people's horses as a kid. Finally, her father had gotten tired of apologizing to the neighbors and bought her one after she was caught.

Bringing her camera along, she walked along the rows of plants, admiring the expertise of the field crew in aligning them so perfectly. Each little head of broccoli was a micro-planet of its own, from stem to head, leaves branching out to collect rain and light.

The clouds cut loose and water traced down her shirt collar pooling in her bra. She crawled and squatted in the driving rain until rivers of mud ran over her boot tops. De-feated, she climbed back into the patrol car, turned on the heater full blast, and opened the file.

Onions. Murray sat thinking for a moment, staring out at the spring fields. How many people around here grew on-ions? This was mainly garlic growing country. Her best bet was the farmer's market held every morning just outside San Luis Obispo. If the man was a grower, he would more than likely belong to the Farmers' Market Association. She got the number from directory assistance and dialed.

"Do you know how many onion farmers there are in this county alone?" The Chamber of Commerce secretary barely disguised her indignation as if everyone should be able to rattle off that statistic at will.

"I have no idea," Murray replied trying for the appropri-ate tone of humility. "I'm just looking for one in particular."

"Well, ma'am," returned the snippy voice, "which one of the one hundred fifty-three would that be? What did he do, sell you some bad onions?"

That's right, get smart. Murray envisioned the secretary as a munchkin with large false pearls and a stacked hairdo. "No, ma'am," she answered sweetly. "He's a witness to a murder."

Sometimes it was fun, playing the wicked witch of the West.

"Oh." The munchkin's voice deflated into a chirp. "Well, what do you want me to do?"

"Just fax me a list of all the names to the Homicide Division."

But Munchkin had the last word. "As if I've got nothing better to do," she muttered as she hung up the phone.

By now, she was sneezing and red-eyed. Remembering something from Carreras's statement about looking for a gas station, she followed yet another hunch, continuing past the intersection and going south until she came to the first and only roadside store for ten miles. It was a small produce stand with two rusting gas pumps in front like gravestones of a less technical age.

The owners, an elderly Hispanic couple, looked alarmed when they saw the patrol car. Suspicion ran through their dark eyes like subtitles in a TV show.

"I'm looking for an older man who grows onions and drives an old Dodge truck." More than a language barrier separated them across the counter. They whispered together while she waited patiently.

Finally, the man said, "We buy onions from one old man, senorita, but we don't know his name."

She was pretty sure they were illegal, always on the fringe of society, never asking names and not giving theirs.

The woman blinked her eyes together and held up a finger. She whispered to her husband. "Aieee. Achee."

Not wanting to get involved was written all over him. "My wife says she thinks it begins with H," the man said. They consulted again. "Yes, H and then O." He shrugged. "That's all we know. Sorry."

Great. Pressing on, she showed them Carreras's photograph. "Maybe you might have seen him. Tall. Latino."

"No, senorita." They didn't even blink. "*No lo conoce.*"

It's no use. Be polite. Leave them with options.

"If you see the onion man again, please call me." She gave them a card with her name, Murray Schmitz, Juvenile Justice Division, and her phone. Then she realized it was one of her old ones. She was now Detective Schmitz. They looked so happy to see her leave, she decided not to ask them for it back.

But at least they had given her a lead.

Getting back in the car, Murray started back up the road away from the intersection. Her mind spun backward and forward over the scene of the Turner murder as she imagined Carreras coming upon the blue van.

Suppose, just for kicks, the man in the old truck was the real killer. After all, he was the only other driver on the road at the time, according to Carreras's story, except the mysterious red Cherokee. Maybe the guy in the Cherokee had just stopped to help, like Carreras, saw the girl was dead and taken off after seeing Carreras coming.

Scenario Number Two: Suppose the Cherokee's driver had killed the girl, then taken off up the road, done a U-turn, switched to a beat-up truck, slapped on a hat and sunglasses, and driven back to find Carreras beside the van. He calls nine-one-one and pins the crime on the innocent passerby. Then how did he get rid of the Cherokee? Simple. He had an accomplice. It was beginning to sound like an old Laurel and Hardy movie.

Scenario Three: The murderer had spotted Alex Carreras limping off the Interstate, came back to see if he was still there by the van, realized he had a patsy, and called the sheriff. It played right in her head, but she warned herself not to orchestrate crimes out of fictional scenarios. Only hard evidence paid off in court. The kind the Crime Scene people said they had and now, the gun. Still for that inexplicable reason she dared to call instinct, at least to herself, she knew Carreras was telling the truth. He was simply too intelligent to make up a story like the one he had given the police. Just as Sanchez had pointed out, he wasn't stupid.

But she also knew better than to congratulate herself too early on just a smart piece of detective work. It would take a lab, not the naked eye, to make a connection between the two sets of tracks at the murder scene and the actual crime. The footprint of a boot might carry some weight, since Forensics could link it to the size and height of the other person at the crime scene. But still, crystal meth in the chassis of the suspect's vehicle was as good as a conviction. She knew that with all certainty.

But it was only circumstantial evidence. The gun and the meth were going to carry a lot more weight than any tire tracks or footprints. Yet somehow, she couldn't figure Carreras, even in some kind of rage, shooting the girl and then flinging the weapon out in the field not fifty yards from the car. But killers had done stupider things.

One the other hand, this was a guy who four years ago had risked his life to save a girl he didn't even know. Gotten a nasty knife scar and a several weeks in the hospital for his trouble. Face it, Murray argued with her inner self, the balance of hard evidence was in the law's favor and against Carreras.

CHAPTER 5

Saying it was on the way to his in-laws' house, Feldman dropped Alex off in front of his condo in Malibu. But it occurred to Alex, this might be Feldman's way of warning him to not even think about leaving town.

"Remember, don't go anywhere, Mr. Carreras. Ten K is a lot of cash to put up for what looks like a slam-dunk conviction, although with your connections, I wouldn't sweat it. We have to appear at eight o'clock sharp Friday morning. Just stick close to home and, please, no more skiing naked. *Oi*, what a visual!"

"Stay home? Are you kidding? I'm going in to work." Alex grabbed his laptop and jumped out. "The day is still young, Pappy. Have a happy Passover."

Feldman looked enigmatic as well as dyspeptic. "Call Crittenden first. Maybe he's got other plans."

"You're my counsel, Eli. I'm counting on your support. Crittenden, as far as I'm concerned, can fuck himself."

The lawyer rolled his eyes and mumbled, "For this, I went to law school?"

Alex stood for a long moment, watching the vintage Mercedes putter quietly down the cul-de-sac. Chelsea's blue Porsche was in the driveway. That was an ominous sign in itself, since she was usually at the office until six. What was she doing home so early in the afternoon? He went inside to face the Arctic storm he knew would be waiting for him.

"Okay, what's going on?" She shoved a mug of coffee into his hand. "You look awful."

She, on the other hand, looked as luscious as an artificial rose in a pink jogging suit.

"And I thought interrogation was over." He headed for the bedroom, but she stopped him, hands on hips.

"Where are you going?"

"To take a shower, do you mind?"

"Okay, but make it quick. We're going to meet Daddy at the club at four-thirty."

"I guess I don't get to know why."

In a voice as cold and efficient as neon lights, she replied, "No, I don't think you deserve that consideration, do you? Since you don't have any for anyone else."

"If you're talking about me being late, I told you what it was about. They've got me mixed up with somebody else."

The night before, the worst fight of their entire two year relationship had graduated from mean to dirty fast. When Chelsea was angry with him, racial equity went out the window and Anglo-Saxon purity took the field.

At first she had given him the cold shoulder treatment when he finally got back, still smarting from the police interrogation. Then as he walked through the bedroom to the shower and attacked.

"Alex, I don't know what is so difficult about facing the truth. Admit that you and your brothers and friends got to drinking and just let time slip by up there in Sunrise. Then you suddenly realized what time it was and took off and had the nerve to cook up some cock-and-bull story about running out of oil, having a flat tire, and finding a dead body." Looking like something downloaded from a soft porn site in her string-bikini and augmented bra, she stood there with folded arms. "I' m beginning to wonder if this isn't a good indication of how you're going to behave after we're married. So I'm really glad we haven't made this arrangement permanent, yet," she added, her eyes icing over into a glacial blue. Here it comes. She was going to using her ultimate weapon in a quarrel, breaking off the engagement.

"Is this supposed some kind of a threat?" He knew those eyes, so much like her father's, never lied unless she wanted them to. "Because it sounds like one. And that's really getting old, Chelsea."

His fiancé's perfectly glossed lips had formed the words with care. "Take it any way you want. But we have an obligation to my parents who were kind enough to give this party just for us." She pirouetted back toward the front door, making certain the filmy dress she had slipped on revealed every curve of her body.

"Wouldn't think of keeping you off the society page or missing the chance for a chat with your mother."

"Obviously, I'm just part of your upwardly-mobile agenda." It was a throw-away line she had practiced for some part in her brief acting career as a TV extra.

Stress gave him the edge and he came up with something equally smart and theatrical. "You having second thoughts about a life with someone who makes less money than your father's cook?"

With the studied cool of a supermarket bandit, Chelsea had given him the old one-two punch. "There are other choices I could make, you know, still open to me. Much better choices, it appears." Her silver sandals tapped across the floor and out to the terrace. "After today."

"Oh, not that again." He had jerked off his sweatshirt, tossing it on the sofa. "You aren't talking about the Silicon Valley wiz kid with the slight lisp and green teeth? C'mon, Chelsea. Do better than that."

"At least he makes over a hundred thousand a year and doesn't have to have a co-signer to buy a car."

That was the final clincher. They hadn't spoken two words since then. At the party, she disappeared somewhere after the champagne toast. He hadn't even bothered to look for her and came home alone. Chelsea had never showed up.

ल৯৯ल

"This looks bad, Alex. The police are saying you had some kind of relationship with that girl they found in Kern County. Is that true?"

At the Marina's clubhouse, they sat at a table beside the window with a good view of the yachts going through the channel to the Pacific. It was the table Crittenden always had, making Alex wonder if he rented it by the year. Chelsea had chosen not to sit beside him, but on Crittenden's side of the leather booth. Together, they regarded him across the table with matching sets of blue eyes as hard as marbles.

"Of course not. Never seen her before in my life! Who did you talk to?"

"I made a phone call to Judge Bailey up there. Old friend from law school. They have pictures and some personal effects of yours."

So that's what Eli wouldn't tell him. He settled back and ordered a drink. "I told you all that I know last night."

He didn't know why he felt uncomfortable except Crittenden has always made it clear he would rather have Godzilla for a son-in-law than a Hispanic kid whose father had been an accountant for the power company for thirty years.

"I got out to see if she was okay and she was dead. Shot twice at close range. Young. Pretty. Two dogs in the back of the van. Some guy in a car similar to mine drove away just as I got there."

Crittenden's pale eyes were trained to give away nothing, but Chelsea jumped in, not bothering to hide anything. "Why did you decide to stop there, at that particular off ramp where there weren't any facilities?"

Alex kept his tone even in contrast to her sarcasm. "Like I tried to tell you last night, I got a flat on the Interstate and right about then, my oil light came on. I didn't have my jack although I'm next to positive I had started out with one. This highway patrolman pulled up and told me to take the next off ramp, that there was a station a few miles up the road. I got off and saw the girl's van."

"Really." Crittenden eased back in his chair, fingers in a tent, sheltering his thoughts. "No one else saw you?"

For some reason he couldn't explain, he changed his story to leave out the old farmer passing him by. He wanted to see if Crittenden knew about it. "That's it."

Crittenden studied him and then grunted. "Strange." The comment carried doubt like a concealed weapon.

"Not just strange. Weird. The whole thing is weird. I know I checked my tires the way I always do. They were fine. The whole car was fine, right, Chelsea? You were the one who took it in for services before I left."

"Fine," she said, staring at the ice in her spritzer. "Nothing wrong with it. Oil was full."

Crittenden shrugged. "You probably picked up a nail in the road."

"And just happened to pull off at the next exit to shoot some girl I didn't know. You can't give their story any credence, Parker. By the way, there wasn't any nail. I had to buy a new tire because the guy at the station said something had punctured the tire just below the rim. 'Almost impossible to fix', he said."

Without commenting, Crittenden changed the subject. "The police say your fingerprints are on the van."

He shrugged, playing it cool under fire. Training had taught him to sweat later. "Naturally. I opened the door to see if she was alive. Let the dogs get some air."

The ice in Crittenden's glass chunked in the silence. "They also say they have some other evidence."

"What kind?"

Crittenden frowned and wiped the glass with a napkin as if it were a communion chalice. "A witness saw you standing by the girl's car. And there were drugs. Alex, were you supplying this young girl with methamphetamine? "

"Do you actually believe I'd do something like that? I have a sister three years younger than that girl. My god, you must think I'm some kind of monster."

It was the lawyer's turn to look uncomfortable. "Look, Alex, I'm not doubting your story. But you do carry a gun in your car, don't you?"

"Sure, but I couldn't find it. When I told the deputy it was in glove compartment, it was gone. Why?"

Crittenden met his gaze just slightly to the right of center. What did he read in it? A certain smugness as if all of his suspicions had been justified. His daughter was marrying a common criminal. "Because they're saying it was the murder weapon. And they found it. Do you want me to go with you to face the indictment?"

"No, thanks. It's really nothing to worry about." He made an effort to sound casual, but they both knew he was bluffing. "Case of mistaken identity."

"I wish I could be so confident," Crittenden said, patting Chelsea's hand. Gone was the fatherly Crittenden. This one was all lawyer, reading off a list of notes from a piece of paper. "Feldman will accompany you to court Friday, but I've called in a bigger gun in case this goes to trial."

"Neither one of you believe me, do you?" He glanced at Chelsea who looked the other way, shaking her head. "Do you?"

Crittenden looked up and cleared his throat. "Under the circumstances, Alex, I think you and Chelsea had better put your wedding plans on hold until this blows over. You know how the media is about corporate scandals."

He tried to engage Chelsea's eyes, but she had averted her gaze, tapping her knife on her cocktail napkin. "So that's how it is. You and Daddy have this all worked out. You can't possibly be engaged to a would-be murderer. Think of how it would look to all your friends."

Cornered, Chelsea could turn nasty, like a sewer rat. "I really don't know what you expect me to do, Alex. There's been a murder committed and they say you knew this girl.

How do I know you haven't been sleeping with her the whole time? How do I know this poor girl wasn't seeing you up there and followed you back? How do I know she didn't threaten to tell me and ruin your beautiful career?" Then she came in for the kill. "Let me tell you one thing, Alex! Your career with my father's firm is over! And you'll be dead meat in the legal business all over Los Angeles after this! So ask me, was it worth it to cheat? On me, of all people!"

"Chelsea, I expected you alone to believe me." His resolve to fight back always melted away under her vituperation. It withered negotiations like a cobalt sun. "I don't even know the girl's name."

Chelsea got her sunglasses from her purse, a sure sign she was getting ready to leave. "If you didn't know her, how could there be pictures of you and her together? Explain that! No doubt, you were having some kind of druggie party and it got out of hand."

"Pictures?" Defeated, he shook his head. "Look, I have no idea. I swear to you I never saw her before." It sounded lame. "Or if I have, I don't remember. It could have been a fraternity party. God, do you know how many parties I have been to? And gotten drunk?"

"And accidently killed somebody?" Chelsea picked up her purse. "Look, Alex, the wedding's off." In a tone as emotionless as the sea beyond the window, she said in her best walk-on voice, "I think we both know it was going to be a big mistake. Thanks, Daddy, I have to go."

"No, I'll go." He slid out of the booth and stood up. Out in the Marina, a three-masted schooner was slipping out of its birth and turning toward the sea. "So this is an easy out. I get accused of a crime I didn't commit and bingo, you're gone! Even cats have more loyalty than that and much smaller claws!"

Her voice was as devoid of emotion as a judge issuing a prison sentence. "Please be gone when I come back. And don't take anything that doesn't belong to you."

"Obviously nothing there does." Her harshness cut like a knife, but he was still numb to pain. "Besides, you forget I can't go anywhere. I'd be jumping bail so I guess you'll have to go." He deliberately raised his voice to cause them embarrassment.

Chelsea took a deep breath. "Fine. In that case, I'll just move back in with my parents. Just don't be there when I come to get my things. I'm afraid to be in the same house with you." She slipped from her seat and walked past him out the door.

In the silence that engulfed the room, he saw his reflection in the glass. It was as if he were looking at another person, as if his whole life had become absorbed into someone else's. He was Alejandro Carreras, whose word no one believed, someone who cheated on his betrothed and, worse yet, murdered of a young woman with long dark hair, who had loved shepherd dogs, and rodeos.

"Oh, just let her go and sit down, Alex." Crittenden waved him back into his seat. "This will blow over, I assure you. Ah, here he is." Parker glanced past him at the front door. His serious demeanor transformed in seconds to the practiced urbanity of the rich and powerful. "The man has no concept of time, but he's a genius." Parker Crittenden signaled a heavy-set man who could have been Feldman's twin. Except that he was better dressed.

Jacob Jacovich looked far worse than his newspaper pictures—paunchy, unshaven with bags down to his chin. He took a seat, all guns firing. "What the hell is this about, Parker? Hello, young man. I presume you're the cause of messing up my schedule?"

Alex couldn't help being impressed. Jacovich was famous for milestone cases involving celebrities accused of serious crimes. His florid face had been on the covers of three issues of Time magazine for his brilliant defenses in criminal cases.

Every time, he had gotten an obviously guilty client off the hook using strategy Disraeli would have envied. But getting Jacovich to represent you was practically an admission of guilt and he knew it.

Jacovich squeezed his bulk into the cranberry leather chat. "I don't know why I can't stay emaciated like you, Parker. But then you always did look like a dried up old bean stalk, even back at Harvard." He turned his gaze on Alex. "Okay, young fella, I'll be straight with you. I looked over what Parker sent me. From what I can tell, the police have a pretty tight case against you and they don't have another suspect, which makes them real anxious. You knew the dead woman—whatshername…Turner?"

"Turner?" It was the first time he had heard her name, and it freed him of guilt in that instant. "Never heard of her. And you're wrong. They only have circumstantial evidence and the fact I was there at the scene. I have evidence, concrete evidence I wasn't there when the girl was killed."

"Really?" Jacovich exchanged looks with Crittenden. "Can I know what that is?"

Something stopped him. What was it? They were both powerful men in the legal business. And power could be used to anyone's advantage. "I'd rather not reveal that at the moment."

He caught their quick exchange of glances. Something was going on and he was outside the loop. Crittenden jumped in. "If Jake is going to defend you, Alex—"

"Thanks, Parker, but Jake is not going to defend me because it isn't going to come to trial. I'll turn what I have over to the DA' s office before they even think about pulling a jury. Besides, the autopsy will definitely prove I couldn't have been there when she was killed. My gun had never been fired. Never even loaded. Clean as a whistle. Open, shut."

The two older men appeared lost for words for a moment. Jacovich recovered first, adopting those earnest tones that had won him the confidence of many a crook.

"Look, er…Alex, I don't know why you'd throw away your chance at—"

"My chances at anything would be through the minute it got out you were going to defend me. You've built your reputation defending high profile clients with dubious guilt and I'm not about to become a media event." He turned to Crittenden who was gearing up for a diatribe. "And you'll be happy to know you'll have your daughter back, Parker. Not that you ever let go of her in the first place."

Crittenden had the grace to look embarrassed. "Now, Alex, let's not overdramatize this. "

Jacovich, looked as if he had heard it all at least a hundred times before, scooped up a handful of cocktail peanuts.

Alex got to his feet and threw some bills on the table. "You never really intended to let her marry me, did you? Afraid you'd end up with a Mexican grandchild? I'm glad I found out before any real damage was done. And did you notice this murder just happened to fit right in with your plans? If I ever find out it wasn't a coincidence, then I'll see you in court." He nodded at Jacovich who was still munching. "And you'd better have your friend here with you."

He strode out of the Yacht Club, tearing off his navy blazer before he even got back to the car. It felt good to be free and too good to last.

Leaving wasn't really a conscious decision. It was purely self-preservation instinct. He had until Wednesday before they realized he had jumped his bail. Reminding himself he still hadn't unpacked the stuff he had taken to Sunrise, he threw in some more clean things and counted on Chelsea to put the rest on the curb. She prided herself on getting rid of live-in's that way.

But the one question that emerged from among all the other trivial ones—where was he really going?

Glancing back once at what could have been his, he felt the finality in this escape of all the escapes he had made in his life. The escape from entangling relationships, the escape from Hispanic-ness and all that went with it. But this one was different. It wasn't just that he was leaving everything he had work so hard to obtain behind. The fact was it would be an overt admission of guilt to everything he was accused of. Besides his brother Ricky, and maybe Sanchez, he was the only person who believed in his own innocence. There was no way he could effectively prove his innocence from inside prison walls, especially if no one believed his story in the first place. Remaining free was the only way he could find the Turner girl's real killer.

✄つ✄つ

The secretaries looked up from their paperwork, startled to see him breeze in the door as if no one had heard the scuttlebutt racing through the office. "Hi, ladies," he said, grinning widely as he passed. "Don't mind me, I'm just passing through."

Only the most intrepid managed a whispered, "After-noon, Mr. Carreras."

Once inside his office, he looked around for what he knew was the last time and then got to work. Something in Crittenden's continuing interest in his visit to Synotech's valley plant prompted him to download the entire file to his laptop.

He followed that with his memos to Crittenden and Harris both concerning the discrepancies in their shipping bills. Instinct was urging him to grapple for a toehold in this avalanche of events that threatened to obliterate him. There was nothing wrong with getting information that might make good leverage in a battle for full severance pay along with health insurance.

He remembered the locked file on the Synotech account that only he and a few others in the firm had the password for. Once in the file, he could access some parts of Synotech's mainframe accounting system as well as shipping invoices. He'd only done it once, when Crittenden had needed something and didn't have time to do it himself. Back in September of last year. What in hell was it?

He ran into a series of locks and almost gave up in frustration. Glancing at his watch, he realized time was against him. It would only be minutes before somebody called Crittenden or Crittenden called Security, whichever came first.

Finally, it came to him. In an old memo book where he kept notes by date—just in cases like these when he had done something, but forgotten who asked him to do it—he found it. There it was, August twenty-fifth. Crittenden had asked him to follow up on a shipment for one of Synotech's customers. Scanning his notes for August twenty-fifth, last year, he found the entry: *Synotech's accounting password and the customer's name, Poseidon.* What the hell was that? He'd never heard of a company called Poseidon.

He typed it in and the screen immediately went into hyperactivity. After a long pause indicated during which the hourglass icon hung suspended on the screen, a single login box appeared.

Type in password, it indicated.

He typed in the numbers and two letters written beside the word Poseidon in his memo book and was launched into some type of shipping log spread sheet. He was downloading the file when Sylvia opened the door to his office with the expression of having caught him with his pants down.

"Mr. Carreras, Mr. Crittenden left strict instructions you weren't allowed in your office unless I was present." He swiveled to block the screen from her view. "And he told me specifically that you shouldn't be using the computer."

"Really?" He gave her a benign smile. "Funny, I just left him at the Yacht Club in the Marina and he never mentioned it. Phone him, why don't you, Sylvia? Otherwise, you're free to join me while I just finish up a brief I was working on, and that I expect to get paid for."

The guardian of the gates of free enterprise wasn't fooled. "I most certainly will tell him, and I'm also calling building security. You'd better be gone before they come. We don't want any more unpleasant publicity around here.'

She slammed the door with a bang and he watched her

return to her desk, glaring at him through the glass window as she went. They didn't need security. They had Sylvia who was worth two Rottweilers.

He only had a few more minutes left, the CD was full. He slipped in a blank and kept looking, even though he didn't know what he was looking for. These entries were all shipments via Synotech transport. The spreadsheet listed the dates, point of origin and mode of transportation, either by overland trucks, ships, or by air.

The origins and destinations were in an alphabetic code he knew partially by heart. The big ones were easy. SD was San Diego, SF San Francisco, PLA, and Port of Los Angeles. But there were others with only a few entries he couldn't identify. The code key was in another program. Whoever figured out the system did a double blind to conceal the truth from casual hackers.

At the bottom on one page, he noticed a notation. *See attached memo. Clicking on the memo link, he got a surprise. It was dated March twenty-second, the day he had decided to check Synotech's operations in the San Fernando Valley. It was from Tim Hardaway to George Crittenden. 'Thought you might find this interesting. Email from MacPherson attached.'

He clicked on the memo link and found a message from MacPherson, the chief of Shipping to Hardaway. Why the hell to Hardaway? As far as he knew, Tim's name had never entered the picture before then. Synotech's account had been his baby.

Macpherson's note read, *Carreras was here today, looking around. What's the story? I thought Crittenden had given him the okay, but then he told me he just come out on his own. I had already given him the grand tour by then. Showed him the entire operation. Did I goof?*

In spite of Sylvia's threat to get him thrown out, his fingers froze on the keyboard, unable to move for a moment. The question kept hanging in his mind like a red flag in the wind. *Why Tim Hardaway? Why would MacPherson have been clearing it with him?*

He copied the email to his disk and went back to the main file of shipments. As his eyes traveled down the list of origins, one particular place jumped out at him DC. Diamondback City. The home town of the murdered girl.

Clicking on the two successive screens he managed to save most of the file. Then he erased the site from his browser and shut down.

He was stuffing his briefcase just as Sylvia buzzed him. "Mr. Carreras, I have Mr. Crittenden on the phone. He wishes to speak with you immediately."

"Tell him I was just going," he said in the speaker phone. "Have a nice afternoon, Sylvia. And tell Mr. Crittenden I'll see him in court."

He wasn't about to leave without seeing what Crittenden had in his personal files. These were the files in yellow folders stamped confidential he had seen Crittenden keep in his own desk. So secret, he had seen Crittenden hide it from Chelsea who had bent over to give him a kiss. *What could be so important, you had to hide it from your own daughter?*

Instead of leaving, he slipped into Crittenden's suite two doors down from his. The light was blinking on the answering machine. Curious, he pressed the message button as he looked for the key to the locked file drawer.

"Parker, Syd Harris here. I just wanted to let you know I made a really sweet deal in Manila today for a Poseidon shipment. It's for an Eye, the whole enchilada, guidance system and all, like one we talked about the other night. Highest quality merchandise, the latest edition. Nice little bit of change, too. Ten million. But get it going by Sunday, or the whole thing's off. I'm letting Willy Wu know it's a done deal but Cecil Martinez has also put in a bid so I can get Freddie to ante up another mil. But don't let me down. You know how naughty little Willy gets when he's disappointed. Naughty, very naughty.

"Make all the appropriate arrangements, that's a good boy, and I'll see you Monday. Have a nice little bonus for us as well. Behave yourself with that cute teenybopper. Cheers!"

As he rummaged through desk, Alex noticed the small redwood box near the desk lamp. The man's voice had a decidedly British accent and turn of phrase. The only person who fit that description he could think of was Sydney Harris, the firm's once and so it seemed, still senior partner. That was it! He made both connections simultaneously. The file drawer key was in the box and Harris worked for Synotech as some kind of advisor. Foreign trade or import taxes.

Implicated in a money-laundering scheme to hide assets belonging to rich foreign clients, he was sentenced to serve six years in prison for attempting to defraud the government. He had been paroled after serving thirteen months. Having been disbarred, he was now supposedly self-employed as an exporter. His son, Frederick, however, was attached as a junior partner out of loyalty to his father, but hardly knew a tort from a golf tee.

Knowing Crittenden kept fresh tapes in his top right hand drawer, Alex traded the message tape for a new one and put the one with Harris's message in his pocket.

Raised voices outside in the reception area told his time was up and trouble was on the way. Rummaging in Crittenden's private files, he loaded his briefcase with the only files under AP. As he brought his hand out of the cookie jar, it bumped something on the underside of the desk.

His own voice began to speak softly from somewhere inside the desk. "The only reason they would lie about it is if what they're shipping is illegal, like contraband arms to banned buyers. And chemical warfare weapons."

Crittenden had been taping their conversations. Alex pocketed the recorder and took the outside stairs down, two at a time. In the lobby, he passed the security guard's desk and noticed it was empty. Glancing at the elevator indicator, he saw it had stopped on the eleventh floor, where Crittenden and Harris's offices were. The realization hit him full blast. He was now a hunted man.

CHAPTER 6

It was four-thirty and he knew exactly where to find Hardaway, Kirkendall, and Harris along with a major portion of Century City's thirty's population. O'Hara's Sports Video Bar catered to young professionals and was conveniently located in the next block from Century City Towers. In spite of hitting the rush hour, he made miraculous time and even found a place to park, good omens in the day from hell.

The three men whose professional life he had shared for nearly three years were so engrossed in conversation, they didn't notice him threading his way through the crowd. Alex added himself to a group of giggling secretaries, offering to buy them beers and inviting himself to sit with them. They found an empty booth across the partition from Kirkendall and the others huddled over their drinks. In spite of the girls' giggling, he could hear the conversation between the three men in the booth. Thanks to Happy Hour, they had to nearly shout to be heard.

"And then he came back to the office and unloaded some stuff off the secure system. Crittenden's having a coronary, for Christ sakes. Says there's big bucks missing from the Synotech account. Carreras, of all people. I think he's lost it. First this murder charge and now embezzling funds. He's definitely lost it!" That was Hardaway. His post-pubescent squeak rose above the rest.

Only Freddie Harris came to his defense. "I don't believe it! Alex is the soul of honesty unlike some of us around here, my dear father included. No, that's a load of crap, Hardaway. I'm surprised you'd believe it yourself, seeing as how you're his best buddy."

Quirky wasn't so sure. "Any idea how much he got away with?"

"I don't know. Crittenden wasn't specific. He just said the Synotech code had been violated and asked if any of us knew where Carreras was headed. Crap, what if he jumps bail?"

Kirkendall played dumb, waiting for the other two to volunteer. "Probably to Puerto Vallarta to live the life of ease with some hot tamale. I'm sure he'd be better off than with Chelsea Crittenden."

Hardaway continued to hammer down his conviction. "Could be that's probably why he iced his little girlfriend. Dear Chelsea had driven him to flee the country and he couldn't carry extra baggage."

"I don't think he did it, and there's a perfectly good explanation for everything." Harris came to his defense again. "Once a rumor starts, it becomes a feeding frenzy around here."

Hardaway played the part of Brutus delivering the last blow. "Then how come they found his stuff in her van?" How did he know that, unless Crittenden or Chelsea had told him?

Kirkendall again. "And her picture with him the night we went out partying."

"I don't even remember her honestly," Harris said. "She must not have been important. But then who would if you picked them up in a bar?'

"You wouldn't have noticed the Playgirl of the Month, Harris, if she were draped over the fucking bar."

"Doubtless. But I do remember thinking the bartender was cute."

"Jesus. Whatever. Carreras's career is cooked. Even if he gets cleared somehow of these charges, everyone's going to associate him with this girl. Here's the down and dirty though." Kirkendall leaned forward across the table to drop the bomb. "Sylvia told me Friday Crittenden had already sent his dismissal down to Personnel. Said the reason was some impropriety. So he must have stepped in some shit somewhere going through the cow pasture."

"No kidding." Tim's reply was barely audible. "That's probably why he raided the secure files. To get some leverage."

"Hell, you've got to hand it to him, the boy moves fast! When did he have time to do that?"

"I just got a text from Sylvia. Alex was just there and skipped when she called the cops."

"Won't do him any good. Murder suspects don't pull off blackmail very easily."

On the pretense of ordering another round, he slipped out of the adjoining booth and stood before his colleagues, beer in hand. "Hi, guys."

It was worth the risk to see their expressions freeze, especially Kirkendall whose bland face rarely registered anything. He looked like somebody had stuck him with a pin in a strategic place.

This time, there were no usual grins of welcome, no shouts of "Carreras, Fearless Warrior!"

Kirkendall was the first to speak, while Hardaway's six foot frame appeared to melt further down into the booth. "Jeez, Alex! Have a seat, buddy! How the hell are you? Want another beer? You look like you could use one or something stiffer."

Alex slid into the seat opposite Tim so he could watch his face. "Thanks, but I'm driving."

"So what's up?" If Kirkendall was glib, Hardaway was tongue-tied. He even tried to slip out of the booth for refills, but Alex stopped him.

"Hang on. I need to talk to you. All of you."

"Is it so important I can't take a leak?" Alex let it go and Tim slipped away to the hall where he would certainly try to contact Crittenden. "I suppose you heard about this morning?"

"Hell, yeah!" Fred Harris almost sounded relieved, as if the conversation had reverted to semi-normal. "It's all the office buzz."

"What's this all about, Alex? Did you know this girl? I mean in the carnal sense?" Kirkendall actually seemed to be amused, leaning back as if he were completely relaxed. Brilliant in a devious way, he was definitely covering something. Occasionally, his eyes slid away toward the restroom where Hardaway had gone.

"Nope. Never saw her before. I wonder if you guys remember Saturday night when we were partying up in Sunrise. Did you see me talking to anybody? "

Kirkendall actually laughed. "Hell, we all talked to every female in the place. And some males," he added with a glance at Harris. "There were some babes over there from some state university and they came by our table."

Alex looked at Fred. "What about it? Do you remember me talking to a girl?"

Harris pressed his gnarly fingers to his forehead. "I only remember the cute little blonde who came up and took our pictures. You gave her twenty bucks. I remember that because I had to lend you some money. You owe me thirty bucks. I tipped her ten."

"So there were pictures? What happened to them? I don't have any."

Kirkendall was almost derisive. "Don't you remember? We gave them to the girls as souvenirs. Man, you must have been scorched. After that, they closed up and threw us out, we went back to the condo and crashed. You were really brain-dead."

"I guess I must have been. And nobody saw me with a girl. Dark hair, pretty."

There was a small pause, brief but significant. He read reticence in it, and something else. It was as if they had reached some kind of consensus.

"Well, we were in separate digs, you know," Harris said. "So I mean, we can't exactly vouch for that, can we?"

The other two shook their heads in unison, and he read that as a no-confidence vote. Friends or not, they weren't about to give him an alibi. "You were with your brother. He obviously can vouch for you."

"In court?"

"Oh, it probably won't come to that." Harris had come back with the beers and, after passing them around, took a sip of his own, wiping the suds of his lip. "What are they going on, anyway? I mean, girls get raped and murdered every day in California. Probably some disgruntled boy-friend or something."

"Because I was the first one at the murder scene, for one thing."

Hardaway spoke up, clearing his throat first. "So you were just the lucky one who found the girl. You didn't run away or anything. I'm with Freddie on this. What's the big deal?"

"How do you know I didn't?"

"Didn't what?"

"Run away."

Hardaway suddenly flushed and looked uncomfortable. "I...you told me that this morning, remember? You said you just found her there."

Maybe all this was making him paranoid, but how did Hardaway know he had stayed with the girl? And why did Tim look so guilty, trading a quick glance with Kirkendall?

"They've got some kind of evidence. Naturally, they won't say what. I don't know what it could be unless..." He rubbed his hand over his eyes. "Unless it could be those pictures. She must be in one of the pictures we took."

"Voila!" Harris snapped his fingers. "You see? I told you it was simple. They don't have anybody else to pin it on. You stopped by, and they found the pictures. As long as nothing else happened, you should be in the clear."

"Nothing else happened. Ricky would tell me if there

was something else. And I don't remember bringing anyone back to the room."

"Besides, you couldn't have banged anybody, the condition you were in." Everybody laughed at Kirkendall's quip. Even Alex managed a wry grin.

"No doubt about that," he said.

"Then, no sweat, man." Freddie extended his hands. "Voila! Case closed."

"Dammit, Freddie, quit saying 'Voila!' like some French whore, will you? Let me get us another round. Relax, Alex. You need a stiff one." Kirkendall slid out of his side of the booth. "Be back in a flash."

"So what did old Crittenden think of the fuzz-busting this morning? I can just see the look on his face now." Harris nibbled at the corn chips and salsa. "I'll bet he nearly wet his pants when they flashed their badges. I would have given anything to have been there. Uh, ah, ahem. May I help you, gentlemen?"

Meanwhile, Kirkendall was moving through the crowd to the hallway, phone in hand.

"Excuse me, Fred, I need to take a leak."

"Seems to be a universal need tonight."

Harris was still keeping up the good-humored patter when Alex slid out of the booth and threaded his way through the crowd.

In the hall outside the men's room, he came up behind Kirkendall speaking to someone in an urgent voice. "That's what I said. Yes, he's here. I told you he'd come. O'Hara's, Century City Boulevard. And make it fast, will you?"

Just then Hardaway walked out. "You calling? I already called Parker. He's sending somebody." Then he saw Alex in the hall behind Kirkendall.

"Alex, I didn't know—"

Kirkendall whirled around to face him. "Look, it's for your own good, buddy. You'll be safer under house arrest, believe me."

"Thanks, fellas. I appreciate your concern for my health and happiness. See you in court."

He left through the side entrance and went to his car. If the police were coming, they would have had to get an arrest warrant in record time and nothing in law enforcement between two jurisdictions moved that fast.

Turning on the engine, he waited to see if they showed up, ready to split when they did. If they did. Whoever they were.

Five minutes later the traffic light changed, several cars pulled into the parking lot, bumper to bumper, none of them police cars. One was a sleek, black Lincoln town car which parked with a screech of brakes as if the driver were desperate for a drink. He recognized the vehicle with a shock. It was a company car used to chauffeur busy attorneys around town. On its bumper came a Jeep. The Jeep was identical to the one that sped away as he arrived at the spot with the murdered girl. This time the plates were blatantly clean, however. They were local plates, standard kind, not vanity plates. And all four tires were standard, not customs.

In spite of his own danger, he had to see who got out of the two vehicles, especially the Jeep. The driver's jumped out of the Lincoln and the Jeep as if on the count of three. They definitely weren't the chauffeur type.

The Jeep driver was tall and dressed like an extra in a budget Western or he was in the Mexican mafia. His black cowboy hat was pulled down low so his features were hidden, but he was wearing cowboy boots and a western shirt. There was something Hispanic about the man, and he had the movement of a combat-trained commando. Slim and broad-shouldered, with a Van Dyke goatee favored by Mexican hoodlums, he pulled on a Western-cut tan sport coat as he went, revealing a leather shoulder holster up under his raised arm. Unless LAPD undercover police had started getting their clothes at Central Casting, these guys were getting paid to pack heat from a private party.

Hired thugs. There hadn't been enough time to get a

warrant out and they weren't plain-clothes detectives. *My god, I'm being chased by goons. At company expense! Where in the firm's budget is there a place for hired heat?*

The cowboy's companion was even bigger and built like a fireplug with a face battered into a permanent scowl. He appeared uncomfortable in baggy polyester trousers and a yellow sports shirt straining at the buttons. Both men wore sunglasses, and were clearly out of place among the thirty-somethings in O'Hara's.

As soon as they were inside, he pulled out of the parking, slipping into the evening traffic. It was clear the company wasn't going to call the police to find him. Not before trying some other tactics first. No, he was wanted in the private sector by somebody who could afford goons, some-one Kirkendall had in his cell phone directory. Somebody with the firm. Somebody that Crittenden had on his speed dial.

Somebody who wanted him badly.

But I am being hunted down.

Alex was still in the line for the light when he caught a glimpse of the two men running back out into the crowded parking lot again, looking frantically around. Splitting up, each ran in a different direction, searching the cars. The light changed and Alex moved smoothly along with the traffic.

It was nearly five, but he counted on MacPherson to work overtime. At his salary level, he was expected to live on the job.

This would be a visit no one had counted on Alex to make. He had been taught, even before law school, to read the situation and find the loopholes, the errors in thinking people would make and how to turn them to his advantage.

His father, the hunch-shouldered, quiet accountant, had taught him how to analyze common mistakes in people's judgment as he clipped his roses in the small front yard.

"And why do you think they did that, Alejandro?"

Though his eyes always seemed focused on the roses, as

a small child, Alex had always thought his father could see sideways like a horse.

"Because they didn't figure out what to do if that didn't work?"

Papa would smile and nod, choosing the next bush as a surgeon chooses his patient.

Now, Alex played that game again and came up with the answer. They would expect him to flee to Mexico, an hour and a half drive over the border. He had a current passport and plenty of relatives to stay with, no problem. They wouldn't expect him to stay here and fight, because they wouldn't do it themselves.

CHAPTER 7

O kay, so where's Rudolf Valentino when we need him?"

Switching primetime games, Jones was shooting paper clips at a small basketball hoop located on the wall of his cubicle. A glass ashtray beneath the net attested to his accuracy in micro-basketball. It was empty.

"Who?"

"Sorry. I forgot you are the young and unschooled in trivial pursuit. I'm talking about Carreras. What's up with that?"

"I thought you'd forgotten." Murray watched Detective Jones launch another paper clip. She'd been working her tail off, following leads, interviewing people, following his trail to absolute dead ends. He had vanished into thin air. How was she going to admit that to a seasoned detective who had taken her on because of pressure from his superior?

Seeing her expression of misery, Jonesy softened his voice. "Look, local cases are going to take priority over some girl from two hundred miles north killed by a guy from one hundred fifty miles south, get my drift? For instance, the missing seven year-old girl that didn't come home yesterday and the guy in question is a registered sex offender who conveniently forgot to register. He's also conveniently missing. Hansen's whole twenty-year career is on the line and so are we, my child, if the truth be known.

Which is why we have to find the SOB and charge him."

He was right. There was a local child missing. They had been working overtime, tracking every lead, every possible contact and come up with a convicted sex offender in their district.

"I'll need a list of all his frequented places." She sighed, putting the Carreras file up on the desk.

Jones handed her a list and cocked an eyebrow at her as he poised a paper clip for flight. "How about starting with all the local schools."

Taking the list, she started the tour of all the elementary schools in the area, beginning with the missing child's. On the way, she dropped by the hospital to see how Sanchez was getting along.

"'You got it?" His eyes glowed when he saw her. "The photos?"

She nodded and tried to look stern. "But Carreras got there before I did."

Sanchez grinned and then grimaced as if smiling hurt. "Sorry about that," he whispered.

Murray patted the hand without the IV attached to it. "It's okay, Gizmo. It's all there, like you said. Thanks for doing that. But one more thing before they throw me out. What do you know anything about Darlene Santana?"

Sanchez rolled his eyes. "Darlene. Only that's she's a druggie. More of a connection than a dealer, though. Rat she married, Santana's big into trafficking. Why?"

"Just something I noticed when I was up there for a bust yesterday. Around that old barn behind the house there were some tire tracks. But she claims her car doesn't run."

Sanchez grunted. "Not surprised. She spends every dime she makes growing pot or hooks up a buyer with the stronger stuff."

"How about family? She ever mention that she has a little girl?"

His eyes closed slightly as if he were hiding something. "Yeah. You know she's not Hispanic, just married one of us. The little girl is grown up now. Santana's not the dad, though. Good thing. He's doing time for meth dealing. Poor Darlene got left high and dry. Almost dry but definitely high." He tried the grin and got it right this time.

There were whispers at the door and an older woman with a little girl tiptoed into the room. In the hall, the nurse motioned to Murray to come out. "Only one visitor at a time, Officer."

"Daddy?" The child stood on tiptoe by the bed. "Do you feel okay?"

"Now that I see you, hijita." He raised his free hand slightly above the bedrail and held her arm. "Meet Officer Murray, the prettiest girl on the force. Murray, my daughter Carlita and my mamacita."

"And just about the only girl on the force." She shook their hands. "I'll let you talk to Daddy. I'm off to find that child that's gone missing."

Mrs. Sanchez rolled her eyes and made a soft groaning sound. "We are so terrified. We keep Carlita in the house the moment she come home now."

But the bright-eyed child continued to hold Murray's hand and gave it a soft pull, as if to get her full attention. "I saw the man, Miss Murray. He came to my school in his car. I saw him from the playground where we were playing kickball." She was the daughter of a police officer, it was plain. "I did, Papa," she said, turning to her father.

Her grandmother sucked in a gasp of horror. "Yes, she say that but I don't believe she is right. You know how children talk. Now, I think she maybe tell the truth."

Sanchez extended his free hand again and the child grasped it with both of hers. "Tell me what's this about?" But his eyes rested on Murray who looked as surprised as he did.

"Everybody's looking for this little girl, Danica Sutton," she said. "And we've pulled in an USO with no alibi."

"But Danica said it's her daddy." Carlita looked from one of them to the other. "He came to see her," she said.

Murray pulled up a chair so she was on the same level as the child's alarmed face. "Did you tell anybody what she said? Your teacher, the principal, anybody?"

The little girl stuck out her lip as if she were going to burst into tears. "It's okay, hijita," Sanchez said from the bed. "You're telling us now."

Carlita wiped tears of frustration from her eyes before they fell. "I tried to tell them, Daddy, but no one would listen to me. Miss Phillips said, "Not now, dear. Don't upset the class.""

Murray took her hand. "Listen, Carlita, you did the right thing to tell us. I'll call it in and make sure your friend is okay, is that all right with you?"

Carlita nodded, letting the tears of relief flow unchecked.

"And I'll give you all the credit for finding her? How about that?" Murray glanced over at Sanchez and winked. "But, one more thing, and then that nurse out there is going to come in and say I'm upsetting the class, I bet." Carlita managed a giggle and Murray got out her notebook. "Can you remember what color Danica's daddy's car was?"

The little girl was back to normal, grinning at her father for approval. "It was black and it was a Mercedes Benz. I know because she told me what it was and that it cost a fortune." She finished with a firm nod. "A fortune. Like more money than a policeman makes, she said."

❧❦

Murray called it in, but Hansen had it already. Sutton was the custodial parent as of the prior Saturday and the principal hadn't been notified. End of all points alert and the search dogs went back to their kennels. The patrol cars went back to their usual beat and Murray back to her cubicle.

"Hey, Schmitzy, you okay?" She looked up from her file to find Jones looking at her around the partition between them. "Listen, Murray." He said her name carefully as if they had just met. "Good work today, finding out what happened to the kid."

"No big deal. Hansen already had it from the school district anyway. But thanks." She returned to Shelby Turner's file, absorbing every detail.

Jones dropped into the only other chair in the cubicle. "Look, I know I acted like an asshole the other night. Sunday, I mean. I kind of left you on your own."

Wondering what he was leading up to, she closed the file. "It's okay. I handled it. I've done it before, that's what you guys don't get. You think I'm just some rookie cop, but I was on the gang unit for three years. You see a lot of …you know, that kind of thing. So I'm okay with it. But it's never easy."

Jones fished restlessly in his pocket for a paper clip. Dragging her wastebasket even with his chair, he readied his next missile. "You heard somebody called in today saying they saw Turner's van and a red Cherokee beside the Interstate Sunday afternoon, right? Said looked like they had a fender-bender. Cops confirmed there was a new dent in her bumper, traces of red paint match the Cherokee's."

Murray had nothing to say. Not without convicting herself of being a dumb twit in front of a veteran detective. "No, I didn't know. I guess some things just aren't making sense, is all."

"Such as?"

"Such as Sanchez took some photographs of the murder scene. Carreras said the Cherokee left the scene just as he arrived, right? Except the other car had bronze trim, Dayton mountain treads. The photos show tire tracks right beside the van, Carreras's SUV parked in front of it. And the imprint of a cowboy boot in the mud on the shoulder."

Another paperclip went into the basket. Jones tilted back in his chair and studied the water-soaked ceiling tiles. "Okay, it goes like this. Carreras bumps the van, they pull over. She sees it's him, tells him she wants to talk, they pull off the exit, she drops the bomb she's pregnant and is going to tell his hi-dollar girlfriend. Her window's rolled down. Bam! She's dead. He has a moment of remorse, blots her head with his handkerchief, then puts it in her hand. He then gets rid of the murder weapon up the road, turns around on his way back to LA. Stops again to see if she's really dead. Says, hello, dear, I'm home and toodles off to his engagement party."

"And called nine-one-one who hears him trying to stop the old farmer?"

"Oh, come on, honey. He's a Century City lawyer for lord's sake. He can do an entire three-act play by himself if he wants to, playing all the parts. You don't think he can act like he's waving somebody down? 'Help, oh, help me, sir!'" He swiveled around to make an over-the-shoulder shot. "You got an open-shut here, girl, as far as we're concerned. Girl freaks out, threatens upscale boyfriend with exposure. He kills her, feels bad about it, then splits. What else, but guilty?"

"I guess I'm just new at this. But I don't like it when all the ends don't tie up neatly."

"Honey, I've never had anything tie up real neatly in fifteen years. There's always doubts, loose ends, maybes. Let me tell you a story." He swiveled back around and this time his sincerity was genuine. "When I first started…I guess almost sixteen years ago…I was like Mr. Affirmative Action-Man. They gave me every case involving blacks—there were three in five years, and any other race other than white. One of them was this fantastic looking Asian girl. Vietnamese, nineteen years old, living with her husband and some other guys like they do…uncles, cousins, or whatever. I saw her picture and I almost passed out. She was so beautiful. She had this hopeful expression, I don't know. It got me and I wanted to know how she died."

"She died? How?"

Jones shrugged. "Oh, yeah, don't forget, this is Murder One. We don't get any live ones. A couple of bullets in the head. Found lying in a ditch about twenty miles from where she lived. Raped and a few other things. It was pretty horrible. Especially since it was my second murder case. Her name was Ming-ahn. She looked like a flower, an Asian lily. An almond-eyed Juliet. Who'd want to kill somebody like her?"

"Who did?" She was caught now, taken in by his obvious pain at remembering all the details of a case given to him to solve.

"I still don't know. Her husband got fifteen years for manslaughter. Seems Ming-ahn had a boyfriend, some high school sweetheart she'd secretly promised to marry, but then her parents had married her off to this older man with money. I guess he discovered the lovers and iced her. Let the guy go or he got away. Later, when the husband got out of prison, he ended up with a bullet in his head so I guess the boyfriend got even. The only one who really lost out was Ming-ahn. I can see her face to this day. Couldn't understand how somebody could kill something as sweet and gentle as that."

"You said you didn't really know who did it? What makes you doubt it was the husband?"

Jones turned back to her with a funny smile and tapped his temple. "Intuition, baby, intuition. Some funny things that didn't add up. Couldn't give enough to the defense to help him out, though. No alibi. No witness."

"In other words, Carreras is in the same boat."

"Or worse. DNA's going to tie him to the murder scene. No, look." Jones leaned forward and knit his long fingers between his knees. "Just don't put your heart in it, is all I'm saying."

"I'm not."

"Yeah, right. It's written all over you. The Alex Carreras Fan Club."

She liked Jones, but he was starting to get on her nerves, treating her like some star struck schoolgirl. As nicely as she could make it sound, she wanted him to knock off the needling. "Look, I don't like killers who get away with murder, okay? That's why I'm in this business, because somebody killed my dad and got away cold. Let's just say the more I put away, the less frustrated I feel every time I go to the cemetery with my mother."

That worked, even though she hadn't wanted to use the big gun, out it came.

He looked stunned. "I'm real sorry. I think I'd heard."

She stopped him like a school guard at a crossing, one hand up. "It's okay. Really, it's okay. I didn't want to have to put it that way, but whatever way I put it, I'm serious about my work. Real serious."

Jones nodded and went back to work. She knew he felt badly, but no worse than she was feeling, having had to drag out the past and wave it around like the bloody bandage from an unhealed wound. He left her alone after that, and he must have told Stockman because even the Super was cordial for a while. Condescending, granted, but at least not making cynical remarks about cheerleaders and Girl Scouts.

The list of produce growers from the Farmers Market Association was waiting in the bin when she returned to her cubicle. There were twelve names beginning with Ho. Some of them were easier to cull out than others. Orchard groves, poultry, organic dairy. There were three general produce suppliers.

She got lucky on the second try. "Yes, is this Mr. Hofstetter?"

"Who wants to know?" Somehow, the curmudgeon voice matched Carreras's description of the old man who passed him without slowing down. Hostile. No, downright mean. When she told him, he hung up. She called back relentlessly until he answered again with a snarl.

"Get off this phone or I'll call the police."

Resisting the urge to identify herself, Murray talked fast. "Mr. Hofstetter, I just want to know if I can buy some onions from you. A whole bushel. For a party."

It took a moment for greed to replace annoyance. "Well, sure! Why the hell didn't you say so, girl? Come on out the county road toward Blackwell Corners where it crosses Fremont Road. I'm two miles up on the right. Can't miss it. Hofstetter's Onions and Garlic. Little roadside stand right there. But it ain't open so come up to the house."

"I'll be right out." She went flying out of her cubicle so fast, she had to go back for her camera and notebook.

Jones looked over the top of his newspaper. "Let me guess. There's a clue in the Turner case," he said.

"It shows that bad?"

"It does when you have to come back and get half your stuff." He went back to the sports page.

ↄꙮↄ

It took her nearly half an hour to get to Fremont Road. The country began to turn rugged here, along the transverse spine of the mountain range. Tumble weed began to roll out of the chaparral across the highway in the evening wind. Yet it was a time of day she loved, when the sunlight slant-ed through the century plants and mesquite turning them to torches of gold.

Abraham Hofstetter lived up a macadam road that had been chewed away in chunks by flash floods and no one had cared enough to fix it. Turning at the sagging gate, she saw three older model trucks, two blue Chevy's and one Dodge, all over ten years old. They were fairly battered ve-hicles that fit Carreras's description of the one that had passed him. The sides of all the trucks had the faded words, Hofstetter's Onion Farm.

It was hard to miss Mr. Hofstetter, an old man with a white moustache in a rocking chair on the porch of the weathered frame house. He was as much of a relic of former times as the trucks in his yard.

But the onion farmer was much more cordial in person

than on the phone. Maybe because she was buying something.

"Howdy. You the young lady who called?"

As she approached the porch, Murray applied her win-
ning smile, which somehow, never looked as phony as she
felt. "Yes, sir, I need some onions."

"Most people come out to the farmer's market to buy
from me. Not clear out here." He got out of his chair with a
slight groan, a tall gaunt man with a slight limp.

"Hate to put you to any trouble," she said, keeping the
smile plastered to her lips. "But I was also looking for my
dog out this way. Wondered if you had seen him?"

Hofstetter's faded blue eyes matched his overalls. "Seen
lots of dogs around here. People just come along and turn
'em loose up here you know. If you've lost a dog, coyotes
probably got him by now."

"Maybe." Most people would have been more encourag-
ing but Abe Hofstetter wasn't exactly a ray of sunshine.
Murray turned away, as if to hide her disappointment.

"Or maybe he got hit or kidnapped or something." Hofstetter shrugged. "Happens all the time. Damn tourists, is
what it is. My Rottweiler got hit just out there right in front
of the house. Always chasing rabbits off the farm. You say
you want some onions? C'mon out to the shed. I got garlic,
too." The onion grower made his way crablike down the
steps.

Murray picked up the thread as she fell in beside him.
"See, he jumped out of my pickup truck yesterday and was
running along the highway back the way we came. By the
time I got turned around, he was chasing something out in
the field. I just wonder if anyone hit him. I hate think of him
just lying there." They had reached the rambling barn and
sheds, all draped with garlic braids.

"What time you say this was yesterday?" She followed
Hofstetter as he went around turning on lights above neatly
stacked bushel baskets of produce.

"Oh, I guess around four-twenty-five, four-thirty. Give

or take a few minutes." Pretending a casual attitude, Murray loaded the wicker basket he gave her with garlic, tomatoes, five cantaloupes, and as many onions as it would hold.

Hofstetter was absorbed in rearranging the tomatoes in cocoons of green tissues. He straightened, hand to the small of his back. "I passed that way around then and I didn't see no dog. What kind of dog was it?"

Murray took the easy way out. "Just a mutt, really. Mostly shepherd. You wouldn't happen to have seen a red Jeep out on the road, by any chance? "

"Yeah, yeah, I did. Wait a second, how'd you know that?" He squinted at her against the setting sun.

She shrugged and tried to look innocent. "Just a lucky guess."

"Sure I remember that damned red jeep! Don't know what this place is coming to," Hofstetter continued, hobbling toward the door. "Some blonde woman damn near run me over when I was coming out of my driveway. People that drive those damned fancy SUV's think they own the road. Got no damned manners. I had to stop so short, it dumped over a whole bushel of tomatoes and onions in the bed of the truck. Damned if she didn't lay on the horn, to boot. Bruised every one of them tomatoes. I sure do remember the red car, young lady! And I'll bet it's the one that hit your dog, too. That's why she was tearing off like that. Going like a house afire, she was."

They walked back to the porch, allowing time for Hofstetter's uneven gait. She wondered how the old man got around the place, he was so crippled with arthritis.

"Was she alone or was there somebody else with her, could you see?" She took a deep breath and held it until it hissed through her teeth.

He was wheezing now and she wanted to help him up the steps. But Hofstetter beat her to it, grabbing the railing and ascending crabwise with practiced ease.

"Naw, that SUV had smoked windows, but I did see her 'cause her window was rolled partway down. Ugliest woman I ever saw, even with sunglasses on. Hair all frizzy and dark-skinned like a man. And that's the strange thing, aside from trying to run me off the road. I no sooner went up the road about three miles and lo and behold this other crazy fool tries to flag me down. I just missed getting mugged because, when I wouldn't stop, he come running after me waving a gun. Come to think of it, he might've tried to pull the same thing on the ugly blonde which is why she was tearing up the road." Hofstetter spat clear of the porch and sat back in his rocker. "Hell, never thought of that angle. Fool tried to chase me all the way up to the intersection, he did."

The farmer rolled a cigarette with shaky fingers while Murray had to choke back the urge to laugh at the thought of poor, desperate Carreras being mistaken for a roadside thug. "I don't suppose you noticed what kind of a car he had, did you?"

He didn't notice the tremolo in her voice as he concentrated on keeping the tobacco inside the paper. "I sure did, sister. Like I told the police, it was a red SUV almost like the one that damned near hit me."

She choked on the words. "You called the police? When?"

Hofstetter held the trembling cigarette paper in one hand, scratching one bushy eyebrow with the other. "Well, it wasn't 'til I got home, see. I don't have one of them cell phones even if my son keeps saying I should. I mean how many days of the week does somebody run after you with a gun?"

She made a note to check with Sandra. "You sure this man had a gun?"

"Well, now, if you was going to get robbed what else would it be?" His calloused fingers finally achieved a crooked cylinder and he licked the paper closed.

"How about a mobile phone? Could that have been what he had in his hand?"

He raised one eyebrow. "You saying I can't see, young lady?"

"I'll give you a test. How many crows do you see on that telephone line up there?" She aimed her pen toward the line across the street and watched his faded blue eyes disappear behind a squint.

He studied the birds and then leaned forward for a better look. "Three. There's three crows up there and if I had my gun out here, I'd pick 'em off. Damn thieves. And I'm a damned fine shot, too, Missy."

Murray sighed and shrugged. "Two. And only one is a crow. I'll watch out next time I come over. You may be shooting crows."

The farmer turned his frown on her. "You said no more tricks, young lady. So you made up this cockamamie story about losing your dog to trap me, right?" Then he started to chuckle deep inside his overalls. Seismic-like, it spread to the rest of his body and he slapped his knee. "Damn, if that ain't just like a woman."

She did her best cop imitation. "I lied in the line of duty. But the fact of the matter is, the man who was running after you yesterday was trying to report a murder. He found the girl in the blue van—you did see a blue van next to the red car, didn't you?" Hoffstetter's bent cigarette was dangling unlit from his lips.

"Yeah. I did, now that you mention it. Thought it was migrants. Come around this time of year looking for work. You mean, there was somebody dead in there?"

Murray nodded and let it sink in a minute. "Yeah, there was. A young girl. And Mr. Hofstetter, your testimony has been the best thing you could have done for her, besides save her life."

Hofstetter's hand came down hard on the rocking chair arm. "I should have stopped. By God! Oh, hell's fire, I feel awful. You should have told me what all this was about. See, that's been happening a lot around here lately. Somebody looks like they're broken down beside the road and flags you down and robs you."

"Yeah, that's true." A string of incidents around the county and in the adjoining ones of robbing good Samaritans who stopped to help motorists apparently in trouble. It hit her like a bag of bricks. Until this minute, she hadn't made the connection, if there was one.

"Unfortunately, she was beyond anyone's help by the time you came by." Murray breathed deeply again. "What you can do is tell the judge exactly what you told me. See, the reason I didn't tell you what it was about was because I wanted to make sure you told me the way you did. Like 'Oh, yeah, I did see the van. And I called nine-one-one. Timing is so important in this case. And now can I have my vegetables so I can go home and cook dinner?"

Hofstetter gave her a hard look, frowning in the setting sun which engulfed the stubborn old farm buildings in amber shadows. "But I didn't."

She was fumbling in her purse to pay him. "You didn't what?"

"I didn't call nine-one-one."

Murray looked up to meet his eyes. "But you said—"

"Naw, I didn't say nine-one-one. I said I called the police. Friend of mine, Arnie Jensen. Played poker with him for years and beat him every time. Called Jensen down at the station. Left a message on his phone. So, see, missy, if you're going to be a cop, you got to listen up when people tell you something."

Lesson taken. Hofstetter was right, she was projecting things in order to make her case for Carreras's innocence. But why hadn't Jensen mentioned the report? "Can you get him any time of day at this phone number where you left a message?"

"Any time I got a game going. Why?"

"Just wondered." Best guess it was his cell phone, not the office number. Which meant Jensen wouldn't have had to report it since it was a personal call.

But if it had to do with the Turner case, why didn't he?

They sat on the porch of the frame farmhouse and talked about how he had once been an extra in Western movies, driving stagecoaches and making up a mean posse. "Made enough money to settle down and buy this little place. Those were the days, though. Met the big stars like Roy Rogers and Gene Autry. Harry James and Betty Grable. They was down-to-earth folks."

She told him she grew up on a few acres of sandy soil very much like this, but with even less rain than the chaparral. A jumbo jet out of Los Angeles cut across the darkening sky, reminding them they were on a tiny island in an ocean of ever-spreading humanity.

"I have to go," Murray said, getting up from the top step, where she had been watching the sun set. "I do have a cat to feed."

Hofstetter tried a couple of times before he got to his feet. "Cats can take care of themselves. I got a pot of the best stew you ever ate. And fresh bread to go with it. Maybe you'd like to stay for a bite." She could tell it was hard for him to spit out and even harder for her to accept. But she had to count on him as a solid witness and she was sick of TV dinners anyway.

"Sounds good," Murray said. "I admire anybody who can cook and grow tomatoes. And play poker." When she smiled this time, it was no effort at all. "I'll take you up on it."

"Plays poker and wins," Hofstetter said, opening the screen door to let her in. "Don't waste your time admiring a loser."

ℰℐℰℐ

It was five-thirty when Alex got to the Synotech plant in the gritty east side of the San Fernando Valley. The winding drive, lined bright green oasis of flowering hibiscus worked hard at trying to give the impression the company gave a flip about absorbing pollution. Instead it worked as a clever disguise for a complex occupying almost five acres with better security than Fort Knox. But Alex flashed his complimentary ID under the laser and the guard waved him on with a respectful salute.

MacPherson was surprised to see him, but not alarmed, which meant the news of his defection hadn't reached him yet. He was busy at his desk, glancing up in welcome. "Carreras, nice to see you. Here for a return visit?"

While he was distracted giving instructions over a speaker phone, Alex checked the banks of security cameras all around the room. Front hall area, shipping room, offices where attractive secretaries powdered their noses, shipping yards full of semis with purple cabs and the Synotech logo, a streamline S. In the front parking lot, his truck was visible at the very edge of the frame.

"Hi, Mac, hope this isn't a bad time to pop in." It obviously was, but he represented Crittenden, Harris, and Lawley which gave him the right to make demands on the company's time, however begrudged. "Just had a couple of quick questions for you."

"Fire away. You don't mind if I keep working, do you? Crunch time and all that." MacPherson was busy jotting things down on a clipboard and switching back to the computer screen. Occasionally, the phone would blip and he would glance up at the terminals in front of him, then mutter into speaker phone a few curt orders. "Five is the witching hour around here. These guys hit the road at night, and I crash the local watering hole. Can I buy you a drink, after?"

"Sounds good but I'll take a rain check, if I may." He dropped into a chair in front of one of the huge screens. "I just wanted to get on the same page as you and Tim Hardaway. He said you could fill me on about some Poseidon shipments made last August."

"Some what?" Macpherson's glasses slid unchecked down on his nose as he glanced up quickly from his clipboard. "Who said that? Hardaway did? Jesus! That's classi-fied info! What the hell is he playing at?"

Alex breezed on. "Yeah, he didn't have time to come himself. Busy in court this afternoon. So he sent me since I knew how to get out here and all."

MacPherson was still staring at him, blue eyes wide. "Which shipments? August 2012? I can't put my finger on it this second…" He was stalling to get hold of Hardaway or Crittenden.

Opening his briefcase, Alex studied one of the shipping inventories he had printed out. "Uhhh, got it right here. The one from Diamondback City, two-thirty p.m., August six-teenth. Entry description in our system says twenty-seven barrels, Herbicide 1212. Destination: SG. But the actual bill of lading says something entirely different." He held up the file printout so MacPherson could see it. "Miscellaneous equipment. That's all. Which is it? Chemicals or equip-ment? And specifically, what equipment? You know they need more info than that in customs. We've already paid half a million to erase past fines. Are we playing Russian Roulette with the Feds again?"

If MacPherson had been shaken up, he recovered quick-ly. "Probably just a piggyback on one of our ships. We do that when there's room in the cargo hold. Let me check it for you," he said, swiveling around clicking a few keys on the nearest computer. Alex was able to see over his shoul-der as the same login screen came up he had seen before in his office. "What's the destination again?" As if he didn't know, Alex thought.

"From Diamondback City to SG. I gather that's Savan-nah, Georgia."

"Oh, yeah. I forgot you've got the destination codes." MacPherson turned back to him again. "Let me ask again who wants to know?"

He didn't blink. "Actually, George asked me to do it."

"He did?" What was in Macpherson's stare? Doubt? Fear? "Doesn't he trust Hardaway not screw up? I sent Tim the stuff back then. He knew all about it. God, I wish I knew what was going on. Between Synotech and you guys, this is like a Chinese fire drill." MacPherson ran his fingers through what was left of his hair.

"You know as well as do, once the Feds are on to you, they never let up. George is just playing watchdog, is all. He's OCD about going up against the Feds again." Alex held up both hands in a gesture of disclaimer. "Hey, don't kill the messenger. You know I'm just marrying the boss's daughter. I'm not the hatchet man. I guess the numbers just didn't add up or something."

"What numbers?" MacPherson was genuinely dismayed now. Was he playing deliberately stupid?

"The weight, for a start. And the final payout on the books. This chemical is worth six figures? And your end said they'd tighten up on discrepancies. The Feds don't look fondly on faking cargo manifests."

"Lots of stuff is considered 'miscellaneous equipment' if that's how they want it considered, you got me? Especially if it comes from military sources. If anybody says anything, we'll just write a letter explaining the manifest was a mistake and send them a corrected statement. It'll be up to them to prove it and I can tell you right now it won't go anywhere. With the war in the Middle East and all, they don't have to sweat the small stuff anymore."

Looking over Macpherson's shoulder, he saw the same file he had pulled up less than an hour ago. The blue trident logo was in the lower right hand corner. "Whose logo is that?"

MacPherson whirled in his chair. "That's them, as a matter of fact. Poseidon. That's the shipper."

Something else attracted his eye in one of the corner monitors. Alex shot a glance at the constantly changing terminals overhead. A truck was being dispatched DC, Diamondback City at fifteen hundred hours. The destination in numerical code with three letters. PLA. He knew that much. Port of Los Angeles.

On the far end of the bank of monitors, there was an aerial shot of a Synotech truck on a highway. For a moment, Alex thought it was from a camera at the gate of the plant. But the truck was definitely on a major road as other traffic passed it. It was definitely being filmed from the air. At the edge of the picture, a digital monitor registered the time and numerical code. Code Letters SD. San Diego. In a split second, the screen changed to the view of another semi, registration code for SG, Savannah, Georgia.

MacPherson caught him watching the monitors. "Satellite photos. You know, in case the driver tries to take a break. They all have a relief driver so they can driver pretty much straight through."

"Love that efficiency. So what'd you find out?"

Macpherson's mind was back on the job at hand. "I pulled it up and it looks like this stuff comes from military sources."

"So the big difference in weight means it isn't chemical drums, even though it's the same shipment, same number and everything. My god, that isn't legal."

The shipping manager shrugged. "Hey, all I do is ship 'em out, I don't ask what's in them, and, if you're smart, you won't either. We have one or two of these a week and you're the first one to raise a question. If Crittenden or Hardaway want to know, tell them to call Colonel Dalton at up in Diamondback about that. I just put the order through and get it there on time."

"Yeah, but your name's on the cargo manifest so that makes you legally responsible for what's in the cargo hold. For all the Feds know, you could be piggybacking all kinds of stuff without their knowledge. I wouldn't want to be in your shoes if they find out."

He made it sound like MacPherson was headed for the electric chair, frowning like Crittenden when he wanted to raise his cut of the take in a law suit. MacPherson swiveled around to look at him, swallowing hard. "Look, Carreras, whatever I do, I was ordered to do. They promised they'd have my back if anything went wrong. And it hasn't so far, has it?"

"They promise a lot of things, Mac. But when it comes down to prosecution, they'll be the first one to throw you under the bus."

He glanced up again at the bank of monitors. On the smaller security screen, a black sedan was at the guard kiosk. It was the same car from O'Hara's parking lot. He snapped his briefcase shut. "You're right, I guess George had better take over from here. Thanks for filling me in." He turned to go.

MacPherson was sweating now. "And one more thing, Alex. We don't ship from Diamondback on Sunday. Officially, that is. If you want to check something out, that'd be a good place to start."

It was as good a tip as he could expect for a man who got over a hundred grand bonus every Christmas and a pair of cruise tickets he couldn't use because he was always working. The wife and mother-in-law always went and sent him postcards of the fun they were having.

"Thanks, Mac. I get it." He noticed another door at the back of the shipping department. "I think I'll take a look around, that is, if that's okay with you."

MacPherson jumped up and followed him to the door. "Hey, look, Alex, I just coordinate the shipping, I don't say who buys what, you get me? Just like you, I'm a middleman, not the lynchpin. So do me a favor and don't go quoting me to Crittenden or anybody else. But I can tell you one thing," he said, dropping his voice to conspiratorial level, "the government knows and looks the other way. You can export any amount of arms you want to and whatever you want to as long as they're purchased from a legit arms dealer."

"Then if it's legal, why does it state the cargo is chemicals or miscellaneous crap when it's really armaments? There's only one reason and you and I both know it. It's contraband."

Macpherson's Anglo face became yellow under sunburned cheeks. "Just between you and me and the gatepost, some of that stuff that goes out is classified. I mean, they know that and they've apparently got permission to do it from higher up."

"Or the higher ups don't even know. We all know military ordinance is about as efficient as three generals trying to change a light bulb in a power outage."

Glancing up at the monitors behind MacPherson, he saw the black sedan was now pulling into the parking lot near his jeep. Old buddy Tim Hardaway got out and strode toward the building. Another man got out of the passenger side and hurried after him. Alex recognized one of the security guards from his building. They were joined by two Synotech guards and the phalanx rushed into the building.

It would take them a few minutes to enter the building and come down the long hall to get to Shipping. He played it to the split second.

"The shipment on Sunday that really wasn't a shipment. Destination: SG. Was it another one of those miscellaneous equipment jobs?"

MacPherson wasn't fooled. "Look, Alex. I've got to tell you. Last time you came, Crittenden told me not to allow you into Shipping again." He followed Alex's stare at the monitors. They were in the hall now. "And I think they've got somebody checking up on you right now. So if I were you, I'd get out fast. Back door to the shipping yard. Get a hardhat and look official. "

One parting shot. "You realize how deep in doo-doo you and I are if we let this stuff go? I could lose my license and you could get hard time like Sydney Harris."

MacPherson winced at the name of Crittenden's former partner, who had just done time in a federal prison for assisting in defrauding the feds of millions in off-shore accounts for bogus companies. "I know. I used to ask questions about this and that. My advice, is the fewer questions you ask, the better. Then you can claim innocence. Now, get the hell out of here."

The door marked *SHIPPING* opened into a long hall with a red arrow pointing to Shipping. As he got to the double doors saying Secure Area. Employees Only, a rough voice behind him stopped him cold.

"Hey, buddy, you can't go out there without a hard hat on, you know. Regulations. Can I see your ID?"

Alex flashed his Visitors Pass under the man's nose. "OSHA," he said. "Sorry, just checking up to see if our recommendations have been met since our last visit."

Immediately, the worker looked contrite. "Sorry, didn't mean to come on as unfriendly. Just that stuff falls, you know."

"No prob," Alex replied, putting his pass away. There were loud voices in the manager's office behind them. "If you could just point me in the right direction." The guard's beeper went off and he sighed heavily. "Hell, I'll be right with you. They always beep when it's just about quitting time, I'm telling you." The man turned his back to avoid the noise as a massive semi in Gate 19 began to gun its airplane-sized engines, pulling slowly out of its birth, Alex saw the number on the rear door. It was one-nineteen and its destination was Diamondback City. Jumping down off the platform, he used it for a shield, it moved slowly toward the front gate.

As it passed his car, he got in and ducked behind the wheel, starting the engine and tailgating the Synotech truck out the gate.

CHAPTER 8

It took almost an hour to get rid of his jeep. His high school buddy Steve let him have a bronze pickup truck with temporary tags with a thousand dollar rebate check.

"You sure this thing isn't hot?"

It was meant as a joke, but his laugh sounded phony. "My girlfriend drives a Porsche and told me I need something to haul furniture in. Guess who won?"

"Hey, I heard you're getting married. Congrats and all that good stuff. I've already been divorced and paying child support for two years." They shook hands over the deal and he got out of Steve's small office only after looking through two photograph albums of Steve's kid. Another link in the chain broken, he thought, pulling back onto the Interstate.

By now, it was bumper-to-bumper and the Synotech truck would be miles ahead of him. But he had the number on a notepad in his wallet one-nineteen, destination Diamondback City. There was no way he could lose something that big.

In the stagnant traffic, he made a call on his cell phone he thought he would never have to make. The answering machine kicked on and his father's perfunctory voice invited him to leave a message and have a nice day.

"Hi, Mama and Pop, it's Alejandro. I just want to tell you the cops think I killed somebody and I didn't. And I've got to prove I didn't. Because otherwise, they won't believe me. I know you will understand I could have never done what they are saying I did. I love you. Elena, I love you, too." At the sound of his little sister's name, he suddenly choked. "Be good for Mama and Boppa." He had to click off, fighting a complete meltdown.

It was six-fifteen and he imagined the small house on the palm-lined street where he had grown up. His father would be in the yard watering his prize roses, wearing his grey cardigan, looking bent like one of his roses that wasn't doing well. In his baggy pants and his gardening sweater with leather patches, he in no way resembled his proud *conquistador* ancestors always portrayed in velvet and lace. Often, he would get on his knees, hunched over his plants as if he were praying over them. Alex ached to say his father's name, but whispered the words he hadn't said as a child instead.

"Goodbye, Mama, Pops. I love you."

His father would be snipping small bits from the roses that had dared to be less than perfect. How would he feel about a son who had failed to meet his demanding expectations? In his father's eyes, he had always seemed to be wanting, in spite of all his achievements. The law had to exonerate him, and full exoneration would be the only explanation his father would accept.

Alex headed for the 5 North at the spaghetti junction just beyond the stark hills of the San Fernando Valley. Keeping his eye on the rear view mirror, he checked the thinning traffic to see if the black sedan was still following him. The speed picked up as commuters dropped off at their bedroom communities along the way and the distance lengthened between vehicles, stretching out like kids playing tag. A Santa Ana wind was picking up and dusty tumbleweeds rolled across the road like beach balls gone mad.

Just as he relaxed a little, it hit him with the impact of a brick to the head. He was headed north, but he could just as easily head south to Mexico, where he would undoubtedly be lost to US law enforcement. So why not? Playing his own Devil's Advocate, he weighed the advantage of both choices, telling himself he would be safe in Mexico, but exoneration would never be his.

Unless her murder had been one of those mindless crimes of impulse by a psychotic hitchhiker, there had to be a motive. Where there was motive, there was a history. A history of relationships, social life, phone calls, and pictures that told a story.

One thing was clear above all the others, until he had that evidence firmly in his control, wherever the chase took him, he would always be a fugitive. Guilty because, in spite of the way the law was written, the reverse was the reality. Guilty until proven innocent. There would be no protection from Crittenden now or the private interests he represented. In fact, he had no doubt Crittenden had put the two goons in the Lincoln on his tail. Remembering they might still be following him, he checked his rearview mirror and took a relieved breath. The lanes behind him were punctuated only by struggling semis hugging the slow lane as it wound through the canyons.

Two more off-ramps and two more opportunities to turn around and head south. He passed the exit signs looming in the twilight like idols to a pagan god pointing to a choice of fates. South, you win but lose. North, you lose but win. There was no turning back now.

An hour later, squeezed in a line of semis going North up the Interstate, Alex realized he was passing the exit where he had discovered the girl the previous day. Although, he was pressed for time, and it was dangerous to be found in the area, Carreras felt the need to be at the scene again. Maybe something would occur to him to shed more light on exactly what had happened in those brief minutes after he discovered the girl—he still wouldn't allow himself to think of her by name. Just the girl in the blue van.

Something had been momentarily lost in the melee that followed within minutes of finding her slumped at the wheel. Something that eluded him as many times as he had been over and over the same scene. He hoped it would come to him if he were actually standing beside the road in the same spot.

Approximately twenty or so yards north of the intersection on Highway 184, he found the spot where the van had stopped. No blood, no yellow tape, or roped off area, no outline of a body on the road. It was as if nothing had ever happened along this weed-choked strip of macadam road.

He stood there with the desert wind beginning to wail above the distant hum of the Interstate. "I'm sorry," he said to the night sky. "I'm sorry I was too late. I keep thinking if I had been there earlier…" The scar across his ribs began to tighten, warning him to be glad he hadn't. "I'm going to find him for both of our sakes."

Then Alex crossed himself and got back in the truck.

As he started the engine, something clicked in his mind. He remembered the highway patrol car with the blue light coming up behind him on the Interstate. He could think of all the reasons a young woman with two dogs would stop on a lonely road. Top priority, to let the dogs out. Car trouble? Most women called road service or just sat on the emergency strip until a cop came along.

Suppose the same cop had pulled her over? LA was full of nuts like that—wackos in Rent-A-Cop outfits pulling pretty women over, giving bogus tickets. Frisking people. Hey, this is a great way to meet in person, not online.

Just as he was about to give up, something white blew across the grass. He bent over to take a better look. It was only a crumpled piece of paper, almost obliterated by mud. He stuffed it into his pocket.

His next impulse sent him in search of the gas station the patrolman had said was just a mile past the intersection. After ten miles up the road, Alex finally gave up the search. Maybe the officer had meant left instead of right at the ramp?

Then, a random thought struck him. Shelby Turner's blue van had been heading in the same direction, half on the road and half off. He was not a great believer in coincidence. The law was not predicated on coincidence. Yet, what else could it be? Both of them heading in the same direction, both looking for the same nonexistent gas station? Checking the other three sides of the intersection for several miles, he found no gas station anywhere.

Finally, he spotted a light outside a Mom and Pop store with one gas pump. It was out of order, but he went inside anyway. The owners, an elderly Hispanic couple, were eating dinner in the back room and looked startled to see him. The moment he inquired in Spanish, they broke into a litany of sorrow.

"No, hijo, there no gas station around here for fifteen miles," the woman said. "We used to operate the only one but we couldn't meet the states *reglas* in the '90s, you know, too much money to upgrade to the fancy stuff. New pumps, new hoses." She shrugged. "Gas was most of our business. So they shut us down. Now, nobody comes." "I wonder if I could ask you about an old beat-up Ford pickup, blue. An old man drives it. A farmer, maybe?"

Immediately, they were apprehensive. "You policia? ICI?"

"No, just looking for someone who might know him, that's all."

The couple exchanged glances and shrugged. "There is an old man who lives nearby. He used to come for gas and burritos here. Maybe it's him you look for? The police girl also look, for him, hijo."

The couple gave him coffee and two homemade tacos which he sat in his truck and consumed. He watched them through the store window as they had a deep conversation and then the man returned. He had somehow earned their trust, he could tell the way the proprietor looked both ways up and down the dark highway.

"I must tell you something, mijo. A police lady was here this morning. She was looking for this man who sells onion and she was looking for you. Tall, she said."

He studied Alex's face through the window. "You in trouble?" he asked in Spanish.

"Yes. But I haven't done anything wrong, I swear to you. I understand if you have to call the police. Just give me a few minutes to get away. Then call. I have to find the one who killed that girl. It wasn't me."

The store owner stood back from the driver's side. "*Vaya con Dios, mijo.* I tell you something. I think you didn't do it, either. The cops here, they think if someone gets killed, it's always us who did it. But they let the drug dealers—" He waved at the night sky. "—they let them run the county go free as birds!"

It was a gift and a sacrifice and he knew it. "If I am free, I can prove my innocence to the law. If I am a prisoner, I can't do that." He started the truck engine.

The reply was a shrug. "If you are guilty, God will find you. If you are innocent, He will set you free. Now, go. *Vaya con Dios, hijo.*"

Oddly, it was the second break in the last few hours, like glimpses of the moon pouring through a stormy evening sky.

As he got back on the northbound 5, Alex briefly entertained the possibility that he was being neatly framed. But who wanted him out of the way so badly? High up, Mac-Pherson had said. So high up, you didn't want to know.

And Tim Hardaway? What part did good old buddy Tim Hardaway play in all this? Good old frat bro Tim who apparently was thick as thieves with MacPherson, taking over the Synotech account so he could rat him out to Crittenden. Not only that, there was Crittenden taping his conversations! Future father-in-law, his ass. Probably the whole set-up was to keep precious Chelsea from marrying a man Crittenden considered inferior by virtue of ethnicity and economic status.

But why murder that particular girl to pin it on him? Was she just a convenience in the wrong place at the wrong time?

Or did something link them other than a photograph of a bunch of people, happily drunk.

That night, Saturday, the whole group had been doing a tour of the pubs in the area, and then landed in this western saloon place feeling no pain. He remembered dancing a lot with numerous pretty girls wearing cowboy hats over masses of curly hair. One of those girls must have been the Turner girl. He felt sick, wondering if anything else had happened he was unaware of. Surely, he had been too drunk to have sex. He had probably posed for pictures with two or three of the girls and she had kept her copy. But why did she have the key to the condo? Had he left it in the bar and she was trying to return it? That was silly.

Or was it just a reason to see him again. *Get real. Don't flatter yourself. A kid that young would think you're a geezer. No, there had to be another reason. What did she ask him? Something about the law. Maybe she was thinking about law school. No! 'I hear you're a lawyer.' That's it! 'Just what I'm looking for,' she said. But why? Too young to be in much trouble except a DUI maybe.*

The purple semi was struggling up the incline from the beach above Santa Barbara, trapped between a commercial dump truck and a commercial horse trailer with a CHP trooper following the pack, just waiting for the drivers to quit driving like their grandmas. Just to put the icing on the cake for the long distance boys, there was a weigh station another few miles ahead with a line as long as a soup kitchen's on fried chicken Sunday.

After an hour, the caffeine jolt had worn off and his head started to throb again. Needing gas and desperate for a toilet, Alex stopped in a convenience store just off the Interstate.

As he was standing in line to pay, the dead girl's picture flashed on the TV screen above the counter. It must have been a yearbook picture, stiffly posed, wearing that special sweater. Dark, wavy hair framing a heart-stopping face, wide white smile that said I'm beautiful but so is my world.

The TV announcer's bland voice ate his heart away.

"Shelby Turner, seventeen, was found shot to death in her van outside Bakersfield. Police are questioning a suspect man found near the scene of the murder after a weapon was found nearby belonging to him."

"What?

The clerk looked at him curiously. "You say something, friend?"

"No, I just thought my wallet was missing." Alex ducked his head, pretending to be fishing for change. "Sorry, I thought I stuck it back in the right place." His hands shook so badly, he was afraid the clerk would think he was a drug addict needing a fix.

"No hurry." This was California where no one recognized people because they rarely looked them squarely in the face. Chewing his gum energetically, the cashier never took his eyes off the TV.

Hunched over as if he were myopic, Alex picked up his groceries and started for the door. The cashier's voice made him freeze in his tracks. "Hey, buddy! You forgot your change! You gave me a twenty. You win the lottery or something?"

"No, kidding, I really need some sleep," he said, going back to collect his change.

"So do we all, buddy." The clerk turned back to watch the rest of the news. "So do we all."

☙☙☙

Alex was counting on the police not getting around to tracing his jeep to the used car lot yet. Nobody in LA moved that fast, and it was only Monday night. No one knew he had even jumped bail yet. Still, the main roads were the first ones to be watched and there were always the two goons in the black Lincoln to worry about.

As darkness fell and the traffic became lighter, he spotted the purple crest of the Synotech truck jutting out above the other semis as they approached the lights of Bakersfield. As the halogen road lamps took over from the sun, that purple cab-over began to take on the appearance of a Jurassic age beast retreating to its lair the craggy mountains rising in the distance.

Although he knew he was taking a chance of being spotted on the Interstate North, following the Synotech truck made him feel like he was doing something on his own behalf. It made him feel less helpless to think this might actually turn out to be a lead somewhere. Synotech had paid up its fines to Interstate Commerce for misrepresenting their weight loads and to US Customs in inaccuracies on their bills of lading. However, what did click in his mind, very clearly now that might impact his life, was that he couldn't remember Synotech actually ever stating to either commission that they were shipping armaments to legitimate foreign buyers. All these buyers had supplied the right papers and licenses. But he could have overlooked, making sure they were on the list of officially approved companies, having been caught up in more recent cases.

It was worth a check to see what they were actually loading. Then, somewhat comically, he remembered he had no way of finding out what the real cargo was anymore. No official position as watchdog, no affiliation with Crittenden and Harris. He couldn't even safely pose as an inspector for fear of being caught. In twenty-four hours, his entire personhood had changed so that he was no longer a member of a professional group, he was a fugitive. The law was looking for him and, if he didn't get out of the country immediately, they would get him.

Anyone with a grain of common sense, he told himself, would get the hell out before they were imprisoned for a murder they didn't commit. Whatever the consequence now, he would never be cleared in the public's eye. No political kudos awaited him, no promising career as a Latino leader, nothing. Only the disappointment in his father's eyes. No, he was going to clear himself, not run, if he had to create another identity to do it.

Staying at least two car lengths behind the eighteen-wheeler, he followed down the off-ramp to a county high-way headed inland. There was very little traffic at this hour and he had to stay behind an older model truck in order not to be seen. Finally, the truck in front of him turned off the road and he was left, following the semi at a quarter mile distance. The truck was making good time at sixty-five miles per hour, now, as if the driver not only knew the twisting road very well, he also knew he wouldn't get pulled over.

The highway yielded to yet another smaller, steeper road and they began to climb around horseshoe curves. Alex checked his odometer, and figured they were almost 150 miles from the shipping center. The time was one-fifteen a.m. so Poseidon's base was near. As they started up anoth-er incline, markers indicated another hairpin turn.

When he got to the top, the Synotech truck was far down the opposite side heading into a small valley. Beyond it, a small pool of lights sparkled in the basin formed by a tow-ering mountain range. As he negotiated the sharp curves, he passed a small sign beside the road which announced he was entering *Diamond City, pop. 1600*. The Synotech truck's tail lights flickered on the dark road ahead, then dis-appeared. As he passed the dirt turnoff, he saw the truck heading up a narrow Macadam road toward the ghostscape of mountains. Pulling over, he turned off his lights and watched the truck until it was out of sight.

Then, ignoring the enormous No Trespassing sign, he entered the dirt turnoff and found the Macadam road with-out using his lights. It was a clear, star-filled night and he could make out a slight rise in the road. As he came over it, he was suddenly electrified by banks of spotlights more ap-propriate on a football field. He braked to a stop as doors slammed and his car was surrounded by uniformed guards.

One of them jerked his door open and he was dragged

out on to the road. The other guard reached in and got his ignition keys. "Where're you going, buddy? This is a private road."

His best defense was the pose he hated most, ignorant and illegal. "No read very good," he stammered. "Sleep."

The blinding lights blotted out the guards' faces, but he always recognized the voices. "Well, buddy, this road ain't no place for taking a siesta, get it?"

"It's only some beaner looking for a place to sleep." The other one peered through the passenger window. "Move on, buddy. I'll back you out."

"Wait a sec," said the other one. "We'd better frisk him just to make sure he's not a narc. You know they said to be on the lookout up at headquarters. Something big going down."

"Okay, okay." He held up both hands in surrender. "No problem. I go, okay? Sleep here no more."

"Aw, let the beaner go, Bill. He ain't no threat to anybody." Something like pity crossed one of the guard's faces. The one who was going to show him the way out. "Damn Mike Sutton's afraid of his own shadow." He turned the flashlight back on Alex, frozen behind the wheel, hands in air. "Okay, buddy, get on out of here. *Vamoose*! And be careful on the road. Imigre's patrolling all around out here. *Cuidado*!" It was the closest thing to a welcome he knew he would get in Diamondback City.

"Hell, I don't know why you baby these wetbacks, Nate. Bunch of parasites, if you ask me. Shit, the wetbacks don't understand a word you're saying. Go on, get out of here." The guard closest to him gave him a shove back behind the wheel. "And turn your lights on, you stupid frijole! You could get off in the ditch and then you'd be a hot tamale. This road is electrically wired to fry your tires! You got to back down all the way."

In the glare of the flashlights, he had caught a glimpse of a dark blue trident on the guard's shirt pocket.

The two men laughed as he backed down the road to the

highway. Sweat dripped from his face and trickled down into his shirt. About a mile away, he had to pull over to light a cigarette. He had found Poseidon headquarters.

CHAPTER 9

The receptionist at Sunrise matched the décor in the central office—sleek, bright, her smile polished diamond-hard. "Good morning, Sunrise Spa and Resort. How can I help?"

Lady, you have no idea, Murray thought. Doing a bad imitation of a falsetto ingénue voice, she said breathlessly, "Oh, hi there, I was just calling to see if my boyfriend had left his wallet there over the weekend. I promised him I would check. His name's Alex Carreras. Maybe he left it in the room or even the bar."

"Oh, hi, Miss Crittenden. I didn't recognize your voice at first. Must be the connection. Anyway, I'll be happy to have a look in the Lost and Found for you, if you don't mind holding."

"Oh, not at all. I'll be so grateful if you found it. He's completely wigged out about losing it."

"I would be, too. Although usually if it's something as important as a wallet, we call the guest to say we found it. But hang on a second, I'll check for you."

"Super duper." Maybe that was overdoing it.

It wasn't seconds, but a full five minutes before the receptionist picked up the receiver again. Murray had visions of the girl checking with the police before she came back to the phone. Unfortunately, she would be butting heads with local law enforcement agency in the resort area. But there was a legitimate reason for the delay.

"I'm so sorry to keep you holding, but the concierge was busy and he's the only one who has the key to the Lost and Found. He says no wallet has turned up."

"How about checking his room? He left Sunday morning. Maybe someone just found it cleaning up today."

There was pause. "Well, you know he always stays at your father's condominium. They have a different cleaning service—a contract company for the owners. I don't know what their schedule is. We here at the hotel have our own staff. But I could find out if you can—"

Whoops! Chelsea would have known that. Murray tried dithering in a higher octave. "I know but, see, like he was having a bachelor party and really partying it up and he might not have spent the night back at Daddy's condo, but crashed with some of the guys like, you know what I mean? There were some of them staying there at the hotel, you know."

The receptionist morphed from robotic to human. "Oh, I remember that party well. Mr. Kirkendall and Mr. Harris and your finance's brother, Ricky. They were living it up, I can tell you. They sure were a cute bunch of guys! They even asked me to come along and I had to say that unfortunately, the hotel frowns on fraternizing with the guests!" The receptionist gave that high-pitched giggle, a signal from Valley Girl to Valley Girl. "My luck is rotten!"

The bogus Chelsea driveled on. "I'll see what I can do to fix you up. Anyway, I'd so appreciate it if you don't let the cleaning service touch that room yet. I'm on my way up there to look for it right now! Oh, I almost forgot. One more teeny little thing. Did you by any chance have a guest named Shelby Turner there over the weekend?"

She squeezed her eyes shut, hoping bad news hadn't traveled that fast to the mountains of the north. There was an awkward silence.

"Shelby? Well, sure. But she wasn't a guest. She works here."

"No kidding! Well, thanks a lot, see you later! Bye-bye for now!"

It was hard to get back to her normal voice. How did they talk like that all the time? It sounded like they were high on helium. She got ready to make her case before Hansen that some kind of evidence could be found wherever Carreras had spent the night. Maybe even evidence of sexual activity with the girl.

But he was out of the office, and she knew Stockman wouldn't okay it.

It didn't take her any time to figure out what she had to do. Murray just got in the car and left, figuring she could always apologize later for not following procedures.

☙❧

Alex hadn't worked two days in the field when he was picked up for work one afternoon by a fiftyish Chicano crew boss named Rudolfo. Rudolfo conducted his group of workers like a mini-labor union. If someone had failed to do their share of the picking, or carelessly damaged crops, Rudolfo exacted punishment. If a man was beating his wife or children, Rudolfo put the matter before the assembled families and justice was exacted. If someone needed money until payday, Rudolfo lent it to them, but deducted the loan before handing over the next paycheck. He was a man who not only commanded respect but deserved it for his kind, but firm insistence on performance standards. If he had been the CEO of a company with a six-figure income, Rudolfo could not have taken more interest in the production of his crew. And he could spot a man on the run a mile away.

Toward the end of the first day he worked on Rudolfo's crew, Alex picked up sound of a tractor-trailer truck hitting airbrakes somewhere above the valley. Straightening up as if to rub his aching back, he saw an eighteen wheeler with a familiar purple cab making its way laboriously up the mountainside. At some point, it turned toward the mountains, he could even hear it whining in third gear. He turned to find Rudolfo watching him.

"Sorry." Alex pressed his hands to his waist. "Just easing up my back."

"No problem, Maestro. Take a break, if you want. We almost finished here."

But Alex continued loading, not wanting to appear as if he were slacking. After showing a few tips for picking apricots, Rudolfo said, "You're not from Mexico, hombre. You from *Los Estados Unidos*. You running from the law or a girl?"

For a moment, Alex was struck dumb with terror. "Both," he said. "Is it written all over me?"

Rudolfo had picked him up after an early morning shift dipping sheep. Like the other crew bosses, he hadn't asked for ID. He simply said the crop was apricots and the pay was five an hour. By noon, Alex's shoulders ached from loading crates of fruit on flatbed trucks. His hands were caked with dirt like the rest of the workers. At break, he joked with them, played a hand of cards, drank some beer and put up with their good-humored jibes about being a greenhorn.

Somehow, either his height or his diligence had impressed the crew boss. "Listen, hombre, you work good, but this is our last day on this job."

At afternoon break, Rudolfo had personally handed Alex a glass of cool tea from a massive container under one of the trucks.

"We go to the same farms every year all the way past Sacramento." He ticked them off on his fingers. "Apples, pears, apricots, oranges. So don't worry about where you will work every day. If you stay, I can keep you busy all summer and into October. You a good worker. And so tall."

The crew boss squinted up at him from under the brim of his straw hat. "With you, we don't even need a ladder."

Without waiting for a reply, Rudolfo wiped the tea from his grey moustache. "Me, I was born in the back of a truck and been doing this for forty-five years. I put two boys through UCLA and they don't even call no more. But if I was as tall as you, son, I'd be retired by now. Where you headed?"

Alex shrugged, pretending to be footloose. "Diamond-back City, I guess."

"Good." Rudolfo nodded. "We got job there tomorrow. You come with us okay, buddy? You got ID?"

That was probably the end of the job offer. "None I want to use."

The crew boss studied his face for a moment, reading the language of trouble. "Your hands don't look like they've been in the dirt much, boy."

"No, I'm a teacher, but they have no jobs here because I have no American diploma. So that's why I am here. I have to survive some way."

Rudolfo raised his thick, gray brows. "You a *maestro*? *Dios mio*, man, what you doing here with us? We need teachers like you, man. You got to be teaching, not pick-ing." He waved the rest of the crew toward the long rows of tomato vines. "Go on, then, get to work. Listen, maestro, I will get you a green card and driver's license. You got forty bucks?" He glanced at Alex's face. "No, okay, never mind, I lend it to you and take it from your pay. Hey, and any time you want a vehicle, just let me know. There's a big market for American cars over the border, comprende? No ques-tions asked."

His new identity was Jimmy Vargas. He had an Arizona driver's license with the photo of a dark face staring back, unsmiling, Mexican. Birthdate: September 9, 1984. Twenty-six years old, a year older than himself. Address: a street in Nogales. There was a good chance Jimmy Vargas had been picked up for some minor offense, but there was little choice. He became Jimmy Vargas, day laborer. Never quite clean, never quite full.

Even his concept of time was changing—minutes and

hours turned to water breaks and lunch, heat and shade. Fear and safety.

As the sun mounted in a cloudless sky, his back began to ache, and Alex straightened for a moment to watch a dozen children chasing each other through the rows of tomatoes and squash. They had been helping their parents, their deft little hands already trained not to bruise the fruit or disturb the blossoms.

"Aren't the kids supposed to be in school?" he asked. "I mean, is it okay for them to work in the fields?"

"Except for having to eat," one plump woman said, "all of us would be in school."

Alex joined in the laughter, realizing how naive he had sounded.

At the next ten-minute break, Rudolfo sat down next to him, offering a cup of tea. "The white lady who's coming to teach our children once a week, usually don't find us, because we move on or she gets sick. She is paid by the government in Washington to come teach us. But they don't pay her enough to get Montezuma's Revenge, she say. And we don't have no clean bathrooms. So, lately, she don't come no more at all. So, our children will grow up like us. Working in the fields."

Suddenly, the crew boss stiffened his dark face snapping alert as if he had heard something. "*Ja, estan vienen, compadres! Guarden los ninos!*" Before Alex could react, the circle around him melted into the rows of plants. Rudolfo swung back to him. "Lie flat and keep your face down, *amigo! En adelante!*"

Across the vast fields which sloped away to rolling ranch country, there was a wink of metal in the sky. Shielding his eyes, he saw a yellow biplane coming directly at them, lowering itself below the telephone lines. The sound of the ratcheting engine reached him as it revved to a steady climb over head. As it climbed nose pointed almost vertical, a jet of gray insecticide vapor gushed from its tail like a peculiar mist.

Then it occurred to him what was happening. "They're dusting!"

Fortunately, nobody heard the very American accent in his voice over the roar of the plane. Across the vast field, workers were all falling on top of the children, like so many mother hens gathering their chicks.

"Cover your face, *maestro!*" they yelled but the sound was barely audible as the duster, made a loop and came almost directly overhead.

Alex dropped down among the dusty vines, covering his face and eyes. A stinging odor closed his throat, as he tried vainly to hold his breath. But the spray permeated infinitesimal spaces between his pinched fingers, burning his mouth and nostrils like fire.

All around him, he heard gagging and choking, but he dared not open his eyes. Even though he had them squeezed them closed, tears streamed down his face, and he groped blindly in his pocket for his handkerchief, the one his mother had embroidered with his initials. Then he remembered it wasn't in his suitcase either.

They lay along the rows like so many dead people almost ten minutes until Rudolfo blew the all clear whistle. Then slowly, they got up, coughing and wheezing. All along the rows stretching the clawed feet of the ridge, he could hear cries of *Dios Mio.*

Alex got up wiping his streaming nose and eyes on his dirty shirt sleeve. "They can't do that. That's a pesticide. I can tell by the smell."

Rudolfo came up beside him. "You okay, maestro? Damn bastards. They knew we were out here."

"Isn't that illegal?" As Alex was about to wipe his streaming nose on his tee-shirt tail, a woman rushed up with a roll of toilet tissue, a precious commodity in the field. "To spray when workers are in the fields?"

"They don't care." Rudolfo wiped his face with a muddy, red rag. "*Bastardos!*"

"Here Senor Maestro. Use this." She offered him the roll

as if it were pure gold. In the field it was even better than gold. "I am grateful." He returned the rest to her.

She pulled around the two undernourished children clinging to her skirts. "This is Miguel and this chiquita is Yolanda. She is seven and he is almost ten years."

Compared to his seven-year-old sister, these children appeared undernourished and impaired in ways he was unable to identify at first. The girl's eyes were crossed and the boy seemed distracted, aimlessly plucking things from the air and examining them closely. "Maybe you can teach them to read sometime," the woman said. "They have only been to school two days."

"*Pobrecitos!*" Rudolfo's gaze was full of pathos as he watched the woman herd the children across the fresh furrows back to the trailer camp under the trees. "It is the spray does these things when the baby is still inside the mother's belly. The Migrant Council says so. But they continue to spray while we are working. My daughter is in the trailer." He nodded toward the little encampment. "She had a tumor in her little head the size of a tomato. Then another. Then another. At the end of the summer, I will take her back home and bury her with the other family in holy ground."

Alex struggled to grasp, the man was speaking in the past tense of his child. "Did she—is she?"

"*Muertos.* I had her embalmed so I can carry her home. She had only ten years of life." Turning away, Rudolfo called in Spanish, "Back to work. Jefe is coming."

As fast as they had emerged, the workers disappeared into the rows of tomatoes. Alternating rows, they popped up again and pretended to inspect plants and catch the action. The foreman rode his quarter horse through the rows, raising a small cloud of stinking, yellow dust that brought the taste of insecticide back into the mouth and nose again.

"Hey, Rudolfo, your people'll have to work an extra fifteen minutes for taking an unscheduled break, ya comprende? I saw you lying down there."

Rudolfo spoke up, taking off his hat to show respect.

"Senor Jackson, there was a crop duster airplane that come along and dusted while we were eating lunch. So we hide."

From his superior position in the saddle, the foreman regarded Rudolfo with a leer. "No excuses, Rudy. There ain't nothing in that stuff to hurt you workers. You quit listening to that damned Migrant Worker council guy and remember because of us, you've got food on the table. First, we had to take the DDT out of everything and now we got cutworm and hornworm and beetles all over the place. You Mexicans bring in new pests and this piss they said we have to use now is next to useless. We got cows over there eating the dusted alfalfa. So don't use your naptime as an excuse."

So angry he almost lost his phony border accent, Alex got up off his knees. "It is not legal to dust when there are workers in the field. The Migrant Workers Union says that. There are children out here."

The foreman looked as if he had discovered a row of gopher holes. "Oh, we've got a really, big guy here! Do you see the Migrant Workers Union around here? None of these work crews are union, or your deadbeat ass wouldn't be here." The rancher leaned forward in the saddle, squinting down into his face. "Hey, you're one of them Migrant Council spies. You get the hell off this place or I'll put my boot up your ass!"

Rudolfo spoke up. "He is not labor representative, Senor Jackson. You know I don't work with none of them. He is a teacher from Mexico. I personally will vouch for him."

The man sat back in his saddle and spat close to Rudolfo's foot. "Teacher, huh? He's got one helluva nerve talking to me like that. I bet you money he ain't legal." He jerked back his horse's head, causing the animal to sling lather across Rudolfo's face. The crew boss didn't move a hand to wipe the drool off his face. "Just tell teacher here to keep his nose out of our business. Or I'll get ICI on you. You won't work on Sutton land again." His horse's hooves spitting up dust, the foreman jogged away across the rows.

Rudolfo lowered his head for a moment. "*Puto*! Better to get to work, *maestro*. We will talk later."

"You ever worked down around the San Fernando Valley?" Alex dropped to a squat and tried to look busy, but his fingers still shook with helpless rage as he pulled fruit from the delicate plants.

"Sure. In most of California," Rudolfo replied.

Remembering the Synotech plant had been using Latino workers, he threw out a line for information. "I worked for a place called Synotech. It's not farm work. It's mostly loading trucks, handling crates, heavy stuff like that. Pays okay, though."

"Bunch of paranoid bastards," a voice said a few rows away. American accent. Alex could only see busy brown hands through the leaves. "Chemical outfit. I worked in their warehouse a couple of months. Always breathing down your neck. Total security, man, total. You know they got another place just up the road?"

"I know." Alex hesitated only a moment. "Where'd you work? The City of Industry or the San Fernando plant?"

"Both, but mostly San Fernando," came the reply. "Might as well have been San Quentin. Must be shipping drugs in those crates, man. The security is so thick, you could spread it on your tortilla."

CHAPTER 10

At the noon break, he caught up with the man named Perez. He looked vaguely familiar and they stared at each other. Perez spoke first. From his lack of accent, he was American-born which put Alex on his guard. Émigré used Mexican-Americans to seek out illegals among farm workers.

Perez spoke first. "Hey, you and me were in the holding tank on Monday in Bakersfield. Perez. Remember me?"

He dropped down beside Alex, holding out a pack of cigarettes. "Smoke?" It was a gesture of friendship, and Alex gratefully accepted, wondering if running into Perez was really the coincidence it appeared. Then he shook off the thought. If he let fear take over his life, he would eventually trust no one.

Perez's questions didn't help, however. "I knew you weren't from Mexico when I saw you in SLO. Where're you from?"

The man's accent was American and, by the looks of him, Perez wasn't a member of the migrant worker class, but a cut above. He looked you straight in the eye when he talked. Migrants, especially illegal ones, always averted their faces.

"What makes you say that?"

The man laughed, exhaling a cloud of smoke. "Hey, I'm not a narc, if that what's you're thinking. I get kind of lonely for someone with a little education to talk to."

"Vargas. Jimmy Vargas." They shook hands. "How about you? What brings you here?"

"My wife. Or I should say ex-wife." Perez shrugged. "Like I said Monday, it was bring in the bucks or jail. She slapped me with a back child support judgment and the judge upheld it even though I'm out of work. I'm an oilfield driller, but right now, they laid my crew off, so I don't even have a paycheck to garnish. Rudolfo's an old friend of my uncle so I got a job out here where what you earn stays in your pocket. Didn't mean to sound like the Imigre or anything." He took another puff on his cigarette.

"So far, Rudolfo's been good to me."

"He's the best. Kind of my cousin. You know, we're all related somehow out here. Got about enough money saved up to pay up my back child support and live until work opens up again. It's not like I'm a dead-beat dad or anything. That *puta* ex-wife of mine has a live-in boyfriend now. I found out my kids don't see support money. It all goes to keep the bum in beer. Where's the justice in that?"

"Where's the justice out here? Spraying workers in the fields. Threatening to fire them if they tell the Migrants Council." He leaned back on his elbow, getting a little shade from the tall tomato plants.

Rudolfo downed his tequila in one swallow and they smoked in silence. The men passed tortilla containers and lemonade while the women chattered about weddings and shopping trips to the city like all other women in town on their lunch hours.

Alex found himself strangely at peace with these simple people. No demands were made on him other than his fair share of the work. They valued his presence which they made known by providing him with small gifts and luxuries in spite of their poverty.

A plastic tortilla box, and a pair of used work boots, just his size from a store of extra clothes in one of the trailers. Each night he had an invitation to share a fire and a hot meal.

They taught him the value of sharing and comradeship that had no place in the corporate world.

Perez took a drag on his cigarette. "I hold my breath every time the crop duster comes around. Thank God I'm not having any more kids. They say there a lot of still births, abnormal babies, things like that. Now that we're back outside Diamondback City, I'm quitting tomorrow."

It was hard not to be won over by Perez's easy laugh. His story seemed genuine—an oilfield worker supporting three children and an amorous ex-wife who'd found used car salesmen more attractive than an oil-drenched husband.

"What's so great about Diamond City?"

Perez pulled out a flask of whiskey and offered it. "My wife, for one. I don't know what to do about this woman. She cheats on me every time she gets a chance and that's a lot because I get sent to the field two weeks at a time. She's used to finer things I can't give her. I mean, we're talking about a babe, man. A real looker. This rich guy was going to marry her and then dumped her at the last minute. She was pregnant, that's how I got lucky. So I ended up with this uptown babe who wanted a father for her kids—they turned out to be twins. I love them like they were mine, anyway. Then we had a little boy of our own and I took a good look at her. She says she loves the kids but she doesn't take care of them. Always hungry and dirty. Man, I want my son back. We can make a home together."

Alex felt a pang of envy. At least Perez, for all his problems, had someone to love and provide for. A purpose in life. On the wrong side of twenty-five, he had no one.

While they were working, Rudolfo had come over and sat down with remarkable ease for a heavy set man, as if he were accustomed to folding up like a plant in the noon sun. The crew boss was watching some workers a few yards away planting tomatoes carefully in wire cones, row and after row of them enshrined in plastic sheeting. "Hey, now, it's time to eat. Go on, rest," he ordered. "They don't pay us overtime. Don't give it to them." He turned his attention back to the men, thoughtfully buttering a tortilla.

Perez continued his story, happy to have an audience. "So I come in there early, just to surprise her and the kids, you know? And there she is with this *puto* used car sales-man. I couldn't believe my eyes. I let her off once before because she is really beautiful and she gets lonely, you know what I mean? I could have married somebody ugly and reliable. The kind you can trust. But no, I got to have this woman! She just beats anything I ever thought I could marry. Like a car magazine cover, I'm not lying. Like Miss Latino America. I guess you got to allow those beautiful women some space, huh? They like to be admired."

He looked at Alex for some confirmation of his weakness.

Chelsea sprang to mind, something he was training himself to reject. "I know the type. As long as she doesn't give you anything you don't want, like the clap or someone else's kid, then it's your call."

"Man, what a situation!" Perez tossed his cigarette away. "I guess I just lost my temper and hit her a couple of times and it was all over. Judge said I got to work on anger management. What about managing that bitch? I got a week in jail and she got everything else. I got it coming, I guess. But damn! You got to be able to depend on a woman, no?"

Alex skirted the question as too close to home. "Tell me something about Diamondback City. Who are the Suttons?"

"The Suttons? In Diamond City, Sutton's the default name for God." Perez studied him, suspicion in his eyes. "What do you want to know for?"

Alex shrugged, trying not to look too interested. "I was wondering about getting a job. Out of the heat."

"Everything for one hundred miles around belongs to Sutton Enterprises. I grew up with Mike Sutton, not that he'd remember me. He's a major pain in the butt if there ever was one. Spoil-ass rotten. His grandfather or great grandfather, I guess, operated the old Devil's Ladder Mine up in the foothills. Old man struck it rich on copper and some gold. But it played out around the early 'twenties and closed. As a mine, anyway. Still, old man Sutton was smart and invested in other stuff and made a mint. His only son, Mike's dad, was a big gambler and managed to get rid of a lot of the millions. But there was still enough to play with. Now, sonny boy Mike's in charge of this Synotech Plant and they employ almost everyone in Diamond City in one way or another. We have a saying 'You owe your living to the Suttons and your soul to the Devil'. But which one is which?"

Alex finished his tortilla, savoring every bite. "So, what do you think the chances of getting a job up there?" He nodded at the mountains.

"At Synotech? Man, I wouldn't want to do that. You already worked for them. You know what they're like. Bunch of damn Nazis." Perez looked up at the jagged ridge above them. "My cousin works there and it's like, he doesn't even belong to the family no more."

Rudolfo grunted in surprise. "Why, what do you mean? People are never lost from family. Just lost, that's all."

Perez lit another cigarette and passed it to Alex who shook his head. "They are when they work for Sutton. Those people up there are weird ass. All gringos, and my cousin, he's the only Latino. The token Mexican thing. All the rest are these Neo-Nazi types. There's something very funny going on."

"I think I ran into some of the Nazis the other night." Alex related how he tried to drive onto Synotech property and was manhandled.

Perez listened with shock written all over him. "I'm surprised you're still alive, in that case. Hear that, Rudolfo? This tin-horn tried to drive into Synotech."

The others on the perimeter of their circle joined in the joke.

"And he's alive! He must be Jesus come back to life!"

"That bad?" Alex looked around. The answer was on all their faces.

Perez nodded. "That bad, man. Those bubbas have shot all kinds of people up there poaching. Even some Yaqui Indians got shot up because they said the mountain is a sacred grave site and they got rights up there. Tried to stage a sit-in and bam! Hell! A Synotech guard killed a seventeen-year-old boy just firing at tin cans up there."

There was a murmuring among the listeners and a man sitting nearby moved closer. "Shot him dead. No trial or nothing. I hope the ghost haunts Mike Sutton forever, man. He was only a kid."

"You think it was an accident?" In spite of himself, he came to Synotech's defense.

Perez focused on him for a minute. "No, *compadre*. And I'm not the only one. My dad was a small rancher up in the foothills and his father, too. You know, sheep and cattle, things like that. I grew up on a horse doing the damn cowboy thing. But Sutton has since run my dad off, him and most all the other small ranchers." Perez threw his half-smoked cigarette in the fire. "Only a few real stubborn ones left, now. Anyhow, like Pierre Bighand."

"Old Bighand, he ain't ever going to give up," someone on the fringe said.

Perez exhaled, sending smoke into the wide blue above them. "Or Turner either. Hell, they'll go down like the damn Alamo. I'll tell you this little story." This was followed by a grunt of approval from those who had obviously heard it before. "My dad and a few of the hands were up there the day Grover Sutton, the old man, got killed. They were rounding up sheep that had strayed into the wash below the Devil's Ladder and they saw some men up on the hillside. Then they heard an explosion. They heard later Grover Sutton was up there in the mine when it caved in."

One of the itinerate workers looked puzzled. "So somebody might have been working the shaft on the other side and he went up to investigate, maybe." The worker looked from one of them to the other. "Maybe it was an accident."

But in their weary faces, he found the answers. "You

mean, somebody set him up? You know, set off the charge after he got up there."

That phrase again, set up. Could the death of a mining tycoon fifteen years ago have some relevance to the death of a young girl living in the same valley? Alex tucked the bit of information somewhere into a space where he could retrieve it again. Fifteen years ago, Synotech had added the Diamondback plant to its subsidiaries.

"Yeah, well, the paper says it was just an accident." Perez took another sip from his flask and offered it around. "Just an earth tremor set off the cave-in. Nothing about an explosion. 'Course the Suttons own the paper." Perez grinned at his listeners who all grunted and nodded. "Right away, Mike Sutton and that creepy colonel what's his name, Dalton, closed the mine and started that chemical operation for Synotech. The old mine shaft is used for a ware house, I guess. My cousin doesn't say what they store up there. Top secret. What's kind of funny is that old Grover's still left buried under the rubble."

In spite of his new identity as Jimmy Vargas, Alex couldn't help but be drawn to the legal aspects of the story. "Did anyone ask your father and the others if they heard or saw anything?"

Perez shook his head. "They went to the sheriff and said they saw somebody on the hillside just before the mine blew up, but nobody ever investigated it. It was open and shut. Bingo. Accident." They sat in silence as the fire died to radiant cubes of heat.

Then out of the blue, Perez came up with an offer. "Hey, maestro, you want to work up there? I'll ask my cousin, the *medio-gringo*. He owes me a couple of favors. He's married to my wife's sister, anyhow, a real bitch. They must be twins. But I tell you right now." Perez took a swallow of bottled water, rinsed his mouth and spat. "Something weird's going on up there. Listen, Vargas, like I said I used to play up in those hills as a kid. There's this old spur track that used to bring oar down from another shaft higher up the mountain. The spur track goes through a tunnel all the way into the next valley. And you know what's over there, right?" Perez watched his face, as if he were testing him.

Not fully trusting his new informant, he replied, "No idea. What?"

"I forget you're not from around here. The air force base. A damned air force base." Perez must have felt the implication was lost on him so he shifted away from the subject. "I'm just saying if you do apply for a job up there, watch your step. Diamondback is owned by one family. The Suttons." Perez patted the dry, sandy earth beside him. "Mexicans are just cheap help to them, not people. But my family has lived there since the earth was cooling. Used to hunt up wild goat there in the mountains until Mike Sutton fenced it off like he owns the mountain. Now they got all these weird ass guys in blue jumpsuits with semiautomatics playing soldier."

"Wild goat is good," Rudolfo put in, in an effort to change the subject. "Got to do it right, though. Or it can be very tough."

"Sounds real sci-fi."

"Sci-fi goat." Rudolfo whooped and lifted his plastic cup in salute. "Aliens, come down to help us, no? Disguised as goats."

Perez looked around at the laughing faces. "No kidding. Jumpsuits like the detox unit. And they carry semi-automatics and fly helicopters. I was in the army four years. It looks just like that."

"Maybe it's the new state prison up there. They run out of space and start stacking the poor convicts in the moun-tains." Rudolfo glanced at Alex to share the joke. He was frowning, thinking.

Perez took another drag on his cigarette. "Okay, I bet you fifty bucks I'm right. When me and Jimmy get there, we prove it to you."

He wanted desperately to bring up Shelby Turner's name but it was pushing his luck.

"Think there's any chance of getting work around here? You know, permanent? Besides the sci-fi Sutton operation?"

Rudolfo put down his beer. "Hey, look. Maestro, I tell you before you can stay with us through the summer. Not exactly the Holiday Inn but you know we take good care of you."

Alex relished the invitation to stay here in relative safety where he was wanted and needed. "Thanks, Rudolfo. I'll keep that in mind. But I wanted to find work on a ranch. I used to work on my uncle's place and my father has some land in Chihuahua he wants me to manage for him. So I need to know the ropes, *no*?"

"No," Rudolfo replied, holding up a warning finger. "You need to know the cows!"

After the laughter was over, the crew boss shook his head. "Your father is a wise man. If you need any help, Jimmy, you know who to call."

Perez agreed. "And if you want a cheap guide, I can show you around Diamond City for a beer."

When Rudolfo gave the order, Alex went back to work smiling for the first time in three days.

CHAPTER 11

When Murray ran her theory on where Carreras would go by him the next morning, Jonesy reacted as if she had said something funny.

"What do you mean, you know where he's going? You're not telling me you're psychic or something, are you? Where do I think he'd run? Mexico, of course! Whaddya think, Iceland?"

He was throwing darts at a dartboard over his computer. Hansen's picture was pinned to the bullseye and Jonesy hadn't missed once. It was a good thing everyone in this unit had a sense of humor, she thought.

He glanced sideways, catching her expression. "Well, the man always says 'What's your point?'" They shared a laugh at the boss's expense. "Okay, give me your take on it. I can see by the way you're sitting on the edge of your chair, you've got another brilliant theory. Out with it!"

"Theory on?"

He shot another bullseye. "Don't get coy with me, Schmitz. Your face reads like a wide-angle screen in living color. Where do you think Carreras has gone to ground?"

"For me to know and for you to find out." Wide-eyed, Murray returned his long, inquisitive stare with a level one of her own. "Anyway, anything I said would be a long shot and you don't believe in long shots, correct?"

"We both know you're lying, but that's okay. I'm just going to warn you that, if Hansen has any inkling, the slightest whisper of an idea that you've got a crush on this guy, your ass is grass, understand?'

"Yeah. Thanks for the warning." She got to her feet, yanking down her T-shirt with the Grateful Dead design on the front. It had cost a mint but she was retro '60s because of her father. "I got work to do."

Jones cleared his throat at a significant level and said, "Not so fast. I've actually been doing a little snooping around myself."

She hesitated. That meant Jonesy, the master of understatement, had uncovered a major development.

"And?"

"Something jingled in the back of my superb memory when I was reading Carreras's life story there, you so conveniently gave me a copy of. And I remembered something kind of weird." He waved her back into her seat. "Just park it a few minutes will you? You're making me nervous, perched like you're about to take off on me."

She sat.

"Okay, this is like weird."

"So you said."

"You remember that thing Carreras got the Governor's Award for, saving this girl from four attackers on the freeway exit one stormy night blah, blah, blah?"

She pretended to yawn. "He was stabbed, almost bled to death."

Picking up a dart with the care of a surgeon choosing a scalpel, Jonesy focused on the space between Hansen's eyes. "At that time, I was working on a case up here on a chop-shop/car-theft gang. Two of the guys we were looking for were involved in the attempted rape case. The big cheese was this Rivera guy. Angel Rivera. I was in court when they sentenced him and he was screaming he was going to get everybody back."

Not giving away anything, Murray watched him carefully aim the dart at the board. Jonesy shrugged with a look of fake innocence on his face. "Well, remember me telling you one of the chop-shop's MOs was slitting the tire just below the rim? Not only would somebody have to change it, they were absolute masters at judging just how far the tire could go before it went flat."

"Carrera's statement said he had a tire going flat and the spare was missing." Murray reflected a minute. "So what's your point?"

"The station where he got a new tire said the flat had a slit just below the rim. Knifed."

"I get your drift. But isn't Rivera still in jail?"

Jonesy nodded. "Supposed to be. But you know these gangster guys are just as powerful in the slammer as out, right? Could've gotten his homies to set Carreras up."

"That's really a stretch." She stood up again. "Can I go now?"

He shot the dart and missed. "Damn. What's up with you? Sit please for the punch line."

With an impatient sigh, she sat. "Okay, go."

"So I phoned the state slammer outside SLO, right?" Jonesy was deliberately holding back, waiting for the impact. "Angel Rivera was released last Friday. For good behavior, would you believe?"

Murray sprang to her feet. "What? You're kidding!"

"And where is Murray Schmitz, Girl Guide, going next?"

"To clear Carreras of a murder he didn't commit."

Jonesy's chair hit the floor with a satisfying slam. For the first time since they had met, he really scowled. "Don't get uppity, girl. Just sit right back there in that chair and tell me who and why and when did Mr. Carreras, GQ, get set up for Shelby Turner's murder? With all his stuff in her van and him big-as-life at the scene of the crime? Holding her hand and saying so sweetly, 'Somebody get this girl to a hospital!' after he shot her twice close range. Now, come on. What else do you need, the smoking gun? We go that, too."

"Just one little problem with that. No prints."

He wasn't impressed. "Registered to him, girl."

"My car's registered to me. If somebody steals it and runs over somebody with it, it's not my fault. Okay, then, I'll level with you! Here's what I think so just check your patronizing damn attitude at the door, Jonesy, okay? Shelby Turner met him at Sunrise, found out he was a lawyer, got that stuff in her van to have an excuse to follow him to give it back. But he got behind her when he stopped on the interstate for gas and food. Meanwhile, some goon knifed his tire at the truck stop, then followed her, and killed her. When his tire went flat, some phony cop steered him in the same direction. Knowing his reputation for being the good guy, they knew he'd stop to help her and called the cops."

Jones sat and stared at her for a micro second. His mouth opened and closed, followed by a grunt of frustration. "You're dead ass serious, aren't you? No court in the world's going to buy that."

"Dead-ass serious. The man has been set up for this murder, and I could give you the facts, chapter and verse, but I'm not going to because you could be one of them and—"

Jones was serious for the first time in their relationship as colleagues. "Whoa—ho—ho! Hold on right there, girl, sorry, Detective Schmitz. First of all, I'm not one of them…whoever they are. I'm not one of anybody by nature of birth, you understand. So anything you say, anything you think, stays right here with me, you understand?"

Murray nodded. "Yeah."

Jones looked sad. "You don't believe me, do you?"

She shrugged. "Would you believe you? If you were me?"

Jones sighed and looked hurt. "And I thought we were pals. Okay, have it your way. What are you going to do?"

Murray pushed her chair into the cubicle. "Bye, Detective. See you around."

"Oh, it's goodbye and see you around, is it? Look at yourself, Schmitz. You could be really sharp, if you worked on yourself. Spruced up, so to speak. The hair a little lighter, maybe. No, some curls. Some makeup. But what makes you think, in your wildest dreams, poor little Carerras's been victimized when he's already engaged to a red-hot dish like this one?" Jones tossed an airbrushed photograph toward her where it fell to the floor, face up. It was Chelsea Crittenden, posing for Miss Teenage Los Angeles.

She stood in the door and gave him a level look that closed the gender gap like a slamming door. "I'm sorry you had to stoop to that level, Jonesy. I thought you were above that kind of pettiness."

"You can't hide from it any more, Schmitzy. I know it was Angel Rivera who shot and killed your dad. And got off with three years because he was a juvie and 'cause he was under the influence of god knows what. If you don't trust yourself to go after him, I'll do it. As far as I'm concerned, he's environmental pollution. Toxic fumes, and I'm Smokey the Bear."

Murray left him looking at the place where she had been two seconds ago.

❧❧❧

When they accepted her proposal without a substantial protest, it was only later she realized Hansen and Stockmen were relieved she was going to be out of the office. She would have felt less insulted if they had really challenged her. Even Jonesy looked as if he'd been relieved of a babysitting chore.

"Sounds like a real great idea, kid. I mean, Murray."

"Murray."

"Er—Murray." Stockman tilted back in his swivel chair, watching her face as if it were on primetime TV. "How long do you figure this'll take?"

She shrugged, knowing she had them where she wanted them, and could play it cool. "A couple of weeks. I have vacation time coming if you…"

The ploy worked. Stockman was always generous to people who demonstrated enthusiasm for their work. "No, don't be silly. Don't use your own time on this. I mean, I admire your dedication and everything but you earned the vacation time. No, I can give you a couple of weeks if you can manage to follow up on your other cases. You know, do some checking on the web on new FBI postings, telephone follow-ups, so on. Send in a written report of everything."

"I thought I'd talk to the girls' parents. Maybe I can find out something that will give us a lead. Get to know some of her friends. Get into their confidence a little bit."

"People just don't automatically reach out to a detective, you know what I mean?" Jones put in. "That's going to take more than of couple weeks. And then they may never level with you."

Murray couldn't resist snapping her gum. "That's what I thought. That's why I want to go undercover."

They weren't ready for that. The two men looked as if she had hit them with something large and heavy, the way cows look before a thunderstorm huddle together for comfort.

"Well, I mean, it's worked for me before. Remember when I helped break up that ring of drug dealers at Saint Anne's High by posing as a student? And when I joined the motorcycle gang to find out about Everett Hopkins's murder? And the time I posed as a cocktail waitress to find out what happened at the ABC Club and, not to rub it in, but I found out what happened to little Danica Sutton."

"Yeah, yeah, okay, we know you can do it." At the mention the hoo-ha over the missing Sutton child, Stockman had recovered and was perspiring along his domed forehead like a flash flood on Mt. Rushmore. "But I mean, you know, this guy could be dangerous. I can't promise you any protection like Hansen did around here. You had guys hanging around backing you up in case anything went down. But up there in…where'd you say you were going?"

Good job of listening, she thought but didn't say. He'd

been so glad to get rid of her, he forgot where she was going. "Diamondback City."

"Up there in Diamond City, wherever the hell that is, I can't be responsible for you, Jones can't be responsible for you. Hansen can't be—"

"I'm responsible for me. I'm weapon-trained, self-defense trained. In fact, I've been a self-defense instructor for three years."

He wasn't easily impressed. "You'll need more than self-defense if you stop a bullet."

Jones was even slightly annoyed, she wasn't sure why. They had gotten along pretty well until he realized she was going off on her own. Then male chauvinism raised its ugly head even higher than before. She might as well have announced she was going to fight crime singlehanded in the inner city with her curling iron.

He just had to side with the boys to look good. "This guy didn't mind shooting his ex-girlfriend a couple of times in the head when she tried to follow him home and explain the hanky-panky to his rich fiancé. What do you think he'll do to you if you get too close? Exchange business cards?"

Selling this wasn't going to be easy, she knew that. But it was her best shot and she wanted it enough to get manipulative. "Okay, I'll take my vacation and do it, that's all. I've got tons of overtime coming and sick leave out the ying-yang, anyhow."

Stockman waved the papers in his hand like a man fanning a fire. "No, no, no, you won't. Forget that. Just let me think about it a little."

She gave him her best smile. "If you think, you're going to say 'no.' So just say 'yes.'"

He sank into his swivel chair, defeated. "I've got an eighteen-year-old daughter that's just like you. She never gives up, Daddy-this, Daddy-that, ya-da, ya-da, ya-da, until I just give in because I don't want to hear it anymore. Look, Schmitz, do this for me." Now he was being condescending and fatherly. "Write this up like you want to play it, see.

What's your undercover placement? What's your operation plan? Time-frame. Technical needs, stuff like that. How many times, how and when are you going to be contacting the office? Are you using secret code? A disguise? You know, the whole enchilada. Then have it on my desk tomorrow morning and let me get an okay from Hansen. Is that something you can work with?"

She took a manila folder out of her briefcase and handed it to him. "It's all there. With Hansen's okay, of course. I made sure I got that first." She flashed the signature under his nose. "Now, I've got to go buy some sleazy chick stuff."

Again, the stunned cow look. "What in hell for?"

"I'm going to be a cocktail waitress at the local watering hole. Every town's got one. So does Diamond City. I already checked it out. It's called the Branding Iron. And it's got an ad for a waitress on its website. They do have the internet up there, turns out."

Jonesy did a bad job of hiding a smirk. "You ever been a cocktail waitress, Schmitzy?"

She was prepared. "I worked at a pizza place in college."

Jersey Joe Stockman got the drift and picked up on Jonesy's indulgent tone. "And you think this Carreras dude will just walk in the saloon and order a drink?"

"I think he's going to try to find out who framed him and killed the girl. He's a lawyer." She stood back, hands on her hips. "That's right, framed."

Stockman didn't know where to look to hide his derision. It always embarrassed him to argue with women. He had been raised to think it was rude. Finally, he gave up because Murray Schmitz wasn't about to. "Okay, you got ten days. Just check in once a week. For updates and all that"

"Yes, sir. Now, if you don't mind..."

He found himself on his feet. "Sure, sure. You need to get ready. Pack and all that. Let me know what we can do." Stockman looked at the others apologetically. They had never heard that coming from him. But she wasn't through with him yet.

"One more thing. Can I charge off my expenses?"

"Absolutely! You know the code numbers and all."

She had him on the ropes, desperate to get rid of her. He waved them off as if expenses were no concern. The other men were sliding glances out of the corners of their eyes. Stockman, who docked you for cigarettes when you had an all-nighter stakeout.

But Schmitzy drove the final nail in his temporary coffin. "Good, here's a bill for a cocktail waitress uniform at the Branding Iron. Eighty bucks." With her hand on the doorknob, she flashed a smile. "But don't worry. I'll make it back in tips and stand you all to pizza when I get back." She left him daring anybody to laugh and knowing they would behind his back. No loyalty among thieves.

Her next task was to prove Jonesy completely wrong about not being able to compete with the ersatz Miss Teen America, Chelsea Crittenden.

CHAPTER 12

They had just stretched out to take a short nap during the break when a young girl, bounding like a deer through the rows of young plants, yelled, "Rudolfo, look, look!"

He turned back to look at the ridge again and saw smoke like an enormous black mushroom rising skyward. "My god," he said, "what's that?"

At that moment, someone shouted, "Fire! Look up there!"

Across the fields, people straightened up like growing plants and looked at the foothills above them. The wide plume of black smoke was spreading along the ridge above them, darkening the sky like the onset of a distant battle.

"Brush fire!"

The shout was one of the most dreaded words in California vocabulary and was met with curses. There was a strong Santa Ana wind driving the onrushing fire in their direction and everyone knew it was a matter of minutes before the fire came over the ridge.

"Get the shovels!" Rudolfo gave orders like a general commanding his troops along a battle line.

A pickup truck came rattling up the road to the grove of trees where the crew's trucks and trailers nestled in the shade. From the edge of the field, the foreman shouted, "Hey, Rudolfo, there's a brushfire up on the ridge. Cover the new plants with plastic, pronto."

"It's done, senor!"

At a word from the crew boss, the workers began unrolling huge rolls of plastic, spreading it like a transparent table cloth across the freshly planted tomatoes. Alex tried to help, but couldn't move as fast as the deft hands around him, anchoring the sheets to the ground with plastic pens. As he worked, a cavalcade of pickup trucks came up the road, carrying men holding picks and shovels.

"Rudolfo, got any men to go up with the volunteers? Five bucks an hour plus a meal." The invitation was shouted over the noise of the truck engines, and workers passed it along. But most shook their heads, fearing it was a ruse to lay them off the minute they left the contracted job.

"Do you want to go?" Rudolfo called to Alex. "It's okay! Synotech's paying. They need help to keep the fire from chemical plant."

Alex responded by running toward the trucks. Perez followed him and strong hands pulled them aboard a pickup truck.

"Now's your chance to check out Synotech," Perez said as they took off up the road, already clouded with choking smoke. "It's just over the ridge there."

Conversation was submerged in the roar of a helicopter's engine as it passed overhead, on the way to dump flame retardant chemicals on the fire. The workers around him were tying bandanas over their faces to protect their noses from the acrid smoke.

Perez did the same and handed him a folded cloth. "It'll take the place of the one with the snot on it," he said.

As they came around the western side of the ridge into the broad valley beneath the rocky face called Devil's Ladder, the seriousness of the situation was immediately apparent to the volunteers. The whole western flank of the foothills was ablaze, driven by the relentless dry winds nicknamed the Santa Ana after the merciless Spanish commander at the Alamo.

"Jesus, it's a bad one!" Perez shouted. "And it's heading

right for the Turner place. And that's Synotech right above it!" He pointed to the craggy ridge barely visible through the smoke.

At the mention of the name Turner, Alex felt a thrill of anticipation unlike anything he had ever experienced. It was as if something intractable as a magnet were drawing him closer by the moment to a destiny he could never have imagined. It loomed above him like a sinister fortress which he had to penetrate like the maw of a great black beast. Whether he emerged or was swallowed whole was as shrouded in mystery as the fortress itself.

As the trucks pulled up in the yard of a group of low, ranch-style buildings, a man on a tractor shouted, "Hey, boys, get the sheep down to the water! And start a firebreak, will you?"

The volunteers leaped from the truck beds and hit the ground running like enthusiastic troops at war. Alex followed the rest, grabbing a shovel tossed to him from the pickup and falling into line with the rest to dig a large ditch to break the path of the fire.

"I knew you guys'd get it in hand! Good job!" The tractor driver waved them on and drove on toward the barn. Presently, he returned, this time equipped with a small backhoe.

They worked ferociously, keeping their eyes on the fire line which came on with the persistence of a well-armed enemy, consuming everything in its path. The smoke was getting increasingly heavy, making breathing difficult.

Alex's eyes watered badly, he had to pause in shoveling to clear them with his dirty fingers. The workers kept their bandanas up over their noses like bandits as they shoveled the soft, sandy soil. Another hundred yards up the slope, the man on the tractor started a ditch with the backhoe just as the flames crested the ridge. There was a shout of dismay as everyone realized time was running out. The wall of flames was bearing down on the small group of buildings.

By then, a number of cows, horses, and sheep were

crossing the ridge just ahead of the flames, the cows lagging behind at a lumbering pace. Even a few deer came leaping in terrified herds only half a mile ahead of the flames.

"Them cattle'll never make it," one man said. "Let's get the stock trailer up there and pick 'em up."

It took precious minutes to hitch up the stock trailer and take it through the pasture gate directly into the path of the fire. Alex sprinted to cling to the sides of the trailer as it bumped over the rough pasture, almost losing his grip a few times. Wheeling in a semicircle, the driver pointed the back of the trailer in the direction of the fire and Alex jumped down, lowering the tailgate. They all fanned out herding the panic-stricken animals into the trailer after their leaders, terrified sheep mingling with bawling cows.

When it was full, the men felt the fire pressing their shirts to their sweaty bodies and the smoke searing their lungs.

"Let's get the fuck out of here!" the driver yelled.

Alex went to hang on to the outside of the trailer again but he fell away with a curse. The metal was burning hot and burned through his thin work gloves, blistering his palms before he dropped to the ground. Someone pulled him into the back of the truck and he rode face up to the darkening sky. He smelled burning hair and realized it was his own beginning to smoke on his scalp.

The driver pulled the rescued stock trailer as far out onto the road and jumped down from the cab. "Leave 'em out here and I'll move 'em if it comes this far," he shouted, racing back toward the barn.

Through choking clouds of smoke, Alex got back to the small shed with the old tractor, hooking up a battered manure spreader. When he began to load the spreader with sand, the others saw his purpose and took up shovels to help. When it was full, he drove through the pasture gate, feeling his beard and face singe in the oncoming wall of flames as he spread the sand in a wide line between the fire and the buildings.

"Hose down the sand!" he shouted over the roar of the fire line. "Get water on it!"

The men wet the sand down, knowing their last hope was to fight the wall of flames as best they could with the yard hoses. Alex made a second trip to fill the spreader again, his face tingling as if he had a bad sunburn.

But as he filled the spreader with sand, he looked up to see the barn roof smoking from embers carried by the relentless wind.

"The barn's going up! Get more hoses on it!" This time, he soaked the sand in the spreader before he went out of the yard. He had just started to widen the strip of wet sand when the fire jumped across the line, and started up in the tall weeds next to the fence.

Risking the gas tank exploding, he swung the tractor directly across the path of the flames, dropping the wet sand over the burning area. A shout went up from the men as he continued to widen the sand margin between the fence and the fire. Finally, the heat was unbearable and he jumped from the tractor, sprinting to the gate. The old tractor went in a muffled explosion of flames.

"The roof's on fire," someone shouted. "Turn the hoses up there!"

"Oh, my god, the barn!" The tractor driver had come from the fire line and was sprinting toward the barn door. "The horses are still in there."

Alex went after him, and they began leading panicked animals from their stalls. Terrified by the smoke, the younger ones shied and balked as he brought them out. A man rushed in to pull the animal outside. It was Perry Perez.

"The roof's on fire! It's going up! Get the hell out of here, Vargas!"

"Can you get a hose in here and wet the hay?"

"Hell, no! There's no more water pressure! Everything's to wet the roof!"

"Buckets, then." The smoke was becoming so thick, Alex could hardly see as he made his way deeper into the barn, opening one stall after another. In one, a prize bull lay on the straw, breathing heavily. The rancher knelt beside him, holding his head, tying a cloth around the bull's eyes and nose.

"You've got to get out!" Alex shouted at him. "The roof's burning through! The beam's on fire!"

"I ain't leaving! Get the cattle prod over on the wall above the tack!" the man shouted back. "I've got to get Buster up on his feet. You better go on out, fella."

Groping his way past the stalls to the tack room, Alex saw the cattle prod through watering eyes. It was already hot to his grip but he stumbled back with it. The huge animal groaned as it got up, first to its knees and then to all fours.

Suddenly, galvanized by terror, it burst out of the open stall, knocking Alex flat on his back. He rolled to one side instinctively, with a terror of being gored. He felt a flash of pain as a sharp hoof nicked his shoulder as the bull fled toward the doorway.

Getting to his hands and knees, he was crawling out under the thick blanket of smoke when he noticed the rancher's hat lying in the doorway of the stall.

With what seemed to be the last of his oxygen, he shouted, "Hey, in there!"

He realized, if the man were in there, his reply was lost in the roar of the fire and the shouting of the people outside. Somewhere, he heard a woman screaming someone's name over and over again, as if calling for someone lost. Reason in the real sense had gone up with the smoke, but instinct told him to keep looking. His vision was blurred, seared by the smoke.

Pieces of burning wood were raining down from the roof now, setting the hay on fire everywhere. Crawling toward the hat, he saw a hand stretched out just beyond it inside the stall. Lying flat on his belly, he groped toward the hand and began to pull the man out of the burning stall.

Suddenly, a roof beam crumbled and fell, collapsing the

stall. In the same instant, with one exhausting lunge, he had just dragged the unconscious rancher free.

Struggling into a crouch, he grabbed the man's hands and was pulling him back toward the door when a pair of suited firefighters turned the fire hose on the burning interior. The water from the hoses hit him full in the back and knocked him down on top of the rancher.

"Hey, there's somebody on the floor!" was the last thing he remembered hearing. Everything began to fade away into darkness.

Even with the pump truck and fire hoses liberating it from the greedy tongues of flame, the roof of the barn burned and collapsed inward, sending pyrotechnic showers of burning beams into the interior. The firemen barely escaped with their lives, rushing out in a reverse charge as, one by one, the groaning beams collapsed. As flames consumed the barn, the weary volunteers sat scattered, faces like Halloween masks with white circles where eyes and mouths had been.

He awoke moments later, looking into the face of Shelby Turner.

She was a little older, but she was smiling now and he smiled back through cracked lips. It was wonderful to see her alive. Then, it occurred to him he might be dead.

"Hi," she said, then, "Lie still. You're hurt. The paramedics are coming straight away."

"No, it's nothing," He struggled to sit up, but she held him down gently, but firmly.

"You're pretty hard headed, aren't you? Just like somebody else I know." Her voice was as sweet as he had imagined it would have been. "I guess you'd have to be to stay in that burning barn to save my husband's life. I'm not letting anything happen to my lucky charm."

His voice rasped from his dry throat like an old man's. "I'm really fine. Please, just a glass of water will be okay."

She gave him a small sip of water that went down his throat like a razor blade. "I'm Marissa Turner," she said, "and I want you to stay right there until the paramedics come."

At the sound of her name, he struggled up again on one elbow, almost in a blind panic. "I don't need the paramedics honestly, ma'am." The last thing he wanted was to be checked into a hospital, especially by someone named Turner. Identification required. Insurance information. Alex tried to find his feet through a blinding firestorm in his head.

"Look at your poor hands. They're burned." Through painfully swollen eyes, he stared at his hands. They were black, with red cracks spreading around his knuckles. Pink under-skin showed on his palm like underdone barbeque. The pain hit him with the force of the fire hose and knocked the breath out of him. "If you're worried about the hospital bill, don't worry. We're taking care of everything. I'm riding with you in the ambulance, so just relax, Mr...I don't even know your name."

Through his pain, he tried to remember who he supposed to be. Where he was from. His birthday. Desperately, he squinted around for Rudolfo to rescue him. But it was Perez who did. "Vargas. Jimmy Vargas, Mrs. Turner."

"Mr. Jimmy Vargas, you're quite a brave young man. I don't know how to thank you, but somehow, I'll find a way. Now, let me go and see about T.C., my husband. Stay right here."

The moment she was gone, he was on his feet, or thought he was. The whole scene seemed to be set on a rocking boat. He saw Rudolfo coming toward him through the smoke, holding out his flask. "Drink this.'

The tequila burned even worse than the water but he felt his heart start again, and with it, the pain returned full force. "You one crazy bastard," Rudolfo said. "You look like carne asada. But you brave, I got to say it."

"I don't want to go to the hospital, Rudolfo. Get me to the truck." But the pain in his hands was killing him and he knew it would only get worse. The paramedic's van came whining through the crowd and he was helped inside by the attendants. The rancher who was on oxygen, had been loaded in first. His wife sat next to him, holding his hand. When Alex climbed in, the man's red-rimmed eyes opened briefly and moved over his face. "Thanks, son," he said. "That's the one, Mama. He saved my life. And Buster, too."

Marissa Turner's smile, so like her daughter's, elicited a different kind of pain. "I know, T.C., honey. He's our hero."

ↄ⌒ↄↄↄ

In the ER, Alex trembled, suddenly cold and faint again as the doctor cautiously removed the burned skin from his palms. Although he'd been given a shot for the pain, the air on the open burns on his hands and arms felt as if they were on fire all over again.

The doctor noticed him flinch and paused. "Take it easy, buddy. You got slightly barbequed. Actually, it's not so bad, it just hurts like hell." He looked up for a moment with something like pity in his eyes. "You use your hands a lot, don't you?" Before Alex could answer, he said, "Of course you do, that was a dumb question. What I meant was, it was good because the callouses on your palms actually saved your hands from worse damage. So that's a good thing."

Alex tried a joke. "I'm glad there's an up-side to this."

The young doctor ordered another shot of whatever took the pain away and went back to work. "Okay, we'll get you fixed up, Mr. Vargas. You've got a couple of minor burns and we'll give you some healing ointment for those and dress them. That's a nasty scar on your rib cage, by the way. It's going to smart where the superficial burns are because it's newer skin. Take care of yourself, and let me check you over in a couple of days. And stay out of the dirt. That's the worst thing you can do to form scar tissue."

Alex looked down at his naked torso, realizing through

his numbed state, that his shirt had been removed so the burns on his upper body could be treated. The two knife scars could be an identifying mark in a police bulletin, something he had never thought of until now.

Sitting up, he looked around for his tattered shirt, but there was nothing in the room. At that point, the nurse returned. Young and Hispanic, she smiled at him so gently, he had to relax a little.

"Mrs. Turner sent these for you," she said, shyly holding out a plastic bag. "She said she hopes they're the right size. We saw the label on your shirt but we just guessed on the jeans. Hope they fit."

His shoulders were so tight, she had to help him slip the shirt over the wound dressings, but he said he could manage the jeans. The nurse giggled and let herself out. "Just be careful pulling them up. Use the ends of your fingers and not your palms, okay?"

Rudolfo and Perez were out in the waiting room looking like performers in an old-fashioned minstrel show. Their faces were smoke-blackened and weary, but when they saw him, wide, white smiles replaced the weariness.

"Hombre, you look a helluva lot better than when you went in there." Perez started to touch his shoulder, Alex shrunk away. "Oh, Jeez, sorry. I know you caught it when that beam came down. You are one crazy dude, going in there like that."

Rudolfo looked down at his hands, shaking his head and Alex realized what he was thinking. "I'm sorry, hombre. It was a brave thing to do. You save that man's life."

"But not so good for work, huh?"

Rudolfo gently touched his arm. "Let's go have some drinks. I'm just glad you're alive, boy. You should be, too."

"Oh, Mr. Vargas! I'm so glad you haven't left yet." Marissa was hurrying across the Emergency Room, flushed and out of breath. He was stunned to see how much she looked like her daughter; as if she were Shelby Turner in twenty years from this moment.

"How is your husband doing?" Embarrassed, he averted his eyes after realizing he was staring at her.

"They're transferring him over to the Medical Center in the morning, but he's stable. I'm on my way over there now. Can you please ask your crew boss not to leave just yet? I need all the help I can get." She looked up at him with honest brown eyes that said so much more than her simple language.

"This is Rudolfo, my boss."

"Thank you, Senora Turner. If you remember, we've worked here once before a few years back. We will be happy to stay. Only we are camping just a few miles away tonight. Tomorrow, we come in the morning, *pronto*, to help you clean up."

Marisa Turner looked less anxious for the first time in hours. "I can pay regular wages and three meals a day. You won't be sorry. Your crew saved the house from burning." Turning back to Alex who was watching her with fascination fueled by pain medication. "And you, Mr. Vargas? Oh, your poor hands." She nodded at the bandages. "I know you can't work and please don't feel you have to. You've done more than enough already."

He shrugged and glanced away. "I'll be okay. I've got a little money put back. Just let them heal up for a week or so. I'll get something else right along."

"Please, I want to pay you something," she said. "Please accept this." From her pocket, she pulled a wad of hundred dollar bills and held it out to him. "It's so little in exchange for what you did."

"That isn't necessary." The pile of bills in her hand was enough money for an airplane ticket to Mexico and then some. He ignored something inside screaming for him to take it. "I just hope he's going to be okay." The most incredible thing came into his mind to say, and he blurted it out, for once, not monitoring his motivation as he had been taught to do. "If you'd just let me stay awhile, maybe I can help out with the crew. Translate, run errands, that kind of thing."

She turned away, and, for a moment, he felt he had crossed the invisible line Jimmy Vargas would have set for himself. *Don't presume too much.*

"I want you to take the money, Mr. Vargas. Nothing in the world I can do for you can repay you for saving my husband's life, but it's a little toward the pain and inconvenience."

"Look," he said, holding out his bandaged hands. "Mrs. Turner. I'm not much use, with my hands in this kind of shape. But if you'd really like some help, I'd like to stay on. If you don't mind, that is. At least, I could look after the animals. Feed and water them, maybe."

"If I don't mind!" Her entire soul seemed to spring to life in her great brown eyes, bringing out depths of feeling he couldn't have possibly guessed were there. "Are you serious? Because, if you are….Oh, I couldn't possibly let you do that! But what a kind thought after all you've been through. I owe you so much!"

"No, really. You'd be doing us both a favor. I've got nowhere else to go, with the crew already gone. And I can at least take care of the livestock. I know a little about it, sheep and horses mostly."

"What's left of them. Oh, I'd be so grateful! Then I could spend time with T.C. up there in the hospital. Otherwise, I'd have to run back and forth." Suddenly, Marisa Turner covered her face with her hands and her thin shoulders hunched as if she were warding off a physical blow. "I just didn't know what else to do. But here you are."

The three men shifted uncomfortably, trading glances. Obviously, she was a woman who had learned not to give in to sorrow although it seemed to be bending her thin frame into a curve of pain. With visible effort, she controlled her emotions and said in a steady voice, "If you'll just follow me back home, I'll show you where to sleep."

"What about you?" Alex said to Perez. "You need a place to stay?"

Perez grinned, an eerie expression in his smeared face. "Hell, this is home. Got to go pay my back child support before the sheriff finds me. You sticking around for a while?"

Alex shrugged. "No choice, it looks like. Get my bandages changed and all that stuff. Can't work at anything else, that's for sure."

Perez nodded, lightly tapping his shoulder. "Hey, you need anything, give me a call, okay? I'm in the book. Perez on Old Mountain Road. We can get together for a beer if you stay around."

"Thanks, I might do that." Alex was grateful for the offer, even though he had no intention of staying more than a night. In spite of his resolution to find the Turner girl's killer and clear himself, he knew his presence here was becoming more perilous by the day. The hospital might stumble on some glitch in his identity and alert the police. It was Wednesday and he hadn't shown up for court. It might have already dawned on Feldman that he had left Crittenden *et al* hanging out to dry, forcing the lawyer to leave the golf course and get a warrant for his arrest. A dozen scenarios ran through his mind, each of them leading to capture and conviction, having sealed his own guilt by running away. He was beginning to think he had irrevocably screwed up his life.

Rudolfo drove him back to the scene of the fire, the odor of smoke greeting them long before they arrived. Smoke had lingered in the moist evening air to the point he choked as he pulled up under the huge mimosa in the yard of the Turner's rambling one-story home. He couldn't avoid seeing where bouquets of flowers strewn across the porch, now withering in the heat. Grimy people with smoke masks protecting their faces, came out to greet them, enveloping Marissa as she got down from the truck. They moved in a murmuring phalanx of sympathy into the house, while more women came out of the house with pitchers of water and beer for the farm workers.

Even through the veil of acrid smoke, Alex could see Shelby Turner here, long, brown hair dancing beneath her straw Stetson as she galloped her pony around the eucalyptus grove. He saw her in her first communion dress standing on the long, wooden porch while her father took pictures. He saw her on her first prom date, proud to look grown up in a long dress, taking the arm of some awkward boy.

As he got out of the truck, a troop of dogs of all sizes and colors swarmed around the truck, welcoming and sniffing. Alex made friends with all of them while Rudolfo introduced them one at a time.

He recognized the two shepherds that had been in Shelby's van and they seemed to recognize him. The older, friendlier one came forward slowly, head down to sniff cautiously. But the younger one with the almond eyes, went back to the shelter of the porch, watching him from a distance.

"I'd leave that one alone," Rudolfo said behind him as he walked toward the aloof animal. "He was with Mrs. Turner's daughter when she died. Still ain't right in the head and maybe never will be."

It was harder than Alex thought to pretend ignorance as he knew he would have to throughout this masquerade. It required a level of deception he never thought he would have to master.

"Oh, yeah? How'd she die?"

Rudolfo was busy directing his crew to clean up the yard and didn't hear him. Alex was suddenly feeling the effect of the strong painkillers they'd given him in the ER. He blinked like a trapped animal in the floodlights from the fire department vehicles. The crew foreman took his elbow gently, sensing his disorientation. "C'mon Jimmy, I'll show you where to bunk."

As he unpacked his things in the simple bunkhouse, it occurred to him for the first time in twenty-four-hours to realize he wasn't the only victim besides Shelby Turner in this tragedy. Marisa Turner had just lost her daughter, and nearly her husband. Her farm was in ruins and, still, she had managed the strength to think of him. Her daughter lay in a morgue across miles of chaparral yet she had taken the time to offer him food and a place to stay. There was survival and there was survival with grace. Marisa Turner had that going for her.

Though she had been in his mind since she had found him lying outside the gutted barn, he wasn't prepared for her brilliant smile as she knocked on the screen door.

"Mr. Vargas, there are enchiladas in the kitchen, so much food I don't even have anywhere to put it. Please join us when you've put your things away." Hesitating on one foot, like a bird ready to fly, she added, "And I can't tell you enough how grateful I am. After you clean up, please come on over to the house."

He was so stunned by her uncanny resemblance to her daughter, he didn't even recognize his new name. He looked around the cabin to see if someone else were there. Then, it dawned on him she was addressing Jimmy Vargas.

"Please, just call me Jimmy. For a minute, I thought you were referring to my dad." *Nice save, and notice how quickly you covered.* He couldn't avoid thinking that deception, which he's always detested in others, was becoming his path to redemption.

Since he couldn't do heavy work, Marisa Turner had asked him to drop off a load of pregnant ewes and nursing lambs at Pierre's. Using what appeared to be a pack of yard loafers who turned out to be efficient herders, Alex loaded the rotund animals into a stock trailer and set off in the direction Marisa indicated. "Take Old Mountain Road and keep going," she called as he started up the thunderous Ford engine. "You can't miss it. It's the only ranch up there. He's the Old Man of the Mountain."

When he met Pierre Bighand, Alex knew he had been right about looking for Shelby Turner's killer in her own home town. Pierre was an old-timer who lived near a wide place in the road called Shoshone Springs. His sheep ranch bordered the Turner's land where his small Marinos were pastured with the Turner's much larger Dorsets. Like the Turner's place, Bighand's land also flanked Synotech's headquarters, providing a window into an operation he could have never even imagined, back in his Century City office. Certainly, his first clue had been the discrepancies in the bills of lading. Next Crittenden's thinly disguised fury that he even had the audacity to point them out. The hush-hush atmosphere of the San Fernando plant and Macpherson's referral to mysterious "higher-ups" had served to ramp up his suspicion.

But Alex never could have guessed the extent to which this Poseidon outfit would go to hide itself behind the camouflage of a simple chemical operation. Not until Pierre Bighand showed him the warehouse in the Devil's Ladder mine.

Finding Bighand's place in the shadow of the foothills wasn't hard. It was getting up the incline with his noisy load that presented the challenge. As the '90s Ford groaned up the steep driveway, Pierre and several giant dogs came out to meet him. Opening the stock gate to a broad but blackened pasture, Pierre signaled Alex to back in and then closed the gate behind them.

Yelling above the bawling sheep and barking dogs, he called, "'Morning, son. You must be Jimmy." Pierre spat smartly in the dirt, barely missing one of the dogs. "I hear you're quite the hero."

Alex didn't feel much like a hero about getting knocked down by the giant, hairy dogs waiting for him to get out of the truck. Some of them were as large as the ewes. "And I take it you're Mr. Bighand." He indicated his bandaged hands. "Sorry I can't shake."

"Never apologize for being brave, young'un. Just call me Pierre." As if he sensed Alex's hesitancy about mingling with the dogs, Bighand added, "And never mind these here dogs. They can pick up a newborn lamb and carry it for miles without hurting it but they wouldn't touch a person. Unless I said so, that is."

Bighand himself could have been carved out of the redwoods shading the house. Like the gnarled trees, he was slightly bent, walking at a slight angle as if snapped in half and mended. Long, graying braids hung down below a battered black hat and his welcoming grin revealed several missing teeth. Only his black eyes were young, taking the measure of a man in an instant, giving away no secrets and missing nothing. Alex had the feeling Bighand could tell more about him than he knew about himself.

Remembering he was Jimmy Vargas, migrant farmhand on an errand, he said, "Mrs. Turner said you might have some lambs to send back and she'd be glad to take them to market for you when they sell their stock. These ewes and new lambs need somewhere to pasture after the fire at their place." He surveyed the blacked lower pasture. "Looks like you got hit, too."

"This side ain't near as bad as farther up the ridge. Still got some acres it didn't touch beyond that, though. But if it wasn't for Trudy, would've been a lot worse. She come and barked until I woke up and saw the smoke." Bighand patted one of the monolithic sheepdogs. "Pyrenees. Best there is. Got to have me a cup of coffee before getting the lambs. Sound good to you, young fella?"

Alex followed him to the sparse, but neat log cabin smelling of wood-smoke and wet dogs. The layout was simple—one big room centered around a great fireplace. The rafters were decorated with curious painted symbols. He walked around, fascinated by symbols that must have read like storybooks to the learned, but were mere decorations to others. "Indian, right?"

Making coffee at the crude sink, Pierre nodded. "Shoshone. My pa and his folks were Shoshone people. My mama was Yaqui from these mountains. There's some Mexican in there somewhere, too. They all got run out of the state in the gold rush days. Those who wouldn't go got rounded up by a bunch of ranchers and shot down like dogs. Around 1900, my grandpa felt like it was safe to come and built this place himself, or the main part of it, anyhow. Each family added something here and there. I was born here, along with four other kids. We had to sleep out in the bunkhouse most of the time. Now, I put the newborn lambs and ewes out there in bad weather. Got no help now, but the dogs," Bighand added, shuffling around banging cupboards.

The panting dogs sprawled everywhere, pink tongues lolling, tails thumping the floorboards as he maneuvered around them. "Don't have no sugar or cream or nothing fancy like that. Coffee's just like good motor oil. Runs you on high all day. You from around here, son?"

Alex knew the question was the gentle examination of a stranger to the mountains.

Deep in conversation like old friends, they wandered out to the truck, coffee cups in hand, talking sheep. Thanks to his summers on his uncle's ranch, he passed the test without sounding like a zoologist talking about wild animals.

Alex told him about Uncle Alberto outside Taft, weighing his experience, sipping his coffee. "Seems to me you're a better hand than that Cooper fella they had over to T.C.'s place. He struck me as some kind of barstool cowboy, kind that plays the guitar and wears designer jeans. My granddaughter Shelby wouldn't hear none of it, though. Thought he come right out of the wild, wild West. Hollywood's idea of the wild West, anyhow."

Alex mentally filed the name Cooper to check out later. He dodged the temptation to pursue the subject and went back to sheep. "My uncle's got Merinos, too. Dorsets couldn't survive where he lives. It's all Chaparral." He nodded back at the milling animals pinned up in the truck. "Dorsets eat up everything in sight."

Pierre warmed to the subject. "You got that right. But they beat those little Mexican sheep all to hell for meat and wool. Long wool it is. Finest there is." Pierre smacked his cup down on the truck's hood. "Too bad the market for wool has gone to hell. All that fake Chinese stuff coming in. C'mon. I'll give you a hand unloading. Looks like your hands got tore up." He nodded at the wrappings around Alex's palms. "Better put on your work gloves."

Unloading the pregnant ewes was easier than getting them in. The lead sheep took off as soon as the tailgate was lowered, capering into the new grass like a school child out for recess. The rest followed, herded toward the lower pastures by the dogs.

That done, at a word from Pierre, they gathered the market lambs into the holding pen for the return trip. One of the Pyrenees was a young pup and chased some of the animals the wrong way. The older two stood by, waiting for Pierre to straighten him out. "Damn dogs. Don't know why I put up with the danged things." He jerked off his dusty black hat and dabbed his brow with a red bandana. "Just run up my food bill."

When they finished, men and dogs sought the shelter of the cabin porch and a cold beer. "I got some stew and biscuits if you've got a mind for some lunch."

Sitting on Pierre's front porch in the cool mountain breeze, Alex felt relaxed for the first time since Monday morning. "You've got a view here people would pay big bucks for. I'm surprised the developers haven't been after you."

Pierre came back with camping plates heaped with stew and set them on the table away from the inquisitive dogs. Before he replied, he took a gulp of whiskey, his first of many for the day. "Legit developers ain't the problem. I wish it was as simple as saying no to a bunch of land vultures. Mike Sutton and his slick friend, the colonel, have wanted me and T.C. out of here for the last three years and we ain't about to go so they've pulled all kind of underhanded shit to drive us out. We've taken our case to the courts and lost because Sutton's got all the judges in his pocket. Hell, everybody's in Sutton's pocket around here, because in one way or another, they all work for Sutton Enterprises."

The way he spat out the words with such venom, there had to be a story behind them worth pursuing. Perez, Marisa Turner, and now Pierre Bighand had all said the same thing. But could a land grab possibly have anything to do with Shelby Turner's death?

Things could get nasty when there were millions at stake that was true. But murder? And why could a young girl barely out of high school possibly be a threat to a bunch of oligarchic land barons anyway?

The horror of the past few days seemed to drift away from him as they ate in creaking willow chairs. When Pierre mentioned Shelby, it was as if her spirit had suddenly appeared beside them on the mountain porch, bringing back the reason he had come here.

"T.C.'s youngest, Shelby, used to say I had the best life of anybody she knew. 'Course, that ain't saying much since she chased off after that air force fella, and I couldn't never prove to her he was no good."

Noticing Alex was listening instead of eating, he stopped to point a fork in his direction. "You're letting your stew get cold. Ain't got the same flavor that way."

Alex noticed Pierre preferred the whiskey to his own plate, and resumed eating so he would continue.

"Foolish little thing, she was. But full of the spirit. Yes, she was." Pierre looked as though he couldn't swallow for a moment. Then, he began a low chant, and rocked back and forth in his creaking chair. Around him, the dogs whined as if saddened by the sound of mourning. His entire body seemed wrapped in pain as if he were trying to crawl out of a roll of barbed wire.

Alex put his fork down. Although he wanted to blurt out, "What air force fellow? What's his name?" he had to be Jimmy Vargas to whom the reference meant nothing. "Who would want to leave this place? I wouldn't, not for anything."

"You must be a lot smarter than I was at your age, son. I used to think it was all happening down in California. When I got out of the marines, I hung around the cities looking for a job 'til I figured out there was no money in washing dishes and working on two-bit ranches. Hell, I still wonder how I got out of some of those bars alive."

Pierre stopped and changed subjects abruptly as if he'd had a sudden inspiration. "Speaking of bars, they got dances in town on Saturday night. Nobody allowed in there over thirty so you ought to feel right at home. T.C.'s young'uns were always over there, getting into trouble. Now, look where little Shelby's at. Going to bury her tomorrow. Damn near want to jump in there with her." Attacking his food, Pierre mopped up his beans with the rest of his bread. With the next breath, he asked, "Got time to take a look at my horses?"

"Sure, why not?" Was he just imagining the old man was trying to drop hints about the Turner girl or just getting absentminded? Could Bighand be making idle conversation with a stranger or leaving a trail of bread crumbs? Still, at this point, Alex couldn't afford to ignore any lead. He resolved to check out the singles scene as soon as he got time off.

But Bighand's peculiar style of embedding important information into what might be considered idle chatter became even more evident as he showed off the distinctively marked horses. He followed Bighand's circuitous lead down to the neat barn, which was in better condition than the house.

"I don't let my babies out much anymore." Before tossing on a thick blanket, Bighand stroked the black-and-white shoulder of the nearest animal.

Alex played deliberately dumb, waiting for the punch line. "Why? Don't they come back?"

It worked. Pierre guffawed, wheezing through the spaces in his teeth like an old donkey. "That's a good one. Naw, they come when I whistle. But if you want to take a ride,

I'll show you why." Under the brim of his battered black hat, Alex felt sharp glances like darts at his face.

Aware he was being submitted to some kind of test, Alex shrugged. "Sure. It's been awhile since I rode, though. Where're the saddles? I'll tack up."

He passed the test.

"Right up there on the sawhorses. Dolly here, she likes the one with silver trim. Typical woman. Likes dressing up. I don't generally use one, but since I'm carrying my pack with my pistol in it, I'll use the roping saddle. Got to be prepared for coyotes and rattlers and anything else gets on my land."

After the horses were saddled, Pierre then began a long chanting prayer as he dusted the horses with ashes from a tin can. It appeared to be some kind of ritual blessing.

Finally the old man straightened. "Let's go. Takes an hour to get up the ridge. "He nodded in the direction of the rocky outcrop outlined through morning mist. "They'll be changing guard by the time we get there, so it should be safe." Pierre slung his pack across the horse's hindquarters.

CHAPTER 13

They left the barn in silence, the paints dusted with sage ashes to obscure their white markings. Alex realized up to now, his entire education consisted of dealing with facts and words. In Pierre's world, he dealt with the moment, with his body, not his mind. It was like being a stranger in a strange country, unable to understand or speak the language, but nevertheless, having to endure.

After a half hour ride, the truth became plain and ugly. Alex had seen dying sheep and cattle down on T.C.'s place after the fire. But the devastation on Pierre's side was on a scale he couldn't even have imagined. As they approach from the west side of the ridge, the odor of burned and decaying flesh hit them downwind. The carcasses of sheep lay scattered across the cropped brown hillside like corpses on a battlefield. Some animals still moaned and struggled to their knees. For a moment, the wind and the drone of flies were the only sounds. It was too much for words to express.

"Damn! Down since yesterday." Pierre stared at the remains of his flock. "My best ewes and some of T.C.'s pregnant ones. He sent them up here to be safe, and now look."

"What the hell happened? Was it the brush fire?" For a moment, he fought the urge to vomit, keeping his nose pinched tight.

Pierre got off and knelt down by a flailing animal. "Looks a lot like anthrax, but even anthrax don't work that fast. They don't just keel over. Not the kind I grew up with.

This is some kind of freak strain, maybe."

"Or something that supposed to look like anthrax. Look at the grass. That's not just from the fire." Alex started to get off his horse, but Pierre waved him away. "Anthrax doesn't kill the grass, does it? Don't get down! Stay away," he said. "We don't know what it does to people. Looks like some kind of chemical warfare weapon to me." He stared up at the Devil's Ladder, the bald stone face of the mountain dominating the ridge. "Damn 'em. Miserable greedy bastards. Somebody's got to stop them."

Alex reached for Jimmy Vargas and found himself instead. Jimmy Vargas wouldn't have given a rat's ass. "You've seen this before, haven't you?"

For a long moment, Pierre didn't answer him. He remounted and started up the ridge without saying anything. Presently, Alex heard the chanting again. The pain of a man trapped in barbed wire. The strange words floated back to him and he understood none of them, but knew what they were saying. They were mourning something lost forever.

As they started down a steep incline, Pierre explained why they had to go through the gorge. "If we approach this way, we're on their blind side. They don't expect anyone to come across the gorge, but then, they ain't the world's smartest people either. Normally, the water's too high and too fast to forge. But just lately, there's a drain-off somewhere further up the ridge. No doubt that bastard Sutton's doing it for his so-called development at Whisper Lake. That's what this is all about, burning T.C. and me out."

Alex tried not to look straight down into the valley. He wasn't good with heights. "Pierre, who are we talking about? Who is they?" He knew very well who "they" were but he wanted to hear Bighand say it. "You keep saying somebody's doing this? Is it this Sutton guy?"

"Tell you later." Pierre urged his sure-footed mare the steep mountain trail. "They change between eleven and noon. For about forty-five minutes, there's nobody up there."

"How do you know that?" It was hard to carry on a conversation against the mounting wind, especially with someone as enigmatic as Bighand.

The answer came back on the wind. "I live up here, remember."

If Alex hadn't expected to be shot at any moment, it would have been a breathtaking ride. The morning light grew stronger, filtering down to a patchwork of spring fields on the valley floor below. An eternity below.

Except for a few tumbled boulders, there was no barricade between them and a hundreds of feet plunge. Alex had just taken that into consciousness when a rabbit jumped across their path and the horses startled. As they danced on the narrow path, Alex gripped the horn and got ready to jump for safety. But at a word from Pierre, they settled down.

"We're heading through the gorge now. Just hang on to the reins. I think ol' Frankie there's got a notion to head home."

"Can't say I blame him."

Pierre's short laugh told him to tough it out. As they descended into the shadows, he heard a stream running through the gorge, but a thicket at the very bottom concealed the water. Above them, loomed the Devil's Ladder with its black streaked granite outcrop casting a dark shadow through the gorge. When his horse slipped backward on loose stones, Alex's boots nearly touched the ground.

"Give 'em a slack rein here," Pierre called. "He don't need any help finding out where to go down."

When it seemed they were going directly through the narrow aperture between two mountains, Pierre pointed upward. "See that little ridge up there?"

Alex squinted through the mist in the direction Pierre was pointing.

"That's where we're headed."

It looked impossible. The ledge was almost directly over their heads, straight up. But he figured there was no turning back now. When they had ridden as far up the trail as the horses could go, they dismounted. Alex found he was so stiff he moved like an old man. Pierre, on the other hand, gathered up his horse's reins and continued briskly up the trail that eventually narrowed to a path the width of the horses' bodies.

When they paused for a break, Pierre took a canteen out of a saddle bag and offered it. "Take a shot of this. It gets the blood flowing again." Alex took the flask, appreciating the many uses of whiskey. Taking a long swallow, he faced the mountain side of the trail, not daring to look behind him to the horizon some fifty miles away. "There's cave 'bout fifty more yards round the gorge side. Watch your step and hang on to Frankie, there if you slip. Don't want to lose you now we're so close."

"Thanks. I appreciate that."

"Just drop the reins, he ground ties. And come on out to the edge. I got something for you to see." Pierre waved him over to empty space.

"I've got a pretty good view from here, thanks."

He'd never worried much about dealing with his dislike of heights, even though his office was on the twentieth floor of a Century City skyscraper. But this was reality. Like his present legal situation, one wrong step would send him plunging over the edge to destruction. This being a moment to confront any number of fears, he picked his way up to squat beside Pierre.

He noticed they were hidden by a boulder from the peak above them.

The old man reached inside his sheepskin jacket and pulled out a small pair of binoculars.

"Now, I'm going to show you why those sheep are dead. Not how. I ain't got that figured yet. But why." Handing Alex the binoculars, he pointed toward the old mine below them. "I keep track of their comings and goings with these. Got the schedule down pat."

"You come up here alone? Isn't that risky? I heard they shoot people for that."

Pierre grunted. "That's right. Don't see nobody around to hold my hand, do you? Now, look real careful at the side of that mountain right below that shelf that kinda juts out." He followed Pierre's gnarled index finger, trying to read the boulder covered landscape the way the old man did. "See those scrubby live oak and pine?"

"They look fake. Looks like they're camouflaging some kind of opening. "

"You hit the nail on the head, boy. When the chopper lands, it opens into a helicopter pad, then retracts back into the mountain. Pretty slick."

"So why have a secret helicopter port on the side of a mountain? Why not just on the ground?"

He felt Pierre's eyes on him again, regarding him with renewed respect. "Knowing that makes you good as dead around here, you realize."

Alex pointed at a narrow macadam road into the compound below. "That's the road I saw just beyond T.C.'s place. The one with a gate and the goon squad." He told Pierre about his encounter with the Synotech guards. "Where does it go?"

"Straight into Sutton's operation. The semis drive right on into the old tunnel and get loaded up."

He played dumb. After all, Jimmy Vargas wouldn't have given two cents about what was in the trucks. Unless it was drugs. "Loaded up with what? Does it have something to do with trying to burn you out? I don't get it."

"You'll see as soon as the guards change which ought to be in about fifteen minutes."

"And that? What's that down there?" Alex indicated a building at a lower elevation surrounded by greenery. The turquoise waters of a large swimming pool glittered in the emerging sun.

"High Point. Mike Sutton's place. There's a road leading out the back down to the operation, but you can't see it from here. Joins up with that other access road just about half a mile from the gate."

Realizing the old rancher was giving him instructions for future use, Alex added the information to his growing knowledge of the terrain. That was exactly what Bighand was taking him up here for, to get the lay of the land. Alex didn't want to even conjecture what that reason behind that might be. Just the view from the precipice was enough to reconsider Rudolfo's offer of sanctuary in Mexico.

At that moment, a semi with the Synotech purple cab pulled out of the plant gate, heading toward the access road, and Alex remembered the girl lying in the van, the tiny trickle of blood running down her cheek like a red tear.

As if reading his thoughts, Pierre said, "Shelby used to love this place. Said she could see around the world from here. Until they wouldn't let us come up here no more."

In spite of the altitude, Alex wanted to grab the old man by the arm and shout, "But she knew the way, didn't she? Maybe she came alone." Instead, he could only manage, "Must be some high dollar chemicals in that semi. Helluva fancy rig."

Pierre turned away from the ledge. "You got to see with your own eyes what's in there."

"Now you've got me going. Is it drugs? Dope."

The old sheepherder turned and gave him a stabbing look. "Cut the crap! If they was hauling drugs, the dogs would've busted them a long time ago, wouldn't they?"

His role of a high-school dropout turned liquor store bandit was wearing thin. He saw himself as others saw him. A Century City Don Quixote tilting at giants of industry, the laughing stock of his profession. *Old Carreras could have had it all,* they were saying in the bars around town, *but he blew it. Man, did he blow it!*

As Pierre had predicted, another purple semi passed through the sentry gate and straight into the mountainside. It was easy to see the old Devil's Ladder mine was doing a brisk business, in something far more lucrative than just copper.

"Let's get some cover. We don't need to get spotted by the motion detectors."

"Motion detectors? You're kidding. Out here?"

"It ain't a low tech operation, if that's what you think. C'mon." They sought the shelter of the outcrop. Pierre nodded at the peak above them. "You want to take a look inside, now we're here?"

"Sure, why not? Isn't that why we came?"

In reply, Pierre gave him a look of approval. "Thought you were getting cold feet there for a minute. Let's go, then."

Leaving the horses by the outcrop, they climbed higher along what must have been a mountain goat path. Somewhere, water was falling from a great height down into the gorge below. Alex felt drops of spray dashed across his face by the wind. If it hadn't been for the whiskey, fear would have made him turn back. He'd been mountain climbing many times, but with grips and ropes, hooks and the rest of the gear needed to scale rock cliffs. Now his boots were slick with mud, his fingers raw from the burns and his bandages shredded after raking across rocks. Adding to his discomfort, the wind whistled through his flannel shirt and vest as if he were naked. *You must be crazy,* a voice in his head told him. *If you get caught up here, you'll live the rest of your life in a jail cell.* And then a whisper, as light and sweet mountain breeze brushed his conscious mind. *Don't be afraid. Do this for me and free yourself.*

After what seemed another hour, but actually only minutes, they reached another rocky outcrop that became a natural respite from the wind. Protected by a slide of mammoth rocks, the trail widened out from the foot wide path they had been following into a natural lookout point. By the time, he had made it up to the point, Pierre had melted into the mountainside. He was alone, trying not to look down.

As he backed up against the mountain, a rope dropped

down in front of him. Looking up he saw Pierre's head sticking out of an opening in the mountain the size of a refrigerator door. Grasping the loose end, he hoisted himself the half dozen feet upward until he could wriggle into the opening. The narrow entry gave way to a natural cave about eight feet wide, with one side disappearing into the mountain's depth.

The two men sat with their backs against the wall, out of breath. Though he had started to work up a sweat during the climb, the cave had a penetrating chill that left him vulnerable and shaky.

Pierre noticed and passed the flask. "Warm up your gizzards."

"Thanks, I needed that," Alex said, wiping his emerging moustache. "You come up here a lot?"

"Now and again. It's my thinking space." Pierre took another drink and replaced the cap. "Funny to think my people ran around up here in buckskins and not much else. And in worse weather than this, if they had hunting to do."

"Your people? The Shoshone, right? This was one of their sacred places, I take it. What did they do up here, talk to the Great Spirit?" Alex tried to sound as cynical as Jimmy Vargas would have. He had him pictured as a person of few values, ancestor worship not being one of them.

But Bighand took the question seriously. "Sometimes. Not everybody's in shape to talk to Him personal. If you got problems, and you're not a pure person, sometimes, just talk to the mountain and hope He hears."

"They say lots of great people in history went up to mountains to get away. Moses. Poncho Villa. Crazy Horse, even."

Pierre shrugged. "And just people like us."

The cave seemed to take on a more comforting aspect. Pierre shone a flashlight along the walls. There were painted symbols and shapes everywhere, almost to the ceiling.

"If you didn't believe in anything before, I bet you would if you started to slip over the edge. Some folks come up here to ask the ancestors what to do about things. Big decisions." Pierre's gaze never left the walls of the cave.

"You?"

Pierre turned the question aside. "Over there," he said, extending his arm. "Ceremonial fire pit. I did that sign." Even Alex recognized the symbol of the upright hand, the hand against the evil eye.

The cold seemed irrelevant now, even though his feet were going numb. He realized that bringing him up here was a gesture of the confidence Pierre had in him. For the life of him, Alex couldn't imagine why.

He leaned forward to study the painted walls. The markings were strikingly similar to the ones on Pierre's rafters. Was the old man some kind of medicine man or guardian of sacred places? "Let me get this straight. If this is a sacred place of yours. Why isn't it protected? You know, like you were saying, the goons won't allow anybody to come up here."

"'Cause it ain't government property, that's why. It's private. Belongs to the Suttons. Old man Sutton come up here long time ago and bought up the whole mountain. Can you imagine anybody owning a mountain? People can do anything they want on private land regardless of what's on it. They set up this operation right on our sacred mountain, to be exact. It ain't part of any tribal land any more. Government took care of that years ago when they forced the sale of it to the Bureau of Mines, see. Said we didn't have mineral rights in our treaty and then they said it wasn't a real treaty anyway. How the hell would we have negotiated mineral rights? We never mined anything, anyhow. Leave Mother Earth alone, we say."

Alex squinted around the cave. "So no hunting, either. No ceremonies, nothing."

Pierre snorted. "And no trespassing. We mainly just ignore the hell out of 'em. It's Larry Sutton runs us off."

"Your tribe can't do anything about it? Take it to court?"

"That takes money. Anyway, nobody owns a mountain.

White people just think they do. No Shoshone would think of owning anything, especially a mountain. It's just one of those things we just got to put up with. Owning things. Never produced a bill of sale for this territory like the white people did. Funny how somebody can take your land 'cause they got a bill of sale for it even if you didn't sell it." He pulled a handful of dried meat strips from his backpack. "Beef jerky. Help yourself." He offered Alex some jerky. "That one's venison. This one's beef. This one's sheep," he said, pointing the cello-wrapped dried meat. "Last good one I got."

"You've already seen whatever's going on in there. They don't want anyone snooping and that's why they want to get rid of you and Mr. Turner. Must be illegal, whatever they're doing."

"Illegal." Pierre sniffed. "Hell, they got a whole arsenal in there. Stuff like chemicals, missiles. Jet fighter parts, especially the classified stuff. They got enough for a small war." He chewed reflectively for a moment.

Alex had to act as if Pierre's off-hand revelation had thrown him a curve. "No kidding!"

Everything clicked together like the tumblers in a lock. He remembered Sydney Harris's voice on the phone. *'I need an 'Eye,' guidance system and all. A nice little bonus for you and me.'*

"Where in hell'd they get that kind stuff? No, let me guess. Sutton's got a connection with the military, right? "

Pierre grunted like an old bear. "His partner, Colonel Dalton's his connection. Retired colonel, that is. This looks like declassified stuff like leftovers from the Cold War. Surplus just gathering dust in a warehouse somewhere. So if it's a legal operation, how come they're packing this up as chemicals? Or hospital X-ray machines?"

Jimmy Vargas would have become cynical at this point. "You better believe there are people would kill to get their hands on this stuff. Like the drug cartels and terrorists, to name just a couple."

He noticed Bighand always sidestepped the truth. He would have made a great lawyer.

"Have some more of the jerky." Pierre pushed another strip forward. Without wasting their energy on words, they chewed the dried meat as if eating had become a duty.

"Good." Alex looked for somewhere to spit out the wad in his mouth "Different taste."

"Squirrel," Pierre replied fondly. "Teriyaki squirrel. Wonder if I could interest one of them fancy outfits in New York in it?"

"How do you know all this stuff, anyway? It sounds like you've been on the inside."

Bighand dodged the question. "The voices from the mountain. Angry spirits."

"C'mon! Spirits don't know details like you do. Besides, you didn't bring me all the way up here to listen to ghosts. What are we going to do in there, anyway? Steal a missile?"

Again, that shrug. "You wanted a look at it. That's what we're doing, ain't it? Just out looking around. Kind of like tourists."

"Tourists don't get shot at, at least not in this country. You want to know what's killing your animals. And when you find out, question is, what are you going to do about it?" In the cave's dim light, Alex met the Indian's dark eyes. Sometimes, he appreciated the protection of Vargas's indifference.

"Don't you think I know?" Pierre shook his head. "Nobody wins against money and the government. Fifteen years ago, my son was up here. He shouldn't have been, I know. But he was only a kid. They shot him dead. I took Sutton and Dalton to court and got nowhere. They had a perfect right, judge said. He was trespassing on private land. Never even knew who the shooter was. I buried him up here because that's where we're all buried. They had to let us do that."

As Alex chewed, he tried to react the way Jimmy Vargas would have. "That's tough, man."

As always, Pierre knew more than he was saying. "That's why they make such big campaign contributions to this guy Roberts."

"Preston Roberts? That figures. He's the champion of the mining industry not only in California, but the entire West. They're even rumors about him in Arizona." And his wife was conveniently on the board of directors for Synotech.

Alex and Roberts had bumped into each other once or twice when the senator was going for his first term and he was active in the Young Democratic Latinos.

Boyish-looking, the son of an admiral, and former war hero, Roberts had all the qualifications the media wanted—big, white teeth and a hairstyle reminiscent of Kennedy. Not only that, he had a juggernaut of party support behind him. The entire Western mining industry backed him against the EPA and environmental groups to open more wilderness areas to mining. Uranium on Indian lands in the Dakotas, minerals in the Southwest, metals in the far West.

"Yep." Bighand settled back against the painted rock. "The same. He's up here more than he is in Sacramento or Washington." Up against the cave wall, he looked like a mummy discovered in some archaeological dig

"Doing what?"

"You'll see."

For a moment, Alex felt himself propelled back in time to the fury of campaigning for the local democratic representative. Though Crittenden deplored his junior attorneys getting mixed up in anything Democratic, he and Ricky had rented a van and driven in through the barrios. Over a makeshift speaker, he had urged people in Spanish and English to defeat the incumbent Republican candidate. When Crittenden had called him in and given him an ultimatum. "Get out of politics, Alex, or it will reflect badly on your evaluation."

Alex gave up the battle. "Why you taking such a risk? They won't hurt you if you just keep your animals out of the upper pasture and sell it to Sutton. Then they'd get off your back."

Pierre Bighand was quiet as an Egyptian tomb, his eyes closed. "If you thought I'd do that, then why did you come? You want to stop the bastards. So do I. I don't know why you care, but they said you were coming."

"They? Who do you mean?" Alex was immediately on the defensive, ready to deny any connection with the death of the Turner girl.

But Pierre went on as if he weren't even there in the same cave. "They said you'd have to climb the sacred mountain and go on a long trail to the heart of the earth. No one can touch you then. People around you can drop like dead flies, but you can't be touched by the living. Only the dead. The heart of this mountain was never dark. There was always a light inside for our people. But then the white man came and dug a hole in it and filled it with bad things. That's why you come here, boy. They can't touch you. You're protected by the living and the dead."

For an instant, Alex thought Pierre was drunk, and he was sitting in a cave on the side of a mountain with a drunk without a clue how to get down. He continued staring at the shadowed walls around him, wondering what nightmare had enveloped him in its dark wings.

"Listen, Pierre, I don't know why you trust me. And I don't know who told you I was coming, but I have to tell you something before we go on. Something important I want you to know. In case I don't make it back, okay?" What in the hell was he doing? It was as if he were talking to the pictographs on the painted wall and only they were listening to his confession. "I'm—not Jimmy Vargas. My real name is Carreras. Alex Carreras. I'm the guy they think killed Shelby Turner." He took a breath and waited. Pierre continued to chew. Waiting for the old man to just get up and walk out of the cave, leaving him here to die. "But I didn't. I just stopped to help her and she was already dead. I think I saw somebody get in the passenger side of a car just like the one I was driving. Whoever it was wore cowboy boots. But I didn't kill your granddaughter. And I came up here to try and get some kind of clue about who actually did kill her. I'm sorry I tried to fool you. I just can't. But if you wouldn't tell the Turners for a while, I'd be grateful. Until I get ready, that is. I'm going to find out who killed Shelby if it kills me. And that's a real possibility."

Pierre was consulting the pictographs on the wall. Strange tall figures, like elongated reflections in a trick mirror. Finally, he said, "I know. I know who you are, just didn't know your name. Not good with names, anyway. So don't feel bad. I knew you'd come up here, look for the truth."

Alex sat there for a few moments in dumb silence. For the second time in as many days, someone had accepted him for who he really was. "How? Why would you even believe a story like that? Shit, no judge in the universe would believe a story like that."

"Because I know who really killed her. Larry Sutton and Colonel Ed Dalton, that's who. And if they didn't put the gun to her head and pull the trigger, they paid the one who did it." Pierre spat out a piece of gristle. "And that's why we're right here where we are now, boy. Now, let's get going."

Stumbling to his feet, Alex struck his head on the cave ceiling. "Shitfire! "

"Caves ain't made for tall people."

They stepped out of the cave onto the fog-shrouded trail into a chill that made the cave seem warm. "Now come on, right behind me. And don't sidestep any to the right or you're history."

"Where in hell else is there to go but down?"

"You get the point. Follow me. We'll take a look inside. Guards change shifts about now. Lazy as hell, these bastards."

⁓⁓

Callie Murphy, manager of the Branding Iron Bar and Grill hired her on the spot without even checking references. "You're just what I'm looking for. Fresh, cute, experienced. When can you start?"

Murray had been hoping Stockman and Jones would back up her references as a cocktail waitress in San Louis Obispo's most popular pub. It had been a summer job in college but that was the extent of her experience with waitressing. But Callie Murphy didn't seem like the type who would quibble over a sketchy reference anyway.

"What I need you've got. Just be here at four-thirty and don't get pregnant," Callie added. "We don't share tips so what you get, you keep. So it pays to be nice. But not too nice, if you get what I mean. These boys get paid on Friday night and lose it all by Sunday morning." She glanced at Murray slyly. "Hope you're not the churchy type. It gets a little rowdy here. You got a man, honey?"

Murray shook her head. "Not anymore. We broke up. That's why I'm…you know…looking for work."

Callie flipped the bar cloth at her. "Hey, just never you mind. Cute as you are, we'll fix you right up. Uniforms are short so don't be scared if you get a feel-up now and then. Just move fast, don't stay in one place too long, and watch the hands. Oh, yeah, and try not to dump beer on anybody. You'll do fine. What's your name again?"

"My real name's Amber but they call me Silk."

"Silk." Callie rolled her round blue eyes. "Oh, gawd, no kidding. I'm not asking why. But I like that. Sounds sexy. Silk. See you at four-thirty."

As she unpacked her things in Mrs. Vasquez's Boarding House, Murray thought about her cat in her mother's care. Would it even know her when she came back?

She fought despair, thinking Hansen would regret his decision to let her go and call her back. Or just simply tell her not to come back. If she failed to find Alex Carreras or any potential suspect in the Turner case, she didn't need much imagination to know what she'd have to put up with when she returned. If they even took her back.

Murray dropped her things at her room in Mrs. Vasquez's Pensione, a cheap boarding house Callie Murphy recommended. "She'll drive you nuts with her gossip, but she's a real good cook and she'll keep a plate for you if you're late. But no guys in the rooms. She's strict about that."

"You sound like you've had first-hand experience."

The manager of the Branding Iron Bar and Grill had fluttered her pretty blue eyes like a comic book character. "Honey, I've had first-hand experience with just about everything you can think of. When Larry and I split up, there was no place around here to go. She'll take good care of you though. Just don't come in too late. She knows what time we close and I swear she never sleeps."

After showering and washing her hair, Murray sat down on flowering chintz to check in with headquarters. She used her cell phone since calls on the house phone could be traced. In fact, she was almost afraid to check in, in case Hansen had changed his mind and wanted her back in the office.

"Jones, Investigative Unit." She heard a thud at the end that told her she had interrupted a dart game.

"It's Murray. What's new?"

"Hey, thanks for calling, Nancy Drew. It's about these long silences. You know, something might be happening down here in Wonderland you need to know about." Another thud punctuated the pause.

"Like?" It must be really evident she was avoiding contacting them.

"Like they found the Carreras dude's car, the red Cherokee, in a used car lot. Apparently, he's driving a bronze 2012 Dodge Ram. I put out an all points on it." Jonesy rattled off the license number. "Oh, yeah, and Sanchez died."

It was a few seconds before she got it together. "Not Gizmo. Oh, Jonesy, he was such a nice guy. How?"

"Yeah. We bastards live on forever. Thing was, Carreras might have talked to him about thirty minutes before he bought it. The Information desk in the lobby said they thought they saw somebody matching his description taking the elevator. And you came in right after him."

"And Sanchez was alive. He talked to me. I told you."

"And you didn't see Carreras? Tell me, Schmitzy, I know you think this dude is innocent. But you'll be in one big cow patty if you're hiding something."

"I would have called for backup if I had." She suppressed the impulse to tell him about the sneaker imprint on the floor in Sanchez's room. "Besides, it doesn't make any sense. Why would he want to kill his only alibi?"

"What do you mean? Alibi." It was clearly a mistake and Jones caught it. "Schmitzy?"

She hadn't told anyone about the pictures, but now was the time, she could tell by his suspicious tone. "Sanchez took his statement, right? And when he did, he took some pictures of the crime scene with a little digital he had. One was a shot of a boot print, cowboy type. See if the CSI people got a casting, would you? And the tire tracks taking off from the shoulder. He got those, too and made notes. Dayton's, mountain-tread. They don't match the Carreras vehicle."

"I remember. So, where are the pictures? Or the camera, for that matter? And Schmitz, don't tell me you've got them, because that would be considered withholding evidence and that would make me your accomplice, get it?"

She took a deep breath, if she couldn't trust Jonesy, there was no one else but Figgy. And it wasn't Figgy's case. "He gave it to his wife to give to his brother-in-law who runs a photo shop in town."

"I'm not going to ask you why Sanchez did that, but did you follow up?"

She told him Carreras had gotten to the photo shop first

and had a copy of the prints. "His brother-in-law still has the camera." Murray winced, hoping he wouldn't ask if she got a copy of the prints as well. He didn't.

"Well, that's pretty clear, isn't it? Sanchez didn't trust somebody and neither do you. How'd you know what was in the pictures?"

"Sanchez told me. And he said something else." She cringed, picking at the chintz pillow as if the pansies would come off. That was a flat out lie. Sanchez hadn't told her about the van's scratched and dented bumper. He had a picture of it. In the dent in the rear bumper, there were definite traces of red paint. She told Jones and there was another thunk in the background. She willed him to miss.

"Damn," Jonesy said, as something metallic clattered to the floor. "Listen, get over it, Murray. The guy is toast. You've got the photos, don't you? Where are they?"

Arguing with Jonesy was hopeless, she knew that, especially when she knew she was wrong. "My desk, bottom left hand drawer. How did Sanchez die, Jonesy?"

It sounded like he was pawing through the papers in her desk to get to the pictures. "They're doing an autopsy, but there weren't any signs of violence. He'd hemorrhaged and drowned in his own blood."

Although she knew Jonesy was just doing things his way, he recited the cause of Gizmo's death as if he were reading it off a prescription bottle. Like a good cop, she would cry after she hung up the phone. Maybe he would, too.

"Just wanted you to know I've got a job in the local singles bar. And I found out Shelby was in love with some air force jet jockey, but they split up over something. She was on her way to meet him when she was murdered."

Feeling as if she had violated the rules of teamwork, she hadn't told Jonesy about how she had gotten that information. Or that she had found out Shelby Turner was working at the Sunrise Mountain Resort cleaning rooms. The information would only put a few more nails in Carreras's coffin, especially when CSI got wind of it.

The day before, on the way up to Sunrise Mountain Resort, posing as a secretary from Carreras's law firm, she was let into the spacious townhouse overlooking the foothills of the Sierras to look for Chelsea's missing piece of jewelry. Still snowcapped, but greening below the tree line, the view was enough to make her pause on the redwood deck. This was how the rich lived, in redwood towers just above the treetops with a Jacuzzi in every room. This is where they would make love, she and Carreras. Go for long hikes, ski, lie in front of the fire in each other's arms. Back home, she had heard from the boys who tried to talk to his fiancé, Chelsea Something, she had spit out enough venomous remarks about him to take rattlers off the endangered species list.

"Pretty view, isn't it? Beats the tips they leave around here. Just bring the key back when you're finished," the housekeeping manager had called with a wave. "I'll be in the break room. Only have twenty minutes for coffee."

She could tell they hadn't cleaned it yet. In spite of being drunk or hungover, the Carreras boys had left it fairly neat. A couple of towels on the floor. She took a body hair with tweezers, putting it in a plastic bag. She checked the rumpled beds for sign of sexual activity. Nothing. A check of the waste baskets revealed only a couple of tissues. But the one by the phone had a wadded up piece of paper in it. Wearing plastic gloves, she picked it up and opened it. In a scrawling hand, definitely not feminine, was written, "Meet you at the bar. Eight-thirty. Party hearty! T." Putting the note in another bag, she had left.

On the way to Diamondback City, she had dropped the note and the samples in the mail to the local lab for analysis with the report to go to Hansen's attention.

Jonesy was still talking. "We're getting phone calls from big folks in Sacramento wondering what they can do to help find Carreras. Some senator's office, I hear. They called in CBI."

That got her attention. "CBI? What for?"

"Yeah, the white boys with the bad haircuts. They think Carreras has split to Mexico or Belize or one of them playboy islands, like he's got money to spend. His law firm is reporting missing dough. I tried to get a date it was missing on, but I got a lot of legal speak like they don't know grass is green or what. So then I followed up on Angel Rivera, and his merry men. Some boys and I paid a little visit to one of his chop shops in Sin City. Guess what I found."

"A lot of Toyotas in pieces?"

"You guessed it. But I also found Santana, erstwhile ex-husband of Dolores Santana, who it is rumored, does a thriving business in meth and coke as well."

"A step up the income ladder for hot cars but too high tech for Delores, that's for sure. She's still growing pot in her window sill. According to her, he was renting the garage for his car repair business, rent being paid in drugs. Pretty generous after he ditched her for a twenty-year old meth addict."

"Romance aside, Santana and the boys were busy repainting a white Honda Civic to send down the pipeline to Mexico's black market with packets of meth crystals in the doors and seats."

She took in a sharp breath. "The woman who Gizmo Sanchez stopped for a ticket was driving a white Honda Civic. She could have ditched it at Dolores's place, Santana returned it to the chop shop in LA and—"

"Hey presto, no evidence."

"So how did Angel Rivera get out of prison so fast and what's he got to do with Shelby Turner's death?"

"LAPD also found Carrera's Cherokee had meth stuffed in the doors. So I did some groundwork on this guy Santana. He and Angel Rivera—remember him? Anyway, they met doing time at SLO. The story goes Santana is kind of like the Godfather Rivera never had. Got him in the same gang, but Rivera decided he wanted to split and run his own operation. Enter Carreras to save the girl and put the finger on Angel Baby. Rivera swears revenge and gets Santana to help him carry out the plot. Seems like that takes care of a lot of loose ends, right?"

The glacier period between them was beginning to thaw, and she was actually beginning to warm up to Jonesy. "I like your story, but I repeat, where does Shelby Turner fit in? Any sign of a custom trimmed Cherokee with Big D tires in Santana's operation?"

"Nope, no sign of it. But it could be baby blue with fringe around the window and major woofers by now, patrolling the streets of Tijuana as a *por puesto*."

She was studying the chipped toenail polish, figuring if she didn't get off the phone, she'd have to go to work with wet toes. "Jonesy, didn't you tell me Rivera could steal just about any car he wanted? He bragged about it in court, right."

"Yeah, his motto was, 'You name it, I claim it.' Why?"

"Maybe the custom Cherokee was stolen, too. Did anybody check it out?"

"I'm ahead of you there, Nancy Drew. I already asked Traffic if they ran it through the hot list."

"And?"

"Sure enough, there was one missing in LA. Fit the description, but it was black and we don't have a license plate number. Trust me, it's already in the pipeline to Mexico." Another thud. She pictured him back at his desk, going through the photos. "And Schmitzy? Something else. I hate to admit it, but you might be right about one thing."

"I know it's hard for you, Jonesy, but spit it out."

"I checked it out with CHP and they didn't have a patrol car in that area Sunday. He was farther down the Interstate covering the interchange. "

"So? Why is that so hard to admit?"

"Because, on the off chance it could have been one of our boys in the unmarked car, I checked the vehicle pool for Sunday. The only unmarked car out was signed out to Stockman."

"Jersey Joe? As they say in the comics, "What the—"

"You thought he was riding with Jensen in the Traffic patrol car. But, no, he came up in the second patrol car on the scene with Sanders whose kid was out at the baseball field."

"Baseball field. Next exit."

"Right."

"I don't get it. I mean, so who was in the unmarked car?"

There was a long pause as if Jonesy were totaling up his pension plan. "Hey, Schmitzy?"

"The way you say that means only more bad news."

"Yeah. The Barrel did a look round on the girl's body that he didn't want you to know about."

"Like he's got something against female law officers?"

"Not against you guys. Just the old chivalry code kicking in."

She sighed dramatically. "I knew it. We're back to Medieval Times." Detecting a suppressed chuckle in the background, she added, "And skip the comments about chastity belts in the interest of time. I have to get to work, you know." That lost him for about three minutes. "Jonesy, I'm going to hang up, now."

"Okay, I apologize for losing it. The Barrel said the kid was pregnant, about four months gone, and this is the tough part."

"Oh, god, that's not it?"

"No, there's more. This kid, sorry, young woman had a malignant brain tumor. He's no expert in the area. His boss the County Coroner did an autopsy at the parents request. Darrel says the damn thing is in a bad place. If she didn't have surgery, she wouldn't have lasted the nine months. Hey, honey, when I said this job gets into the tough side of life, it was an understatement of the facts. If Carreras killed this kid, I'm going to hand in my badge and tear him into little pieces. You still there?"

She answered from somewhere around the North Pole. "Yeah, last man standing."

"Hey, Murray, listen. I'm not doing anything Friday. I ride mechanical bulls after a couple of long necks and even have shit-kicking boots for such occasions."

"You mean Hansen wants you to keep an eye on me. He put me up here to get me out of his hair, you know. What hair he has left. I'm going by the name of Silk. So, if you come up here, for Pete's sake, don't call me Schmitzy'"

"Okay, Silk," Jonesy could barely contain a chuckle, the way he did when the phone was tucked under his chin. "I can't wait to see what kind of little waitress outfit this gig's got you wearing."

"I'm hanging up, Jonesy."

He backpedaled faster than he spoke. "Okay then, Silk. Look, I'll go along with this. Let's have one of these secret codes things. I'll text it to you when I happen to be in the area. What'll it be?"

"How about eight-nine-nine-five?"

"What's that, a lottery number?"

"My birthday. Got to go. Have to redo my pedicure. Try not to hit anybody with a dart." She rang off and sat staring into nothing, her nail polish brush suspended above waiting toes, thinking of the Turners and imagining them as her own parents. *I only want you to be happy*, her father and mother use to say. Is it too much to ask for?

❧❧

Clinging to the rocky face of the mountain, Alex and Pierre Bighand made their way upward to a slight widening in the trail protected by an overhang. Another cave, even smaller and darker than the first, permitted them to wriggle through its entrance into primeval darkness.

Pierre's voice reached him in a rasping whisper. "Stay right behind me. Move when I move. Stop when you feel my boots. The guards are down there, sleeping off a good drunk. This is the upper level so they shouldn't even be coming up here unless we make noise. One thing is, they don't have is real good lights up here 'cause they work off a generator. But they got motion detectors. Anything passes the beam, it goes off. So stay down on your belly, no matter what."

The cave gradually widened into a manmade tunnel in which they could move at a crouch. Whether this had been part of the old Lucky Seven works or been built by others long before old man Sutton arrived, it was hard to know.

Alex felt his breath come more rapidly either from fear or lack of oxygen or a combination of the two. This was farther inside the earth than he had ever been and he fought a feeling of profound claustrophobia, as if he were being squeezed to death in the maw of a giant beast. It seemed as if the rocks were moving forward to crush him and it was all he could do to keep the rising sense of panic from overcoming him.

At some points, the passage was so narrow they had to go sideways through narrow apertures in the rock. Then, abruptly, they came out of primal darkness into an eerie greenish light. The hand Pierre held up looked like a cartoon Martian, with long green fingers.

Alex heard a sharp hiss and then, "Drop!"

He immediately hit the cool ground hard.

After that they made their way on their bellies, Pierre leading the way along a serpentine tunnel until they came to a steel catwalk. At that point, Alex could hardly conceal an expression of sheer amazement. Directly across an enormous cave was a manmade platform containing towering stacks of wooden crates.

Over his shoulder, Pierre made the silence sign, fingers to his lips.

There was a growing buzzing sound like a giant hive somewhere below them, like the whine of hundreds of machines at maximum capacity.

Like soldiers in trenches, they crawled out of the tunnel across the catwalk. Whatever the old man did, he mimicked to the last gesture, knowing his life depended on it. On elbows and bellies, they snaked across the catwalk toward the platform.

Alex lifted his head slightly and peered over the edge of the ramp. At least fifty feet below was a track nearly the width of a rural highway which moved continuously toward an enormous door in the outer wall. It was flanked by two guards in orange jump suits, armed with assault rifles who watched as the crates on the track were diverted to ramps feeding the cargo into the depths of Synotech eighteen-wheelers.

Lowering his cheek to the cool steel he crawled on, following Pierre's narrow behind to the relative safety of the platform. There he wedged his body between the stacks of boxes, sweat dripping off his chin in spite of the cold.

Pierre jerked his head at the crate beside him. In the dim green light, he could make out *Dangerous Materials* in two-inch letters stamped on the sides of the crates. *Property of US Air Force. Toxic Chemical. Caution. Do Not Open.*

Below the warning was a detailed description of the chemical components. Alex fished a pen and paper out of his jacket pocket and wrote them down. Instantly, directly above their heads, an earsplitting alarm went off. A rumbling sound like the preface to an earthquake made the steel platform vibrate like a tuning fork beneath them. At first, he thought he had set off the motion detector and got ready to spring across the catwalk into the tunnel. Then he saw Pierre's green face.

Again, Bighand jerked his head toward the floor of the cavern. With a deafening rumble deep within the mountain, an immense opening let in rolling waves of fog. As they watched, the fuselage of a dark gray jet aircraft, its wings and tail section off, came along the moving ramp as if the mountain itself had birthed it.

As it moved along below them, it resembled a strange

truncated insect shorn of its wings and nose cone, with only the main body intact. Directly behind it on the conveyor belt came the missing pieces—engine, wings, and nose. The tail section passed by almost on the level with them.

As the dismantled plane moved along the track, Alex could make out the purple cab of a Synotech truck, its rear doors yawning to receive the aircraft body. The conveyor belt brought the jet fuselage up to the truck's ramp and came to creaking halt.

Like ants over an insect carcass, a team of mechanics with drills and wrenches swiftly dismembered the plane into smaller parts. Another team loaded the parts into the waiting truck. As the dissected body of the jet was loaded into the semi, another pulled up to take the rest of the parts along with the engine. It was swift and so efficient, even Alex had to admire their rapid fire technique. Following the aircraft on the conveyor belt came an all-terrain vehicle, and crates marked *Hospital Equipment* and *X-Ray Equipment*.

Another stripped jet waited behind the first, and another. Three altogether. There were no classified aircraft or all-terrain vehicles in Synotech's manifests. In his idle moments during the Board of Directors meeting he had attended, Alex remembered glancing over their shipping manifest. Aircraft, missiles, assault rifles and toxic chemicals were definitely not on the list. Industrial chemicals and hospital equipment were. But from what he could ascertain, there was not one x-ray Machine or MRI lab within the Lucky Seven mine.

His face must have registered his shock because in the green light, he saw Pierre smiling at him. Then, without any warning, except a beeping noise below, the platform on which they lay began shudder, and warning lights flashed along the edges to alert any personnel its contents were going to be loaded in the yard below. Lunging forward on his elbows, Pierre barely made it back out on the catwalk with Alex glued to his heels before the platform began to drop. The intent workers below, scrambling to set the crates with the aircraft body on grappling hooks to load it into the truck, never bothered to look up.

They were almost home free when it happened. Alex instinctively raised his head to avoid getting kicked by Pierre's boot heel and a hideous, whooping, shriek filled their ears. The motion detector had registered that slight movement. He froze in the middle of the catwalk, too scared to go forward, wondering if his next move was his last.

"Move, kid!" On the cave side of the catwalk, Pierre Bighand crouched, not caring who heard him yell. The catwalk groaned and squeaked as a half dozen guards in orange suits ran around pushing buttons and shouting for reinforcements.

"The dogs! Get the friggin' dogs!" somebody on the level below them shouted. "God dammit, doesn't anybody know what to do around here?"

Galvanized by the mention of dogs, Alex wriggled off the platform, past Pierre.

"Go first," Pierre ordered, flattening against the opening of the tunnel.

Alex needed no urging. Digging his bleeding elbows into the floor of the tunnel, he pulled himself forward until they reached the place where they could move at a crouch. Pierre came in backward, dragging a piece of raw meat along the tunnel surface. There was no time to ask him what he was doing. The chilling sound of snarling dogs came toward them from somewhere below. By the sound of them, the animals were out for blood.

"Get back to the tunnel. They're coming up the ramp," Pierre hissed back at him. "Look out for an opening on your left. It's coming up right around this little bend. Past that gray rock bed. You'll feel the cold air. Get in there!"

The greenish light was fading as they widened the distance between the platform and themselves. Alex was certain he could never find the opening to the spur tunnel in the dark.

Then his groping left hand felt a draft of cold air. "Got it!"

"Back up into it, butt first."

Completely blind, one misstep away from dropping hundreds of feet into an abyss, Alex went feet first. Pierre came after him, blocking what little light had penetrated from the arsenal. They were in total darkness again, but this time, darkness became an ally. As he pushed his way backward through the tunnel, the sound of the guard dogs barking echoed eerily through the warehouse. They held their breath as the sound centered around the opening of the tunnel and then faded.

"Hot damn!" Pierre whispered, "They missed us. Keep going!"

Alex could hear Pierre's breath coming in sharp rasps with the effort moving backward up the slight incline.

"Keep going. You're almost there. Ten, fifteen more feet." Pierre's boot tips crushed Alex's grappling fingers as he felt the surface level out. The air was much colder which meant they were nearing the tunnel entrance. But there was no telling what was waiting for them outside. Suddenly, his foot swung into air, grasping nothing. His legs were outside, dangling in the air.

He emerged like a breach birth from the side of the mountain just as the sun slid back behind the curtain of fog. His moment of jubilation was replaced by stark terror as he looked down into the gorge yawning below. The flirtatious sun lit a grayish spume of water rising from the waterfall for a fleeting second. There was nothing for at least twenty feet below. Pierre's feet coming up in front of his face, threatened to send him plunging into empty space.

"What in hell do I do now? There's a twenty-foot drop. Sprout wings and fly?"

The reply was calm, as if they were discussing shoeing a horse. "Reach out your hand, boy. Just over your head. Other end's tied up to into the rock. When you hit the edge, let go and hang on to something."

"You don't have to ask twice." The rope fed out as Alex rappelled down the rock surface of the mountain. In three jumps, his feet hit solid earth. Bighand was beside him, as nimble as a mountain goat.

Pierre glanced at his hands, oozing blood through the gauze wrappings. "You okay?"

"Besides scared shitless, just peachy."

The old man chuckled to himself. "It takes a man to admit he's scared."

The horses were only a few hundred yards below, sheltered behind an outcrop of rock. As the sun parted the clouds, they were already hidden from the guards on the Devil's Ladder by the foggy ravine.

CHAPTER 14

Only a day had passed since the fire, but things were beginning to take shape at the Turner ranch. Neighbors pitched in with backhoes and tractors. Local contractors replaced the damaged roof beams on the barn and, by tomorrow they would put the shingles back on. Inside heavy leather work gloves, his own hands were beginning to mend, but he kept them bandaged anyway. The ER doctor had told him to come back for a check on the following Monday, but he could tell from the lessening pain they were beginning to heal, in spite of the heavy workload.

Then Alex remembered Shelby Turner was being buried tomorrow in the little windswept cemetery at the foot of the mountain range she fought to defend.

He was about to clean up for dinner and tequila drinking with Rudolfo's crew when he noticed something green by the back door of the house across the yard. He stared in amazement at rose bushes sprouting red leaves, encouraged by the warm sunshine.

Unlike the dry trees around the house, their leaves hadn't been seared by the heat of the fire. Remembering his father's fondness for roses, he put on clean bandages and ointment and went over to dig around the bushes, circling the little garden with stones. Looking up, he saw Mrs. Turner standing on the porch watching him. They exchanged polite nods.

"It looks very nice, Jimmy. Thanks so much for every-thing you've done."

Her resemblance to her daughter was so striking, it threw him into sudden reticence. "I hope it's okay, ma'am." He brushed the dirt off his jeans. "I'm just amazed they survived the fire. Kind of like a sign."

Her conversation was awkward as if she didn't talk much. As she was married to T.C., he imagined why. "Why, that's true. Even survive at all. It's too dry out here for roses. They like moisture. But they've survived." The woman's fixed expression didn't change. "Would you like some iced tea?"

It was his chance to speak to her alone, and he took it with some trepidation. "That would be nice, thanks." The more she saw of his face, the faster she would recognize the photographs of him in the paper.

"Please come in," she said when he hesitated at the kitchen steps. "I'd like someone to talk to."

He indicated his jeans. "I'm really filthy."

Then she smiled. "This is a ranch, Jimmy. Don't you think I'm used to dirt? Come on into the kitchen."

The iced tea was made with mint and lemon, the way his mother always did it. Marisa kept busy at the sink making small talk above the clatter of dishes. All at once, her dark head bowed and her shoulders began to shake. He sat awkwardly at the kitchen table for a moment, resisting the urge to go to her. All he could offer were platitudes.

"It's going to be all right, Mrs. Turner. You'll see. Everything will work out."

"But she won't come back. That won't work out, will it? I keep wondering if God could just reverse the universe, turn back the clock, she would've been home Sunday. Not way down there. Not in that cold awful place. What was she doing? I want to pray, but I can't. It's too much if I had a lifetime to pray. I just don't understand why. What have we done to deserve all of this?" She sucked in her sobs and wiped her eyes with her apron. "I'm so sorry." She apologized without turning around. "I didn't mean to break up all to pieces." She faked a wobbly smile again, her face streaked with tears. "I'm really a much more together person than this. Really."

"I was wondering when you were going to be human and let it all out. You'll blow up if you don't." He looked around as if he had made a social gaffe. "Just let it all out."

They both laughed because they both knew he hadn't meant to be so blunt. "I was never good with small talk. I guess that's plain by now, huh?" For an instant, he appreciated his role as Jimmy Vargas. Not schooled in false etiquette. Meaning exactly what he said when he said it.

"Me either." She dried her hands and kept smiling at him. "I'm so glad you're here, Jimmy. It's such a comfort."

They made small talk after that, talking about the livestock and how the new barn was going up so fast. Nothing could beat good neighbors. Alex could tell Marisa wanted to concentrate on the present problems and plans for the future, rather than reliving the profound depths of recent loss. After helping with the dishes, he was leaving the kitchen just as a small pickup was coming down the road.

❧❧❧

As Murray drove out the county road to the Turner ranch, Hansen's questions rolled though in her mind like subtitles in a foreign movie. *Why do you think he's heading for Diamondback City? Why don't you think he'd make a beeline for Mexico. I would if I were him.* They were questions she didn't have real answers for. She didn't know why she figured he'd head for Diamond City, she just felt that if she were in Alex Carreras's shoes, that's what she would do.

On her way to the Turner's farm on Little Spur Creek, she had tried to reason it out the way a hunter justifies following one path rather than another. Sure, he could split to

Mexico and blend in with the higher end of the Hispanic population in the tourist meccas. Jonesy's theory made more sense. It just wasn't Alex Carreras's MO. Then she mentally gave herself a swift kick. The Alex Carreras Fan Club of one. What did she know about his mode of operation for that matter?

She smelled the acrid smoke long before the neat aluminum out buildings of the Turner ranch. The closer she came, it began to sear her nasal passages and then she saw the fire trucks still hosing down the pastures. It became increasingly clear as she pulled into the yard. Turners had suffered yet another terrible blow. They were burned out.

The scattered buildings clung to the scowling mountain like begging children to an unresponsive parent. There were dusty farm trucks scattered throughout the yard and, as she parked next to one, a tall man in work clothes left the house by a back door and walked toward the barn. She called to him, but he apparently didn't hear her. Surrounded by a pack of curious dogs, she didn't think it was a good idea to chase him.

She wondered if Mr. Turner had gone down to claim the two that had been in Shelby's van. While she was petting the dogs, a woman came out on the porch and stood looking at her suspiciously. Murray knew she was unrecognizable dressed as her present cover. Her hair was curled and she had on makeup which she never wore. Her skirt was short and so tight she had to walk knock-kneed.

"Hi, Mrs. Turner. You probably don't remember me. I met you at the hospital day before yesterday."

Who would want to remember someone under those circumstances? She saw the pain flicker across the face of the small, dark woman on the porch. "I'm sorry. I don't—" Then something like relief replaced the pain. "Oh, sure, the sweet little police detective. You look so..."

Awkwardly, Murray held out a bouquet of flowers. "Different. I know. Can I come in for a moment? There's something I'd like to tell you."

The woman nodded as if the sight of the flowers reminded her of death all over again. "Of course. Aren't they lovely? How sweet of you! Please come in. I've just made some
ice tea." Her voice was robotic and flat, letting Murray
know her visit was only one of many Marisa had endured.
But suffering platitudes was just another painful pat of loss
and they both understood the gesture for what it was.

While Marisa was in the kitchen, she had an opportunity
to study the wall of photos over the fireplace. Then she got
up for a closer look, attracted by a photograph of what must
be Shelby with a man.

"I so sorry, I didn't get your name yesterday, Miss..."

Caught snooping, Murray immediately retreated to the
couch as Marisa came back from the kitchen carrying a
tray. "Around here, I'm going to be known as Silk. Kind of
a nickname."

"I see." Marisa Turner's expression registered no curios-
ity nor ridicule, nothing except a forced politeness. Murray
had the feeling her remarks fell like coins dropped down a
well without registering a sound.

"I see your daughter liked to rodeo. I used to barrel race
myself as a kid." That at least was true. She had grown up
on a horse like many girls in rural Southern California,
spending dusty hours cleaning sour smelling stalls just for a
chance to ride.

"Is that right?" It sparked a little interest and she saw
Marisa's eyes flick to the mantel where a picture among
those of the Turner children stood out. It was a large framed
photo of Shelby in a white Stetson and white Western shirt
clutching a huge trophy. But it was the man beside her that
interested Murray. "Shelby was passionate about it."

"Wow, she got Best All Around Cowgirl! That's a real
accomplishment!" Murray's admiration was genuine. She
hated to ferret information out of people without first estab-
lishing a common bond. "I never got more than a Third."

Marisa came barely up to her shoulder. "Yes, she is—
was very good at it." Her voice snagged and stopped ab-

ruptly. "I'm sorry if I've been unwelcoming. There've been so many reporters, I just can't—"

"I understand, believe me. But I'm not one of them. You do remember me? We met Sunday night and I've come up here just like I said I would. But I don't want it to get out that investigating your daughter's death. That would scare everybody away and compromise my investigation. So for now, I'm just Silk, a cocktail waitress at the Sidewinder."

It was like watching life flooding back into Marisa's pale face. "Oh, I see!" She reached down and took Murray's face in her cold hands. "You're so brave to do this. I never thought you meant it, that it was just something you were told to say. But here you are. I feel like there's some kind of hope now. Some kind of justice. You know, she didn't deserve to die so soon. Oh, God, she didn't deserve to die at all. She was such a sweet thing. Always trying to help out. She was going to be a nurse, you know. Or a vet, depending on how long we could keep her at university." Her voice spiraling to wail, Marisa fell to her knees in front of Murray, racked by sobs until it seemed her frail body would break in two. Murray gripped the grief-stricken mother with both arms, as if literally keeping her from breaking apart.

There they sat in a kind of *pieta* until Marisa wiped her face and sat upright with a great sniff. "Thank you. I needed that."

"I was wondering when you were going to stop acting like nothing was wrong." Murray smiled. "I was beginning to think you had been abducted by aliens or something."

"That's funny. Somebody else just told me that. I must have looked like a time bomb ready to explode."

Marisa poured the ice tea and offered Murray a cookie. "Who're those men in the picture beside her?" There were two men in the photograph with Shelby Turner. On her right, a tall, freckled man whose hand rested familiarly on Shelby's waist. Slightly behind her on her left, was a darker type in cowboy regalia and no smile in his eyes.

"The one on her left's Duke Cooper. He used to work

with Shelby training the horses. And the other man is called Burnside, Sutton's man. Larry Sutton always put up the prize money and usually Darla Sutton, Larry's sister, wins. That's why it was such a big surprise when Shelby won last year. But I'm so glad she did." Marisa took the picture down and cradled it to her thin chest, tears running unchecked. "She was my baby."

"And she'll always be, that's the good thing about it. My dad's still a young man in my mind and, by now, he'd be…" Murray set her glass carefully on a coaster and wiped her nose with her napkin. "…almost fifty. Hey, I'd better be getting along. I got a job at this place called the Sidewinder and I've got to be at work by six. I just wanted to stop by and let you know I'm around, if you need to talk. Anything you might remember you think might help track down Shelby's killer, just call me any time." She wrote down her cell phone number. "Just leave your name and I'll call you right back, okay? I'll let myself out." And as she had done the other night after Darrel the Barrel had finished his tour of her daughter's body, Murray wrapped the small, sobbing woman again in her arms. "Don't worry. We're going to find him. Whoever did this, we'll find him."

When Murray looked in her rearview mirror, Marisa Turner was still standing under the trees, waving. She looked so little and forlorn, Murray was determined never to give up until she found who left this woman without any hope at all.

Promptly at four-thirty, she showed up at The Branding Iron feeling like she was in costume as a French maid for a soft porn film. Skimpy enough to fit a ten year old, the outfit contrasted sharply to the Buffalo Bill-era paintings of bosomy ladies above the bar.

When she arrived, the place was empty, but the odor of food and sounds of laughter directed her to the kitchen. As she was heading down the back hall, she nearly collided with a stocky, sandy-haired man coming out of Callie's office.

From his picture on the manager's desk, she recognized Larry Sutton, the owner of the bar and just about everything else in Diamondback. The photograph had been touched up because his looks weren't great to begin with. Still, some women would have found his wide-shouldered aggressiveness attractive. Murray, however, thought he was attempting to compensate for his short stature.

"Hi! I came a little early." She nodded at the kitchen. "Callie said I could have something to eat."

"Sure, whatever you want." From his expression, she knew she had passed the Barbie Look-A-Like test. "You're new, aren't you?" Then he stuck out his hand with a lopsided grin that fell just short of a leer. "Sorry, I'm Larry Sutton. What's your name, honey?"

She had forgotten French maids were supposed to have limp little hands. "My name's Silk. Silk Rogers."

His easygoing grin was deceptive. The man was as tense as a tomcat. "Callie didn't underestimate your looks, for once. You're a knockout in that outfit."

She did the whole girly thing, with a giggle and blush that would have made Jonesy eat his words. Or at least miss a shot. "Oh, thanks. I hope it fits okay."

"Turn around and I'll check."

"Hey, I walked into that, didn't I?" They shared a silly laugh and she tried to edge past him. "Got to find out what to do. My first night and all."

His eyes never left her. "Sure, honey. But Callie's not around right now so I'll be glad to introduce you around." Taking her elbow, he steered her down the hall. "By the way, she tells me you broke up with your boyfriend and you're scared he'll find you."

"That's right. I'm kind of…incognito, you might say. He can really make trouble."

"Just let me know if he does show up. I'll have him out of town in a New York second, you got me? I don't like having bullies around." Larry Sutton gave her elbow an intimate squeeze. "You'll tell me, won't you, honey?"

Freeing her arm, she edged toward the kitchen, but he neatly blocked the doorway. "Sure. Thanks, Mr. Sutton. I appreciate it."

"How about just calling me, Larry, honey. And maybe we can do lunch tomorrow? On my boat, would you like that? After the county fair, naturally. They always expect me to give out the prizes. Naturally, since I paid for them. Come on over to the grandstand and I'll meet you there."

"But I already promised Callie I'd help her out tomorrow." The last thing she wanted was to be alone with this wolf.

Sutton's expression clouded. "No, let her stay and work. Serves the little bitch right. She hasn't been following orders lately." Realizing he was coming across as a tyrant, his artificial smile returned on cue. "Hey, you met my sister Darla yet? She's about your age. Actually, she's my half-sister which accounts for the age difference."

"No, sir, I haven't had the pleasure, but I'd better get going." She noticed the laughter in the kitchen had stopped and conversations reduce to whispers.

"Oh, you will. She hates everyone prettier than her. And you are, definitely. Just to warn you, she'll run up a tab here if she comes in. And she'll leave without paying. Just let her go and I'll tend to it later, okay?"

His eyes were taking inventory from her long, slim legs in black mesh stockings to the front of her frilly apron. "Silk. I like that name. It suits you. You from around here?"

"Buckley. You've probably never heard of it." Quick save. It was a wide place in the road she'd chosen because it didn't have a local high school where inquisitive people could check yearbooks or the phone directory.

"Buckley? You're right, never heard of it."

She grew uncomfortable under his intense scrutiny and glanced toward the kitchen, hoping someone would come along to break up this interview. "If I were your boyfriend, I sure wouldn't give up that easy." He eased into the subject of personal relationships with the expertise of a born womanizer. "Anyway, I'd like to show you around, if it's okay."

She deliberately played dumb. "Callie's already showed me what to do. I just came a little early to get the lay of the land, so to speak." Did she sound as dumb as she looked?

"Not around here. I mean around the town. Like a real date." His indulgent grin was cosmetic white in his tan face, reminding her of a predatory animal.

"I thought you and Callie were—"

He waved away her objections to his ex-wife. "Callie won't mind, and if she does, too bad. She and I were quits long time ago. We just have our little girl, Danica, in common. And I gave her this job here as manager so she could make a decent living. This is the thanks I get."

She hoped her face didn't give her away. There couldn't be two Danica Suttons in this part of California. A black Mercedes Carlita had said. She'd put money on it he had one. Her father had neglected to tell the principal he was picking her up. He said he had spoken to the office, the principal denied it. And the grandmother had been the one to call the police.

Her eyes strayed past him as Sutton consulted his cell phone calendar. The child who matched the photograph county law enforcement had circulated was the same sweet six-year old missing a tooth, but smiling anyway. Red curls, big bow. In fact, she bore a striking resemblance to another little girl from another era whose sun-faded photograph lay in the bottom of her desk drawer. The one she had taken from the trailer of Delores Santana to keep while she was in jail.

Sutton snapped his phone shut. "So how about I'll have my driver pick you up at eleven tomorrow and bring you to the fairgrounds. Don't dress up, we're always casual around here." He glanced at his watch and whistled. "Now, I've got to skip so I can get to the school in time to see my daughter be the star of the school play. I know she'll steal the show from all those other little kids, she's such a ham."

Resisting the urge to ask how the child could miss him,

Murray played straight man. "Wait a sec! How do I know it's your car? I mean, I usually don't get in strange cars, if you know what I mean."

"Honey, it's the only black Mercedes stretch in town. Can't miss it."

As a police officer, she wanted to ask him what his beloved daughter was doing in school in a neighboring county and why he had to virtually kidnap her and then lie about it if he was such a great father.

But Sutton was reaching out for a bare, perfumed shoulder to cry on. "Naturally, Callie didn't even tell me about this play tonight. I only found out when someone said their kid was in it. That's okay, you don't have to cover for her. I know she's already over at the school so I'll look like the bad guy." For the space of a blink, a sudden murderous rage brightened his pale eyes, then faded as his neon smile flashed on again. "Anyhow, I'll get one of the kitchen staff to help you wait tables tonight. See you tomorrow." He rubbed his hands together in anticipation. "Can't wait."

ღოღ

Her first night as a waitress began with switching orders of customers, mostly all male, who good-naturedly called out, "Okay, who got the New York Strip rare? Anybody got my deluxe burger with fries?" After returning two orders to the kitchen, she worked out a numbering system that solved the mix-ups. Sutton had said one of the kitchen staff would help her out, but throughout the rush hour until seven, she was all alone.

From the very beginning of her shift, Murray hated the hands. Besides the smoke and the constant music, she hated the squeezes and the feel-ups. They touched her waist, her legs, sometimes her arms, even groped an occasional foray down her ruffled blouse as she leaned over to set the drinks on the table. Twice on her first evening, she had seriously considered dumping the contents of an entire tray on a customer who had insisted he got to stuff a tip in her bra. She opted for stepping very neatly on his toe with the pointed heel of her shoe. This proved effective and he left the tip on the table, a whole dollar and fifty cents.

In fact, there was very little about the job she didn't detest—the sleazy customers, the stupid costume, and heavy trays. The twangy electric guitar music and the overhead wide screen TV blaring the latest sports news. It was a virtual man cave, and she felt like cave woman delivering slabs of the latest kill.

Then there was Duke Cooper. His photograph on the Turner mantel didn't do him justice. In the flesh, Cooper was even uglier. "You the girl they call Silk?"

His hound yellow eyes wandered over her, only to be followed too soon by calloused hands. As much as she wanted to say no, she had to admit she was. "Then how about me taking you for a little dinner when you get off?"

"I don't think my boyfriend would approve. But thanks, anyway."

He stuck out a long, freckled arm to bar her way. "Look, I don't mean to be nosey or anything, but I already asked Callie and she said you and your boyfriend broke up. Give it a try, okay? I really got a heart of gold."

Be nice to the customers, Callie had said. There was money in it. "Look, I don't even know your name, for a start."

"Duke. Duke Cooper. Callie's known me forever. Went to school together. Just ask her. I'm okay, she'll tell you."

Murray tried to keep her assignment in mind as she side-stepped his extended arm. "Look, Duke, I don't know what Callie told you, but—"

At that point, the canned country western music drowned out her reply and he said, "How 'bout a dance? Can do you no harm, can it?"

"Sorry, I'm on duty, sir." Holding up her tray like a shield in front of her, she backed away as he stood up. As tall as she always considered herself, Murray found herself looking up.

Duke snatched the tray from her hands, yelling, "Hey, Callie, I've got your girl. Okay if we dance?"

"Sure! It's on the house!" From behind the bar, Callie waved a bar towel in his direction. As she tried to put space between his body and hers, Murray resisted the urge to knee him in the groin. Then she thought about Shelby Turner who would never dance again, and gritted her teeth in a smile. She was here to do a job and she'd do it, in spite of this creep.

"So, Duke, what kind of work do you do?"

"Airplane mechanic over at the airbase. I get paid Friday. You want to go dancing and get dinner some place fancy? This bar ain't no place for a girl like you."

Murray relaxed as they two-stepped around the little patch of dance floor. Things were going to work out after all.

CHAPTER 15

Alex had just returned from Pierre's place when Rudolfo pulled up on the old tractor. He was still covered with mud and dirt from his boots to his flannel shirt, looking as if he'd been working in the pasture all day instead of crawling through old mine shafts.

"Hey, son, you're starting to lose that city polish." The crew boss grinned. "Damn if you don't look just like a real *obrero!*"

Alex continued measuring feed for the few animals left in the pasture. "I know you didn't come up here to tell me how pretty I look." He smacked his sweat soaked straw hat on his knee, driving the dust off the brim. "So what's up?"

Rudolfo expression grew sober. "Man, I got something for you to see. You want to take a ride up to the top pasture. We can take the truck up there."

"I know already. Dead animals. Swollen up like they've been poisoned. I saw the same thing today up on the ridge. Somebody's spraying around here to drive the farmers out."

Rudolfo stared down at their shadows in the later afternoon sun. "Yeah, like they spray on us in the fields, *los bastardos.* But there ain't nothing you can do about it, maestro. The union already try, but this company up there—" He jerked his head toward the ridge. "—it belong to the government. That's what they say. They doing something top secret over the ridge at the airbase. That's why they can't have nobody up there."

Alex slowed a step. "Who says?"

"The Migrant Workers Union rep. He say this company, *como se llama,* Synotech, it got government protection. Can't take 'em on. They got all the guns and ponies, *comprende?*"

At that point, Alex would have given anything to confide in Rudolfo what he had seen going on in the Devil's Ladder Mine. But he had already laid his entire life on the line twice today—first by telling Pierre his true identity and again, by following the rancher into the depths of the old mine.

"I don't get it. Why would the government be involved?" Unless the chemical they were producing had a military use. Like Agent Orange back in the '70s. Then what was 1212? And where were they sending it?

Remembering the assembly line of armaments he had seen inside the cavernous Synotech warehouse earlier, it suddenly struck him the operation was totally legal! No wonder Crittenden had been in such a filthy mood when Alex had tried to call attention to the company's books.

"Hey, I only work here." Rudolfo swatted away the flies with his hat. "But you know, Perez knows all about He's got a cousin who works up there. Ask him."

"Perez? He still around?"

What was it about Perry Perez that made Alex uncomfortable? Too with it. Too educated and too knowledgeable for a simple migrant worker. But then, hard times made for simpler lives. Alex only had to look at his own situation for the best example of that.

"Sure, maestro. He lives here, up in town. He was here earlier looking for you, but he left. He said call him when you got time." The crew boss cast a sympathetic glance at his filthy bandages streaked with blood. "Looks like you got a lot of that for a while."

☙❧

The dead animals in the Turner's upper pasture were a repeat horror show from this morning. Eyes popped and swollen tongues sticking out of gaping mouths, they still looked as if they were in agony. Flies already covered the carcasses, rising in thick squadrons when the two men came to inspect the damage.

Pinching his nostrils against the odor, Alex commented. "They died exactly the way Pierre Bighand's sheep did. Choked to death, not by the smoke but by something else before they died. He had some dead sheep that looked exactly like these, but hadn't been caught in the fire."

Rudolfo kept muttering prayers under his breath or curses, it was hard to tell. "Dios mio, who would do this, eh? Some kind of monsters they are. After this family suffer so much, losing the daughter, now this thing. Curse them for it."

But the sight had a different effect on Alex. "Keep them here, Rudolfo. Don't let anybody move them. I'm calling the Ag agent. We're going to make somebody pay."

Rudolfo looked up and Alex could see there were tears settled in the wrinkles around his sad eyes. "I got news, amigo mio. He already come out here today. Say he got to quarantine the farm for the anthrax."

"What?"

Rudolfo lifted his arms in a gesture of futility. "Happens all the time in Mexico. They want you out, they put you out of business in a heartbeat. Don't make no difference how they do it." He took off his hat and waved the flies away as if they were sorrows.

"Maybe if it's proved not to be anthrax, the Bureau of Agriculture can help stop the spraying. Whatever happens, we've got to try to stop them."

"Not we." Rudolfo looked at him. "I got kids and a wife to take care of. You gonna lose your job. Then what? Some time you got to think about you. Come on, let's get out of here. It ain't our fight. Don't get into it."

Alex turned away, sick of the sight of death. "You need me for anything tonight?"

"I want to say yes, but you going to do whatever anyway. So I won't waste the breath."

They walked away from the pervasive stench and breathed deeply. At the bottom of the pasture, Rudolfo held up a finger. "Oh, I know. I got a bunch of ewes need a dipping. Keeping them all over in a separate pasture."

"Dipping?" He Alex the idea of running squalling sheep through something that stunk like a cess pit. "How many are we talking?"

"'Bout thirty." Rudolfo frowned and replace his hat. "Why? You had some other plans?"

"Yeah, and they don't include dipping sheep."

For a moment, the two men faced each other, each trying to measure the resolve of the other. Then, the crew boss began to shake with laughter from the shoulders down. "Son, I was just playing. Go on and get cleaned up. Hell, *hombre*, you go on in town and give some of those girls a good time. But better get some of that sheep smell off you first or they won't even get close enough for a kiss."

Alex could see why his crew would have followed Rudolfo anywhere. He had only been into town once with Rudolfo, to buy groceries at a Latino grocery and take clothes into the Laundromat. But now, something besides sheer loneliness was making him take the risk of being spotted. He had to call the agriculture extension office and report the dead sheep at Pierre's place. He knew better than to use his cell phone any more. The police might already have put a tracer on it. He doubted any law enforcement would move that fast, but he couldn't take a chance. He was too close to pay dirt to get caught now.

Showering and trimming up his faint moustache and beard, he tried to think clearly about the risks of getting himself involved in a local territorial dispute. After all, it was plainly out of character for a migrant farm hand like Jimmy Vargas.

For another thing, Pierre Bighand had hinted today Shelby may have chased off to find her pilot boyfriend who according to Bighand was no good. And then there was this Duke Cooper who had worked for the Turners. Maybe he was in love with Shelby and she rejected his advances.

Then why would his own picture have been in the van? And his keys? He had an answer for that, too. After they had their pictures taken together, he lost his keys or left them there in the bar. Ricky and his drinking buddies had said they had to carry him back to the condo. The keys might have fallen out of his pocket. The Turner girl found them, took his business card, and the photo—might as well because what would she do with it?———in the van with her as she chased after her boyfriend. Being the nice girl she appeared to be, she was going to mail them to his office when she got the chance.

The next morning he had used his spare pair without thinking about it. Simple. The boyfriend or rejected lover killed her and he had just happened to stumble on her body.

Flat tire, phony cop, drained oil. Leaked story to the press. All paranoia. And yet they existed unresolved, like nails in a spiked road.

He wiped his face clean and studied it in the plain mirror in his equally plain room. The operation inside the Devil's Ladder was motive enough for the deaths of ten Shelby Turners. It was motive enough to destroy anyone who betrayed it, those who fought against it, or anyone who even called attention to it the way he had.

"What in the world inspired you to do that?" He pictured Crittenden in his office, tailored, and urbane, martini in hand against the expensive view of the Palisades. "Why not visit the plant itself and look around, if you represented a board member? Why skulk about, pretending you're some workman inspecting the facility?"

The answer was in his own reflection staring back at him. He had to get to Diamondback to call Perez.

Before he left, he decided to water down Marisa's flower

garden. The searing heat and smoke from the fire had snatched moisture from the ground already, leaving it parched and shriveling some of bushes to stalks. Some of the Pink Talismans were gone, no doubt finding their way to a vase beside Shelby's picture in the living room.

As he stood at the side of the house, winding up the hose, he heard Marisa talking to someone. At first he thought she was on the phone, but then his blood seemed to stop flowing as a familiar voice answered her. He slipped along the side of the house to listen to the conversation that was taking place on the porch. Then he realized who Marisa was talking to and his mouth went dry with panic.

"He was the kind of guy who got the Mayor's Award for rescuing a kid and his mother from a burning apartment two years ago. My brother was the type of guy who pulled over to help people on the freeway. He got the Governor's Award for saving this girl from getting raped. I think you'll agree that's not a very smart thing to do, especially in LA. I'm just asking you to listen to me, Mrs. Turner. My brother Alex did not kill your daughter. They've made a big mistake or confused him with someone else." His brother Ricky sounded like a defense lawyer trying to convince a hanging judge.

Marisa's voice came back faint and sweetly sympathetic. "Sometimes those closest to us are still the greatest strangers."

Ricky was giving up. "I admit that, ma'am. But I know my brother. He was an outstanding person in every way. And he was engaged to be married to a beautiful and wealthy girl. Why would he throw everything away like that?"

Without seeing him, a mental picture of Ricky came through, standing there looking earnest, his square hands outspread in a desperate plea.

Marisa's voice followed his appeal, unconvinced but still sympathetic. "I know you believe your brother is a good person, Ricky. But maybe he was afraid his fiancé would discover his relationship with our daughter?"

"That's just it. I know my brother didn't even know your daughter. One of the guy's at the bachelor party got them together to take a picture, is all. He called me and told me he'd never seen her before, but I reminded him he was so drunk, he wouldn't remember anything."

"But then why would his things be in her van?"

"I don't know, but we were all partying that night. I remember we went over and asked those girls to dance. Your daughter was with a whole group of girls. They all said she never left them."

Alex tried to move backward but it was as if his feet were glued to the sandy earth. If Ricky somehow spotted him, he was finished. Slipping around to the front of the house, he saw a dusty red pickup parked in the drive way. The kid had even driven his own truck up here. Furious, Alex bolted into the bunkhouse and scribbled a note on the back of an envelope. *Get back to town and wait for me. I'll find you.* Running back to the yard, he tossed the note through the open window of Ricky's pickup and then jumped behind the wheel of his own truck. Taking the back road to the pasture gate, Alex fought both fury and absolute delight at seeing his brother.

It didn't take Ricky more than five minutes to wind up his fervent appeal for justice and start back to town. Waiting for him at the crossroads, Alex followed him and blinked his lights, pulling him over just outside the city limits. After waiting to see if anyone was following Ricky, he got out of his truck and walked up the truck. Ricky lit a cigarette trying to look cool.

"*Que paso?*" Alex touched the brim of his hat. "And don't even think about saying my name."

He had to hand it to Ricky for cool. His brother jerked imperceptibly and then just nodded back. "*Que tal?*"

"Tell me what in hell are you doing here?" Alex pretended to be examining the bottom of his boots for gum, keeping his hat covering his face.

They were both fighting tears. Ricky, always the baby, kept running his sleeve under his nose. "Quit looking around. You think I'd set you up?" The road was clear so they risked a quick handshake. "That hat and the half-past-five shadow look awesome. Hey, you're starting to look like—"

"Hey, I know. Don Pedro, no?"

It was good to hear Rick laugh again. "More like King Kong. Look at you, man." He waved his cigarette at Alex. "The look, the smell—Hey, Granpa would be so proud."

For a partial second, they were back home and into sibling rivalry. Alex punched him hard in the arm and Rick tried to punch back even harder. Then they laughed. The sound brought them back to the present and they were quiet. Alex had forgotten what it was like to really laugh. It had become a forbidden sound.

"Honest, I didn't have any idea you would be up here in the boonies. I mean this is like where we used to spend summers and I couldn't wait to get back civilization. I just really wanted to apologize to that poor lady. She looked like the Madonna. And then I see this burnt-out place and her husband's in the hospital." Ricky ran his hand through his hair. "*Dios mio*, I just came up like on the spur of the moment and decided they aughta really hear your side of it. They only know what the papers said and what the cops told them. They had never considered the cops might be wrong."

As a truck passed them, Alex examined his boots again. "Okay, so now you've seen me. Now, beat it, little brother. Go home as fast as you can, and tell Mama I'm okay. She'll worry herself sick. I know how she is." He thought he had learned not to choke on his emotions. They were somewhere on ice, to be unearthed in the future like artifacts from another civilization. "If they find out you know where I am and didn't tell, the cops will consider you as an accessory, get that?"

"I got some news for you." Rick touched his arm as if he

couldn't believe his brother were real. "I've been doing a little detective work myself."

"Oh, god! I told you to stay out of it." Alex took off his hat and rubbed the sweat off his forehead. "You don't know what you're doing. You'll only screw things up even more."

"Then okay, here's a question for you. Who owns the condo where we were staying in Sunrise for your bachelor party?" Ricky used to do this with bad jokes when they were kids.

"That's easy. Crittenden does. Why?"

Ricky snapped his fingers like a classroom teacher conducting a review. "Right! Next question. Who made the reservations for our bachelor party weekend?"

He knew Ricky was avoiding a confrontation by trying to put him on the defensive, but he played along. "Chelsea, I guess. Why? What does that have to do with anything?"

"Wrong. George Crittenden. Big Daddy himself. Well, his secretary did, anyway."

"How do you know this stuff?"

"Easy. I asked your secretary, Sylvia. Nice lady. A little old for me. Face like a hatchet." Ricky looked smug and lit a cigarette. "Like I said, bro, I've got my sources."

"Yeah, okay. So what? Maybe he did. I should know Chelsea'd never do anything herself. So what's the big deal?" Alex waited for the payoff, but Rick was enjoying the moment. His eyes glowed through the barbeque smoke.

"Company digs, right?" Ricky flicked a mosquito off his arm. "The condo is one of Crittenden's perks as a board member for Synotech. They actually bought it for him, but all their top people stay there. There just happened to be a meeting of all the bigwigs last weekend. Head honchos. They even had a senator at the deal. And wait until you hear this. Guess who worked at the condos over the weekends, cleaning up and such." Ricky always viewed life as a series of super bowls, games he had to win.

"Okay, who?"

"Shelby Turner, the dead girl. The cops are saying the girl appears to have been pregnant."

"What? No. Oh, god." The news crushed the slender hopes he was starting to nurture. Then he thought of Marisa and his pain doubled. "But you were there, too! Nothing happened. We left the bar and came back to the condo."

"Remember Hardaway and the guys carried you back. I drove your car with your spare keys. After we came home, you crashed and burned. That's it."

Ricky made a gesture that said he was sweating the small stuff. Nevertheless, Alex was used to reading the fine print of contract law. "Listen, you told me there was no oil light on and the tires were all right when you drove the Jeep, right?"

"Right. They're saying it was your gun that killed Shelby Turner. The one you always kept in your glove compartment—no, listen, will you?" Ricky raised his voice over Alex's protest and continued steadily. "They found your gun out in the field. Wiped clean as a whistle. Two bullets fired."

"But I didn't kill her, Ricky. When the cops searched my car, it wasn't in my glove compartment where I always keep it. Someone is setting me up. You've got to believe me. Even if no one else does, you know I wouldn't kill anybody. I didn't even know the girl."

He felt Rick's hand on his arm. "Of course, I believe you, stupid. It's all just too perfect a crime scene. The best thing you could have done looked like the stupidest at the time. You stayed right there, trying to help her. That's what you've got going for you. And that little slip of paper that says you were at the one stop shop at Gorman when the girl was killed. Thanks to your lawyer Feldman, the convenience store security camera has you pegged at least twenty minutes behind the girl. The coroner has set the time by now. Where's the receipt, by the way? Is it safe?"

"I put it in my safety deposit box along with a printout of Synotech's phony bills of lading. I found out for sure today,

Synotech is shipping weapons as bogus medical supplies and they use some kind of chemical on the pastures to drive the locals away."

Ricky whistled softly through his front teeth. "You think that's maybe why the Turner girl was killed?"

"I'm certain it had something to do with it. She must have known about the whole thing."

Ricky exhaled, deep in thought. "So maybe she wanted you to help her. That's why she had your keys and stuff in her car. *Dios mio.* I also found out some blonde that works in a bar in Diamondback got Shelby the job with house-keeping services. Seems like she always worked for this girl in the winter ever since high school. Cool job. Tips, free lift tickets, gourmet meals. I had to work bagging groceries."

Alex regarded his brother with newfound respect. "How do you find out this stuff? You surely couldn't get some girl in bed that fast. Not even you."

Rick grinned that smile which apparently unlocked many doors in his love life. "Want to bet?" Then he laughed at Alex's look of amazement. "No, but I did chat up the recep-tionist at Sunrise before I came on up here. Cute little red-head, but engaged. I just told her I had lost touch with this blonde who works the bar during the big conventions like the one last weekend and she even gave me her name."

Rick fumbled in his pocket. "I wrote it down some-where. Began with a C. Carol. Cassandra. And anyway, this blonde C-something also takes pictures of the guests. You think they had some kind of extortion racquet going? They've got a lot of high dollar guests there. Movie people, corporate front-burners, guys cheating on their wives. It could be a big business. Maybe they used the Turner girl to trap these guys into forking over big bucks"

Alex studied his brother who was too good-looking for people to take seriously. Usually, Rick took advantage of that fact to challenge the stereotype. He favored the Cauca-sian side of the family, rather than the Hispanic DNA. His nose was not hawkish like Alex's, and though shorter, his build was muscular rather than lithe. "So Sylvia told you Crittenden reserved the condo and you just followed your nose up there? Rico, do you realize someone could have been following you?"

"I was careful and I bought one of these universal cell phones to use. And no, I haven't used my credit card either. Took a helluva lot of cash to come this far so got to go to work now."

He was aghast. "What? You can't! You've got to get out of here, Rick. I told you. You'll lead them straight to me."

"I'm staying, man. I've got to. Can't leave you to fight this thing alone." Rick started the pickup's tinny engine and they lingered in silence for a minute, Ricky smoking, and Alex listening to the sounds of the world going about its business as his own slowly crumbled.

"I also found out who owns Sunrise." Rick exhaled and then tossed his cigarette on to the macadam where Alex stamped it out. "Some outfit right here in Diamondback. I wrote it down too along with C-girl's. Phone number and everything. Sutton and Something."

"That's beautiful. Sutton and Dalton." The pieces started to form a picture now, a strange mosaic. "If Shelby Turner worked at the condos why didn't I ever see her? I've been up there with Chelsea dozens of times."

"I don't know, it's a big complex, man." Ricky shrugged. "Just one of those girls who pays no attention to the Do-Not-Disturb sign and tiptoes in to change the towels. The cops are saying you got mad because you had sex and then she followed you, blackmailed you with the picture, and threatened to tell your fiancé. You lost your temper, shot her, and they practically caught you in the act."

"But they haven't got anything but circumstantial evidence. And if she was twenty minutes ahead of me, I couldn't possibly have gotten all the way there in time to kill her with a tire going flat and the oil light on. Then there was the cop who stopped to help me and I asked him directions. He's a credible witness." Maybe fear had heightened his senses, but he read doubt into Rick's silence. "Do you think I killed her, Rico?"

Again, that hesitation. "Even if you did, I'd defend you to the last, man. I'd lie for you. You're my brother. But hell, Alex, there's always room for a last fling, that's what they're going to say. Bachelor party got out of hand. And I forgot to tell you."

"Just lay it on me. It can't get worse." But it could.

"The deputy you were counting on for an alibi, Sanchez. He didn't make it out of ICU."

"Oh, god, no."

Alex threw down his own cigarette where it glowed in the road for a few minutes and died like an abandoned hope. "Jeezuz, what is happening?"

"Apparently, he was doing okay, making progress, and then, whammo!"

"What does whammo mean?"

"Best they can tell, his IV went on the fritz. They found him in the morning, dead. The poor night nurse got accused, but she had a witness with her when she changed the IV bag. So it could have been somebody who slipped in there when they changed shifts."

"So there goes my alibi. What a coincidence!" Alex had stayed in one place long enough. Looking up and down the road, he said, "Listen, I can't talk anymore now. Write me at the Turner's place. Address it to Jimmy Vargas. Sign it Miguel Vargas. You must have the address since you already showed up."

Rick nodded. "Jimmy Vargas, got it. Listen, *hijo*. I'm not going home. I already got a job in town at La Taqueria. We're in this together." He tried a dry laugh. "Hey, who knows? I might even learn how to cook."

"You'll just lead them right to me, *comprende*?" Alex put his hand on his brother's shoulder. "And think about Mama and Papa. I bet you didn't even tell them where you were going."

They shared a laugh over the formidable image of Don

Pedro scowling down from the dining room wall. "Hey, man, you think I'm stupid? I took all my finals and told them I was going to visit my roommate in New York. By the time they find out, you'll be cleared."

"You lied to Mama and Papa?" Alex pretended shock—part of Rick's charisma was created by stretching the truth just to the point of a lie but not beyond. "*Dios mio*, you are a bum."

His brother smiled in the way that always meant trouble. "I know, but I'm a helpful bum."

It brought Alex pain even to bring up the subject of his father, grayed and stooped from so many hours doing people's taxes.

Ricky's smile died. "You know Papa. You were always his shining star. Hard. Doesn't talk to anyone. Goes into his office and sits with the light off."

Alex's stomach turned over, framing the picture in his mind. "Go home. Forget you saw me. I mean it."

Again the shrug. "Okay, you don't want to know the rest of the bad news?"

Alex hesitated, keys in hand. He had heard about all he could stand.

"Chelsea wasted no time announcing she's going to marry Tim Hardaway." Ricky said it carefully, glancing at him sideways to see how he took it. The whites of his eyes became brief half-moons in the setting sun.

"How do you know?" It didn't hurt as badly as he would have thought earlier. She'd dropped enough hints she was seeing someone else.

"Her cousin, Allison, called me. You know the one I took out a few times, preppy Ali? I guess she wanted to rub it in because I dumped her. Too Valley Girl for me. You know the type that says 'That's just too funny!' to everything?" He checked Alex's face in the growing dark, and kept talking. "When I think how close Chelsea actually came to being my sister-in-law, I have nightmares."

Her face came back to Alex, bitter and accusing. "Of

course, I don't blame her. It's over, anyway. Why should she wait around? I think she had somebody else for a while. I knew it when she broke off the engagement. She'd been with him when she said she was staying with her parents or with a girlfriend."

Ricky grinned and exhaled with a relieved sigh. "I wouldn't have called it bad news except for one other little thing. She's pregnant as an alley cat."

Alex thought he was prepared for anything, but not for that. "What?"

"And I'll give you two-to-one it's yours. Hardaway doesn't look like he could father a joy stick. Dear preppy Allison must have been given the mission to pass the information on to you."

It was like Rick to take the news lightly. Not much in his young life affected him especially the pregnancy of some girl he detested. To Rick, it was payback for his brother's humiliation at the hands of the mainstream culture.

"Sorry to shoot down your theory, but Chelsea and I haven't slept together for the at least the last two months. And even then, she was on the morning-after pill. Said she didn't want kids to tie us down so early into marriage and a lot of other crap to cover up sleeping with Hardaway at least since Christmas, if not earlier. I really lost her before then, though. Just didn't want to admit I didn't belong, I guess. But now I see why she wanted to keep up the myth of the poor Latino making it with the boss's daughter. "

His brother bristled at his self-deprecation. "Listen to yourself, Alex. We're not poor, bro. We're not in Crittenden's tax bracket, but Pop's always earned a good living. You haven't got anything to apologize for. Those girls in Santa Barbara fought over you to take them to the Country Club."

"It isn't the same." Alex drew a breath and stepped back from the pickup. "We're not movers and shakers. People like Crittenden are. They inherit it along with their name. And Parker isn't going to let anyone mess that up for him, let alone me. Now go home and forget about it. You've got to be the man, now. Be there for Mama and Papa, and all that good stuff."

"Sure." Rick started up the engine, and Alex knew by his sideways smile, his brother had no intention of going anywhere. "Hey, if you're ever in town, I make a mean carnita taco. Check it out at La Taqueria."

He slid back on to the road, leaving Alex in a cloud of dust, no doubt in revenge for all those times he had been called chubby or *gordito* by his taller, skinnier brother. Revenge was sweet. Then he stopped and backed up just as Alex was getting in his truck.

"Hey, I remembered that blonde's name. The one who took the pictures of us the other night."

Alex squinted at him through the settling dust. "You know, I just took a shower, Rick. Did you have to give me a dirt bath, too?"

It was just too good not to savor the moment. "Just wanted to make you look authentic, man. Anyway, her name was Calico. Isn't that cute?"

"Just ducky. Haven't you got somewhere else to be? Peeling onions or something?"

"You know where I am, baby!" Rick burned rubber as he took off down the road toward town.

CHAPTER 16

Outside the decaying strip mall in town, Alex found a battered public phone still standing and called the Agricultural Extension agent, hoping there would be a machine to take his message.

But on the second ring, a voice with a weary banjo twang answered the phone. "Extension, this is Wilson."

Caught off guard, Alex stumbled. "I thought you'd be closed. It's almost six."

"Then why'd you call?"

Country bluntness jolted him into his rehearsed speech. "I got a small spread off Old Mountain Road and Highway 420. My pasture adjoins T.C. Turner's place on Little Spur Road. I think some of my stock are down with anthrax and some of his, too. Dead sheep up there in the north pasture by Devil's Ladder. I was wondering if someone could come out tomorrow and take a look."

On the other end, the drawl picked up a faster cadence. "Anthrax? Hell, son, I'm gonna be out there tomorrow morning, eight sharp. Now, bear in mind, I'm just filling in for the regular agent. Tommy Bartlett's been took real sick and all. My name's Wilson. I'm retired after cancer got to me. What's yours? Name, that is."

He coughed. "Vargas."

"Bargrass? You must be that little Mexican place other side of Little Spur. Kind of new, aren't you? Hope to hell you didn't buy acreage as close to the chemical plant as

Turner's is. Something coming out of there's killing every living thing around. Now where's my pen at?"

Wilson sound more promising than anything he expected to find under the shadow of Devil's Ladder.

"I'll meet you at the Turner's place, eight tomorrow. Thanks, Mr. Wilson."

"How's he doing, by the way? Heard about the fire, damn shame. But I'm not surprised. I ain't surprised by nothing that happens around here. I'm from Idaho, by the way. Came to California to retire. Hell, I'm going back soon as I get my place sold. Living here ain't what it's cracked up to be."

"But I'm sure glad you're here. See you in the morning." Alex replaced the phone and drew a deep breath. Something was working.

He put in some more change to call Perez. A Hispanic woman answered the phone and screamed for him. He gathered that was the woman Perez could not live without. Perez sounded grumpy until Alex identified himself.

"Jimmy! Hell, man! How are you? I heard you got toasted bad? You doing better, now?" Perez had left the crew as soon as they had arrived in Diamondback and he collected his pay. "I came by this afternoon to see how you were getting along, but they told me you went up to Pierre Bighand's up on the ridge. How was it up there?"

"Guess. What in the hell is going on around here, Perry? It's like everybody's scared as hell to cross this guy Sutton. And he's got some kind of war zone up there, man."

There was a pause while Perez lit a cigarette. "Told you something's going down. Whatever the hell they're spraying up there's killing livestock and I swear making people sick. So one of my kids has got some respiratory thing the doctors can't even diagnose. Have to send samples up to the state lab, for god's sake. Sutton wants to run those ranchers out of the area and he's doing a damn good job of it. People packing it in every day, man.

"I just called the Ag agent. He's coming out tomorrow."

There was a snort. "Hell, he won't do anything if it's got the government okay." A child wailed in the background and Perez covered the phone and yelled. The wailing subsided. "Man, I never knew what pressure was until a kid's waiting for dinner to heat up."

"Maybe I've got a chance. There's a retired guy from Idaho filling in for the regular agent who's sick. We'll see if he's got a different take on it. Listen, Perry, can your cousin get me hired on over there at the Synotech plant?"

"You're the wrong color, man. He's the token Hispanic, the rest are gardeners. But he can get you through the gate if you want. You want to see what they got over there real bad, don't you? Hell, man, you just go looking for more trouble, don't you? Like you don't have enough."

Alex still didn't fully trust Perez, but there was something—he couldn't put his finger on it—comforting about his company. "It looks for me. Meet me for a drink tonight, Perry. You can tell I'm at loose ends."

"I'd love to, man, but I can't. Hear all that squalling behind me? Promised Mama I'd babysit while she hangs out with the girls over at Tico Town. *Dios mio*, the things I do for that woman."

"Has she dismissed charges yet?" Alex had to laugh without Perez hearing him—which wouldn't be hard with all the kids hollering in the background. Here was Perry Perez, macho oilfield worker, jack-of-all-trades, street-smart, literate and wrapped up tight by a bimbo.

"Hell, no. The frigging used car salesman's got the spare room. Can you believe it?"

Alex couldn't hold the laugh any longer. "Another time, man. See you."

"Hey, Jimmy, wait. I don't know why you want to see inside the Synotech plant so bad, but if you really think it will do you some good, my cousin doesn't want to work tomorrow. Wants to go hunting with his buddies. Great work ethic, but what can I say? Come by tonight and get the key to his lock. Number Twenty-Two, Perez, same as me. If you come late, don't ring the doorbell and wake up the kids, okay? They'll all get in bed with us and ruin my plan for Isobel to drop charges because I'm a better lover than ol' Retread in there, *comprende*?"

"You are a dog, Perez. Leave the key in the mailbox. I'll put it back tomorrow night. And, Perry, thanks."

"If you end up back in the slammer, I don't know you, Vargas."

"Tico Town. Where's that?"

"It's the Mexican side of Diamondback. That's where all the action is, man. You can find the hot chicks by the dozen down there. Only the redhead with big boobs is hands off. That one is mine."

"You're in enough hot water already, Perez. Do you have to borrow trouble?"

Perry Perez gave his version of a mariachi laugh. "*La vida loca, hombre. La vida loca.*"

"Nice to know where I can get a decent meal, anyway. Everything around here is chicken-fried or barbequed."

Another baby wailed in the background. "Hey, Jimmy, I'll get back to you, okay? In the meantime, stay out of trouble for a change. *Adios.*"

Putting down the phone, Alex stood there at loose ends, leaning against the graffitied mall, watching families going by in quarreling, laughing groups. He and his own family used to go out to eat Friday night and then shopping at the upscale malls in Santa Barbara. His father always said it was so Mama wouldn't have to cook, but they all knew it was so he could buy them something for good grades. He remembered watching his father ritually studying the check to see if it were correct, adding in the tip to the penny, and then opening his wallet to count out the bills while they all unwrapped their peppermints or fortune cookies, heedless of his mental gymnastics. Only Alex knew he was mentally subtracting from this college fund or that savings account to pay for a meal that meant nothing more to them than a peppermint.

The memory suddenly make him ache with loneliness. Making up his mind to put Jimmy Vargas's name and ID to the test, he sought the company of strangers and a solid whiskey at the only trendy thirties-something saloon in town. If Rick was right, and the blonde photographer Calico worked there, then she was the link between Sunrise and Shelby Turner.

As he pulled up to the too-cute hitching rail bordering the sidewalks, the sound of swinging country music and cowboy catcalls nearly soured the plan. The thought of having to make the rural singles scene, with its custom boots and earsplitting electric guitars caused him near physical pain. It was the kind of place he would have avoided at any cost in Los Angeles.

The place was hardly spacious, filled with crowded tables and couples two-stepping around the tiny dance floor. Remembering cow palace etiquette, he left his hat on. When the petite blonde behind the bar gave him a come-on smile, he tugged at the brim.

"Hi, sweet lips, what'll you have?" For a moment, leaning across the bar and smiling, the girl reminded him so much of Chelsea, it put an ache in his throat.

He was invited to look down at her name tag and even farther. He stopped there. It said *Callie*.

She followed his eyes. "That's me. Short for Calico. My folks were big into square dancing. And other things, needless to say." Her laugh was the kind that made others laugh.

"Hey, Callie, what're you into?"

A few of the customers exchanged laughs.

"Too bad you'll never find out whatever it is, Eli," she snapped back.

She didn't recognize Alex. That was plain from the way she smiled unblinkingly at him.

He tried hard not to look down the front of her low-cut blouse, but what was there was obviously not a secret. An undone button invited looks and generous tips. She caught him looking. "That's okay, honey. They're real." She laughed even harder, noticing how he quickly looked away. "Are you old enough to drink? No, just teasing. That beard makes you at least twenty-four. Let me see some ID just in case."

"I'm twenty-six, and I'd like a draft beer, please." He flashed Vargas's driver's license and put three dollars on the bar. She bought it.

"Okay, Jimmy, I'll settle for twenty-six. We don't stand on formality at the Big B." She whirled back with the draft beer so fast the suds flew off behind her. "Drafts are two dollars here, honey."

"The other one's for you." He took a sip of his first draft beer in three days. It was almost worth getting caught for. The small blonde kissed the bill and tucked it down her blouse with a pretty smile.

"Hey, you come on back anytime, Twenty-Six." It was safe to look at her retreating up the bar.

"Don't get your hopes up, buddy," the man next to him said. "She don't go out with the likes of you."

"Hell, or the likes of you either," the man next to him retorted.

At least, this girl wasn't some ghost with an everlasting smile who seemed to haunt every room. But that barroom laugh and her ample cleavage brought back last Saturday night, searing them on his brain as he recalled her bending down to take their picture.

"Now, smile pretty for the birdie," she had said as the whole group of them lined up together without a care in the world. Small wonder she worked in a place called the Branding Iron. How could he ever forget?

It was safe to lean back on the bar and just absorb being around carefree people for a change. Not sad ghosts of peoples whose dreams had vanished but whose dreams were still embraced in a love song. The singles scene in LA cut to sexual relationships without the slow dancing first.

He wasn't prepared for things to happen quite that fast in Diamondback. He was to learn Darla Sutton never practiced patience when she saw something she wanted.

"Hi, cowboy. You look like you'd be hell in bed. Want to dance?"

He looked beside him into a stunning face nearly on the same level as his own.

"My name's Darla. What yours?"

Her eyes weren't a color he had ever seen in another person, rather in the aqua waters of a tropical lagoon. They invited him to strip off and dive in.

Apparently the girl was accustomed to the kind of reaction. She swung her long copper red hair back and forth like a flag at a stock car race. "The quiet type, aren't you? Have you got a name or are you just having trouble remembering the right one?"

"I'm not sure. I think it just slipped my mind." He ran his hand across his new moustache, checking for suds clinging to his upper lip. She didn't miss an uncertain gesture.

Touching his lip, she said, "That's real cute, but I hate whiskers. Irritates my skin. Are you really glued to the bar or do you dance?" She put out her arms.

He became acutely aware of heads turned in their direction. The unwanted attention caused him something near physical pain. Feeling panic rising, he looked at the fast two-step on the packed dance floor. "Sorry, not really my style. I'm afraid you'll get stepped on."

"You can handle it. And if you can't, I can."

There was no getting out of it. She pulled him by the hand to the crowded dance floor. Since she did most of the leading, he only had to stumble after her.

Before the music stopped, he had picked up the beat. "I hope you don't have sensitive feet." He looked down at her expensive, hand-tooled cowboy boots, remembering Shelby Turner's plain ones beneath her jeans.

"It's okay. I've got good medical insurance." Her height almost matched his, but she moved like a giraffe, in one fluid motion as she guided him easily around the dance floor. He was relieved clever conversation was made impossible over the whooping and shouting. "Just relax." She smiled into his eyes. "I can see you need a little fun, cowboy. And I never did get your name." She tilted her head, waiting.

"Jim. Jim Vargas." He made sure it was clear over the noise. Her copper hair seemed to move from side to side as if she were swaying to an ocean current. He was fascinated with her eyes which never left his lips as he said his name as if she were memorizing it.

"Hi, Jimmy. Welcome to Diamondback City. My family owns it. I'm Darla Sutton. You're the one who saved T.C.'s life, aren't you?" She indicated his still bandaged left hand. "That was real brave. I admire brave men."

"News really gets around fast here."

"Especially bad luck stories. It was so hard coming so soon after Shelby's…passing." He noticed she hesitated before she said the word as if it had a bad taste. "She was a terrific gal. You ever sleep with her?"

In spite of the fact she was drunk, the remark hurt for some reason. "Never met the lady."

"Just checking. She used to go out with Duke Cooper who worked for the Turners and they were a thing until she met the jet pilot." Moving close, she whispered in his ear. "It was love at first sight for Shelby just like this is. God, you're just so cute, I can't keep my hands off you."

Pretending to be slightly drunk himself was much simpler than he thought. He controlled Darla's hands which roamed over his butt as if he were an extension of her own body. "Jet pilot? I thought there were only cowboys around here."

The music stopped and she sighed, tossing her hair as if she were tired of the subject. "You're not from around here, are you? There's an airbase near here. They come here, sometimes, the guys that work over there. In fact there are a few here now." A brief sobriety flitted across her face. "I'll bet anything he had something to do with her murder. Scott

Mason did. I know it wasn't Duke Cooper. He was working for my brother Larry by then."

He pursued the lead as if it were a bubble, afraid the topic would vanish. "Was she as cute as you are?"

"You're kidding, right?" Darla lifted her copper hair off her shoulders impatiently. "Darling, I'm not only the cutest thing you're going to find in Diamond City, I'm the richest. Stick with me if you want to have some fun. Ol' T.C. will work you to death and you'll have no time to play. And, from what I can see from here that'd be a real shame."

She kissed his ear and then stuck her tongue in it. "Come on over tonight. We've got a little party going."

"Sorry," he made a point of looking at his watch, "I get up real early. Maybe some other time."

That brought a laugh. "You can't work tomorrow, honey, it's against the law to work on the day the county fair opens. T.C. would say the same thing, bless him. Just get up early, feed your stock, and come on." Something snagged in her mind and she frowned, a strange puzzled look foreign to her face. "Oh, yeah, I heard he lost some sheep. We're really sorry about that. I'll get Larry to replace them with some real fine stock." A mist of uncertainty drifted across the girl's beautiful face. "Terrible about that fire."

"Especially since it was started on purpose." It slipped out and fell between them like a lit fuse.

She didn't stop dancing, but he felt her stiffen against his arm. "Arson? Who told you that? I didn't hear that. Who would do such a thing to the Turners after Shelby just died and everything?"

"I've got no idea. Do you?"

Her aqua eyes slid away, beckoning his to follow. They were looking at a table where a rowdy group of locals were gathered. She evaded the question, and shifted to another subject. "I really loved Shelby, even though she won last year. I should have, but now I'm glad she did. I was Rodeo Queen for three years in a row, anyway." With a sudden shake of her head, Darla snapped shut the book of unpleasant memories. "Look, just come on over and I'll shave off that horrible beard. I like men with skin like babies' butts."

He wasn't entirely sure his luck was turning, but making friends with one of the Suttons wasn't the worst thing that could happen, even if it was just for the evening.

While the perspiring band took a break, Darla pulled him from table to table, introducing him as Jimmy, the new guy who works for the Turners. It was almost sensory overload after his long hours alone. He felt slightly dizzied by the acceptance where he had expected rejection.

A hand clapped him on the shoulder and he turned to face a tall, freckled man. "Kind of out of your territory, aren't you, hombre?"

"Didn't know I had one."

They traded hostile stares.

Darla introduced them, sliding a calculating glance between the two tall men. "Duke, I want you to meet my friend, Jimmy. This is Duke Cooper, Jimmy. He used to work for the Turners, too."

So this was their former handyman turned mechanic. The one in the picture with Shelby at the rodeo.

Cooper turned to Darla, ignoring his outstretched hand. "You into Mexicans now, Darla?"

"Learn some manners, Duke," she snapped, "Don't be so damned rude! Now, go away, will you? You're drunk." Darla slipped her arm through Alex's. "C'mon, Jimmy, I want you to meet some of my real friends."

"I'm not your friend, Darla. I'm your brother." As Alex turned away, Cooper grabbed him by the arm. "Listen, hombre, you need to go back to Tico Town."

Alex realized he was being pushed into a fight, but it was too late to opt out. "Take your hand off my arm."

Their voices had caught the attention of the tall blonde waitress who came up quickly and slid her arm around Cooper's waist. "How about that dance now, Duke?"

But Cooper pushed the girl out of the way. "Not now, honey. Beat it, I said, buddy!"

Alex jerked his arm from Cooper's grip. "When I finish this dance and my beer." He glanced around checking his options. The dance floor was about the size of four tables put together and the minute Cooper had raised his voice, it had cleared off.

The waitress surprised him by speaking up again. "He doesn't have to leave. I have a table for you and the lady, sir, if you'll just bring your drink and follow me, please." The waitress looked at him with a slight shake of her blonde curls. She didn't want to clean up a lot of broken glass and he didn't want to call attention to himself above all costs. He turned to follow the girl but Cooper gave him a hard shove that spilled beer all over him. From the table behind them, Cooper's friends cheered him on.

"Way to go, Duke! Way to go! Throw the beaner out!" They pounded on the tables with their glasses.

"Knock it off, bud." A girl full of surprises, the tall, blonde waitress whose nametag read Silk whirled around and blocked Cooper's wild punch with her tray. Cooper recoiled, cursing and gripping his hand. The girl whistled through her teeth. "Bouncer, get this guy out of here!"

But the bouncers remained by the door, glancing at Callie for a signal. Silk was about to turn back to him, when Cooper shoved her roughly out of the way again, causing her to stumble against a table and swung at Alex. With the reaction of a trained fighter, Alex took the man out neatly under the chin. Cooper sailed backward over a table, upending it, and landed in a heap in front of the jukebox. It was a neat set up.

At that moment, two other men passed right by the bouncers, carrying baseball bats. The bouncers didn't make a move, clearly staying out of the fight.

"Too bad you don't take a hint, beaner." The first of the men came forward, his gruesome face made even uglier by the greenish-yellow light from the jukebox.

Knowing he was surrounded, Alex balanced himself and circled the small empty space. "Get 'em up, Beaner. You going to get a little boxing lesson tonight on the house. Come on, now, it's one-two, one-two, just like you was dancing."

The goon feinted a few mock punches and then landed a painful jab on his shoulder. Alex saw his chance as the move opened the other man up for a neat belly punch. The blow clearly caught the goon off guard and knocked the breath out of him. His small eyes narrowed, and he moved in for real blood. As he crouched, Alex caught him hard in the ribs.

"Better move a little faster, buddy. You're getting old and rusty."

The big man was breathing a little harder. The second punch had cracked a rib. "C'mon, Springer, nail the bastard," somebody yelled.

But most of the patrons were just anxious to see a good fight. It was better than the orchestrated fights on TV and they gathered to watch as Alex ducked and weaved around the tables. Springer followed him, kicking chairs out of the way, but at a slower pace.

By now, it was clear Springer was unprepared for an aggressive stance from an amateur. Out of shape from an easy life and age, he tired quickly. The few solid punches he had landed on Alex hardly more than bruised the younger man. Soon, he was doing more ducking than punching as Alex backed him in a corner and finally landed another uppercut on his square chin. The bodyguard staggered back, obviously dizzy.

Out of the edge of his eye, Alex saw the other two carrying bats edge toward him. In desperation, the goon came at Alex with a head butt. Alex avoided the attack, sidestepping at the last minute. Springer splintered a wooden table and then whirled around, coming at Alex with a wrestling hold. Alex had to hand it to him, the old guy was tough. Alex danced back, knowing if he fell into that bearlike grip, he was as good as dead. Springer had manslaughter on his mind, it was plain.

"Fight fair, Springer. Give the kid a chance." The voice was educated and without the twang of the local ranchers came from the circle of spectators.

Now, thoroughly winded, Springer resorted to chasing Alex around the tables. At one point, Alex got him with a rabbit punch that split his lip. Blood spilled down the body-guard's shirt.

"You're just making an ass of yourself tonight, Spring-er," someone else said. "Give it up,"

That taunt sent Springer into another rhino charge, head down toward Alex's midsection. In mid-lunge, the big man tripped over a fallen chair and fell to the floor, taking a ta-ble with him. The climate in the bar began to change. Muff led laughter and even some applause went up from some of the crowd.

One man raised his beer mug to Alex. "Damn good fight!"

"Better than Pay per View TV, that's for sure. Way to watch 'em, buddy!" The patrons began putting the over-turned tables upright and a few clapped Alex on the shoul-der as they passed.

The punches had made his blistered hands bleed and the waitress was doing her best to wrap them with clean nap-kins when a sheriff's deputy came cautiously in and sur-veyed the damage. "Geeezuz, what's going on in here?"

One of the men with the bats pointed at him. "He started a fight in here, Officer."

But he was shouted down by the crowd. "No, Springer started it. Jumped him. The kid fought clean. Self-defense."

The man who had raised his mug in salute walked over to the deputy. "I saw the whole thing. He picked a fight with the Mexican kid." He jerked his head at Alex. "Kid just defended himself and did a damn good job of it, too."

A beefy gentleman with a familiar accent nodded in agreement. "I agree with him, Officer. I'll be happy to make a statement to that effect."

When it dawned on Alex where he had seen that unctuous face before, the flashback sent the room spinning around him. He had been at the board meeting at Synotech, the one Crittenden had asked him about. Same voice, same educated accent he had heard on Crittenden's answering machine, calling from Hong Kong. Sydney Harris, the ghost partner and ex-convict.

Alex was dead if the man recognized him, but there was no sign of it. Only a patronizing expression and lingering look that made him uncomfortably aware he was naked to the waist. The fact that the man had called him a Mexican kid was reassuring. There was no way he could connect an LA lawyer with this dark-skinned, unshaven cowboy.

"If I was you, buddy, I'd watch myself," the deputy said to Alex, coming only to his chin. "Clean up this mess in here and go on home. We don't tolerate drunk fights around here." He looked uncertain about his next step. "You want to swear out a complaint or anything, Miss Callie?"

With a wide smile, Callie put her hands on her hips. "I guess that won't really be necessary since nobody seems to think there's anything to complain about," she said. "But Larry is gonna be pissed about the broken furniture when I send him the bill."

After the deputy had left, Sydney Harris strolled over, holding out his hand. "Wonderful job, my boy. Wonderful! The name's Harris. Sydney Harris. Let me buy you a drink."

Something told him to avoid the offer at all costs, but there was no one closer to the company's overseas operations except MacPherson. Nevertheless, associating with him might be a two-edged sword that cut both ways. While Alex might get some information about Synotech's secret arms shipments, there was also the chance Harris would eventually recognize him.

As Alex pulled on his shirt, Darla came up and rubbed his shoulders. "Leave him alone, Uncle Sydney," she said, wrapping herself around Alex's waist. "I saw him first."

"I should have known you'd get your hands on this one,

Darling." Harris wasn't giving up easily. "Then how about both of you joining me at the Royal Gorge for a drink and a chat?" He looked around the bar which had resumed its high decibel clamor. "I could do with something a little more upscale."

"Sorry, Sydney, honey." Darla gave Harris a smile as perfect and as phony as a paste jewel. "Jimmy and I have a date tonight, don't we, Jimmy, baby?"

Harris sighed dramatically. "Another time then. Nice to have met you, Jimmy is it?"

"Yeah, Vargas. Jimmy Vargas." Darla answered for him, tugging on his arm. "Say hello and goodbye." She dragged him away. "We're on our way. Ta, ta."

Harris lifted his glass hopefully as they left. "Don't forget that drink, Jimmy. I might have a little deal for you."

"I'll bet he does. Don't worry about Uncle Sydney. He such an old fag," she added in a low voice. "That's why he hangs around here, chatting up the young guys. When your shirt got torn, he started drooling." With a giggle, Darla slipped her arm through his with a triumphant smile at Callie. "Sorry about the mess, Callie. Just send Larry the bill. His man started it, and if he has a problem with it, tell him to take it up with Springer."

The fury in the bartender's blue eyes was evident in a hostile stare. "Gee, thanks, Darla. Why don't you tell him? After all, the fight was over you."

"At least I'm worth it."

Darla pulled him along into the street. He desperately wanted to talk to Callie Murphy about her job at Sunrise. Darla, however, had other plans. "Why don't you come on over, Jimmy? You won't be sorry. After all, the night is young and so are we. Besides, when me and my friends leave, this place will be dead anyway." She leaned closer, pinning him down with her turquoise eyes. "I'm always so alone." Her voice had an appeal that was nearly genuine, and she tugged on his hand like a child. "Please come and keep me company. I don't want to be alone."

When he turned slightly, he saw the tall blonde girl waiting on a table just behind them. He met her eyes wanting to thank her for trying to intervene. She appeared to get the message with a little nod, and, after ducking a patron's wandering hands, busied herself cleaning tables.

Callie tried a firing the last shot. As they went out the door, she yelled, "Watch out, Twenty-Six. She's got a hunting license this season. And plenty of traps."

"Oh, piss off, Callie." Dropping his hand, Darla went back inside, one hand on her hip. For a moment, the little bar teetered on the brink of a cat fight. "You'd better go on home early tonight. Your bags are showing. Callie. This place is so boring, even the TV falls asleep. Anybody who wants to party, follow me."

Alex got Darla out before the two women tangled but the others swept him along to the street in a raucous wave of bad jokes and laughter.

Darla became a dancing flame in front of him, swinging her hair and hips like an image on a Balinese temple come to life. "Come on, Jimmy" she said. "I promise you, there's nothing else to do here unless we do it." She gripped his arm, drawing him closer under the streetlamp. "I just want to get to know you better." Her voice dropped to a whisper with a certain urgency about it. "I can't believe you whipped Springer. You know he was a pro boxer, don't you? You're my hero!"

He shrugged the victory off. "Think he's a little past it now. Still he landed a couple of good ones. You know how it is. New guy in town has to prove himself. Same everywhere."

'Yeah, I know. But tonight's tonight, baby." She jumped into a red truck with gold chrome trim. "Just follow me for a good time. You won't be sorry. I promise you."

Following Darla turned out to be more of a challenge than he had anticipated. Darla's stretchcab took off so fast, he had to stay at eighty just to keep her in sight.

The truck streaked up the two-lane highway, the noisy

caravan of partygoers behind her like a bright comet's tail. Alex's old Ford was the last to make it up a steep incline to a sprawling complex lit up like a space station. It seemed to float at the top of a plateau high above the sprawling valley. He didn't have to be told this was High Point but an enormous sign on the hillside lit by spotlights reminded him anyway.

Trying to get his bearings, he put the estate exactly below the ridge where Pierre Bighand and he had stood this morning. From this angle, it looked more like a hilltop fortress than someone's home.

Darla was standing in the drive way at the top, directing cars to park to one side of the complex. When Alex drove up, the parking lot was full and Darla ran to meet him. "This is home, if you want to call it a home," she called to him. "Park right behind me. I'm not going anywhere."

"Look, Darla, I'm not dressed for a party. There's blood on my shirt and I worked up a sweat fighting that guy Springer. Let me take a rain check."

"Oh, nobody dresses up for these things. In fact, they end up with less clothes on than they came in with. And I love the smell of sweat. Turns me on. I'll find a clean shirt for you, if you're so worried about it. Please come in, Jimmy. I think I love you."

Behind the main house, a pavilion with a vast pool hosted a country western band which struck up a fanfare of fiddles and banjos as Darla made a dramatic entrance, Followed by a congo line of her chums, she danced around the pool and then jumped in the shallow end. Following her like sheep over a cliff, the other guests jumped screaming into the pool fully clothed. Most all of them landed in the shallow end, wading around splashing each other. This was apparently a kind of tradition with Darla's crowd since, after a few minutes in the water, they melted mysteriously into the sumptuous pool house to change their wet clothes. Champagne was circulated among the guests by waitresses in western shirts. From what he could see, there was little else underneath.

A shout from a tall, graying man brought the dripping crowd out of the pool. "The bar's open, boys and girls. Tank up at this water hole 'cause the food's hottern' blazes."

Darla came up to him soaking wet, laughing at his obvious discomfort. He hadn't joined the others in the pool, but hung back near the door. "Don't worry, honey, I'm going to change into something that don't drip or smell like horses. Hang out with the gang until I come back."

Although they had all met at the Branding Iron in the first five minutes of joining them, Alex had to repeat his own name half a dozen times, simple as it was. It was a treatment reserved for outsiders and it suddenly dawned on him he was the only Hispanic in the room beside the waiters.

"Jimmy boy, we thought you'd been abducted by aliens. Come have a seat." A red-haired kid he had seen at the Branding Iron waved him to an empty chair at the table beside him. He had no idea what the young man's name was but joined the group who were all wet to the skin.

"Who's he?" he heard a girl ask her neighbor.

"Darla's hot tamale for the night. She found him in the Iron."

"She is such a kick. Picks up all the strays."

"What else? She's got more money than sense."

They were joined by the tall, graying man who took up an at-ease position in front of Alex and extended his hand. "I don't believe we've met, young man. My name is Ed Dalton. Colonel Edward Dalton."

Alex knew immediately, without being told, this must be the colonel Pierre had spoken of. Colonel Dalton of Dalton and Sutton. Alex was in dangerous territory, he knew. But as Pierre had said, danger was part of the journey.

Dalton let him know, in a few short sentences, he considered himself Darla's guardian, not only entitled to monitor her behavior, but to screen her friends. Keeping up an interrogation that would have made an intelligence officer proud, Dalton found out as much about Jimmy Vargas as Alex himself knew. If the conversation had gone any deeper than surface exchange of information, the colonel would have had him figured for a fraud.

Dalton read people the way people study the telephone directory, looking for the numbers he could call on and those he couldn't. The ones he couldn't call on automatically became his opponents. Uncle Miguel would have called him a master of the People Game. "I hear you're pretty fast with your fists. Where'd you learn how to fight?"

It was like getting into another fight, this time without blows. Dalton led and Alex countered. The whole table became hushed, listening for his reply. "I can defend myself, if that's what you mean."

"I think there's a place here for somebody like you, Mr. Vargas. You looking for a job?" The colonel rattled the ice in his glass and a passing waiter refilled it with whiskey as if on signal.

Alex played it cool, even though working for Dalton and Sutton was a break he hadn't even counted on. Jimmy Vargas would want to know what the catch was. There was always a catch for men like Vargas.

"Depends. I'm working at the Turner's until Mr. Turner gets better. I don't know how long it will be."

Darla rescued him from the inquisition. "I see Uncle Ed's got you pinned down and hog-tied, poor baby." She was dressed in something like a long sarong slit up the side to her tanned hip. Above that was only a bikini bra. The rest of the bikini was probably under the skirt, but the point was to guess. Darla could change the focus of a conversation just by what she was wearing, very much as Chelsea could. It was a talent both women played to the hilt to redirect the conversation in favor of something they wanted.

Her appearance couldn't have come at a better moment. She grabbed his arm. "C'mon, Uncle Eddie, let me have him back, now that you've found out he's not on the FBI's list of the Ten Most Wanted."

"Just checking." The corners of Dalton's mouth turned up, posing as a smile. "Run along and have a good time. Nice meeting you, Vargas. Keep in touch, now."

Within an hour, Darla's intense interest in him drew a great deal of notice among the men in her circle. Like a pack of dogs protecting their territory, they drifted over while Darla entertained them with the story of Alex's fight with Duke Cooper. No one noticed him slip away and take cover with the Ferguson brothers. Their dip in the pool seemed to have made them sober enough to drink even more.

"You got some place I can hide?"

The Ferguson brothers, Jared and Clint, made room for him at their table where a semi-coherent argument was underway. The brothers seemed to be closer to Darla than her more sophisticated friends. They supported every frenetic search for entertainment she came up with, almost as if vying for her attention. Sons of a local rancher, the Fergusons occupied their time hunting, drinking, and comparing feats involving prowess with girls or horses.

After a six-pack of beer, the Ferguson brothers were friends with anyone, although freckle-faced, gregarious Jared appeared less judgmental than his narrow lipped brother Clint. Clint, however, seemed to the real source of information and a little less drunk than Jared.

"Any good hunting around here?" Alex figured it was a good opener, given the arguments centered on guns and shooting.

"Depends what you hunt."

That brought a laugh from Clint's fan club of young girls until he shot them a hooded glance. Ferguson tilted his long neck beer bottle to his lips, but Alex noticed he was measuring every sip. A careful man, nothing like his affable brother.

"You hunt? Something else besides ass and money, that is."

Alex played dumb over the reference to Darla. "I was just wondering if there were any Bighand sheep left up there in the mountains."

Jared and Clint erupted into a chorus of hoots, lost in the big amps of the Sutton's night-club-quality Karaoke system. "He wonders if there's any Bighand sheep up there."

After the laughter died down, Jared was the first to get it together. "This is the home of Poseidon, baby. I wouldn't hunt nothing up there. Or you could be the big game."

Clint's immobile face shifted itself into a frown. "Shut up, Jared, you ain't supposed to talk about it."

Trying to look unimpressed, Alex played Jimmy Vargas to the max. "That's okay. I've never heard of it, anyway."

It worked wonders and they all relaxed, except for exchanging looks around the table.

Clint flicked his bottle. "Naturally, you wouldn't. I take it you hunt, Jimbo?"

Jared got enthused immediately. "Yeah, you ever hunted in the mountains before?"

Clint rolled his eyes at his brother as if he were talking to an idiot. "Still don't get the message, do you? Shut up. Jared. Go take a piss or something."

Jared's face flushed, nearly matching his hair. "What's such a big deal about it? It's only a game."

"Sure, I hunt." Alex had gone hunting in the Sierras with Uncle Miguel a time or two. Nothing like these boys who had a rifle in their hand at twelve. "I wouldn't call it a game, though. Going after some game, that's what I'd say. Unless you've got something else in mind."

Clint sat back. "We're talking New Age hunting here, man. With night-vision lenses and rubber bullets." He flicked invisible dust off the toe of his custom boots with a linen napkin from the table.

"Oh, playing at hunting. Like paintball stuff? Haven't done that since I was a kid."

Clint rankled at the perfect put-down.

Subtlety wasn't Jared's strength, it was easy to see. He had to jump in with both feet to prove his manhood to a stranger. "It's more than that, it's a game of survival of the fittest. See, there's one real bullet among the rubber ones. If you don't keep moving, you can catch it."

All the guests looked at Clint for his reaction. "Shut up, Jared. You don't know anything." His look at his brother was a warning. "He don't know anything."

"Sounds a lot like Russian Roulette."

"Hell, no, it's Western Roulette." Clint was quick to jump to the defense of local industry. "Colonel Dalton says the military does it all the time, only we just don't know it. Keeps everybody on their toes. And he should know. He's seen action in the whole Middle-East war, Iraq, Afghanistan."

Again, Jared chimed in. "Yeah, he was working undercover for military intelligence when some war lord took him prisoner in the mountains tortured him 'til he and Roberts escaped. Shot their way out."

"Damned towel-heads." Clint gave his bottle a savage push, sending it into the glasses crowding the table. "Coming over here making trouble. We ought to nuke 'em and be done with it."

The brothers Ferguson launched into a well-rehearsed campaign for self-defense. "Next they'll be coming over here trying to take our land away. That's why we need to get ready, right, Jimbo?" Jared nodded at Alex as if expecting him to contribute something.

Alex stood up and pushed back his chair. "In that case, I need another beer."

Clint leaned back in his chair. "What if they come over here and take us over? The Red Chinese and the rest of 'em? You just going to sit back and let 'em move in your house."

Alex shrugged. "When the time comes, I'll fight, I guess. If somebody really came over and tried to invade us, then

I'd fight, sure. But I don't t see it happening any time soon. Besides, they like burgers and fries over there."

His apparent neutrality clearly annoyed Clint who set out to convince him in earnest. "That's the whole point." he said, leaning forward. "See, that's what the spy planes are for. To detect any kind of spy activity in the States. We know there're even Commies running the government in Washington right now. We know that for a point of fact. You want to know who owns just about half of the high dollar real estate in America? The fucking Chinese and the Russians, that's who."

"I don't know." Alex gestured at the lavish pool area with marble columns and an indoor waterfall. "Can't get more high dollar than this."

The Ferguson brothers exchanged looks that asked and answered an unspoken question. "C'mon," Clint said, a secretive smile crawling around his lips. "Let's see if you're ready, Vargas. Let's play Real Thrill, everybody." He stood up, swaying slightly on his feet. "Real Thrill, gang! We're going to introduce my friend Vargas here to Diamondback the right way!"

CHAPTER 17

After shedding her sarong and dancing solo around the pool, Darla seemed to have disappeared into the house, no doubt so drunk she fell asleep somewhere. "Sorry, but I just came here because Darla invited me along. Got to get back to the Turner's place before it gets too late. I'll take a rain-check on this game, though. Sounds like fun."

What it sounded like was a bunch of drunks running around with guns, one of which was loaded. Darla's playmates played for keeps. "See you guys later."

Clint raised his bottle in salute. "Sure. Anybody who sleeps with Darla is like a brother to us, even if he's a Mexican."

"That's cozy. I never thought of it that way."

Something about the drunken fire in Ferguson's narrow blue eyes was a warning. He was pushing for a fight.

Jared started to intervene but at a glance from his brother, thought the better of it.

Clint kept it up. "See Darla's real taken with you, Jimbo. Which means, if you're going to hang around with her and us, you got to be part of it, you get the drift? Like you got to fit in. After all, it's one big country made up of all types."

"Hey, I think the boy's just being modest," Jared said, clapping Alex on the shoulder in an awkward effort to divert Clint's attention. "Let's go see if he knows a butt from a barrel."

"He sure knows Darla's butt from one," Clint said. "C'mon, let's go outside, Jimbo. Show us what you know about guns."

"Hey, we're not going to shoot it out over Darla, are we?"

That brought another hee-haw session among the listeners until Clint finally collected himself. "Goddamn, that's a good one. Shoot it out over Darla? No, son. Hell, Darla'll show you a good time but she ain't worth getting shot for. Shoot it out over Darla? That's a hoot."

Alex followed the pair outside to the veranda. As they passed the other tables, Clint collected empty bottles and glasses, continuing the conversation.

"Besides, around here we've all slept with her at one time or another, right, Jared? But she'll marry one of us some day, you can count on it. We got too much in common, you know. Same race, same class."

Outside, the Fergusons set the bottles up on the veranda wall, facing the Devil's Ladder ridge. From this vantage point, Alex could see lights at the foot of the mountain, and the movement of vehicles down in the yard of the plant. He glanced at his watch. Though it was nearly midnight, the place was lit up like a county fair, he didn't want to leave. Not until he found out more about what Dalton and Sutton were up to.

"Light's not the best out here. But good enough for the really fun stuff. That happens in the dark. Here take your pick." Clint produced two twenty Magnum pistols, lovingly polished to a leaden shine.

Something warned him to make his excuses, but as he suspected they would, the Fergusons weren't buying any. It was a setup to make him look like a greenhorn.

"Look, I'd rather not go shooting off somebody's balcony. It's kind of close range and I'm not that good with handguns."

A crowd had gathered in the doorway behind him and they booed their disapproval.

"Now, you're not going to be a bad sport, are you, Jimbo?" Clint was needling him and his dislike was barely disguised.

Alex did what he always did, he took the bait. "Okay, whenever you're ready, then. We have to make this fast."

Surprise replaced contempt in Ferguson's face. "You don't want to practice a little bit?"

Alex shrugged off the suggestion. "Why? Do you?"

"Hell, no, bud. Here goes." Clint took aim at the bottles on the ledge, but beer had clouded his aim and he shot only three out of five.

As smartly as a pin boy in a bowling alley, Jared lined them up again. "Your turn, Vargas."

Four beers had also altered Alex's own vision somewhat but he had always been a good shot. The men in his family had taken him hunting every summer since he was old enough to carry a gun.

Firing steadily, he took out all five. There was a slight hush and then sporadic applause.

"This boy knows his way around women and guns, that's clear to see," someone said from the doorway in a distinctly British accent. He turned to see Sydney Harris standing in the doorway. The mysterious Sydney Harris, former federal prison inmate, now Synotech executive, held a martini in his hand. =

"Well done, young man. Smart shooting."

"Hellfire," Jared remarked, "he didn't miss a one!"

Clint looked as if he were sucking lemons. "Real good."

"He definitely needs to come hunting with us," Jared said. "We got this little club, Jimbo. Maybe you'd like to join up, right, Clint."

"A hunting club? Sure." Alex played along, waiting for Clint's next move.

"You could call it that." Clint gave Alex a practiced, lopsided grin designed to be appear genuine. "Except we don't always hunt animals."

"Yeah, sometimes it's people." The buzz around the table stopped as if someone had pulled a switch. Jared looked around puzzled. "What?"

"Shut up, Jared. You talk too much when you're drunk," another man with a saddle leather face said.

Jared stopped sweeping up the broken glass on the veranda. "Well, it's the truth, ain't it?"

Clint bridged the ensuing silence. "Hey, you guys," he yelled at the uneasy onlookers. "How about a game of Thrill? What do you say?"

The suggestion was greeted with raucous cheers and the young people swarmed outside, following Clint down the balcony stairs on to the lighted lawn.

Alex stepped out of the way to let them pass, but he noticed Harris was still watching him. Could he possibly have guessed his identity? The thought sent him down the stairs after Jared insisted he join them on the lawn.

"Hey, Jimbo, you coming?"

"I don't know." Pretending hesitation, he moved out of the direct light of the balcony and shook his head. "If this is one of those weekend warrior things, shooting paintballs at the enemy and the losers buy the beer, then I pass."

The younger Ferguson glanced over his shoulder at the guests milling around Clint. "Hey, we're not amateurs. We compete all over the country."

Surprisingly, Sydney Harris took up the defense. "Mr. Vargas is probably not into frivolous pastimes, Jared. He works very hard for a living. Besides, I'd like to talk to him privately for a moment. Now, run along before your brother gets a knot in his tail or whatever that quaint expression is."

Jared knew he was overruled. "Okay, then. Maybe later."

"Exactly," Harris said. "Some other time."

Jared took the hint and disappeared down the stairs.

Alex kept his face averted in the shadows. "Thanks. I've got the feeling they would've ganged up on me."

"No doubt, my boy No doubt. Like jackals do with lions." Harris stepped out on the veranda, carefully avoiding the broken glass, and stared down at the lawn, where several groups of both sexes were opening boxes of paintball guns. "It seems so odd young people would want to play at war and killing, when my generation did all they could do to avoid that."

"Seems kind of funny somebody would have the equipment around to let them play war."

Alex wished he hadn't said it the moment the comment was out, but Harris simply nodded. He had an aristocratic air about him, but his gaze often slipped away in the middle of a conversation. His son, Fred, who had replaced him in the firm, was a pale imitation of his father's distinctive presence.

"Indeed," Harris answered and then was quiet a moment. "Let's talk about you, Mr. Vargas, for a moment. That was quite an impressive feat with the pistol a moment ago, and your encounter in the bar earlier tells me you are equally adept at defending yourself."

"I grew up tough." Alex became Jimmy Vargas, avoiding eye contact, ashamed before someone speaking perfect English. "You had to fight to survive where I lived."

"I understand. Which is precisely the reason I would like to offer you a job. That is, my friend, Ed Dalton and I would like to offer you a position with our company. We work together, you see." Harris was about as transparent as the smoke from his pipe. "Security work. Bodyguard type thing. I do extensive traveling in third world countries. It's not terribly safe at the moment and you can't trust just anyone. We do a lot of business in South America and I thought, since you undoubtedly understand the language, it would be the perfect opportunity. We'd pay very well and give you some professional training to boot. We have some former mercenaries in our employ who know the ropes. Sixty-five thousand a year to start. How does that sound?"

Jimmy Vargas would have given a body part for sixty-five grand. He whistled softly. "Sixty-five K. I'm in."

It was the break he'd been waiting for, the inside track to

Dalton and Sutton. Then he thought of Marisa Turner, her face dominated by tearful eyes as she thanked him for staying. Rudolfo could only stay through next week and then he and the crew had to move on.

"But what about the Turners? I promised Mrs. Turner, I'd stay on until Mr. Turner could take over again. I don't like to leave a lady high and dry like that."

For a moment, Harris looked puzzled. "The Turners? Ah, of course, the people who had the fire at their place. Terrible thing, that. How is the poor man doing? I understand you're the hero who rescued him from the burning wreckage of the barn." Suddenly, he notice Alex's left hand, still bandaged from the burns. "I say, that fight must have hurt your hand! You're quite a Titan, Mr. Vargas. Your concern does you credit, but don't worry. Let me arrange some help for the Turners. It will be my pleasure after the terrible loss of their daughter and now Mr. Turner in such wretched condition."

Either Harris was a consummate actor or he was genuinely affected by the family's misfortune, because Alex found himself believing the man.

"There you guys are. I thought I told you to leave him alone, Uncle Sydney. He's mine." For the second time during the evening, Darla stepped through the French doors, this time in something short and filmy, clinging to her as if she were still damp from the pool. He smiled, thinking how Chelsea would have envied her long slim legs in stiletto heels "There you are, Jimmy. I was right! Uncle Syd had you cornered. Let him go, now. He's got to dance with me."

Harris smiled almost wistfully. "I remember when you used to ask me what I had in my pockets," he said. "Now, you ask me to give you a young man. Well, take him along. He's a fine fellow."

They left him staring at the mountain from the balcony as if he were suddenly faced with an awful truth. Ten years ago, Sydney Harris would have thought nothing of climbing the Matterhorn or going on a white rhino safari in Nepal. He hunted big cats in an African nation where the endangered species list was ignored.

However, in the world of finance, the same risky behavior had met with disaster, since he was risking other people's money to the tune of billions of dollars, pounds, and yen. It put him away in prison where he lay awake all night to afraid to sleep, listening to men howl like the animals he hunted. Maybe that was what Harris might be thinking as he stared into the darkness at the Devil's Ladder.

Meanwhile, two other men had joined Colonel Dalton at his table beside the dance floor. Alex recognized Springer from the fight in the bar. Although he had only seen them briefly, the man's size and build reminded him of one of the thugs looking for him at O'Hara's.

The other man was cold-eyed and stocky with a roosterish arrogance in the snap of his fingers and incline of his head. Alex guessed immediately he was Larry Sutton, Darla's older brother and his host.

CHAPTER 18

When Darla pulled him out on the dance floor, Sutton gave him a long, disapproving stare that would have been an insult in any social setting. Then he pushed back his chair and strode up to them.

Without waiting to be introduced, he demanded, "So you're Vargas. *Hablas Espagnol?*"

Alex kept his smile cool. "Probably not as well as you do."

From the edge of the dance floor, he heard the Colonel chuckle. "Well said, young man. He's pretty smart, Larry."

Sutton addressed his partner over his shoulder, keeping his eyes on Carreras. "Pretty damn smart for a ranch hand. You the fellow who saved T. C. Turner, aren't you? One of the day laborers?"

Alex felt the sting of inferiority in the term. Larry Sutton was an expert in dishing it out. "That's right." His pride made him get careless. "Mrs. Turner asked me to stay on and help out."

"That must be a real break for you, then. Getting a steady job."

Alex shrugged off the inference. "It'll give me a few tips on the ranching business."

"Oh, it will?" Sutton was amused by pretense from a ranch hand and closed in for the kill. "A few tips, huh? I've got a good one for you, Mr. Vargas. Stay out of it. The ranch business won't make you anything but a lot poorer than you already are. So you won't have any reason to stay on, will you?"

Alex felt his Latin temper was melting the edges of his studied cool. "I appreciate the advice, Mr. Sutton." He relaxed and took his time, pointedly looking around the extravagant pavilion where chefs in tall, white hats were preparing a buffet. "But if this is poor, then I can handle the ranching business."

Darla laughed and clapped her hands. "Bravo, Jimmy! C'mon, Larry, leave us alone! We want to have fun!"

Her brother studied her dress with an undisguised look of disapproval. "I thought women only wore things like that in cheap bars, Darla."

"I wouldn't know, Larry. That just shows where you been hanging out." Darla's smile turned deprecating as she stared at her brother. "Only thing cheap about this dress is, it don't have a zipper. Now, let's dance, Jimmy. And leave these old men to spit and chew."

"The young man has balls, Mike." Colonel Dalton toasted Alex's one-up-man-ship with a raised glass as Sutton retreated back to the table. "I like that. Never back down from a put-down, Mr. Vargas. That'll only cost you later." His greenish eyes glinted above the rim of his glass.

Alex returned his gaze steadily. "Cost me what?"

The reply was soft. "Why, the chance to get even, of course. What better reason is there?"

Sutton was not amused by the compliment and left the group abruptly, followed by Springer. The colonel glanced at the retreating pair and grinned. "Kind of like the dog of the same name," he said. "Right at his master's heels. Mr. Harris has spoken to you about our little offer?"

Alex nodded, doing the Jimmy Vargas impression. "Yes, sir."

"And you're thinking about it?"

Darla clung to him as if she were flaunting her power to do as she pleased. "Oh, talk business later, Uncle Ed. Right now, he's mine." She dragged him away to dance. "Are you really thinking about working for Uncle Ed?" she asked the moment they were together. "Because I want you to, Jimmy. So we can be together. Please, please, please."

There was something close to fear in her urgency and Alex wondered what this mountain princess knew that frightened her. Her frenetic behavior reminded him of LA kids on uppers and speed. She was never tired, even though she couldn't have had more than a few hours' sleep the previous night. In spite of the lavish buffet, she never touched a bite of food other than a bit of cheese here, an olive there. Still her energy seemed to accelerate as the night wore on. Her wide eyes looked even brighter, and her behavior more out of touch with reality. He knew the sign of cocaine addiction. It was an affliction of their generation and more widespread in circles that could afford the drug.

Finally, he slipped away, using a trip to the bathroom as an excuse. He thought he could easily let himself out the front way and hitch a ride back to town. But finding anything in the Sutton mansion could be a sobering experience. He went through the terrace doors into the living room area where the vastness of living space made him pause just inside. The entire back of the house was glass with a panoramic view of the distant mountain range. The house fronted on the valley below where Diamondback sprawled to the North, obscured in a rancid cloud of agricultural dust.

The expensive appointments of the room were devoted to an upscale version of ancestor worship. Fine paintings and bronzes from Europe disguised the humble beginnings of the Sutton family fortune like jewels on a madam. The founder of the empire, Chester Sutton, who had come to the region as a peddler, was portrayed as a white-haired tycoon in three piece dignity. Photographs of subsequent Suttons who had ruthlessly expanded his prospecting venture into an empire were pictured in order of financial worth. The last photograph was relatively recent. He figured the graying executive in the picture must have been Larry and Darla's father.

According to the brass plaque, Calloway Sutton had been fifty-seven when he died.

Turning down a long hallway which seemed to branch into more rooms, Alex encountered another painting of Chester Sutton making the old miner look like a banker with bowler hat and cane, an obedient greyhound at his feet. Just beyond it there was a door with a GENTS sign.

He was heading toward it when he heard a familiar voice somewhere down the hall. He froze and listened.

"Poseidon said, you idiot!"

Alex edged closer toward a sliding door where the man's voice was becoming louder, punctuated with determined profanity.

"Dammit, I don't give a shit about matching serial numbers! Synotech needs the stuff as of late yesterday. Don't give me this song and dance about security after you already promised MacPherson the shipment a week ago. It should've been to Manila by now."

The distinctive nasal twang immediately identified Larry Sutton. At the mention of Macpherson's name, Alex stood by the door holding his breath to hear better.

"It needs to be crated as hospital equipment, understand? Hospital equipment, you dumb ass! Do I have to spell it out? Like X-ray machines. Big stuff. Hell, I don't know. The biggest stuff in a hospital. Magnetic radiation imagers or something. Just get them crated up. No, in parts, stupid. How in hell are you going to crate a jet? Send it to Macy's for gift-wrapping? If you don't know, get somebody who's done this before, dammit. And make sure the bill of lading says Hospital Equipment, you got it? We've got clearance for it." There was a pause and then, "By tonight. I don't give a damn about serial numbers. That's your end of the deal. Make 'em up out of your head. Get 'em off your Wheaties box tops. I don't care. Just have the shipment ready for Synotech pickup by midnight tonight, okay? The entire Eye system. Don't leave one screw out or Freddie Wu will have Poseidon's bad boys breathing up both our asses like bloodhounds. And I do mean blood."

The slam of a receiver propelled Alex past the doorway toward the bathroom, but it was too late. He had almost reached the end of the hall when he collided with Springer.

"Looking for something?" The former boxer was even uglier close up. His face, pulverized by years of blunt force, had taken on the appearance of a rubber Halloween mask.

Alex tensed to defend himself. "Where's the bathroom? I couldn't find one outside."

"By the pool house." Springer didn't look convinced. "Go on back out there."

Alex made an effort to look distressed. "Sorry, don't think I'm going to make it. Can't I use the one in here?" He nodded at the Gents door.

"Who in hell's out there?" Larry Sutton came to the door of his office and faced Alex with repulsion. "You! What're you doing in the house?"

"Says he's looking for the terlet." Springer grabbed Alex's shoulder like a steel clamp. "I told him go outside. He's gotta go bad."

"I don't care if you wet your pants, Pancho." Sutton clearly enjoyed the moment of total power with Alex pinned between the two men. "Hired help always use the outdoor facilities. And let me tell you this. Let this be the last time I catch you in my house, Vargas. I don't like the fact that my sister's taste runs to ranch hands, especially Beaners. So don't let me find you in Diamondback when the sun goes down tomorrow, understand? Just say adios to Mrs. Turner and get the hell out of here, understand?"

Alex considered hitting Sutton, but the enjoyment of punching him out was not worth facing the law just yet. "Okay, this is your backyard, Mr. Sutton, and you make the rules. But I'll bet anything Darla makes her own decisions about who she sees and where she goes."

Sutton only managed to reply in a whisper. "Get Macho Man out of here before I kill him!"

He snapped his fingers and Alex felt himself being lifted almost off his feet by one arm.

Springer's viselike grip threatened to separate the muscle from the bone. "C'mon, Beaner. You can use the terlet outside. I'll show you. Then beat it off the property like Mr. Sutton said. If I was you, Beaner, I wouldn't make Mr. Sutton no madder. He's king around here. It ain't healthy, you get me? Be smart and don't go out with his sister no more."

Alex tried an end run. "But I need to tell Miss Sutton goodbye. She's going to wonder what happened to me."

"I'll tell her youse got called away sudden-like. Now, get out of here."

"Leaving so soon, Mr. Vargas?" Except for a sinuous curl of pipe smoke, Sydney Harris was almost invisible in a massive leather chair. "How about one for the road? Let him go, Springer. I assume he can get along without assistance."

Springer dropped his arm, looking confused by having two orders at once. "But Mr. Sutton said—"

"I don't care, let him alone, Springer." Dalton's voice rang with unquestionable authority. The lanky colonel leaned in the doorway across the room, drink in hand. "Go find something else to do. Now." He nodded at Alex. "Have a seat, son. Springer's kind of over enthusiastic about his job."

Alex should have felt relieved, but being alone with these two powerful men was anything but a relief. "You can say that again. But I better not hang around anymore tonight. Mr. Sutton really don't like me."

"Have you considered our offer any further?" Dalton stepped down into the enormous room and folded his lean body into a chair. "Because if I were you, I'd make a quick decision. When Larry doesn't like somebody, he can be real hard to get along with. You kind of have to watch your back, right, Sydney?"

Harris was sinking into a stupor of alcohol, his way of avoiding facing what he had become and might have been.

"Right you are, Ed. Watch your back, my boy. Especially among such company as we."

"I thought I'd find you in the Man Cave." It was his night to be rescued by women. For the second time in the evening, Darla wrested him from the two men, who if they weren't aware of his real identity now, would have the information at their fingertips by tomorrow. "No, you don't, Uncle Eddy. He's mine, and you're not getting your hands on this one. You got Benjie Mason and Duke Cooper. Now this one's all mine."

Dalton chuckled through his cigar smoke. "I didn't think you needed any more boys to play with, baby. You've already got the Ferguson boys. Besides, nothing wrong with getting the boy some gainful employment is there, sugar? But okay, run on and we'll talk later when you've made up your mind we're the best offer you'll ever get. Remember what I warned you about though."

As they started to dance, Darla moved her perfect body in time with the music and stuck out her tongue invitingly. Alex ignored the invitation, aware of Larry Sutton watching them intently. "You'd better chill out, Darla. Your brother really doesn't like me."

"That's his problem. I hate him, and that doesn't seem to bother him. His hating you shouldn't bother you." She put two fingers between her lips and whistled at the DJ. "Hey, play something slow for a change." Throwing her arms around Alex, she ran her hands up and down his sides. She was so tall, their noses touched. "I love tall, skinny men. I'm never letting you go, Jimbo, baby. I said you're my hero and I meant it."

He put his arm gently around her waist and set her back four inches. "And Dalton? What's he all about?"

"Uncle Ed? Just an old soldier. In the Middle East doing something for the government for several years. Got captured by some kind of rebels. Made him kind of...funny, you know. Like suspicious of everybody. He was a friend of my daddy's before he died." A shadow was passed through

Darla's exotic eyes. She glanced uneasily back at the bar where Sutton jerked his head at her. "See, Uncle Ed grew up around here. He's a lot younger than my dad was. He was in the air force so when he got out, he came back to McTigue Air Base." She nodded at the foothills. "Just over those mountains. When my daddy died, he kind of took over helping Larry run the business. They're business partners."

"'What kind of business is your brother in? All this doesn't come from ranching, I know that."

Darla shrugged as if she didn't want to talk about it. "Mining or something. I don't know what they do and I don't care. Something up there in that old mine where my dad was killed. I hate the place and I hate Larry's guts, but I guess it's okay as long as my bills get paid." Looking back, the shadow was gone, her face lit with naughtiness like a spoiled child. "Now, let's forget about it, honey! We've got to get to know each other much, much better. You dance like a dream."

"More like a nightmare." He tried one more question, knowing he was losing by fishing for information. "So, is your mom around?"

As she did when asked anything she didn't want to answer, she flipped her auburn hair back and looked at him through a veil of eyelashes. "We're just poor little orphans, Larry and me. My mother ran away when I was four and I never saw her again. His mama died and I heard my mama died, but I don't know. My father died ten years ago when the mine caved in on him. That's it." In spite of his resolve to keep his distance, Alex held her a little closer. The subtle movement wasn't lost on Larry Sutton who rarely took his eyes off them.

A whooping crowd of guests poured up the steps and chased each other around the patio, firing paintball guns that exploded small pellets of paint when they hit their target. Sutton interrupted his conversation with Harris and

Dalton to go to the patio doors and order them off the terrace.

"Get the hell out of here and keep that stuff down in the bushes or go home. Better yet, go home right now! Clear out, all of you!"

Darla immediately rushed to her friends' defense and a screaming argument between brother and sister developed. Finally, Clint Ferguson and Ed Dalton intervened, pulling the two gently apart as if they were accustomed to settling quarrels. Alex didn't miss the whispered exchange between the two. He didn't have to wait long to find out what it was about.

"Hey, Darla," Clint shouted, "get Romeo over there to join us this time. He acts like he's kind of wimpy about virtual sports. Maybe he just wants to look like a cowboy, not be one."

It was another open challenge. Sutton's venom became poorly disguised as gracious hospitality. "Hey, great idea, Clint! Why don't you take our guest, Mr. Vargas here, out to the shooting range and show him around. Maybe he'd like to do a little shooting with you."

Everyone cheered as Alex was dragged and pushed down the terrace stairs into a floodlit area covered with bushes and clumps of fir trees.

"Welcome to our world, Vargas," he heard someone say from the terrace above him. "Now, let's see if you survive in it!"

Colonel Dalton was leaning on the railing, raising his glass in salute like an emperor to a gladiator on whom he had placed a large bet.

The group was divided up into platoons and lined up to receive paint ball pistols and bands of ammunition from white-coated waiters. Guards were posted along the course's perimeter in all-terrain vehicles and the area nearest the patio was floodlit with banks of lights.

The platoons boarded a fleet of all-terrain vehicles to climb the rough hillside toward the ridge where thick forest formed an apron to the foothills. When they stopped just at the edge of the floodlights, the platoon leader shouted the order to attack over a megaphone. With murderous shouts, the players leaped out and raced toward the ridge which enveloped them in darkness.

Alex followed Jared Ferguson into the last of uncleared timber left below the ridge. Orange flags marked the course as it climbed a rocky hillside toward the Devil's Ladder face of the ridge, disappearing into the last of the virgin forests skirting the foothills. One of the all-terrain vehicles assigned to their unit took Jared's group up to the starting line where the others in their platoon had assembled.

"Hey, Jared, wait up a second!" Alex caught up with the only person who had at least been cordial to him. "What are we supposed to be doing? Who's the enemy and how do we recognize them?"

"Yellow bands." Jared sounded slightly out of breath. "Shoot at yellow bands only, okay? Stay close to me." Then, in the growing darkness, Jared melted into the thicket.

Losing track of him quickly in the impenetrable dark, Alex kept moving, following the sound of crashing of feet through the underbrush. Occasionally, he heard the pop-pop of paintballs and cries of "Man Down!" coming from somewhere in the dark. Negotiating his way through so many trees was only going to get him lost and he decided the best defense was to stay crouched among the rocks at the base of the slope. From there, he could get a better view of the course. Making his way to the upper part of the thicket, he squatted in some thick mesquite, waiting to see who emerged from the dark line of trees below him.

Beneath the waning moon, the ridge appeared to be the craggy profile of a fallen prehistoric behemoth. Presently, the shadowy forms of men passed him, fanning out as if they had been trained to scale the ridge. The steady popping of guns followed from the thicket area and a few of the men fell suddenly, hitting the ground with curses.

"Geezuz," he heard a voice call out just above him. "Somebody's firing real ammo. Hey, who's playing the Real Thrill game? You didn't say that was it. Get the medic, I've been hit!"

Just then, Alex ducked as something whistled by and tore into a nearby tree, splintering wood into his face. A bullet chewed up the tree at his back and he knew he was in trouble. He dropped flat until the firing stopped. Finally, he got to his feet and touched the tree where a deep groove still warm and oozing sap creased the bark. It was certainly no rubber bullet could have torn up a tree like that. He was being targeted for a kill and he had to make a move.

Taking advantage of the darkness, he darted up the ridge, stumbling to his knees over rocks and the stubble of bushes. Behind him, bullets tore up the ground at his heels. Someone had an infrared telescopic lens.

"Look at the beaner go!"

A dark figure emerged from the thicket behind him. Throwing himself behind a rocky outcrop, Alex saw the moonlight glinting on the copper-colored hair of Clint Ferguson.

"It's a flying burrito!"

He was coming straight up the hill toward Alex's hiding place when a shout stopped him.

"What the hell? This isn't Real Thrill! Knock it off, Ferguson!"

A helicopter's searchlight swept across the hillside just as Jared popped out of the thicket and came up the hill at an oblique angle. Seeing him coming, Alex shouted a warning that was lost in the rattle of gunfire.

Either Jared didn't hear him or he didn't take the warning seriously. The helicopter pinned him with the search light, struggling up the hill side, his freckled face was contorted as he shouted battle cries.

"Jared, get down, damn it!" Alex gave away his position and stood up yelling the warning. Jared stopped and turned toward his voice just as Clint fired in the same direction.

With a choking cry, Jared fell forward, rolling downhill.

Running up and sprawling next to his brother, Clint cradled Jared's head in his hands. "Jesus God, Jared, get up. I didn't mean to! Get up, Jared!" He tried to pull his brother upright but Jared's head lolled onto his chest. "My God, somebody call nine-one-one."

Alex slid down the hill beside them, pushing Clint away from his lifeless brother. "Give him some air and let him down real easy. He's losing blood."

But Clint beat at him with his fists until someone dragged him off. "You get away! You should've died, Beaner! I should have shot you!"

Ignoring Clint's blows and kicks, Alex took off his shirt and twisted it into a tourniquet. In the pale floodlights, he saw blood spouting from the base of Jared's neck where it met the collarbone. Gently, he applied pressure while another pair of hands applied the tourniquet across his shoulder. Jared moaned and rolled his eyes.

"Stay with us, Jared. Help's on the way, buddy," Alex whispered.

One of the guards rolled up an ATV and jumped out with a walkie-talkie. "How bad's he hit?" he asked laconically.

"Looks real close to the coronary artery. He's bleeding like hell." Alex kept the pressure on Jared's neck near the wound. "Get a doctor fast."

"Bring the chopper in, Doc," the guard said into the walkie-talkie. "On the double. Kid's been shot. Okay, here they come. Let me take over, guys. I got combat medic training."

The guard kneeled and replaced Alex's hands on the gushing wound. Getting back to his feet, Alex felt the chilly mist of midnight settling down like a curtain over the mountain.

Above them, from somewhere on the Devil's Ladder, a helicopter rose skyward, coming toward them with a searchlight playing across the terrain. They watched as it passed overhead and landed on a helipad on High Point's grounds.

In minutes, a team of paramedics raced up the hill toward them with a stretcher followed by Darla screaming Jared's name at the top of her lungs. With the paintball soldiers standing around, holding their weapons, the scene had all the eerie impression of a battlefield evacuation of the wounded.

When the chopper had left, the now sober guests gathered before the castle-sized fireplace in High Point's great room.

"I want to know what happened this evening." Looking out of place in faded jeans and work shirt, Joe Ferguson appeared poised for a fight, murder in his eyes. Ferguson was a local rancher as his father before him and apparently not one of Sutton's rich allies. His red-haired sons, however, had been given all the advantages of money and privilege including an education. Joe had dropped out of high school to help his father and uncles on their vast cattle ranch.

The subdued party guests stared at the floor or at each other. Some wore clothes stiff with paint, others stood in dripping swimsuits still clutching their drinks.

Larry Sutton took command of the investigation, his arms crossed, legs apart in the center of the room. "First, I want to know who in hell was using real bullets out there." His eyes rested on Alex. "Nobody we know would do anything like that. But maybe somebody we don't know would."

Alex caught some incredulous looks among the young people. He quickly intercepted Sutton's challenge. "All I know is, someone was shooting at me and Jared stopped one of the bullets when I stood up to warn him."

"How do we know it wasn't you doing the shooting? You're the only one we don't know around here." Sutton moved toward him, still keeping the strategic distance that didn't emphasize the difference in their heights. Someone had lent Alex a shirt but his jeans were spattered with Jared's blood.

"Because this guy here—" someone said from the group at the fireplace. "—he was ahead of Jared, up the hill." His defender stepped forward and Alex recognized the man who had helped him with Jared. "He couldn't have shot him from that angle because the bullet entered Jared's neck from the side. Besides, he saved Jared's life. And I saw him coming down the hill and pushing Clint away. Clint came from out of the thicket on the same side as the bullet. I saw him fire and I heard him tell this guy here—" He nodded at Alex. "—that he meant the bullet for him."

Joe Ferguson swung around to stare at his son who was staring at the floor in shock. "What do you have to say now, Clint? Was that real ammo you were firing? From a real gun? Come on out with it. You know Smitty here don't lie."

Clint continued staring at the floor, his jaw set as if he were gritting his teeth. "I'm telling you the Mexican guy fired and hit Jared. I know because I was the one who put the real bullet in his gun."

Ferguson gaped at him for a long moment. Then he looked around at the group huddling by the fireplace. "What in hell were you playing at? Sutton, are you crazy, letting them shoot real bullets at each other? "

"That's right. Clint was behind both Jared and me." This time the speaker was a girl dressed in camouflage with grease daubed on her face. "Jared started running up the hill and this guy," she nodded at Alex, "he stood up and yelled at him to stop. I did, too, but then there was a shot, like a regular pistol shot and Jared fell down."

"It wasn't me, Lily. Honest, it wasn't." Clint's voice began to wobble. "What if he dies?"

"Of course it wasn't you," Larry Sutton broke in. "Somebody call the sheriff and tell him to come get this dirt bag. He's been nothing but trouble since he got here." He pointed at Alex. "Look at him, over there smirking. I even caught him sneaking around my office tonight. Probably looked for something to steal."

"Excuse me, Mr. Sutton." The guard who had given Jared first aid earlier stepped forward. Dressed in camouflage, he had all the appearance of a combat veteran. "I retrieved two weapons from up on the course where they were dropped by these two young men." He held up the standard game pistol Alex had been carrying in a bloody rag. It was the sleeve of Alex's shirt. In his other hand, also in a rag, was a Glock. "The one was dropped in the bushes where the shooter was standing to Jared's left. It's been fired several times. Not rubber bullets, real ones. "When I got to the wounded, this guy—" He nodded to Alex. "—was making a tourniquet out of his shirt to hold the wound closed. "This standard game weapon was on the ground beside him along with Jared's weapon. He was making every effort to save the victim's life."

Sutton looked ready to send him to the firing squad for insubordination.

"And this, I'm pretty sure—" Alex added, digging a shell out of his jeans pocket, "—comes from an automatic. Before Jared got hit, somebody shot at me and barely missed. They weren't playing any game. They were shooting to kill." There were grumbles among the guests, but no one came forward to contradict him. The truth was acknowledged by their mutual silence. "Seems like everybody knew it, but me."

Dalton and Syd Harris had entered the room with brandy snifters. They appeared mildly amused as if they were watching a form of entertainment. The colonel was playing the Man Game in his head, watching the reaction on the various players' faces.

"You don't expect us to buy your story, do you?" Sutton was still determined to rally a lynch mob, but Dalton interrupted him.

"Why don't you put an end to all this 'he said, she said' stuff and just run your security cameras back. That ought to tell you who's telling the truth and who's lying." He looked around to the others for affirmation. "Right, boys and girls?"

"Yeah, why not, Larry?" Ferguson turned away, looking disgusted. "But I, for one, trust Smitty who was right there." He nodded at the stoic guard. "And Lily wouldn't lie about it. I've known her from a baby. This boy's hands are still burnt because he pulled T.C. out of a burning barn. It was probably killing him even to hold a rifle. You and your god-damn games! I got to go to the hospital now to see about Jared. I thank you for saving my son's life, mister," he said to Alex. "And I'll talk to Clint. If he was shooting real am-mo, he's going to be prosecuted just like he's not mine."

Darla had returned from seeing Jared off in the helicop-ter. She was leaning in the doorway, looking drained and tired. "I'm sure it was all just a mistake. Somehow real ammo got loaded into Clint's gun by mistake."

Clint leaped to his feet and started toward her menacing-ly. "Oh, shut up, Darla. It was all your idea to shoot the beaner, anyhow."

Sutton rushed toward her, grabbing Darla's arm. "You don't know what you're talking about, little sister! You're drunk! Go to your room and sleep it off."

"Wait a second," Ferguson said slowly. "How did you know that, Darla?"

Darla appeared surprisingly sober. "It wasn't my idea at all. It was Larry's and he said to get Alex to play. Because we had kind of decided to play Real Thrill instead of just plain old paintball that gets so boring. And Clint drew the short straw tonight."

Clint staggered back a few steps. "What the hell? Don't blame everything on me. That's just like you Suttons, blam-ing everything on somebody else when you started it."

She turned on him. "Don't act like you didn't know!"

"But—but I wasn't supposed to get the real ammo! He was!" Clint pointed at Carreras.

Sutton clapped his hands together, dismissing the whole

matter. "So you see? It's a kid's game gone wrong. Whole thing was a big mistake. Jared's wound is not fatal. Bullet just nicked his neck. He'll be fine, the medics told me."

Ferguson grabbed his hat and stalked out the door. As he passed Sutton, he said, "It ain't no game when somebody could get killed, Larry. You're going to jail! See if I don't put you there."

"I'll have your son Clint for company, in that case," Sutton fired back. "Only he'll be in for attempted murder."

Silence settled across the great room as people began to slip away. The sound of cars in the driveway signaled a retreat from complicit guilt.

Only Harris appeared genuinely amused by preoccupations of bored farm folk. Swishing his brandy in the glass, he observed, "You're still doing that old manhunt thing, Larry? What do you call it? Real Kill, Real Thrill? Capital idea," he said from his leather armchair. "Pick a victim and try to shoot him. Beats fox hunting. People are much more worried about foxes and deer than shooting other people."

Clint followed his father out the door, jerking angrily away from Darla's desperate attempts to stop him. "Get away from me, bitch. It was all your idea anyway."

"Okay, if that's how you're going to be, then get screwed in court!" she screamed at him.

Running back to Alex, she slipped her arms through his. "Here's the brave one. He saved Jared's life."

"Here, here," Harris said, lifting his glass. "Well done, Vargas."

Alex shrank from the unwanted attention. "Not me. That's the real medic," he said, nodding at the guard who had stood watching the scene with folded arms. "Thanks for sticking up for me, mister."

The guard shrugged, his gray eyes giving away nothing. "I only said what I saw. It's what I get paid for. Correction. Did get paid for, anyway."

"I better get going then." Alex started to unbutton the borrowed shirt, but Dalton stopped him.

"Keep it, Vargas. We'll be seeing each other tomorrow, right? Royal Gorge—say, about nine in the morning? Just ask at the desk. They'll take you up."

Alex thanked them and walked out to the parking lot. Darla followed him, slipping her arm through his. "But, honey, I thought we were on for tonight." She put one hand inside his shirt, running her fingertips over his bare chest. "Does that mean you don't want to sleep with me?"

"I know this sounds dumb, but did you think I wouldn't mind getting shot at tonight?" He set her back again at arm's length. "You and your buddies had this set up all the time, didn't you? You came to the bar looking for a victim, and you found me. What were you going to do with my body, dump it on the road and say I accidently shot myself in the back? And how many other people have you killed this way? Maybe Pierre Bighand's boy?" He backed away as if she were carrying something contagious. "And now you want to sleep with me?"

Darla combed her long, fragrant hair with metallic aqua fingernails. "Okay, play hard to get, if that's the way you want to be. But you came out the winner tonight. I knew you would. See, it was like a contest of the best man wins, don't you get it? And you won!"

Inside, the pulsing music began and the guests gathered at tables around the pool, laughing as if nothing had happened. "Oh, sure, now I get it. And you'd be the prize, is that it? If Clint had shot me, he'd get to sleep with you. Either way, you wouldn't sleep alone."

He left her standing in the doorway, the light behind her shining through her clothes as if they were butterfly wings. "But I don't want to sleep alone, dammit," she shouted into the night. "I'm afraid of the dark."

"Strange. I thought that's when most predators did their hunting. Good night, Darla."

෴

Alex was on the way back to Little Spur Creek when his headlights picked up something moving in the road just ahead. As he approached, he made out a slender figure dressed in a short skirt and white blouse, a pair of high heels dangling in her hand. His first impulse was one of aversion—the days of rescuing women in distress were definitely over.

He had suffered too much for gallantry lately, or whatever that urge to do the right thing was called. Even though it was about five miles into town, he had decided to keep going when he recognized Silk, the tall waitress from the bar. She had given him the impression she was tough enough to resist any situation except one she couldn't physically control. Something about the urgency in her walk and the way she was dressed told him she had just encountered one of those situations.

He hit the brakes and rolled down his window. "Hey, miss. You picked a strange time to go jogging. Want a ride into town?"

She slowed for a minute, squinting at him through the glare of the headlights. "You're the guy who works for the Turners, Jimmy Something?"

"That's right. Vargas. I'm harmless, if that's what you want to know. Honest, sober, and hardworking. Could I drop you off somewhere? I wouldn't try walking home from here unless you're into marathons."

The tall blonde slowed a little, confusion showing through a surface hardness. "Sure, that would be nice if you don't mind. I was going to call Callie for a ride, but my cell phone isn't in my purse." As she started to come around to the passenger side, another vehicle's headlights came toward them. Alex caught her anxious look as she turned to face them. "I just want to warn you, this could be some more trouble coming," she said in an even voice. "You don't have to stick around, if you don't want to. It's the guy you had the fight with in the bar. The one who looks like a coon hound."

"And has a glass chin. Trouble's my middle name. Hop in." As she climbed in beside him, he noticed her blouse sleeve was hanging loose. "Bad date, I take it."

"What?" She nervously glanced behind her, and then saw her sleeve. "Yeah, a real prince of a guy. What's your excuse?" She nodded at his ripped jeans and then smiled. "Looks like tonight was kind of hard on your wardrobe, too."

"Same. Real bad date." As they pulled away, he kept his eyes on the oncoming vehicle in his rearview mirror. "What kind of car was your date driving?"

"Maroon stretch cab. Why?"

"I think he's got something else to say. This the guy who grabbed you in the bar?" He remembered the man called Cooper and how he had grabbed her in spite of her protests.

"Same. Please don't stop or I might have to kill him."

"People around here really shoot from the hip, don't they?" The truck suddenly swerved around them, pulling sharply into their path. Alex barely avoided a collision by slamming on the brakes. "See what you mean."

When they were stopped, he took charge. "Just sit tight, and let me do the talking. Whatever you do, don't get out of this truck. We don't deal with crazies, got it?"

Murray glanced at him with new respect. "Don't worry, I've got no intention of going anywhere with that moron. I wasn't prepared for his grabbing me the first time. Now, I am."

Her calmness set him back a little. The girl was cool, he had to admit. She didn't appear rattled, except for gripping one of her green stiletto heels in her hand like a weapon. "Maybe we'd just better back up and get out of here. He could have a gun."

"He'd just follow us and do something stupid."

"Looks like he's too drunk to be real dangerous. Put your other shoe on, if you don't mind. There's a wrench under the seat if you have to use it on him."

The driver of the truck jumped out and came running over to them.

Silk reached under the seat and grabbed the wrench. She rattled on nervously in college-educated English without the phony barmaid twang. Her beautifully structured face was taut with anger. "If you're expecting him to listen to reason, his brain doesn't work that way. What little brain he's got."

"Sounds like a wonderful evening. What's his name, again?"

"Duke Cooper."

It was the third time he had heard the name in one day. Pierre had mentioned he had worked for the Turners and Darla had identified him as a former boyfriend of Shelby Turner.

"Oh, yeah, now I remember. You're right, he does sort of look like a hound. Big floppy ears, long nose."

Freckled and rawboned Cooper loped up to the driver's side and tried to stick his head in the window. "Silk, you c'mon and go with me, now."

Close up, with the smell of cheap liquor on his breath, he could be mean, that was plain. Alex wondered if he were mean enough to kill a girl who dumped him for someone else.

"I promise not to pull anything on you."

Silk used a business-like tone not customary with waitresses in singles bars. "Mr. Cooper, you need to understand one thing very clearly. I do not like having my clothes torn off or having to walk home at one in the morning because some sorry ass pig like you thought I would be easy prey. You owe me money for this blouse and you will pay for it because I will send you the bill. You are lucky I am not going to have the sheriff arrest you for assault, but I swear to you, if you lay one finger on me, or my friend, here, I'll have you arrested. Now, get out of the way before I ask my friend Jimmy here to run you down like the dog you are." She leaned across Alex to deliver the message, brushing him with her silky, perfumed hair. It smelled wonderful, like flowers. Something inside of him ached to touch her hair, but, for now, he had to be content with just the odor of it. Loneliness had suddenly become sexual, as well.

The hunting hound at the window yowled a whining apology. "Now, c'mon Silk, honey, you know I didn't mean nothing by that. You just jerked away from me and I—"

She withdrew back to her seat. "Please get me out of here before I do something illegal with this wrench," she said politely to Alex. She sat back beside him and stared straight ahead.

"Sorry, buddy, you're out of chances with the lady." Alex put the truck in reverse, and began to back the truck up slowly. "You need to send her some flowers or something tomorrow."

"Aw, Silk, come back here. You bring her back here, boy! She's going home with me!" Cooper tried to hang on to the door as they backed away, but Alex whipped the steering wheel around to the left and dropped him in the road. "How come you want to run off with a beaner? Look at his truck! He ain't nobody!"

"Persistent dude, isn't he?"

They took off toward town, leaving Cooper stomping small clouds of dust, silhouetted in his own headlights. Next to him, Silk still held the wrench, prepared for a second assault.

"I liked the way you told him off. You're very good at it. You must run into a bunch like that at work."

He glanced at her in the light of the dashboard. Her skin was golden-shadowed, her features as clean-cut as those of a prom queen. Finding herself still clutching the wrench, she replaced it under the seat.

"I think they must have cloned the world's worst chauvinists around here. Thanks for bailing me out, by the way. Except for the suggestion about sending flowers. You party kind of late, don't you?" Silk glanced at her watch. "Two-thirty. I'm glad I don't have to get up with the chickens." She smiled at him for the first time that night.

It also occurred to him for the first time that she was beautiful. He thought about Darla Sutton's outrageous come-on tactics, and how different this girl was. In spite of her torn blouse and blood on his jeans, she managed to keep the conversation banal.

Maybe it was her training as a cocktail waitress, but she was very self-possessed in spite of the fact he was a complete stranger on a dark country road with blood spattered jeans and a serious start on a beard.

"Hey, it's Friday night. Even the chickens party late. But I'm starting to wish I hadn't already." The agriculture agent would be here around at eight, he remembered. It would be at least three by the time he got back to the Turner's place.

"I know it's none of my business but I kind of gathered Callie and your date don't get along," she said, a little hesitantly as if she didn't want to pry. "She didn't have very good things to say about her after you left. Miss Rich Bitch was about all I can repeat in mixed company. It's strange because Callie used to go with Larry Sutton."

"I got the feeling it was mutual."

They shared a laugh.

"Still, Callie got the bar out of it, or at least a living. And their little girl. End of story, I guess. It sure wasn't a friendly parting of the ways."

They were silent a minute, each looking into their own futures.

"Think I'd like a little more out of life than that," he said, more to himself than to the girl beside him. "But these days, it's so hard to stay together what with all the pressure on you."

Silk nodded, her hair hiding her expression. "I know," she said, as if she really did. Then she deftly changed the subject again. "Is that really what they call you around here? Twenty-Six?"

"That's what Callie calls me, anyway. How about you? Is Silk your real name?"

"I'm twenty-two," the girl said, sidestepping the question as neatly as any defense lawyer. "It sounds like a shot-gun. Kind of suits me, I guess."

For the first time in days, laughter came easily for both of them.

He dropped her off at her apartment in an old frame boarding house squeezed between the coy main street Victorians. As he cut off the motor, a lace curtain on the ground floor was pulled aside and a woman peeked at them.

"I think Mama's still up. I won't come in, in that case."

"That's not my mom." Silk put her heels back on to walk upstairs. "It's my landlady. She thinks my night job includes hitting the pavement. This will confirm her suspicions."

Something about her fresh directness made him smile again. "I'll wait until you're inside. If that guy gives you anymore trouble, call the sheriff like you promised him."

"We don't need the sheriff now. My landlady can take care of him." The girl called Silk swept her shiny, jiggling hair aside as she looked for the key. He couldn't help noticing she was naturally blonde to the roots and then wondered why he did. "Thanks again, Jimmy. I can see why Darla Sutton likes you so much."

He tried to figure out the reason behind the phony compliment. Obviously, the girl thought he was a local. "Really? Somehow I didn't get that impression tonight."

Silk smiled a shy smile and was even prettier under the overhead light. "She doesn't look like the type to hide much."

With a wave that said nice knowing you, she walked up to the porch. His last glimpse of her was Silk putting on her missing shoe like a fairy tale princess in a set for a bad Western.

Somehow he hoped she would ask to see him again. Then he remembered who he was supposed to be and why.

When the old truck was out of sight, Murray Schmitz leaned up against the closed door and burst into tears. Brushing away Mrs. Rodriguez's scolding with a wave, she went upstairs to her room where she swallowed a glass of beer in one gulp. That gave her enough nerve to go to the bathroom to examine the bruise on her shoulder where Cooper had grabbed her. When she turned on the light and saw her torn blouse, she fought to stay under control all over again. Her first instinct was to call Hansen at two in the morning and get him out of bed to tell him she was an idiot and was coming back. Giving up the quest for Alex Carreras was easy because she didn't have to let herself get mauled by the likes of Duke Cooper.

Standing there with the neon light turning her bruises green, Murray role played how she'd handle her reception back at headquarters as Jonesy and the crew welcomed her back.

"How'd you handle all those horny cowboys up there, Silk?"

"What'd you do all those long nights in the hills, count sheep?"

"I'd like to get a job working in a bar. I'd drink up all the profits."

And on and on. They'd never let her forget she was a woman again. Never. And neither would she.

Murray straightened and stared at her face in the mirror, made-up to look like a teenage cover girl. Watersprite eyes with mascara puddled in murky pools. Hair like a teenager's worst Monday morning.

She splashed water on her face and drank some more beer. Something had to make all this worth it. She wasn't going back until she had a real lead.

As soon as she threw herself in bed, and turned out the lamp on the bed stand, the phone rang. She picked it up, hoping it might be the tall one with the beard who had given her a ride home. It wasn't. It was Duke Cooper whining something about being sorry, and she slammed the phone down. It rang again and she unplugged it. Unable to drift off, she saw a spotlight drift across the lace curtains. Getting up to lower the shade, Murray went to the window and looked out on the deserted street. Parked some distance away, under the only street lamp on the block, was Cooper's truck. She had really ended up in a world apart.

CHAPTER 19

Before Alex fell asleep on the bunk bed, Shelby's young face slipped back into his mind. This time, she was alive, and smiling as she appeared in the photograph on the Turner's mantle.

Then her image faded and he found himself staring at the springs of the mattress on the top bunk above him. The tip of something white was sticking out of the corner brace. It took him a moment to realize it was paper and not part of the bedding. Reaching up, he pulled it out of the brace and several small squares of white paper cascaded down on his chest. There were even more wedged in the wire mesh supporting the mattress.

Alex sat up and collected the notes in a small pile beside him. He used to get notes like this from girls in school, filled with round feminine handwriting on notebook paper. They were from Shelby. Every one of them was addressed to this guy named Scottie. With lots of love and decorated with little hearts and Xs. This was the jet jockey who had lured her out to Sunrise for a few nights of love on the wild side.

After reading several, Alex fell asleep with one still in his hand. He awoke to doors slamming in his head. Then he realized the banging was on the bunkhouse door and he was naked in the morning sun streaming through the window. Grabbing last night's damp towel off the chair, he covered himself just as the door burst open.

Darla stood there dressed in a glittering western shirt and skintight jeans with fringe down the sides. She took in his nakedness without a blink.

"Whew, baby, you've gotta wear more than that! The ladies won't complain, but the bulls might get jealous!"

Slamming the door again did no good. Darla simply opened it and walked into the room where he had sought refuge in the bathroom.

"Here, honey, get dressed and I'll put things right in here. We've got to hurry. In case you forgot you're interviewing for a job with Uncle Ed this morning." She threw his jeans and shirt at him and looked around. "Lord, if this isn't a mess! Leave it to men to live like hogs."

"I seem to remember getting shot at last night at your house. How's Jared this morning?"

"Fine," she said, gathering up dirty clothes in a pile while Alex ran the water for a shower. "I just went by to see him. He was lucky the bullet just nicked his neck, the doc said. He's lost a lot of blood but he'll be out Monday."

"It doesn't seem to bother you that somebody could've gotten killed, particularly me. I've heard about blood sports, Darla. I thought they'd gone out with the Roman Empire." He tried closing the bathroom door but the lock didn't work and Darla came right into the closet-sized bathroom. "You get out of there this minute or I'm going to jump in there with you!"

"There's not room enough for two midgets in here and you'll get your cowboy outfit wet. Now get out and let me get dressed."

"Okay, this damn steam is making my hair frizzy anyway."

But as he got out of the shower, Darla was putting his shaving gear out on the sink. Before he could speak, Darla wrapped herself around him and gave him a long kiss. "Now, I'm going to shave off that's awful beard," she said waving his razor.

"Can't." Struggling free, he covered his face protectively. "Teenage acne scars."

"Talk about scars." Her long fingers traced the white scar across his ribs. "That looks like a knife."

"At least, it's not a bullet hole. Come clean about the ammo or get out."

Like a little child begging not to be punished, her voice changed to an odd singsong voice like a child jumping. "Clint wasn't supposed to…you know."

"Yeah, I know. Shoot him. He was supposed to shoot me." Throwing any attempts at modesty aside, Alex retrieved his clothes from the chair and put on his shorts.

Darla looked hurt at the accusation. "Not to kill. Only wound you a little, baby. That's all. Just a little nick."

Alex was aghast at her complete lack of remorse. "That one little nick could have killed me, you silly idiot! Like it had Jared spouting blood all over your brother's expensive grass. Doesn't that bother you just a little bit?"

She looked so much like a person sleepwalking, he wanted to take her by the shoulders and shake her, but Darla would only want to embrace him.

Instead, he walked away with an incredulous shake of his head.

"Okay, okay. See, Jared's kind of like my best friend. Clint and Jared are the closest thing I've ever had to a real family. They both really, really care something about me. And it's just like, I just have this thing for Clint. You know, sex is better with him than Jared. And he's not afraid of Larry. You can't say that about most men I know. Except Uncle Syd and Uncle Ed, naturally. They don't take anything off him."

He pushed her away. "You are sick, Darla. And this is a sick situation. Now, let me get dressed." He brushed past her into the bathroom.

She followed him back into the bathroom. "I don't know what you're so upset for, it was just an accident!"

"Two good reasons: one because I got blamed for it, and

two because I was the real target. Or maybe it was Jared. Whatever it is, I hope Clint's ass gets fried!"

"Well, the guard and that ugly little Lily girl stood up for you, so you're in the clear. I don't know why you're getting so upset just because of that."

Like a lost puppy, Darla followed him back to the bunkroom where he looked for his boots thrown somewhere in the room the night before. Before he could stop her, she flung herself down on Shelby's letters without noticing she was crushing them under her. Calling her attention to it would only draw her interest to them. He wanted to go through them himself to see if they contained any leads to her death before he turned them over to Marisa. The last thing in the world he needed was Darla broadcasting Shelby's personal correspondence all over the Branding Iron.

"Clint called me later on. He was so broken up I could hardly make head or tails. Said Jared must've dropped his own gun. That's just like him. A complete klutz." Then she burst into tears. "But I was so scared, I had to take another snort just to make it through the night." In the next millisecond, her flood of tears had given way to a deep sadness, a void, she claimed, only love could fill. "Stay with me tonight, Jimmy. Larry's going away again and I don't want to be alone up there. It's haunted. I think I see my poor dad walking around, moving stuff around in the night. I think I'm going crazy or something. Really."

"Darla, understand one thing. Your brother intends to kill me, preferably sooner than later. I wouldn't be surprised if he wasn't the one who loaded Clint's gun with real bullets last night so he could get rid of me. I don't know why but he hates the sight of me."

Darla twisted her hair around her finger the way his little sister did when she was deep in thought. She stared into space, ignoring the little triangles of paper she had sent cascading to the pine floor. "Well, I think that's a really mean thing to say, Jimmy. Larry is truly awful, I admit, but he wouldn't kill somebody. Not himself, anyway. He'd pay somebody else to do it."

"No doubt. Like Clint, maybe." He pulled on his shirt. "By the way, Shelby Turner's funeral is tomorrow. You going?"

Darla sighed with her usual indecision. "I know. I did send a huge arrangement of flowers to the funeral home. Shaped like a heart with two fake doves in the middle. Are you going to be there? Clint won't be there since he's in jail and Larry's out of town. I need somebody to take me."

"Darla, you set me up to get killed. Why would you want me to take you somewhere? Get Uncle Syd or Uncle Ed to take you."

She writhed on the narrow bed, crushing Shelby's messages beneath her. "Because you are such a stud, baby. That's why. Clint and Larry were jealous; it was oozing out of them every time they saw you." Stretching out seductively, Darla stared up at the mattress above her." I don't know how can you sleep like this. It feels like you're lying on a stretcher. And all alone. What a shame! People like you and me should never sleep alone, Jimmy."

"Did you know Shelby Turner very well?" Hoping to catch her in a vulnerable mood, he turned the questions back on her,

Sprawled across Shelby's letters, she became quiet. "She was my friend. We grew up together, went to school together, rode together. She was like my very own sister. Until Larry…"

"Until Larry what? "

She stared at the bunk above with fixed eyes as if she had fallen into a trance. "Larry and T.C. started fighting about something. Larry had made T.C. an offer for this place and T.C. told him to go to hell. Since then, he wouldn't let me even call Shelby on the phone. But when I got my own cell phone, we used to talk every day. And we'd ride together up there in those hills or we'd take our trailers somewhere and ride together. That was until Scottie came into the picture. She met him one night at the Iron and that was that. Shelby went out of her mind about him. Wanted to marry him the night she met him. Said that was the one she'd been waiting for." She stopped and her eyes drifted over to him. "Come make love to me."

She was tempting, lying there stretched out in the morning sun, but he took the easy way out. "It's like the shower. There isn't room for two people on that bunk."

"That's the whole point." Darla lifted her arms. "I need holding."

The mattress springs creaked as he lay down beside her and cradled her to his side. Her fingers wandered down his body, teasing him.

"I don't want to talk about her anymore. It makes me too sad. I just think it was Scottie Mason's fault. If she hadn't gone to meet him, she'd still be here. Isn't it funny? Everybody wants what they can't have." She sighed like a child ready for sleep and her fragrant hair fell across his face as she rolled on to his chest. "It's Clint's real punishment. He's thinking about me being here with you while he's in jail."

"Does that give you a charge? Why?" He could never understand why women did that. Chelsea, too, made a habit of that kind of power play until she realized it didn't affect him. He wondered now why it never had. Maybe because he didn't love her the way he thought he did.

Her hands played down his body, more insistent than before, touching places only she would know. "Because it's proof he really wants me. Just like you're going to want me before this morning's over."

He brought her hand back and held it firmly. "And you're going to make sure, aren't you?"

Her turquoise eyes looked deep into his. "No, that's the trouble. I'm never sure about anything anymore. It's all just games."

He rolled off the bunk to his feet. "Forget it, Darla. You'll marry either Clint or Jared or both of them and your two fortunes will be one. What Larry can't do by force, he'll do by whatever way he can and what he wants is the Ferguson's land. Tell me he doesn't." He put on his jeans and tucked in his shirt.

"Well, he probably won't get it. Mr. Ferguson doesn't like me. He thinks I'm not good enough for either of his boys. He's already told them not to come over to High Point."

"I noticed how well they obeyed." At the sink, he splashed cold water on his face.

"Hey, this is Shelby's writing. I'd know it anywhere." Idly, she picked one of the scattered papers under her arm. "Where'd you get these?"

Stifling the desire to rip them out of her hands, he said, "Under the mattress. Just leave them for Marisa to read first, will you?"

"But you were reading them, weren't you? She was such a good writer. I used to have her write letters to boys for me. She could express herself so well. Listen to this. 'I feel you right beside me even though you're miles and miles away.'"

"If you want me to get to that interview with your uncle, I've got to get some coffee first." He tried to keep the desperate edge from his voice. "C'mon, I've got to leave."

But Darla only sat up, leafing through the little pile with a curious frown. "That's funny. I wonder why they never got mailed? And they're all to that Scottie guy she was so in love with." Something changed on Darla's face and then was gone like morning mist in the sun. "Oh, god!" She jumped up as if she were scalded and began gathering the letters with shaking hands.

"Now what's the matter?"

"I just realized something. Duke used to bring the mail to the post office. I know that! I know for sure because I met him a couple of times when he was picking up the mail. Does she mention me? Does she say anything about me?" Her reaction to finding the letters wasn't at all what he expected. Darla's usual bravado was gone, and she looked terrified. What could she possibly have to fear?

"See, she said she was going to Sunrise to meet Scott Mason. Callie Murphy had invited her out there and she told me she had asked Scottie to come for the weekend. That was last week."

There was no deception with Darla. Only the kind she created for herself. "So? Why wouldn't Cooper just mail the letters? Was he jealous or something?" Trying to sound as if he were making small talk, he combed his hair. "Come on, fold them back up, will you? We're wasting time."

"She told me Callie had a little job for her out there, working as a maid. She'd done it lots of times, all through high school. She and Scott used to meet there, go skiing, fool around. Her parents never caught on to what she was really doing. They didn't like Mason much, so they had to sneak around. Then she found out he was married with two kids."

"But he never got the letters so she must have called him. End of story."

Darla tried folding the notes but gave up and piled them flat. "Maybe, but she told me once it was hard to get him on the phone. He was always flying some kind of special plane or in some training program. I think he wanted to break it off. Mason was a player. He had a wife and a kid all along and, all the time he was playing around with her. Poor Shelby. She really thought he was going to marry her, but he was just stringing her along." She kissed the letters in her hands, kneeling beside the bunk. "We could have grown old together, two grandmas, riding around with our kids." Darla burst into sobs, holding the letters to her chest. "Now, she's gone and I haven't even been able to cry. I keep seeing her everywhere I look. I keep expecting to hear Shelby laughing, the way her voice went way up and then sort of slid down."

He let her cry, not even being able to tell her he felt the same sense of loss. How could he say that, when he didn't even know the girl? But Darla had provided more pieces of the puzzle around Shelby' death, that much alone was gratifying.

It figured Duke Cooper had read the letters, knew when and where she was going and had probably followed her. Mason hadn't showed up and Shelby decided to go find him. Cooper followed and killed her.

It seemed strange that if Shelby had been that broken up about Mason not meeting her, she would have left Saturday night instead of staying on. Maybe those were the terms of her job, but even so, why had she been partying Saturday night as if she didn't have a care in the world?

His thoughts went back to Saturday night in the bar at Sunrise. The group of girls at the next table was having some kind of celebration. He and his bachelor party were making equally as much noise and finally, the two groups had mingled. He remembered they were all pretty with several attractive blondes among them, the kind he always fell for. Several groups had taken pictures together in various ridiculous poses. Shelby must have been in one of those groups, but he couldn't remember her clearly. Callie Murphy had made certain they all had drink refills and he had accepted every time. *Someday, I'm going with him, going with him someday soon.*

He put his arms around Darla and tilted her tear-streaked face upward. "If you care as much about your friend as you say, you have to go to the police with what you know."

"I can't. Don't you see? I can't. Duke Cooper is my half-brother. He's my father's son, but Daddy never married his mother. Jimmy, he's blood kin to me and I just can't do that to him! Larry has all the money and the property and he won't give Duke or his mother their fair share. He gets treated as if he's dirt, and I try to help his mom out when I can. But she's proud and doesn't want to take anything. She works at the supermarket as a clerk. I can't do anything that would get her only son in trouble."

He gathered the scattered letters and folded them up. "Then, let's go find Marisa."

☙❧

Marisa Turner was out in the yard feeding the peacocks as she always did early in the morning. When she saw him with Darla, she appeared to light up all over. He realized the sight of Darla provoked memories of happier days. Darla broke into a run and flung her arms around her. They both stood in a hug, rocking back and forth weeping.

Finally, Marisa pulled slightly away. "I'm so glad you came. I needed that hug."

With a tenderness he had thought Darla incapable of, she replied, "That's for all the hugs you gave me growing up. You're the only real mother I've ever known. And Shelby was my sister."

Marisa embraced her even more, tears slipping down her cheeks. "I've missed you so much. But I knew you would come back, sooner or later." Then, still holding Darla's hand, she realized he was just standing there, giving them to mend past differences. "I've got fresh coffee in the kitchen. You must need it. I know I do."

It was an oblique reference to his coming in so late last night. "Sorry, I came in so late. I was up at Pierre's, helping him bring down the last of the sheep. Then we had to celebrate a little." He glanced at Darla. "And she had a party going on."

Marisa brushed off the reference to Pierre's drinking with a good humored chuckle. "No need to give me an excuse, Jimmy. I know how boys are, even big ones. Don't forget, I've got two of my own. Anyway, good news. They've moved T.C. from the Burn Unit to the step-down unit. He's not going anywhere very fast, but it's progress. I told him they were probably just passing the buck because he was such an awful patient, but he said he'll make it to the funeral on Sunday, though. We put it off until he could make it, of course."

Darla heaved an audible sigh of relief. "I'm so glad he'll make it to the funeral. Because I sent this big heart of roses with two fake doves. It would be too bad if T.C. didn't see it. Maybe he'll see I really loved Shelby. And him, too. It was all Larry. He twists everybody's tail."

Marisa kept her arm around the girl's waist and hugged her closer. "He knows you always have, honey. Jimmy, he said to tell you thanks again. Neither of us can say it enough for everything. You'll stay on a little longer, won't you? As long as you want. You've got a home here, you know. If you want it."

He hesitated, knowing he had to say the inevitable. "I don't know. Ed Dalton offered me a job doing security for him. It pays well and—" He held out his raw palms. "—I can't do much with these."

Her face froze. "I see. No, of course, you can't. The colonel knows talent when he sees it." Keeping Darla close, Marisa tossed the last handful of grain out to the iridescent flock around her with her free hand. "Now, come on into the kitchen, both of you. You can't leave without having some breakfast."

"Mrs. Turner—Marisa, please." As if she knew what he was going to say, she walked ahead, chattered on about coffee and something to eat.

"Marisa, we've got something to tell you." Darla hadn't let go of Marisa's hand. "Would you please just stand still and listen for a minute."

Marisa stopped on the walkway to the kitchen, shielding her dark eyes to look at them. "Don't tell me you've already decided to get married! "

Darla must have inherited some of old Chester's backbone. "Don't I wish!" After sliding a glance at Alex, she dug the notes from her skintight jeans. "No, it's something else. Something about Shelby. We found her letters in the bunkhouse. Duke never mailed them." Taking Marisa's hand, she deposited the small heap and curled up the numb fingers. "Jimmy says the police should see if there's any clues in there about…you know."

Marisa's delicate face reflected a range of emotions from confusion to pure joy. "I knew she'd find a way to tell us. I told T.C. she'd get in touch with us, no matter what. These are proof!"

"We'll let you read them and be back later. A couple of my horses are up for judging and Jimmy's got to see Uncle Ed. But don't worry about help. Larry said he was sending a crew over today." Darla slipped her arm through his elbow.

"I don't think she should be alone right now, Darla." He slipped from her grasp. "I'll get over there and then come on back."

She gave him a desperate look. "But you don't how to get there. It won't take me but half hour."

"The Royal Gorge is hard to miss. It's the only thing with more than two stories in town."

"That's all right, you two run along and do what you have to do." Marisa was pressing the little pile of notes to her heart. "But, honey, tell Larry I've got all the help I need. Rudolfo and his crew are staying here until T.C. gets home. And that goes for you, Jimmy. I know how much Ed Dalton pays his guards and it makes what we can do look like peanuts. You go on and take that job. But be careful. Ed Dalton isn't like he used to be. He's changed, and not for the better, I feel."

He wanted to know what that meant but she turned away and walked into the kitchen, her dark head bent as if blessing her daughter's letters with her tears. Alex glanced at his watch. It wasn't the moment to tell her Wilson the Ag agent would be arriving shortly, but there wasn't a good time.

"Marisa. Mrs. Turner, I've got something to tell you."

She stopped and turned, tear-wet cheeks glistening in the sun. "If you're going to tell me about Mr. Wilson coming out, Jimmy, I already know. I told him he could come ahead, but it won't do any good. I take it you were the one who called him."

"I called after I saw Mr. Bighand's place yesterday. His sheep up near the ridge were caught in the fire. But the sheep in the lower pasture who survived the fire died anyway before the fire even started. I think they were killed by the spraying of some chemical."

"Those animals up there—" She gestured toward the pasture. "—were perfectly healthy the day before the fire. I know because I was up there looking for lambs. The fire was set just to cover up the fact that the herd was already dead. And they knew I was down there doing what I could for my baby. My Shelby baby. Oh, I hate them. It's bad to be so full of hate."

He was talking to a woman who had reached her limit for emotional damage.

"That's why I called Mr. Wilson. Somebody's got to know what's going on."

"You know what? I don't care. What else have I got to lose? My life? I don't care about me anymore. Do you think I do? No, I want to save my husband from those murderers. I know they killed my Shelby Anne and I just can't prove it, Jimmy! I'm so tired. I can't fight anymore. They'll just keep on running people out of this valley until they own it all. Let him come!"

He had to play his last card, hating himself for having a lawyer's instinct, glad it was still alive and well. "Then, we can't let her die for nothing, can we? "

"No. You're right" The storm passed and she began to smile with a glow that matched the morning sky itself. "Of course, you're right. That's why, isn't it? I've been asking myself that same thing. That's why you've come."

Beside him, Darla made a little hiccup sound and vomited into the rose garden. Then with a moan, she folded up on the walkway before he could grab her.

It turned out Darla had washed down two amphetamines with an energy drink truck drivers use on the long haul.

When she came to, there was a bluish pallor beneath her tan that told of lack of oxygen. "I nearly snuffed it, didn't I?" She studied the two of them as if they were aliens.

"Yeah, you did. Proud of yourself?" He knew it sounded harsh, but he was sick of people his age or younger throwing their lives away as if it were a dirty tissue. "Like Mrs. Turner didn't have enough to worry about, you have to overdose in her living room."

"Jimmy!" Marisa's voice stopped him, and he turned on his heel. "She just needs some breakfast in her, that's all. And you need your coffee, that's obvious! It's in the kitchen."

"Too bad Shelby didn't have that choice, to play Russian roulette with her life." He meant it to hurt and it did.

"Well, Shelby popped pills, too, didn't she, Marisa? I saw her popping big white ones." Darla got to her feet, and sat down hard on the arm of the sofa. "Didn't she?"

Marisa put her arm around Darla's thin shoulders. "That was just her pain medicine, honey. Now, let's just get some orange juice in you."

"I hate orange juice! Makes me puke! Jimmy, you come right back here. I know I'm bad, dammit, but I'm pretty, aren't I? And rich. So why don't you like me?"

Dodging another reprimand, he left by the kitchen door; heading to meet Wilson. Behind him, Darla burst into tears with Marisa's croons to comfort her.

☙❧

Wilson and Pierre were already at work up on the ridge, examining the stiff carcasses one by one, taking tissue samples in plastic bags. Putting on his fence gloves, Alex took soil and grass samples and put them in separate plastic bags he had borrowed from Marisa. Following the agent's incisions, he used his own pocket knife to carve off sections of the sheep's lung and flesh. As he worked over the carcasses, his eyes met Wilson's. Behind thick lenses, they held little hope, but he hadn't really expected any.

"Well, I can tell you one thing, this isn't hoof-and-mouth or anthrax." Wilson stood up with a grunt, and stripped off his gloves. "For one thing, it don't kill animals this fast. This is some kind of weird virus or something. See the way they've swelled up? Eyes popped like that? Black sputum? They couldn't breathe. Choked to death, damn near on the spot." He spat as if the air left a bitter taste in his mouth. "I've seen horses with a rhinovirus like that. Take one step and then drop dead. But it don't usually affect sheep unless it's some kind of mutation. It seems more like a chemical reaction."

He stumbled around through the burned underbrush and then squatted painfully over an untouched clump. The tips of the grass were brownish and the stems were yellowed. "This isn't for lack of water. Looks to me somebody's been spraying some kind of chemical around here." He indicated the animal carcasses with a wave of his hand. "See how their eyes bug out? Their tongues out? They died before they had a chance to swallow like something shut down their lungs. Let's take a look-see."

Poking through the burned carcasses, he found one and made a neat cut down the chest of the upturned body. As Alex watched, he neatly exposed the sheep's lung with his blade, letting out a hissing burst of foul air. A bloody, black liquid spewed from the incision. "Look," he said, pointing into the emission. "Beats the hell out of me. I've never seen anything like this." He squinted at Alex. "Did you say you've notified the newspapers about this?"

"I was waiting to hear what Mr. Tate had to say. After all, this is his herd. But mine looks the same."

"And mine," Pierre put in. By the look on his face, he took a dim view of the Ag agent's power to do anything. Or his willingness, for that matter.

"I'd hold on, if I's you, young fella. You'll start a panic around here among the livestock owners. Give me a chance to quarantine this whole area." Wilson swept his hand over the rolling pastureland. "Off limits to anyone except government agriculture officials." Ignoring Pierre's expression of disgust, he turned to Alex. "You say you still got livestock down at your place?"

In spite of Pierre's snort of derision. "They're at Mr. Bighand's."

"Then they don't go anywhere else. Same goes for you, Mr. Bighand. No stock leaves the premises. We got to watch and see if it's biological or chemical. But whatever it is, I'd sure like to know."

Some corner of Alex consciousness became aware of a powerful engine throbbing just below the ridge. "Listen," he said, jerking his head in the direction of the sound.

The three men interrupted their conversation and stood still, listening.

"Sounds like a chopper." Wilson turned to the other two men for corroboration, but they were hurrying back down the slope. "Hurry up! We better get to cover."

Wilson looked blank. "What for?"

"You'll see," Pierre shouted. "And cover up your nose and mouth. Get moving!"

With Pierre leading the way, they hopped and slid down the mountainside to the shallow outcrop a few hundred yards below them.

The sound of the helicopter grew louder as the machine rose in a long arc, up from the valley below, banking sharply in their direction. Alex pulled his bandana up over his nose and face, the way he remembered Rudolfo showing him. Wilson wasn't wearing a bandana and seemed to need both hands to keep his balance scrambling down the hill. "Pull your shirt up over your nose!" he yelled at the bewildered man, but Wilson looked blank and even annoyed by the command.

They reached the shelter just as the helicopter rose above the ridge, circling and banking back in their direction, even though they huddled against the rock hidden from view.

"Face into the rock!" Pierre shouted above the throbbing engine nearly on top of them now. "He's going to spray."

Just as he shouted the warning, the helicopter ejected a broad swatch of red spray as it passed overhead. The burning moisture seeped through Alex's shirt, making it stick to his skin, and on the backside of his jeans. Spread by the strong north wind, the red droplets drifted back, leaving a fine spray over their faces.

"Oh, crap," Wilson shouted. "That's just the forest service spreading fire deterrent! That don't hurt nothing!"

The helicopter continued on, spreading a wide blanket of red foam over the entire hillside. As it disappeared beyond the hillside, the men stepped out from the outcrop and looked around. Everything was drenched in red, the symbolic color of danger—sheep carcasses, burnt stubble, the backs of the waiting horses, their saddles.

They rode down in disgruntled silence, Alex and Pierre bemused by Sutton's latest trick to prevent any investigation of the brushfire. Most of the livestock carcasses were burned to the point where any etymological investigation was impossible. Now, the last few animals were soaked in flame retardant which had a chemical residue all its own. The combination of smoke damage and chemical damage would make finding the original cause of death nearly impossible. Nevertheless, he had managed to bag a few tissue samples and so had Wilson. That ought to be enough for a good lab to go on.

At the barn, the agent dismounted, barely able to stand and furious about the condition of his clothes. "I'm too old for this. I'm going to ask you to donate one of your healthy animals as a blind study. For comparison, you know." He looked at the ridge. "But I'll tell you one thing. It's going to be hard to get a good picture of exactly what killed your animals with that fire deterrent all over everything. It's a real pervasive chemical compound. Soaks right into the tissue. Combine that with the fire damage—"

"Amazing how their sense of timing was so perfect"

Pierre spat and leaned on his saddle horn. "You tell any-body you were coming up here?"

"Just my wife. Don't worry, we'll get to the bottom of this." Wilson ignored the insinuation and walked to his truck as if there were a board between his legs.

Pierre slipped to the ground like a cat from a tree. "There've been agents up here before, but nothing's ever been done about it. Not expecting much different from you, no offense intended."

In spite of his pain, the agent looked as if what he really wanted to do was take a swing at Pierre. "What'er you say-ing, exactly, Mr. Bighand? That we're not doing our job?"

"I'm just saying, Mr. Wilson, that you asked us why we hadn't reported this crap before, and I'm telling you we have. And not one damn thing was ever done about it."

Wilson looked as if he had just stuck his hand in a hor-net's nest. "It just takes time to autopsy and grow cultures. You got to allow for that."

"In the meantime, we're getting run out of business, sir." The discussion was getting tense, aggravated by the pound-ing wind, an intense itching over their skin and the flies. "The last man they sent out said exactly the same as you. Made a big deal about chemical poisoning and that's the last we ever heard of it."

The agent took off his hat and slapped it against his leg to scare off the flies. "Listen, folks, I'm doing all I can. Like I told you, the agent in charge of this area died unexpected-ly—"

"How?"

Wilson blinked, his round, honest face free of deception. "How what?"

Pierre watched him the way a snake watches a gopher hole. "I asked how did he die?"

Wilson hesitated, looking at the rim of his hat which was beginning to fray. "Lung trouble. Sudden, just like that. 'Course he was always a heavy smoker."

"Amazing, ain't it?" Pierre spat again. "It's what we've

been telling you people for two years, now. No telling how many people've died around here 'cause the government's just not interested. Now, we've got little kids with brain tumors that kill 'em in six months and women that have deformed babies. We never had that before and I've lived here all my life."

Alex had wearied of the entire debate to the point he forgot who he was supposed to be. "Mr. Wilson, you have exactly twenty-four hours to come up with an explanation for the deaths of these animals or we go to the newspapers with this story. And the television nationwide news." That surprised even Pierre.

Wilson recoiled as if he'd been shot. "Nothing can be done in twenty-four hours. It takes days to go through labs. Even weeks before—"

"Twenty-four hours or I go to the papers," Alex repeated. The words were hardly out in the chilly air when a sudden wave of dizziness swept over him and he fought vomiting. His entire body itched and his brain began to pulsate like a neon sign. He had to put his hand against the fence to steady himself..

"I'll sure let you know if I do find something." Wilson glanced at Alex. "Right away. You okay?"

Alex shook his head. "It's not good enough. We want answers now."

"Well, buddy, that's about as good as you're going to get around here, like I told you."

As he and Pierre watched the agent's truck negotiate the rutted road out of the pasture, Pierre read his mind. "How do you know he isn't on Sutton's payroll like the rest of these flunkies?"

"Because I think he's scared as hell he's going to catch whatever killed the guy before him, that's why. Wilson's already got prostate cancer and he's not from here. Other guy's in the hospital having something out." He looked at Pierre. "What about you? Aren't you scared of this stuff?"

Pierre spat into the blackened soil. "Now, that's a dumb

question. You really going to go to the papers?"

"I told you already. I'm in this to win. You still with me?"

"That's a really dumb question, ain't it?"

Suddenly, Pierre buckled like an old tree, squatting on the blackened earth. Alex thought the old sheepman might have had a stroke under the strain of losing just about everything. The edges of his frayed hat hid his face, but a single tear, hitting the black dust like a rain drop, told him Pierre was simply overcome with emotion. Finally, he squinted up at Alex as if he couldn't believe what he was seeing. He made no effort to wipe his face as if he had lost the will to be part of civilized society.

"I never told you, but my little Shelby was sick."

"Sick?" Alex's mind flew in several directions. HIV? Drugs? Crazy? He remembered her as exuding health at Sunrise, so much so Harris had referred to her companions as farmer's daughters. "What kind of sick?" He almost dreaded the answer.

"Brain tumor. Right on the base of her spinal cord. Growing like a weed and they were going to have to operate to stop it. Thing was, she might not have been the same Shelby afterward. Blind, maybe. Or just never wake up. A vegetable. Haven't touched as much as a carrot since."

Though his skin was now on fire, and he wanted to plunge into water up to his neck, Alex waited for the rest.

"She says, 'I know what they're doing up there, Papaw.'" Pierre's voice wavered. "She says, 'I'm going to talk to the governor about what's going on around here,' she says. 'I'm going to sit up there on the steps of the capitol building so he's got to step over me when he comes out. Maybe, I'll even make the news,' she said. I can see her now, laughing. She made the news, all right."

"Does Marisa know? Sorry, that was dumb. I heard her mention pain medication to Darla. I thought it was for the cramps or something simple like that."

"Yeah," Pierre said, finally wiping his nose on his

sleeve. "If only something simple as that. You know, they said you'd be coming, but I got to tell you I lost hope you would. I lost faith in the old ways."

Alex stuck out his hand to help the old man to his feet again. "I guess that makes two of us needing reminding. Come on, let's go kick some butt."

"Hell, haven't kicked any in years. Makes me feel right young again." Beside him, Pierre spat, mixing saliva with tears in the earth beneath their feet. In the wake of their footsteps, the moisture washed the soot from a tiny blade of grass. It rose green toward the morning sun.

Alex tapped on the screen door and heard Marisa's voice calling, "Come on in, Jimmy."

He lingered in the kitchen, not wanting to set Darla off again. From the sound of cutlery, she was actually eating. The kitchen smelled of bacon and eggs. On the counter there was homemade sour dough bread with two slices gone.

"Can I see you a minute, Mrs. Turner?"

"Sure, come on in the living room."

"My boots are dirty. Socks, too. If you wouldn't mind, I just want to tell you what Wilson said."

Marisa came into the kitchen without even glancing at his fouled clothes. Always the gracious hostess, she asked, "Want that coffee now? Or something stronger. You look like you could use a shot of T.C.'s medication, he calls it."

"No, thanks. I'm supposed to be at that interview and it would look kind of funny to come in half-looped. The coffee'll be fine, though."

She filled a mug and passed it over the kitchen counter. "Now, tell me what I don't already know."

"He says the toxic spray is just to drive ranchers off the ridge. Which is obviously working. He can only prove it by taking it to the state labs which he promises to do or—" He took a sip of coffee. It tasted better than any coffee he had ever had, probably because his mouth still tasted like burnt flesh.

Marisa waited, dark eyebrows raised. "Or?"

"Or I threatened to go to the newspapers with the story. And the television. Not here, naturally. But in Sacramento. It's an election year. Nobody wants this dropped in their laps."

"Okay, I know it's about me. You know you don't have to hide from me, Jimmy." Darla hung on to the doorframe, weaving as if she were drunk.

"Drink your coffee before it gets cold, dear. We're only talking about business, not you. Now go sit down and finish up. I need to visit T.C. and I wish you'd let me take you along. A little checkup won't hurt you, seeing as what Shelby had—" Marisa cut off the sentence and turned abruptly to the sink, busying herself with dishes.

"It's all my fault, isn't it? That's what you both really think, Marisa?" Darla reeled her way to the counter stool and plopped ungracefully. "I took her there. I know she told you. She wanted to go to the tunnel and I took her. We thought it would be such a hoot, sneaking in past the guards when they were playing cards and then hiding up in the catwalks, watching them ship all that stuff out. A guard saw us up there and chased us and we ran all over the place, laughing our heads off until he finally cornered us. They lowered the bay doors and we were trapped but I showed the way to the outside stairs. See, there's an escape staircase in case something in there blows up or something. So we hit those stairs and almost made it out, but somebody had ratted me out to Larry and I guess he ordered them to lock the staircase door. But that Shelby baby, she was bold. She was a gutsy girl and stood right up to Larry. Called him the Godfather of the Northern California mafia, baby killer, drug runner, everything she could think of. I could hardly stop laughing, I've never seen him so mad. Later on, she showed me something she'd grabbed when we were running. It was just an old label off one of those big oil drums or whatever they are. But it was a souvenir of our adventure, she said."

When Darla stopped talking, they both were staring at her.

Finally, Alex found his voice. "So I don't get it. Why does that make anything your fault? Do you think she got killed because you guys went in there? Then why haven't they tried to kill you?"

Darla's face froze in a dumfounded expression. "Maybe they have. Larry gives me all my drugs. Anything I want. Nobody would believe anything I say, especially the police. He's threatening to put me in one of those fancy detox hospitals. That's why I sent Danica to her grandma. I have to run away, but I can't leave my baby behind."

Here was yet a new quagmire of relationships threatening to swallow him whole should he dare to put a foot in their midst.

Once again, Marisa came to the rescue, apparently familiar with Darla's capacity for impulsive behavior. "You'll be eighteen in August, dear. Then you can do whatever you choose for yourself and Danica. In the meantime, you just stay with me and I swear I'll press charges against him if I have to. You understand what it would mean for Callie, though. You have to consider the fact she's been a wonderful surrogate mother to Danica."

Darla gave a horsey snort. "Aside from the drinking, you mean. But I'll have to admit she did what I asked her to do and got in real trouble for it. That's why, when Shelby got pregnant, we hatched a plan to move in together with the babies. It would have all worked, too. If Scott would've gotten her letter, he'd not have taken off like a scared cat."

Marisa picked up a letter from the pile she had only put down to make breakfast. "This is the last one. She wrote it on May fifth, ten days ago. She says, 'I know you think I'm just a crazy kid, but I love you with all my heart, Scottie. Now that the baby's coming, I want us to be together forever. I've told the doctors I'm not going in for surgery until after he's born because of the anesthetic and all. Also, if I'm going to die, I want to see him first. See, I know it's a boy.'" She put the letter back on the pile and started furiously washing up. "She didn't tell me, but she told you."

Darla got up and enveloped Marisa in her long arms. "She was afraid of what her dad would say. You know how men are about that kind of thing. Especially old farts like T.C."

He wasn't able to stand anymore and made his excuse to leave. Marisa walked him to the door, wiping her face on her apron. The sad smile she had glued on her lips hurt him more than her tears.

"I hope all this hasn't been too much baring of souls for you, Jimmy. And I wish you luck with your interview. I really do. I just hate to lose you." She patted his arm and he felt like a dog, leaving her in the kitchen doorway. "But you'll be among the bigwigs today. They'll be coming for the air show at the base. Even Senator Fulton Roberts, I hear. And Frankie Caprelli, the singer. Oh, go on now. I hope you get the job."

"'Course he'll get the job." Behind them, Darla was draped like colorful bunting in the doorway. "I'm going to come up there to Uncle Eddie's place to make sure, Jimmy. As soon as I check to see what the horses won. Can't wait to see you in that uniform you have to wear." There was that plaintive note in her voice again, the "lost child cry." It stopped him midway across the yard, midway through a thousand thoughts flying through his mind like a swarm of bats. If Shelby's painful confession to Scott Mason revealed him as her real lover, Darla's admission that she had allowed her friend a firsthand glimpse of Poseidon's operations also provided that company with a motive for murder. She was as much at risk as Marisa.

"Thanks, Darla. Feel better, okay?"

She took off for the bathroom and he took the opportunity to warn Marisa of the dangers of staying there. "You need to wait until the EPA gets involved. Find out what's killing these animals and making people sick."

Her dark head stayed bowed for a moment, and then she

straightened, pale and strong as a lily in a storm. "Oh, I know all these things are happening, but other people have tried to protest and they're gone now, too. Mrs. Kennedy across the ridge. She had an avocado orchard for thirty years. It had been in her family for three generations. She died two months ago from cancer. Her whole body was just riddled with tumors. I can name at least twelve cases around here right now." Touching her narrow fingers one by one, she ticked them off. "There was the Winters boy. Football player in high school. They had to amputate his leg because of a tumor in his knee. Cecile Bergstrom has only a few months to live. Cancer of the stomach. The Deiseldorfs, Smiths, Netherfields, and on and on. Dozens of local ranchers and farmers put out of business, unable to get farm loans at the bank, bad credit reports, health problems. No, after this thing with the fire, we're leaving, too. They can have the land because that's what they're after. Most of those people I named live on this side of the ridge or the other." She turned away, shaking her head. "They didn't deserve to die and neither did Shelby. "No, Jimmy, I appreciate you trying, but I've already called the auctioneer to come in. They can have it."

"Then, that's it. Sutton and Dalton are going to win."

Her voice rose to a scream as she whirled around. "I've been asking God, why? And there's no answer." She gestured toward the mountains, purple shadowed in the distance. "The answer's been up there all the time. It took so much losing to realize that we can't win." Marisa kept talking, almost to herself with an odd detached look. "One day, she was riding up there. She used to love to ride along that ridge. And a crop duster came along and sprayed her, right there on her horse. Her horse, the one she loved almost as much as us, she used to say, that horse died about four months later. His heart gave out, the local vet said. None of us believed him. He's on Sutton's payroll, just like almost everyone else here. So we got a vet to come over from the university at Chico State. He said the horse's lungs had hemorrhaged. Just like those poor sheep out there, only it took him longer to die. I raised those from lambs just like I raised my own lamb. What do they say about sacrificial lambs?" She nodded at the pasture. "I've lived here all my life. I grew up in these mountains up there. I'm the daughter of Pierre Bighand and I know sheep. This is the first time I've heard of animals dying like that. My Shelby swore up and down it was from the spray. And God forgive me, I didn't believe her. I was even mad at her for getting pregnant, Jimmy. For putting off the operation that would have saved her life! Because she would have been in the hospital this month and never died."

Her voice caught and hung on a sob. "Yes," she said slowly to the mountain, "let him come. We've got nothing else to lose. She died to save these people and this place." Marisa waved at the pastures flanking the mountains. Rudolfo and the crew were camping up there under some cottonwoods. Her laughter was slightly off-key and he wondered if she were on the edge of reason. "Sometimes, I think He did us a favor, letting her go like that."

Darla was back, her confidence in her ability to charm restored with mouth wash and a lot of perfume. She waved like a cheerleader to an adoring crowd. "I 'm better already." The orange juice and toast brought a little color back to her face, but she still looked as if nothing but water flowed in her veins. "See you later, honey!"

CHAPTER 20

urray sat straight up in bed and stared at the alarm
clock. She rubbed her eyes and looked again. It
was nine-thirty and she said she'd meet Larry
Sutton at eleven. Automatically, she reached for her cell
phone and then remembered. That dog-faced yokel, Duke
Whatever, had it and she had to get it back from him if she
had to break his arm. It would have her call records back to
headquarters in it and, if he started calling the numbers,
he'd find out who she was. Even scarier than that was the
possibility Jonesy would find out.

The underside of her eyelids felt as if she had slept in a
sandstorm. The only thing left in the room to drink was flat
beer and warm water. She took a little of each, reviving a
little. Snatching her big box store outfit out of the armoire,
Murray found the chartreuse capri pants fit looser than
when she had bought them last week. Waitressing was
harder than it looked and Murray made up her mind to always tip twenty percent even if the service was lousy. Who
knows, the girl might have had to put up with likes of hot-
hands Duke?

Matching it up with a frilly midriff top, she stepped the
platform heels that went with the outfit. Glad she took the
salesgirl's advice to accessorize or lose your guy; she added
a fringed purse, checked the tops on her false fingernails,
put on enough mascara to coat a stealth bomber and took
off for town. It was an easy walk and Murray got noisy ap-

proval from the half-ton pickup trucks roaring down the main street.

"Hey, baby, wanna ride?"

Adjusting her rhinestone rimmed sunglasses, she failed to notice as she usually would have, that two men in an SUV with smoked windows were slowly moving down the street behind her.

Larry Sutton was waiting for her in front of the Branding Iron. As she approached, he was on the cell phone which was usually glued to his ear. Seeing her, he snapped it shut and put it away, flashing his augmented smile. "Well, wowee! Look at this gorgeous chick I've got a date with! You are worth waiting for."

She picked up on the not-so-subtle hint that she was seven minutes late. "Sorry, my alarm didn't go off. You been waiting long?"

"Not a minute too long. May I say I admire your outfit?" He looked as if he couldn't keep his hands off her.

"You may. Before we go, would you mind if I checked with Callie to see if I left my cell phone in the ladies room last night? Will only take a jiffy, I promise."

Before she could take a step toward the bar, he said, "No need. I've got it right here." He pulled her phone out of the pocket of his tailored khakis. "Callie said Duke Cooper brought it in this morning." Murray had a moment of relief which didn't last long. Larry Sutton stepped up to her side, pulled her to him and, pressing his face to her ear, he said, "Why didn't you tell us you were an undercover detective, sweetie?"

"What?"

"He just said you're a cop, girlie, so get in the car nice and quiet." In tandem, two gorillas grabbed an arm each, and stuck a pistol in each arm pit. "Or you'll be one dead cop."

"It's a federal offense to kidnap a..." But it was lost in the roar of dooleys rumbling down main street.

Larry Sutton turned away, cell phone to his ear again,

taking up his conversation where it left off. "Take her up to Dr. Wu, boys. Let me know when she talks. I'll be at the Gorge."

"You're making a big mistake, Mr. Sutton." She tried to yell at some of the passing trucks, but the drivers just tooted their horns at the sight of a drug bust so early in the morning and right on Main Street.

In the back seat of the SUV with smoked windows and a screen for vicious dogs, she managed to touch the cell phone in her front pants pocket. Though the ugliest of the two goons was turning around watching her, and handcuffs on her wrist, using one finger she texted Jonesy the numbers *8995 Nancy Drew*.

❦

Detective Ronnie Jones was stuck in the drive through line of the fancy coffee chain, wondering why he hadn't been content with the donut place's plain cup of joe. But, no, he had to have a cappuccino caramel latte with extra caramel and one of those sticky buns with nuts on top. *That's what happens when you get spoiled*, he was thinking when Murray's text came through.

He called back but the phone was on voice mail. Uneasy, he dialed Figgy and then remembered Figgy had this Friday off for a reunion or some Italian thing. He called Hansen who had his voice mail on. Then he called Stockman, who of course, answered. He would already be there."

"Good morning, Jonesy." *Why aren't you here in person?* went unsaid. He was such a prick.

"Look, I think something's up with Schmitzy."

"Why?"

Jones told him and got a satisfied chuckle in return.

"Told you she couldn't handle it. So what do you want me to do, send out the Swat Team."

On the verge of telling Jersey Joe what he could do with

the Swat Team, Jonesy decided to stay cool. "No, I just thought I'd cruise on up to Diamond City and check on her, that's all. Look around. See if she's okay. No biggie."

"Oh, great! Figgy's out, Hansen's in some all-day conference on pornography so I'm stuck at my desk."

Better than stuck in the drive through. "Hey, I covered for you when your daughter got married. Again. Besides, you can watch the Sports Channel all day. Listen, Joe, I've got to check it out, okay?"

"Okay, but you're out of our jurisdiction up there, just remember that. That's strictly a no-no, to butt into someone else's jurisdiction."

"But I'm backing up an officer who's following a suspect in our jurisdiction." *Like I was born yesterday.* "Just tell Hansen I called in. I'll try to get back this afternoon but might just stay the night. Off the expense account. That ought to make his day. Ciao, baby." Unable to listen to anymore of Stockman's whining, he rang off.

It took him an hour and a half to get up to Diamondback City. It was Friday, after all, and the semis were having some kind of drag race through the rising terrain. Finally, he took the turnoff marked Diamondback City some local sniper had shot full of holes. He hated these little bergs trying to pretend they were something else besides rural industrial parks. As he turned into Main Street, he could tell it was one of those places where people always asked where you were from, knowing you weren't from there.

Schmitzy said she was working at the only singles bar in town and he found it without even consulting his phone memo. It was the only one that looked like it could afford to hire a waitress. The Branding Iron, for Pete's sake. How cute! He was glad Friday was dress down at work because he was wearing jeans. Otherwise, he'd look like he was selling something or, worse yet, CBI.

Getting out, he put money in the meter and a quarter slipped out of his hand. He followed its path to the gutter. It landed beside a pair of rhinestone chartreuse sunglasses.

Chartreuse. Hadn't Schmitzy mentioned a chartreuse something being part of her new undercover wardrobe? Leaning down, he picked them up and put them in his pocket on the off-chance someone would recognize them.

Someone did. The place didn't open until ten, but a very cute blonde woman responded to his ringing the doorbell. She looked as if she'd been crying, mascara underlining her blue eyes. He flashed his badge quickly to dispel the salesman image.

"Oh, thank God! Come in!"

They sat in her cluttered office where she immediately burst into tears when he pulled out the sunglasses. "Those are hers, poor baby! Oh, there's no telling what they'll do to her, Mr. Jones. They think they can do anything to people. I don't care if she is a police person. She's a darling girl and so kind."

Jones waited patiently until the pretty blonde had waded through a rambling account of her ex-boyfriend making a date with Schmitzy only to be told by some guy named Cooper she was a cop and then Larry called his goons and then kidnapped her broad daylight. After Callie, the blonde, stopped talking she began crying all over again.

"How long ago was this?" She told him and he realized it was when he received the code message waiting in line for his latte. "So did you call the police?"

Callie was aghast that he should even have brought that up. "On Larry? He'd only say I was lying and come back later to get me! And then I'll never see my baby again!" She broke into another wail and snorted into a tissue. "Never!"

Whoever this Larry dude was, he definitely alpha dog around Diamondback. "First, we're going to tell the police, Miss Callie. And then you can tell me and them where they took Schmitz…Silk."

"No, she won't and you won't." The man in the door was short and Jonesy could have taken him out if he hadn't been pointing a gun at him. Another man who looked like a reject from the Sumo circle, barged in and frisked him.

"No heat, Mr. Sutton. Shall I cork him?" The man with the gun nodded and Sumo hit Jonesy with a side chop to the neck. While he was on the floor, Sumo started closing his windpipe with two fingers until he was thrashing for air. The blonde screamed and everything went black.

෬෬෬

Before going to Colonel Dalton's room at the Royal Gorge, Alex dropped by Silk's boarding house on the pretense that if she had any further trouble with Duke Cooper, to call him. Or call him anyway. He really just wanted to see her in the daylight, and then refused to admit to himself that was the real reason. He told himself how stupid that was when Mrs. Rodriguez, the sentry turned landlady, said she wasn't there.

"At breakfast, she said she was going to meet a friend for lunch today. And she'd better watch the kind of friends she makes down at that place where she works. Not the type of people a young girl like that should be around, if you want my opinion. However, seeing as how I had been busy with breakfast and had stepped out to run to the bakery, you can go up and check to see if she has left yet on her date." Rodriguez was less than hospitable. "Second door on the left. And don't stay for more than a minute or two. I don't allow male guests in girls' rooms," she called as he ascended the narrow staircase.

Upstairs, the second door on the left was wide open. Cautiously, he rapped on the door and then stepped inside. The place had been ransacked. Drawers pulled out, their contents strewn around the room. Her suitcase was open on the bed, and for a moment, he wondered if she were trying to pack in a hurry. Then he heard the clatter of things falling in the bathroom and the sound of male voices. In an instant, Alex was back out in the hall, snatching up the morning paper from the doormat. He was sitting in the window box at the end of the hall, pretending to read when two men came out of Silk's room.

"Hell, let's get out of here. There's nothing in there except a lot of cheap underwear. I ain't about to tell him we didn't find anything. At least come up with some drugs or something. It makes me feel stupid." One of the men had the Tex-Mex accent of a Hispanic born in the Southwest.

"Shut up, will you? There's a guy right down the hall. You want the whole world to hear you."

Although he was half-turned away, he heard the floorboards of the old frame house creak as their footsteps hesitated. His whole body tensed, ready for action. He exhaled slowly as they continued on down the stairs, still griping about the useless errand.

Slowly lowering the paper, Alex caught a glimpse of them as they turned on the landing. There was no doubt in his mind the dark one was one of the men he had seen at O'Hara's. The other was a rat face he'd never forget. It was Angel Rivera.

⌘

The Royal Gorge was hard to miss. It was the only building above two stories in Diamondback City with no hint of Victorian bric-a-brac or cowboy charm. Sleek and ultra-environmentally friendly, it made no bones about being a five-star hotel and spa. Subtle hints were plastered all over the boulders forming its site just under the gorge falls. Mineral Spa this way, heated pool that way. Riding trails, nature walks, green living space—whatever that was. Tennis courts, the works. Since he was in the mood to kill somebody, it hardly registered on Carreras. The fact that this paradise existed within ten miles of suffering residents was like a slap in the face of humanity.

The snotty doorman registered his lack of luggage and stained boots. "May I help you, sir?"

"I'm here to see Colonel Dalton," Alex said.

The doorman dropped the snootiness. "I'll get someone to escort you there in a jiffy."

"If you just tell me the room number, I'll escort myself."

The doorman oozed over to the wall phone. "Can I say who's calling?"

"Vargas. Jim Vargas. It's okay, he's expecting me."

Alex didn't know if Dalton even remembered him and didn't care. Instead of the elevator, he took the stairs two at a time, to the penthouse.

A man he could only describe as a paid bodyguard opened the door. He had the look of a combat veteran, not caring a flip who you were, ready to kill if you weren't who you said you were. "You Vargas? How come you're so damned late?"

"I'll ask the questions, thanks, Burnie. Come on in, Jimmy. Never mind his manners. Burnie doesn't know what they are."

As he entered the penthouse suite, Alex tried to do a Jimmy Vargas impression—dazzled by fake Spanish revival décor that came off more like Italian mafia. As he hesitated in the entry hall, the colonel waved him impatiently to a vinyl monolith.

Dalton wasted no time, lighting up a cigar to join one of many butts in the ashtray.

"I said last night I was offering you a job and since you showed up this morning, I take it you want it."

Alex sat forward in his chair, as Vargas would have. Uncomfortable with authority, wary of traps. "Maybe. What kind of a job is it?"

"Security. Just bodyguard kind of stuff. By the looks of you in action last night, you'll know what to do if the time comes."

"Do I carry a gun?"

Behind him in the entry way, Burnside laughed. It wasn't a pleasant sound. "He's asking if he packs heat. What a greenhorn."

"I'm not deaf, Burnie. And find something else to do beside butt into other people's conversations, will you?" By the looks of it, risking Dalton's displeasure was on the short list of things not to do. Burnside faded into the depths of the suite, still chuckling about a pistol.

"Not yet. As you probably guessed, Burnside has dibs on that part of it. No, you just use your fists and that'll be fine. Later on, Burnside can show you some stuff that hopefully you won't have to use. Right now, I just need you to back up Burnie in a little soap opera we've got going on here. You just do what he says and that'll be fine. We'll break you in slowly. Two thousand a week sound good to you?"

For that kind of money, it wasn't hard to fake the Vargas-looking-amazed expression. "You kidding me, right?"

Dalton sat back in his overstuffed quasi-Mediterranean chair and took a long pull on his cigar. "I don't kid, Vargas."

"I don't have to kill nobody, do I?"

That got a chuckle out of the stoic colonel. "Not yet, Jimmy."

Burnside came back, cell phone to his ear. "He's coming. Limo's downstairs now."

Dalton nodded. "Good. Jimmy, you can go behind the bar and serve drinks. You know how to do that."

Sure, all Latinos know how to wait tables. "I guess so."

"Know so, flacco."

"That's it, Burnside. Knock it off." The edge in Dalton's voice could have cut a steak.

"I'll go on downstairs to meet him, that is, if you want." Burnside checked his slick-backed hair in the hall mirror and put his sunglasses on. "Think I look threatening enough?"

"I think you look like an idiot with those shades on inside a hotel. But get on down there. Roberts always expects bowing and scraping. That's your job, thank God, not mine." The colonel got up and went to the club-sized bar. "Come on over here, Vargas, and mix me a drink. Just

Scotch on the rocks, that's enough mixing for me. Just whiskey and ice."

Going behind the bar, Alex poured the Scotch over ice and gave it to Dalton who was studying every move he made. "Never done this before? You seem like a natural. Knew right away Chivas Regal was scotch and which glass to use. Ice in ice maker."

Alex did the dumb-ox look and shrug. "It ain't rocket science. I can read labels."

"Don't kid me, Vargas. Correction, Carreras. A punk like you're trying hard to be wouldn't have known Chivas Regal from Diet Pepsi." The wrinkles at the corners of Dalton's eyes fanned out as he took a long sip. "Elixir of the Gods, Wu called it."

"'Scuse me? I don't get it."

"Get it quick. I know who you are. And I've got to say you've got balls, Carreras, coming up here trying to get on the inside of Poseidon's operation. Last couple of guys who tried that ended up as toxic dust. "

"Man, you got me mixed up with somebody else. I'm outta this place." Playing dumb now was the only way to counter Dalton's dovetailed moves. Alex stormed out of the bar, heading for the door.

The colonel held up the glass he was holding. "Got your fingerprints? Care to compare, Carreras?" When he tried to open his mouth, Colonel Dalton just waved his hand. "Oh, just cut the crap and let me talk. We don't have time to play charades anymore. Like I told you last night, I've got a job for you to do. Right now, the police are sniffing up your butt. You're wanted in connection with the Turner girl's death and embezzling millions. They're even saying you visited Sanchez before he died."

Alex fell into the trap with such ease, he later wondered about his courtroom skills. "Sanchez? My god, you killed Sanchez! You set the whole damn thing up!"

"And if you don't play ball, you'll get two consecutive life sentences without parole." The colonel leaned against the bar, regarding Alex over the rim of his glass, his eyes reading even the pulsing vein in his neck. "They've got you coming and going."

Ed Dalton turned his back and strolled back to his chair. For a brief moment, he considered bringing down the bottle on the man's head. "Don't even think about hitting me with something. It'll only get you in deeper shit than you are now."

Alex decided to fight fire with fire. Fire seemed to be something Dalton liked to play with anyway. "Okay, I'll cover your ante. I've got enough on you and Sutton to put both of you away in federal prison until one, you die, or two, you pay somebody really high up enough to get out of smuggling classified military equipment. And don't threaten me with Shelby Turner's murder. I've got almost enough to make it a party of three with Duke Cooper."

The colonel was amused. "The key word there is 'almost.' You and I both know 'almost' don't do it in federal court. Not with a man like Fulton Roberts connected with this operation. Even 'damn sure' doesn't do it. Why don't you listen to my proposal and then decide whether we're just chump change in this little game or the high rollers?"

There was the word "game" again, the way men with power used it. A game played to the death with real people. A globalized version of Real Kill, Real Thrill. Alex thought about Sanchez, his wife just delivering a child. Shelby Tate, pregnant and ill. Marisa, so full of pain and sorrow, she was a walking tombstone. But Dalton kept talking, watching him the way a predator watches prey, and waiting for the first indication of fear and anger.

Alex struggled not to display either and he couldn't tell whether the colonel was impressed or not. Not that he cared.

Returning to the bar, Dalton poured two more neat whiskies and handed one glass to him "Come, sit down. You see, Alex, we've been steering your career right along. The 'we' being Crittenden and I."

"And then you destroyed it. Excuse me if I don't quite get that." Alex found himself gulping the whiskey down and immediately needing another stiff one.

Dalton rattled the ice in his glass as if it were dice. He leaned forward, greenish eyes glinting like broken glass. "Lots of good reasons. Number one, we needed you for a specific job. Number two, we needed you out of the way. You screwed yourself when you snooped around Synotech's LA facility. You caught on too quick and we had to put a stop to it pronto. And, three, Crittenden wanted you gone so it was perfect."

"And you just had to kill Shelby Turner as part of the game. You know she had two things growing inside her, a brain tumor and a baby. You and that ass Sutton are spraying toxic chemicals around here to drive the farmers off their land. Sanchez was a good cop. His wife was having a baby while he was upstairs in the ICU. What kind of scum are you that you couldn't let them live to see their children?" Alex put down his glass and walked over to where Dalton sat, slumped in his massive chair. "How can you live with yourself, Dalton?"

He saw something new in Dalton's face as the colonel looked at him, something like admiration. "That's why you're here, Carreras. You're smart. Too smart. You've got the files on the shipments, and you know the drill on the doctored manifests. That's why your ass is so hot; I'm surprised you can sit on it."

"Go ahead. You could turn me in, and I could spill what I know about this whole operation."

Somewhere, deep in the leather chair, he heard a laugh. "Hell, ain't this grand? Dog eat dog. You won't live to go to court but you'll be an exonerated corpse."

"Better than a dishonored one." Alex started for the door.

"Sit down. Where're you off to, anyway?"

"In case you'd forgotten, I've already got a job helping the Turners. Now, if you don't mind, I'll get back to work."

Something froze Dalton in his interrogative position, but he went on, filling in the moment neatly. "I grew up around here. Used to date Marisa before T.C. moved in on her when I joined the air force. Crittenden and I, we had something bloodless in mind, like your misusing funds. Padding your expense account. Accepting gifts from clients, that sort of thing. Something that would enable the firm to get rid of you quietly. The Turner girl thing was set up on the other end, not by us. Apparently, they had specific reasons."

"Why in hell should I believe you? Why do you keep saying 'they,' when it's really you and Sutton and Crittenden? And should I add Syd Harris to the list?"

Dalton shrugged as if he'd been asked why the sky was blue. "As I see it, Carreras, you really don't have a choice. Your career is ruined any way you look at it. And you will be very valuable as well as well paid if you take us up on our offer. I believe you are a bright enough fellow to grasp that." He blinked and smiled urbanely. "No, the way to look at this, Carreras, is that it's the opportunity of a lifetime. The end of one phase of your career and the start of a brilliant new one if you help us."

"Now, why the hell would I help you? You sit around destroying people's lives and, for all I know, murdering them. So far you've been unchallenged, covering up smuggling arms as medical supplies and chemicals to third world countries. All that's going to stop right now, because I'm turning myself in. And I'll get my day in court. Help you? I'd rather help a bunch of maniacal terrorists." Carreras started for the door again, half-expecting Dalton to pull a gun on him after two steps.

He wasn't prepared for the weary note in Dalton's voice. "To get your day in court, Carreras, we have to stop Fulton Roberts from being re-elected to the senate. If we expose his connection to these shipments, we're going to ruin his chances of becoming President of the United States and maybe, out of politics for good. And you can help us do that. Combined with what you know and what we know, we can bring him down."

It was the last thing Alex expected the colonel to say.

Dalton took advantage of his speechlessness by continuing. "Now, let me show you something." He picked up a remote from the couch and pointed it at the wall. A panel pulled slowly aside revealing an enormous entertainment center. A film began running on the theater-sized screen and Alex was startled to see himself, beardless and impeccably dressed in casual clothes at a packed bar. He was talking to a group of other young lawyers about something unclear because the sound was muffled by a television blaring. More clips of himself doing various things and Dalton fast forwarded to Sunrise the previous weekend. The times and dates were noted digitally at the corner of each screen. He was stunned to see himself drinking with Rick, Kirkendall, and Tim Hardaway as well as the others at his bachelor party in the local singles bar. He saw Kirkendall get up and talk with a blonde girl behind the bar. Their conversation wasn't audible behind the noise and the twanging of country music but he had no trouble recognizing Callie Murphy in the brief Western outfit he remembered the waitresses wore.

Reaching in his wallet, Kirkendall deftly folded a bill and shoved it across the counter. Callie picked it up and nodded, then called to another girl with a camera around her neck. She took the camera and swished over to their group and then to the group of girls at the next booth. There was Shelby Turner alive in a red sweater and jeans, laughing with her friends. His heart lurched in his chest, at the sound of her voice, lilting and full of spirit. She was so animated and alive, and just as pretty as he had imagined she would be. A girl to love.

Callie's husky voice rose above all else. "Hey, those dishy guys over there said they want to take a picture with you gorgeous chicks. They're all lawyers from LA, looking for high country fun!"

The girls giggled and whooped at the suggestion. "Hey, why not?" one of them yelled. "C'mon, Shelby! Let's go."

"Yeah, come on, girlfriend. No use crying over that Scottie loser anyway. Have some fun. Find another guy. Hey, LA lawyers and cute, too."

She was reluctant and had to be pulled and cajoled out of her chair.

In a cluster, they made their way over to the bachelor party to have their pictures taken.

"This is the good part. Watch this." Dalton smiled as if he were actually enjoying this setup.

Tim Hardaway played host, getting up to welcome the girls with open arms. "Right this way, girls. I'm single and in line for a very big promotion. Come on, guys. Grab a gorgeous babe and let's boogie. And, Alex, I've got Miss Sunrise herself for you. Sweet as violets in May, right?" He slipped his arm around Shelby's shoulder. "Get him up here, boys. This is his last chance at freedom."

Alex watched himself, really drunk, being pulled out of the booth by Kirkendall and shoved toward Shelby. With a wink at Kirkendall, Hardaway changed places with Shelby, pressing her against him.

"Okay, everybody grab a mug and say, "Cheese!""

Callie showed the deep cleavage she was known for as she bent over the lens. "Closer, everybody! I've got to squeeze you all in!"

"You heard the lady, squeeze, everybody. Say, Squeeze!" The whole line of them made an effort to press together, Hardaway and Kirkendall shoving Shelby almost under his chin. He even remembered how she had been laughing, but slightly uncomfortable.

After the pictures, he danced with her. Then he heard the music to the words going around in his head. "There's a young boy that I know, his age is twenty-one. Comes from down in Southern Colorado." That's when she asked him what he did for a living and he said he was a lawyer.

The room phone rang and Dalton shut off the VCR. His

conversation was brief. "Well, when he's finished, he can come on up here. I'm not going down there, I told you." He slammed the phone down. "Damn politicians anyway. Hardaway and Kirkendall. Two very ambitious young men. And all ambitious young men have a weak side, including you. Yours is trying to be a hero." He sipped his drink with narrowed eyes. "There was something in it for everybody. You put a burr up Roberts's ass by getting out the Hispanic voters in the race for the district seat. He had to do some fancy dancing to keep his man in the seat. Cost him no small change. Crittenden's daughter was pregnant with Hardaway's child. Crittenden never wanted you for a full partner in the first place. It was always in the cards she would marry Hardaway. His father is an old friend of Parker's, an old yachting buddy with plenty of cash. When her taste strayed to you, Crittenden saw red, threatened to cut her out of his will, all that stuff. When you started getting suspicious of the Synotech account, the order simply came down from Poseidon to get rid of you. To give Parker credit, he never thought it was for a murder rap. They were going to charge you with skimming company money or something. So, everybody got what they wanted. Kirkendall repaid a very large credit card with the proceeds, I understand. Wife, baby on the way. Easy mark. Hardaway will get your slot and keep Kirkendall in the perks. Watch now." The VCR sped forward to the intersection of the country highways. There was his red jeep limping toward the blue van and the custom Cherokee. It was all there. Dalton shut it off. "Seen enough?"

Alex sat down feeling ill, as if he had been drugged. "Who killed her?" Not a hard liquor drinker, the whiskey had gone straight to his head.

"Hell, I'm not sure, but Roberts knows. It was edited out when I got it. The point I'm trying to make is we've been tracking you since you hooked up with Chelsea."

"But why? Why did they kill her?" Cold fury was eating his stomach lining, and Alex jumped to his feet again, this time pacing the room. "She was just a kid, dammit."

"And she was Darla's best friend and they're on the way up here." In the silence, the elevator bell dinged Robert's arrival. Dalton's unwavering stare was battle-ready, armor-tight and dead level. "You in or out with me, Carreras? Tell me now. They're here."

Alex stood his ground. "I don't care if all hell comes through that door. Tell me who killed that girl first."

The colonel sat back as if satisfied. "If I tell you everything you want to know, then you're in by default. That film was taken by Poseidon's Eye, the missile guidance system Senator Roberts has been trying to get the Arms Committee's approval for to target suspicious civilians. Homeland Security is the umbrella agency that supposedly supervises it and, without public knowledge, has implemented it eight years ago. Now there's a navy blue blazer and khaki pants in your measurements third room on the left down the hall. Go change out of the cowboy gear and get behind the bar. Now."

Burnside came in first, holding the door open for Fulton Roberts who was followed by a couple of efficient-looking babes in business suits, and Angel Rivera. "Don't get pissed, Ed. I know we're running behind schedule. Damned Caprelli wanted photo ops in the lobby. Then we had re-takes just to make sure they got his best side. Can you get over what an egomaniac that guy is?"

For one of the few times in his life Alex Carreras obeyed a direct order. By the time the party had made its way into the living room, he was down the hall looking for the third room on the left. From the front room, Dalton's voice came back to him, strong and deep as the whiskey in his glass. "No, Fulton, I can't say that I can."

✃✃✃

When the car stopped, Murray got a glimpse of some

kind of industrial park. Before she was roughly blindfolded, she committed it to memory. A few struggling palms. The sense of being at the foot of a high elevation from the slight shadow cast down over the area despite noon sun. Then she was dragged into an area echoing with the sound of machinery, especially the repetitive flip-flip sound of a conveyor belt. After a short trip on an elevator, she was pushed into a small enclosed area with a medicinal odor and tied to a chair. The door slammed and locked, and for a moment, she thought she had been left alone.

Fighting panic, she busied herself trying to loosen the blindfold by shaking her head.

"That won't be necessary," a mild voice said behind her. "Here, let me remove that for you." The cloth dropped from her eyes and Murray looked into the bland face of an Asian man in a white lab coat. "There, that's better, isn't it?"

"Who are you?"

He looked like the neighborhood dentist, carefully setting out his instruments on a white towel. His emotionless smile frightened her more that the fact she was helpless. "My name is Dr. Wu. And you are a young lady who goes by the charming name of Miss Silk." He bowed slightly from the waist. "How do you do, Miss Silk?"

"I am not Miss Silk. I am a police officer. And I am ordering you to free me immediately, unless you want to lose your license by being an accomplice to the kidnapping of a law enforcement officer."

In dealing with run-of-the-mill criminals, that statement alone could send them into recanting vows to the local drug dealers or gang lords. Dr. Wu, however, with an Asian sense of irony, thought she was just being droll. "Oh, my! Lose my license! I am quite impressed by your knowledge of the law, Miss Silk." Wu made an effort to master a good humored smile as if sparing a child embarrassment. "I am not a physician. Well, not in the United States. I am research scientist. And, if you will forgive my correction, you are not being kidnapped. Merely detained."

"Correction, Dr. Wu. To merely detain someone against their will is to kidnap them. However, they might refer to it in your country as temporary detainment."

Intrigued by the nuances of semantics, Wu countered with equal certainty. "I think they refer to it as detainment for the purposes of obtaining information. The question of whether or not someone wishes to be detained unfortunately never arises."

"Let me remind you this is America and the question always arises because that's the law. So please untie me and I will be on my way without mentioning your part in all this stuff." She looked around. "Where am I anyway?" The constant hum of machinery permeated the walls of the small room which appeared to be some kind of laboratory fitted with stacks of shelves and metal cabinets.

"I believe that was the whole point of the blindfold, Miss Silk. Now, if you will excuse me, I have a little more work before we go."

"Go?" She tried to swivel around to see where he went. "Go where? I'm not going anywhere, you hear me?" But the only reply was the soft sound of a closing door. *Oh, God, Jonesy. Where are you now?*

Inching the chair across the floor, she loosened the rope around her arms enough to hook the rope binding her hands on the drawer pulls. But the pain of trying to lift her arms against the tight rope became almost unbearable and the drawer kept opening as she worked the rope. Finally, she swiveled around enough to see if there was anything sharp enough in the drawer to cut the rope with. A knife. Anything. Looking sideways into the drawer, she saw nothing but cotton swabs and hypodermic needles in plastic bags. Hypodermic needles! Where had she landed, in a mental hospital?

Footsteps approached outside the door, and Dr. Wu was back, accompanied by a pretty Asian nurse. The door opened as they carried on a lively conversation that sounded as if it were not about medicine. The young woman's face lit up with delight as she saw Silk and she nodded her approval to Dr. Wu. He looked very pleased, and they both nodded again to her. For some reason Murray couldn't identify, the affable Dr. Wu and his pretty little nurse frightened her more than Larry Sutton's goons.

"I see you have been trying to escape, Miss Silk. Very good action. Shows much spirit and courage." He signaled to the nurse to swab her arm with an alcohol pad.

Murray tried to match his attempt at formal conversation. "I'm really glad you approve. That's shows you've had a lot of experience with kidnapping victims."

"Excellent joke. It is sarcasm, is it not? I went to UCLA, you know. We studied sarcasm in English Literature." He was busying himself with something he had pulled from his pocket. Her eyes walled sideways, making out a hypodermic needle. "Sarcasm," he said as if relishing the syllables.

"Listen, Dr. Wu, I'm not kidding now. I don't know if you're familiar with American law, but detaining people, especially a police officer, is a federal offense. And I don't know where you're from, but—" She broke off as he began rolling up the sleeve of her shirt. "What are you doing?"

"Not to worry. Just administering a little sedative to calm you down. You are very nervous, no doubt." He rubbed an alcohol swab on her arm, and she felt a sudden prick. Detective classes had not prepared her for this.

"I don't need a sedative. I need to get out of here."

"Don't worry about a thing, Miss Silk. You will get out of here very soon."

"Why doesn't that reassure me?" she thought she said.

Before he had even closed the door, she knew something very wrong was happening to her. A sudden rush of warmth flooded her entire body and she began to perspire. The room began to blur in and out, like bad television reception. She fought to keep her head up until a curtain of darkness came down, pulling her chin toward her chest as it descended. One last, desperate thought formed in her mind. *Dad! Help me!*

CHAPTER 21

He was serving drinks—a soda for Roberts, third set-up for Dalton when Syd Harris arrived with Parker Crittenden. Alex kept moving, head down, eyes averted when taking drink orders, passing the deluxe mixed nuts as he had observed other waiters doing. At any moment, it was inevitable Crittenden would point an accusing finger at him and, in rich, urban tones, say, "Carreras, we've got you at last! How foolish to think you could escape."

Alex had already put together an escape route—third door down on the right led to a bedroom with a balcony in jumping distance to the one next to it. It worked in movies, anyway, unless Rivera or Burnside or both decided to use him for target practice. In that case, Alex would drop like a stone down to the balcony below, no doubt landing on some banker deep in the *Wall Street Journal*.

Stocks are falling today.

However, the inevitable never came. He should have known Crittenden treated all servants as if they were interchangeable parts and barely glanced at him, except to request dry Vermouth on the rocks.

Alex caught Dalton's eye. The colonel smiled his humorless smile with eyebrows raised as if saying, *See I told you so.*

However, Roberts's eyes darted around the room, making a mental list of discrepancies. "Who's he?" he asked, jerking his head toward Alex as if he couldn't understand English.

"Oh, let me tell him, Eddie. He's really my discovery." Syd Harris put his drink down and fastidiously wiped his hands on a cocktail napkin. "His name's Vargas. He's one of the best impromptu fighters I've ever seen, and I've already offered him a position as my personal bodyguard and traveling companion."

"I'll bet you have, Sydney," the senator replied, with a smirk at the others. "He speaks Spanish too, I take it. Ought to come in real handy in some of those bars in Puerto Rico you like."

If Harris got the point, he didn't care. "I just thought he might come in handy today, Fulton. He needs a little polish in this type of operation. But as a street fighter, I saw him take out Larry's goons single-handed."

"As long as he knows enough to keep his mouth shut, then okay. Angel's not always around and Burnie's Dalton's sidekick, right, Eddie?

"Right, Fulton."

"So what's the deal with Caprelli? Won't he cough up the money or what?"

Alex got the impression Dalton was leading Roberts into a trap.

Apparently satisfied Alex wasn't an FBI informant, the boyish senator relaxed from the defensive crouch he had assumed. Although his wide shoulders and lean build made him appear taller than he really was, Roberts was a short man. A favorite with photographers, he was being hailed as another John Kennedy in the making—the smile, the boyish look, even the hair. He commanded people's attention when he spoke with that Type A energy hammering every word in place like ten-penny nails. "His excuse is he's had this hot tamale from Ecuador who's pregnant again and the wife— you remember Dagmar Jorgenson, the Swedish bombshell from Minnesota?"

"Dagmar Jorgenson. I always thought she was gorgeous." Crittenden put in a rare remark, proving he was still alive. "Especially in those centerfolds. Had one on my closet door in college. I used to lie in bed imagining every bikini waxing. Which reminds me, I'd better freshen up before I leave for town." His slight smirk let everyone know he was sleeping with Sherianne, his eighteen-year old mistress.

"My point, Parker. You're going to end up in the same boat as Frankie without a paddle. Dagmar's in Mexico having her third body sculpt combo with facelift and he's whining about the bill. I got him the Vegas date and a couple more supper clubs since then and he's still whining about the contribution to the campaign. Bottom line, I need some muscle behind me."

"You came to the right place, Senator." Syd Harris waited for Dalton's affirmation of his loyalty. It didn't come. "We've arranged delivery of the Eye system tomorrow. As planned, I'm proud to say."

To Crittenden's credit, he delayed his trip to the bathroom to take issue. "Exactly what does muscle entail, Fulton? I don't want to get into a situation which attracts attention to Synotech's operation or, for that matter, Poseidon."

Washing up the glasses behind the bar, Alex heard more than he saw.

Roberts's transition into a malignant force simply stunned everyone in the room. "You, of all people, Parker, shouldn't be questioning my judgment. I am, after all, the person who got rid of this Carreras, the so-called threat to your firm and your daughter's happiness, aren't I? I do all these things out of the goodness of my heart for people who are disloyal to me? How do you think that makes me feel? In the instance that you yourself should be implicated in anything illegal, wouldn't you think I'd stand by you?" Quickly, before Parker Crittenden had time to reply, Roberts continued. "If you're with me, you'll approve of me calling in some favors. If you're not, then I will remember who you are."

In response to Roberts's not-so-veiled threat, Crittenden

became as sincere as Alex had ever seen him. "Look, Fulton, I just meant I don't approve of violence to achieve political advantage. Never have, never will."

Roberts held up his hand to deflect apologies. "Never mind, Parker. I understand your aversion to violence. Which is why when we were captured. you wanted to negotiate our release with Tiger's forces instead of ordering commandos in. But we were the ones suffering, not you back in your air-conditioned office in Kabul."

Crittenden remained detached, even unconcerned in contrast to Roberts. "I've explained all that before. It would have cost American and Afghan lives as well as yours. You're forgetting Tiger rebels behead and mutilate prisoners if they aren't paid off. Really, Fulton, you're caught up in the past. It's time to cut our ties with the Tiger and his little oligarchy."

Roberts became his media persona by getting to his feet and pacing around the room, hands clasped behind him. "Never mind, Parker. We're in two different camps on this. I respect choices, but appeasement doesn't work. Only power does and with your support, or without it, I'm going to get that power. You talk about Tiger with the same wimpy attitude you showed then, but you don't want to be his nemesis. I do. Now, let's get Frank Caprelli's support. Burnside? Vargas? You with me?"

Colonel Dalton nodded at Alex. "Go on. Do what Burnie says and you might learn a few things."

Rivera had been out in the hall smoking with the suite door ajar. While Alex took his time behind the bar, he saw Fulton Roberts stride to the foyer and call Angel Rivera inside. It had been five years since Alex had seen Rivera, but rats never changed, except for a slight paunch as they matured. While Roberts was bending his ear, Rivera remained a true rodent, sliding glances around the room as if he smelled green cheese. It was clear he was looking for anything worth stealing. Not that he would break in himself. No, he was big-time now. Hobnobbing with politicians like

Roberts. Men in gray suits instead of guard uniforms.

Powerful men like Roberts who slipped a set of keys with a brief exchange. "It's an easy one, this time. Black Jaguar in the second level of the garage. It's got an alarm system."

Rivera caught the keys with a snap of his hand. "No problem. When do I get paid?"

"Same way. It's already in your account."

"I need cash tonight. Traveling expenses. You know."

Fulton slapped him on the shoulder just as Crittenden emerged from the bathroom still smoothing his hair. "You'll get it. Now, shove off." He caught Dalton's eyes burning green with a warning look over Harris's balding head. "How about a drink for Mr. Harris, Jimmy. Gin and tonic. No ice."

Parker Crittenden sat down between the other two. "I'll have one of those for the road."

At Dalton's call, Burnside returned to the room. Walking briskly over to the colonel, he leaned down to speak softly in Dalton's ear.

"Aw, shit! Larry's done it again."

The colonel got on the cell phone again while Roberts joined them, crouching into a chair. "What's the matter, Ed? How did he screw up?"

Dalton cradled the phone between shoulder and chin. "He hired some waitress who turns out to be an undercover cop. Vice squad or some damn thing."

"So? Did he take care of it?"

"He sent her up to Freddie Wu to work over. He'll call us as soon as he gets something out of her. Springer and Rivera searched her place for clues, but Cooper got her cell phone last night. That's how he found out who she was. Yeah, Larry, what's going on?...Yeah....Yeah. Fulton's here. Get the hell on over, quick time." Dalton hung up, cursing under his breath. "Jimmy, fix me another one of these, will you? This looks like a full-pint morning."

Conversation erupted from everyone present. Behind the

bar, Alex took his time filling orders, thinking in the next breath, he would be revealed as the person who rescued Silk from Cooper early this morning.

Fortunately for him, Roberts was under a fund-raising deadline. "As long as he takes care of it, I don't care what he does. We have to get Caprelli before he goes on tonight. That's when he doesn't want bruises showing."

Dalton stowed his cell phone in his pocket.

Roberts exchanged looks of disgust with Burnside. "I knew Sutton would screw up. Hates to take orders. Burnie, you and…you," he said over his shoulder to Alex and merely motioned to him, "come with me."

"It's Vargas," Ed Dalton said from the chair. "Jimmy Vargas."

"Whatever," Roberts muttered as he cannonballed out into the hall. "Just follow me."

As Alex followed Roberts's gaggle of the faithful out the door, something told him Dalton, Harris, and Crittenden were clustering together behind him like the petals of a man-eating plant. Dalton, however, never took his eyes from the action. When Alex glanced back, he raised his glass in the silent salute of Romans to their gladiators.

They waited for the elevator in a silent, twitchy group, Alex lit a cigarette. The reaction was as if he had set off a four-alarm fire. "Hey, no smoking, mister," one of them said. "Fulton doesn't allow it."

The senator turned around. "Who's smoking?"

"The new guy," Burnside said. "He's used to bodega bars where you get the habit just by breathing."

The group flattered Burnie with a little wave of giggles, all except Roberts. "Have a talk a talk with him, Burnie. I don't like it around me."

Alex wondered if he ever addressed anyone outside his entourage in the first person.

"And what's that on his boots?"

Everyone turned to look down at Alex's worn cowboy boots.

"That's cowshit, Senator. We've got a lot of it around here."

"See that he stays off the carpet, will you?"

The elevator finally arrived, spilling out Darla in a wave of French perfume. "Uncle Fultie! I'm so glad I caught up with you! You didn't come out to the fairgrounds to give my horses ribbons like you promised." She had to bend slightly to hug him. Over his shoulder, she winked at Alex.

"Hi, beautiful! I'm on my way there, but I have just a little bit of business first. Did you win a bunch?"

She waggled four long fingers. "Four, baby. Four blue. I'm going to hang out here until you're ready, if that's okay. Want a bunch of pictures with me on the grandstand like you promised. Oh, hi, Jimmy, you look sharp. If you don't need Jimmy for a minute, Uncle Fultie, I have to borrow him." Like a sockeye salmon going upstream, she parted the group to get to him. "Promise I'll return him in better shape than he started out."

"Lucky man," Roberts said, hiding his annoyance behind that boyish grin. There were subdued snickers as looks were passed around like canapés before the real party began.

"But we're short one man. We need him pronto, Senator," Burnside complained.

"Five minutes, Darla, honey," Fulton said, stepping into the elevator. "I give the orders, Burnside, in case anyone forgets."

"Five minutes, Vargas," Burnside warned through the closing door. "Fourth floor, Suite twenty-one. You've got five."

The second the elevator left, they fled to the exit stairs and started talking at once. "No, you've got to listen, Jimmy. They've got that girl Silk up at the plant. God knows what they're going to do to her. You've got to come with me to get her out!"

"Silk? How do you know?" Her hands were shaking so badly he lit a cigarette for both of them.

"Callie saw them through the front window of The Iron.

Said she met Larry and then his thugs dragged her at gun point into their car. She just called me. You don't know what he does to girls. He raped me when I was fifteen. Danica's my baby, not Callie's. For a while, I thought she wanted to take her away from me. Now, I know why. Tell me what to do. I'm not afraid of him. It's crossed my mind to kill him before and I swear I could do it."

"Do you want your daughter to be an orphan just like you? Then forget about killing Larry and, instead, put him where he can't hurt either of you. You got something to write on? Wait!" He pulled a piece of paper out of his pocket and wrote a name and number on it. "Call this number and ask for Ricky. He's my brother. Tell him Chucho said Don Pedro needs him. I'll get out there as fast as I can, but I've got to see what Roberts is up to first, okay?" *Ricky, you wanted to get involved. Get involved, dammit.*

Darla closed her eyes and repeated "'Chucho said Don Pedro needs him.' Kiss me first."

He kissed her full mouth and had to admit it wasn't all that bad. "Now, take the elevator down. I'll go downstairs. This is one show we've definitely got to get a first in."

They split in opposite directions, she to the elevators, he down the stairs two at a time. Roberts and Burnside were just getting out of the elevator. Everyone else must have thought the bar was a good idea. The senator nodded his approval as Alex fell in behind them.

Frankie Caprelli was practicing his famous lopsided smile in the mirror when the buzzer rang. After striking several more poses, he assured himself he was better looking than he had ever been. That's what people said, anyway. "You look good, Frankie. More mature than back in the '70s."

Of course, those people had been around as long as God so anybody looked good to them. But he could still sing, although he had a definite warble in his chords. Some women thought that was sexy.

"That'll be Senator Roberts, Elena. Let him in, will you?

And make sure you ask me if we want drinks, okay?" He blew her a kiss. "You look dishy tonight, baby."

The slightly overweight woman smiled and winked at him as she went to the door. "And you look good enough to eat. How about tonight, Frank? What are we doing later on?"

He held out his arms. "What d'ya want to do, baby? I'm all yours. The old bat's in LA getting a remodeling job."

The buzzer rang again and then someone thumped on the door. Elena scowled bringing her eyebrows into one line. Pressing both hands into the small of her back where the ache had settled, she muttered, "Geez, I'm coming. I'm coming. Keep your shirt on."

Caprelli patted her firm behind as she past him, fastening a flashy necklace. "Hey, be sweet, okay? Buy you something pretty after this show."

Outside the door, their voices came over a receiver in Burnside's lapel. He and Roberts exchanged glances. "Still as bad as ever. You'd think he'd learn by now. Getting kind of past it for a player."

Roberts rocked up and down on his toes, as if getting ready to jog. "Maybe tonight's the night to teach him."

Burnside nodded and gave some quick commands. "Stay close, okay, Vargas? But not that close. Geez, we got to get you some new boots. Stand at ease right inside the door and fold your hands behind you. Just watch me. I can tell you never been in the military."

Caprelli himself came to greet them, wearing his famous smile and a bathrobe. "Senator! What a tremendous surprise! Isn't it, darling?"

His pregnant mistress nodded without enthusiasm and showed big white teeth in a perfunctory smile. "Yeah. Real tremendous, honey."

Roberts held out his hand, but didn't go for the hand-over-hand clasp he used on the campaign trail. He kept his distance after a brief handshake. Possibly because he was considerably shorter than Caprelli's good six feet, but it was more likely to indicate this was not a social call.

"Frankie, my boy. Sorry to interrupt you when you're getting ready for a show." Following Burnside's orders, Alex stayed by the door and tried to look as ominous as possible. According to Burnside, that was all he had to do. A glance at the bodyguard gained approval with a nod.

Roberts dropped into a chair and rested his hand back over the back of the chair. He flicked up one finger. "I wish I could stay for your performance, Frank. But I've got some business in LA."

"Are you sure? I was going to introduce you during the show. You could turn on the old charm. Maybe we could sing 'God Bless America' or 'Yankee Doodle Dandy,' hey, yeah. Get some votes going. You know the drill."

"Yeah, I do. That's why I'm here, Frankie. To make sure I can count on you to support me."

"Was there ever any question?" Caprelli pressed his hand over his heart as if somebody had stabbed him. "Senator, you know I've been your loyal supporter right from the get-go, right, Elena?"

She nodded vigorously.

"Then why are you holding out on me, Frankie. There's a little question of fifty-thousand in campaign contributions. I haven't seen it yet. And you promised me down in LA if I squashed all the stories about you and Elena, here, you'd come through."

Caprelli looked as though he were onstage playing Paliacci. "Oh, that. Well, you know, Fulton, things have been really slow lately. Elena, how about some drinks for the senator and his…his friends."

Caprelli's glance went to the doorway and Alex saw fear in his eyes.

"No, thanks all the same. We've got to be going."

"But we haven't had a chance to visit. Hey, you still play golf? We could stay over, get in a few holes. They say this hotel's got a decent nine-hole course."

"Maybe next time. Look, Frankie, this isn't a social visit." Roberts leaned forward. "I want the money in my campaign account by Monday, is that clear?"

Caprelli's voice dropped to a whine. "But I haven't got that much in cash, Senator. Honestly. You know, my two ex-wives are like vultures, and I've got four kids. You know what it's like. You're married, twice as I recall."

"Frankie, man, don't let me get unpleasant. If Dagmar finds out about your little girlfriend here, who if I'm not wrong, looks like she's pregnant with kid number five, you're going to have one more ex-wife. Knowing that Dagmar thinks she's still worth a lot after two B-movies, I'd say you were heading for bankruptcy court." Roberts held up a CD. "We've got enough stuff on your little affairs to send her running to the lawyers the minute the plastic surgeon says go." Elena had dutifully gone to the kitchenette to make somebody a drink. Roberts nodded in that direction. "Frankly, I thought you had better taste. She's a little porker."

Caprelli ran his fingers through his dyed black hair as if outrage had somehow revealed his bald spot. With a fire that surprised them all, he said, "Listen, damn it. You know what you're doing isn't legal. This is blackmail, and if I let the FBI know about your strong-arm tactics, this'll be the last run for office you'll ever make. I've still got friends, you know. A lot more powerful than you, Fulton. Make no mistake."

Roberts lifted his finger up and down twice. "Let's find out about that, shall we, Burnside?"

For a heavy man, Burnside moved with catlike efficiency. Before Caprelli could react, the bodyguard had his arm around his neck and smashed his fist into Caprelli's lower back.

The singer screamed and struggled as Burnside tightened his arm in a strangle-hold, delivering more blows to his kidneys. Finally, a blow to the back of his neck stopped his flailing arms. With a moan, Caprelli dropped to the floor at Roberts's feet.

They were startled by a scream from the doorway of the bedroom. Caprelli's mistress stood horrified, staring at her groveling lover and then rushed to him. "*Assasinos! Robados*! Leave him alone!"

Burnside looked annoyed. Jerking his head at the woman, he said, "Vargas, get her out of here and shut her up. Or I will. She's getting on my nerves."

His hesitation brought a quizzical look from Roberts. "You heard him! Remove the bitch!"

The woman screamed as Alex approached her. Then she dropped Caprelli's arm and ran back into the bedroom. Before she could slam the door, he pushed it open.

"Don't hurt me! I don't have any money, but I will give you what I have! *Por favor, no molesta me*!"

"*Callate*, senora," he said, pushing the door behind him closed. "If you keep screaming, you'll get hurt."

She kept backing away around the king sized bed. "Who are you? What are you doing to Frank?" Her glance slid to the room phone on the bedside table.

"Better not ask. And don't touch the phone. They will hear you." When he spoke to her in Spanish, she replied with a rusty Tex-Mex accent. But her terror appeared to diminish.

"Are you going to rob us?"

"No. It's not about that kind of money. It's about politics." No one had ever been afraid of him before and he stared back at her, wondering how to behave. "Like in Mexico. They want money to buy votes."

There was another muffled cry and the woman's eyes strayed to the phone. "You're not going to hurt me?"

"Of course not. I don't beat up women. So just be very quiet in here. They'll be finished soon."

"You are not like them, but still you work for them. I'm going to call the manager before they kill him," she said in a shaking voice.

"It will only make more trouble for him."

Her hand was on the receiver when Burnside burst into

the room. "Okay, let's go. What the hell? She's going to call the manager! Get away from that phone, lady!"

"I told her not to touch it."

The terrified woman sat down on the bed as if her knees had just given out. "Bring her in the living room, Vargas. You got a lot to learn."

Caprelli was on the sofa, looking pale and shaken. When he saw the woman, he said, "It's okay, Elena. I'm fine. Just bring me the checkbook, will you? The business one."

"But, Frankie, you don't have to pay these *pistoleros*. You're famous man. You can make big trouble for them and they know it."

"Make it fast, please, Elena," Roberts said. "Unless you want us to start hitting him where it shows. That's a good girl," he added as she rushed back into the bedroom. A knock on the door startled them all. After a brief consultation, Elena opened the door. It was the night manager with a strained smile as if he were expecting trouble. The celebrity suite was always trouble for the staff, night or day. The occupants either demanded extra service or were disorderly and tore up the furniture or their checks bounced.

When Elena answered the door, he immediately stepped inside. "Is there anything wrong, Mr. Caprelli? Someone reported a woman screaming." His practiced glance inventoried the room. No apparent damage. No blood. Burnside was at the bar, and Roberts was sitting relaxed in his chair.

"Not a thing," Caprelli said, oozing his famous charm. "It was just a little mouse, wasn't it, Elena? Ran right over her foot. Actually, it was kind of funny. I mean, I had to laugh. She was almost the first pregnant woman in space!"

Everyone shared a laugh except Elena and the manager who remained grim.

"A mouse? In here? That's awful!" The manager was having a meltdown. "I'm so very sorry, Mr. Caprelli. And Senator Roberts! We don't often have mice, I mean, we never have mice. Oh, maybe downstairs in the kitchen, you know the food brings them in."

Caprelli raised his hand to calm the man, and Alex had to admire his acting job. "Take it easy, man, it was only a tiny little mouse, not King Kong. Just send somebody up tomorrow to look around, that's all."

"I can send somebody up right away, in fact, I should. Or I tell you what. Let me move you to another suite, a little smaller than this one, but just as nice. Jacuzzi and everything." He looked around hopefully.

Caprelli revealed his famous teeth, most of which were still his. "Never mind, man! It's fine, isn't it, honey?"

Fulton Roberts stood up, and like a well-trained dog, Burnside came to his side, blocking the manager's view from the door. "Loved seeing you again, Frankie. Sorry I have to miss your show. Best of luck, but you always get them on their feet." He reached out his hand, palm up, and Carprelli placed the folded check in it, slapping his own palm over it. Roberts graciously bowed to Elena, who looked as though she would explode into pieces if he touched her. "Goodbye, lovely lady. And no more close encounters with mice, okay?"

Elena stared at him, terror and loathing in her eyes. Caprelli put his arm around her. "She'll be just fine when we get downstairs."

With Burnside and Alex at his heels, the senator patted the manager's shoulder as he went him. "Great place you've got here, sir. On the top of my list of places to hang loose and relax."

It was obvious he had picked up yet another vote through the personal touch. "Thank you, Senator. So glad to be of service."

"Remember that in November," Roberts called back. "Every vote counts in our great country."

✑✑✑

"Hello, Miss Silk."

She tried to locate the cheerful voice coming from somewhere between two moons as they orbited through dense fog. Murray tried to speak, but only a rude gargle came out.

"Can you hear me?"

"Uh."

One moon issued a brief order in code. Her arms relaxed, sending a rush of relief to her head. Her vision cleared a little. One moon came closer. It was a face. She felt fingers lift up her eyelids.

"Are you awake?"

She wanted to scream but nothing came out. Murray hung in her chair like ripe fruit ready to fall from the tree.

"Adrenalin." This time the word made sense.

Murray felt a prick in her arm, and then a rush of warmth suffused her body.

Dr. Wu's face came into focus. Her brain began working as if it were under a snowpack. He was her dentist and she had fainted in the dentist chair.

"Hi." This time it came out as a word instead of a sound.

The dentist smiled. "Ah, that's better. Much better. Now, what's your name?"

Murray thought it was funny he didn't know her name. He must be getting old. He'd been her dentist since she was eight.

Wu was becoming impatient. "Silk Murray? Is that your name?"

That sent her into a giggle. "Uh-huh." Her heart was racing now and her entire body suffused with sweat.

The dentist took a chair, propping a clipboard on his crossed his legs. "Now, Miss Silk, what is your occupation?"

"Huh?"

"Your job. What do you do?"

"Nothing." A warning alarm, dulled but sentient, went off somewhere in the spongy interior of her brain. She had translated the question incorrectly. He had asked what she did, and she wasn't doing anything at the moment except sitting there drooling like an idiot.

"You don't do anything? No job? This is misinformation."

The moons had a brief consultation in the coded language. The satellite moon was female. Probably Leslie, the dental assistant. She moved her hands, but they were still loosely tied together.

"You are a prostitute?"

"Ahhhh."

Another spate of code language.

"You have sex—never mind. What is 'vice'?" Dr. Wu appeared rattled, having lost his train of thought. "It says you called police last night. That you were under the covers."

"Huh?"

"The police. Why did you call them? Are you working for them? Were you looking for Poseidon's Eye?"

Here was a sticky part. "He lost it?"

Dr. Wu was getting irritated. "Do you work for the police? Are they interested in Poseidon's Eye? Missile guidance systems. Are they looking for missile guidance systems up here?"

She tried to wrap her tongue around the words. "Thistle Midas Thistem?"

"Ah, ha! You know the word. She knows." Quick lunar consultation. Wu leaned forward, hissing garlic in her face, his nose inches from hers. "Are they coming up here, Miss Silk Murray? Did you tell them to come?"

"Vice squad informant." The female voice spoke crisp American English with a slight nasal twang. "Hooker, profession. We are wasting our time, Doctor.""

"Ah, hooker," Dr. Wu repeated. The term was on his list of American slang. "Yes, of course. Noble occupation. Very old indeed." English-speaking Moon cleared her throat.

"Thirsty. Water."

Moon Number Two took over. "Yes, we are going on the water soon. You like the boats? Do you get the sea-sickness? Me, too."

Back to the encoded commands. One of the words sounded something like Savannah.

English Moon's voice faded and Murray felt a cold rush of air as the door opened, cooling her perspiring face. Somewhere in space, she heard another female voice, not as pleasant as the first one. It sound somehow familiar and then she heard, "Okay, then, Larry Sutton says so."

There was a smothered scream, and the door slammed closed.

The next thing she heard was Wu addressing someone in deteriorating English. "Who are you? What are you doing here?"

There was the sound of breaking glass and a grunt.

A male voice said firmly, "Just shut up and do exactly what I tell you and you and Madame Butterfly here won't get hurt."

There was a scuffle, bottles fell to the floor, and Dr. Wu's chair tipped over. A pair of feet in shiny black shoes flailed in emptiness. A man flashed by her line of vision, the ropes fell away from her hands, and she slipped off her chair to the floor.

"Oh, great! She's out cold. Okay, Dr. Death, get in the closet. You, too, lady."

"If this is robbery, I have money." Dr. Wu scrambled to his feet, walking backward with his hands in the air. "Plenty money."

"I'll bet you make a fortune doing tattoos. In the closet! Now!"

Through the fog hovering over her vision, Murray saw the nurse lunge for the hypodermic needle on the table. Adrenalin, real and artificial, kicked in.

Picking up a full bottle of alcohol from the table, Murray threw it at the woman. The syringe dropped to the floor, and the nurse swung a back kick at her which Murray blocked with her foot. Lashing back, Murray's longer leg length sent the woman flying straight into Dr. Wu. The couple fell in a heap at the door of the closet. Grabbing the loosened rope, she tried to help her rescuer tie them up.

"Nice shot. Now, that's what I call togetherness," the young stranger commented, as he locked the closet door.

"She's here! Oh, thank God!" A voice somehow familiar came from the doorway. "Hurry, Rick. They're calling Larry! We need to get out of here fast! What's wrong with her? Drunk?"

Her heart was trying to get out of her chest over the sudden movement, and Murray started weaving on her feet.

"Whatever it is, she's out of it. Stoned or something." For a moment, they regarded Murray, swaying like a cobra listening to a flute.

The girl pulled up one of her eyelids by the lashes. "Stoned. That damn Larry. He's done it again."

The closet door began to rattle to the sound of hammering and kicking.

"We'll sober her up later. Right now, the natives are restless. Get hold of her before the Siamese twins get out. C'mon, grab an arm and let's go." Together, they pulled Murray out the door and along a hallway. "Okay, Treetop Goddess, let's walk."

"Who you?"

"Forgot to introduce myself. I'm Rick Vargas. And you must be Silk."

"Mice to neet you."

Darla looked at the girl who nearly matched her height. "Does she speak English when she's sober? Whatever they gave her, I could use some right now."

Murray tried to focus, but her eyes crossed, showing two tall redheads. "Hey, Darlene. You here, too?"

"It's Darla, honey. Darlene is…was my mother's name."

"Oh. 'At's too bad. Pizza tonight."

They guided her to the freight elevator, but Rick took one look at the indicator and turned her around. "Hit the stairs! Can you make it if you hang on to me?"

Murray started off confidently, missed the first step completely and shot down three before they could stop her. In a cluster of three, they half pulled and pushed her the rest of the way.

"Not drunk," she mumbled. "Swear."

"That's okay. We're just glad you're not driving."

As they passed the open door to the office, the guard shouted at them to stop.

"Keep going!" Behind her, Rick pushed forward. "Just keep going!"

The guard followed them. "Hey, Darla, your brother called. Says you'd better get your ass down there, if you know what's good for you!"

"You know she got stoned at one of Larry's parties. If you don't want her to crash on you, just open the damn gate, Zeke or I'll drive right through it."

"And what if I don't?"

Darla turned around and stared. "Who are you talking to, Zeke? I know what size jockeys you're wearing. Do you want him to know that?"

"C'mon, damn it, Darla. Don't pull that crap on me. You know I'll get in trouble if I let you guys out."

"Just do it! I'll make it up to you."

The guard turned away. "Yeah, that's what you always say."

They were through the gate and on the access road when Springer's SUV and another truck followed by a fire truck screeched to a halt across the road.

Darla gunned the engine. "Hold on, I'm running it!"

Beside her, Ricky turned and yanked Murray down on the back seat, and then held on to the dashboard. "You go, girl."

They hit the drainage ditch tilting on two wheels, so that if he hadn't grabbed the strap handle, he would have landed in her lap. In his side view mirror, he saw the SUV trying to turn around. The backup truck ended up fishtailing, but the fire truck let loose with a blast of fire retardant foam as they passed.

Darla hit the windshield wipers, but the stuff smeared the window in white grease. "I can't see," she yelled. "I can't see, dammit!"

"Put it in four-wheel, and try easing up on the right shoulder. This thing should drive on ice."

The rear tires dug in and up to the macadam. Suddenly, Darla swerved sharply to the right and they lunged on to a spur road.

"Where the hell are you going? I thought we were getting out of here." In the side view mirror, he saw the SUV do a donut and head toward them.

"To get Danica. I'm not leaving without her ever again."

"I don't know who she is but she better be worth getting killed for. That SUV is catching up with us."

"Watch this." Sliding to a halt, Darla threw the truck in reverse and tore backward down the road, forcing the SUV driver to drop off the narrow shoulder. It tore a long swatch through the rocky chaparral, hit a boulder and promptly flipped on the driver's side.

"Faked him out," she yelled with a wild laugh, continuing on up the hill.

Rick could only look at the auburn-haired maniac beside him with admiration.

"Awesome," he whispered from a dusty throat. Awesome was the word since the moment she had stalked into the Taqueria in that cowgirl outfit and said, "Hi, I'm Darla and Chucho sent me. And something about Don Pedro. He said you'd know."

"I knew he'd chicken out." Darla continued on up the hill, laughing as if she were playing bumper tag with her buddies on some desert highway. "We're going to switch cars now. There's another set of keys in the glove compartment. My car's up in the front parking lot. I'll run and get her and meet up in front. This girl needs to see a doctor. No telling what they gave her."

That said, she pulled into a garage large enough to house a theater. She flipped her remote and closed the bay doors behind them.

"Get her and run," she said. "Follow the stairs to the ground floor and go!"

She waited until he had pulled Murray to her feet and headed for the stairwell. When he glanced back, Darla was punching in a code in the alarm system. A deafening alarm went off and the sprinkler system kicked in as she followed them up the stairs.

By that time, Murray was capable of toddling on her own, content to be dragged along by the arms by her rescuers. Below them they heard a screech of tires and Darla pushed them both into the hedge of hibiscus bushes.

"Leave her and run start the car," she whispered to Ricky, her face deliciously close to his. "She'll just go to sleep and we'll go get help. Run."

He made a quick choice. Pulling the tall blonde farther behind the hedge, he made his way around to the front of the house. Hidden from view by a profusion of bright poinsettia bushes, and bougainvillea that tumbled over the railing, he crouched and surveyed the parking lot. Antique lamp posts at intervals skirted the area large enough for at least twenty cars. Horticultural masterpieces in enormous containers provided cover as he darted from one to another.

Among the handful of vehicles parked in front of the sprawling house, a metallic blue sports car winked back when he pressed the unlock key on the remote. Using the other vehicles for cover, he slipped behind the wheel and the engine purred. Then Rick lay down across the bucket seats and waited, air conditioner blowing full blast in his face.

In less than five minutes, the passenger door opened and the redhead jumped in the front seat. In her arms, great brown eyes full of questions, was a little girl. "Let's go, Romeo," Darla said. To the child she whispered, "He's really Superman, baby. Let's see if he can fly."

They were down the winding driveway and out on the road before the men in Poseidon uniforms came into the parking lot. Their booted steps and frantic calls stomped out the sound of snores coming from behind the thick hibiscus hedge.

⌦⌫

Alex took the stairs two at a time down to the hotel garage. Glancing up and down the rows of expensive vehicles, he searched for Crittenden's personal baby, the silver Rolls, when a puff of cigarette smoke in the second row indicated someone was working on one of the cars. Following the trail of smoke, he saw the Rolls's hood up and then Angel Rivera straightened up and slammed it shut. He walked rapidly down the line of parked cars, still smoking and disappeared into the elevator. Before he entered the elevator lobby, however, Rivera looked both ways, certain he wasn't being observed.

Alex took the stairs back up to Dalton's suite. Then he wondered why he should bother telling the colonel what he probably already knew anyway. After all, this was dog-eat-dog. It was also the perfect opportunity to take off running for the nearest exit out of town. If it hadn't been for sending Darla and Rick to get that girl, he would have. But he'd put their lives on the line and he was responsible for their safety.

As he stood outside the door, it opened and the lanky colonel said, "Well, son, are you just going to stand there or did you ring the bell and I just didn't hear?"

After Dalton had heard about Rivera, he barked brief orders. After so much to drink, Alex was amazed the man was even coherent. "There's a set of keys right hand drawer of my dresser. Get them and I'll show which to use. He might have rigged my Mercedes for that matter so I'm giving you a dummy. Yeah, don't look at me like that. I know what

Roberts is like. When you get back, I'll tell you a story. Now, get the dummy car—it's a beat-up-looking Prius with a dented left rear fender, but the damn thing goes like a rocket. Special engine I had put in it. Don't mind the dust, never drive it, myself. Follow Crittenden and flash your lights. He drives that thing like an old lady so you'll catch him in a heartbeat. Pull him over and tell him to call me, got it? Be sure and wear your shades though. The beard and shades make you look like one of Fulton's boys."

Alex was back down the stairs before he wondered why he was trying to save the life of the man who ruined him. Who didn't care if he went to prison for murder? As Alex reached the garage, he'd figured out why. Because he didn't want to become one of them, using any means to an end. Fraud, violence, murder. He found the Prius where Ed Dalton had said it would be and it was as much of a wreck as he claimed. But when he punched the gas, he burned rubber and caught the attention of the parking attendant. The man stared at him in disapproval as Alex took the exit out. At the bottom of the ramp, the Prius took off under him like an old warhorse hearing the call to battle.

The narrow highway hugged the steep sides of the canyon just outside of Diamondback City. Like the drivers themselves, the road clung to the rocky walls as if it, too, were afraid of plunging several hundred yards into the stream far below. Because earthquakes were frequent in the area, that possibility was all too real.

After weaving through the town's agonizing traffic, Alex caught up with a tight caravan consisting of Crittenden's Jag, a semi, and his Prius, just as they were beginning to negotiate the switchback mountain pass leading to the Interstate.

Since the curves offered no opportunity to pass, he had to remain behind a semi with out-of-state plates, although he was risking losing Crittenden who drove as if he were on an LA freeway. Even out here in the kind of territory where mountain lions still hunted, there was always a chance Poseidon's satellite cameras were keeping the lawyer's car in view. It was a strange thought that never would have crossed his mind a year ago. Now there were eyes in the sky, no matter how rugged the terrain.

After a mile went by, an SUV pulled up to his bumper, flashing its lights in an arrogant signal for him to move over. In LA, Alex would have rolled the window down and given the driver the middle finger. Although he could only take his eyes off the road for seconds to glance in his side view mirror, there was something familiar about the SUV. It was a Grand Cherokee, the mud splattered license plate, the smoked windows, the snow bumper, and oversize tires. The same model as the red one that had fled the murder scene, except this one was black, so shiny the noon sun's reflection on its surface gave the appearance of an exploding star.

Just as the road went into another sharp curve, the SUV suddenly whipped around him, passing the semi to cut in sharply behind Crittenden's Jaguar. The semi's brakes hissed and its horn blasted a furious protest, as the driver flicked his lights. No doubt, the driver was cursing the SUV into the next eternity.

As if in reply, the SUV rocked on two wheels around the curve, tailgating Crittenden's car, its tail lights flashing, signaling to pass. This guy was either drunk or had a death wish. Alex lost sight of both vehicles as the sluggish semi braked to take the steep grade. When they rounded the turn and straightened out, the only vehicle in view was the SUV's tail lights, zigzagging ahead.

Crittenden's Jag was nowhere in sight.

Alex first thought was the hulking shape of the SUV was blocking his view of Crittenden's car. Then, as he hugged the inside curve, a peculiar chill crept over him. Glancing left, he saw an enormous jagged hole in the guardrail and an ominous glow far down in the ravine.

There was nowhere to turn around on the steep grade for the next several miles. When he finally was able to pull over and go back to the place where Crittenden's car had gone through the railing, a column of noxious, gray smoke rose, and then a sudden flash as the Jag caught fire. Pulling up beside the shattered guardrail, Alex slid down the embankment toward the burning car, searing his healing palms against rocks and gravel. He almost slid past Parker Crittenden, spread-eagled head down, only a few yards from the flames. Either thrown out or crawling out of the burning car, he was still not clear of the wreck if it exploded. Grabbing the lawyer by the feet, Alex pulled him back upward an inch at a time, feeling the gravel digging into the blisters on his back.

In spite of the eminent explosion of the gas tank, he could not move any faster up the incline, hauling Crittenden with him. The lawyer was a big man, over six feet tall and heavier by fifty pounds than he was.

For every foot he gained, he lost half slipping backward in the loose top soil of the ravine.

"Hang on, buddy, we're coming!" Two men appeared at the roadside above him, and a rope snaked down the ravine, landing just a few feet away.

Alex tried reaching for it, but the risk of letting Crittenden slip down toward the wreck was too great. A pair of feet dangled just above his head and a hand reached down to grasp Crittenden's other foot.

"I got him," a man said. "Looks like just in time, too."

With their combined strength, they pulled Crittenden toward the road. Just as they reached the railing, there was another explosion and pieces of metal vomited upward. They flattened against the asphalt shoulder as molten fragments showered around them.

"Thanks for bailing me out."

When Alex could speak, he looked over at the man lying beside him.

"Shit, I've been in worse when my rig jackknifed. I wouldn't be here if somebody hadn't pulled me out." They rose to their knees cautiously. "I saw him go over, but I couldn't stop my truck that fast. Damn idiot SUV cut me off. You know something weird, though? The guy in the Jag never hit the brakes. He just kept going over the side. And there wasn't any traffic in the other lane. He wasn't even going that fast that he couldn't have got it under control."

Emergency vehicles materialized from somewhere and blocked the road off, damming up the traffic on both sides. Men in firefighting gear climbed down the steep slope to the flaming wreck. Two paramedics dropped down on either side of Crittenden.

"What happened?"

The trucker was explaining as Alex went back to his car. "Some guy in a SUV cut me off and then tapped the Jag's bumper. Jag just keeps going right through the railing. It happens all the time around here. This highway's not called Suicide Alley for nothing."

Alex didn't know what feelings to experience first as he drove away from the narrow pass. Crittenden would probably never even know to whom he owed his life. But he would know who tried to kill him. What was important was that he would see he grandchild, something Shelley Turner and Sanchez would never do.

Alex could run now. Dalton had given him all the rope he needed to hang himself. By midnight, he could be safe in Mexico, doing the smartest thing he had done in days— taking care of Alex Carreras.

Starting up the Prius, he pulled out into the traffic, actually beginning to smile. He had just now noticed a little button on the console of this urban assault vehicle Dalton probably had customized somewhere in Bulgaria where it would pass inspection. The button lit up green when he pushed it and the colonel's voice rumbled through speakers loud enough to satisfy a South LA hood.

"Good work, Carreras. I'm proud of you, kid." The Eye had been on him all the time. "Now, come on back. The big game's tomorrow and we've got work to do." It was suddenly clear as the sky breaking through the shroud of smoke from the wreck. Ed Dalton was getting ploughed and he knew he needed somebody clear minded and sharp to accomplish whatever he had in mind to defeat Roberts.

Alex gunned the Prius as he came back into the garage of the Royal Gorge. It would have to do for a victory lap until the real thing. It was then he realized he was determined to win the game, even if it meant an alliance with Ed Dalton.

Once again, he took the stairs up to the penthouse suite from the garage, glad he used to exercise by running up and down the ones in his Century City office building. When Dalton opened the door, he saw his guess was right, the colonel was three sheets to the wind. From the looks of Sydney Harris, they both were. What he hadn't figured is that Perry Perez was sitting there with a great big grin on his face.

"Vargas, you are one crazy dude, man. I would have just let that *gringo* who screwed you toast! No, but you, you got to jump into the fire with him! *Que stupido!*"

❧❧❧

When Murray woke up, it was dark. Her mouth felt as if it were growing grass. When she ran her tongue around it, she actually located a few blades. Inside her head, a nest of really angry wasps were plotting an attack. Her entire body hurt as a whole, and as individual parts. Then she realized she was tied up. Bound and gagged. Thirst raged through her like a forest fire, touching every nerve. It was profoundly dark. Where in hell was she?

In panic, she began to struggle. Her legs, bound at the ankles, were otherwise free and she kicked out, though not very far. Her feet collided with something wooden. A wall? A door?

Her heart racing, she twisted counter clockwise, using her legs as the dials. She seemed to be in a box. It was long and so wide, she couldn't even find the far side. So there was oxygen except for an obnoxious odor, almost like kerosene.

Then her feet hit something metal. Flat on her back now, Murray raised her feet along the side of the metal thing. It was higher than her legs would reach. Bringing her feet around the side, she found it was round, as well. An oil drum? Then it all came back to her, causing her feet to fall to the floor. It was a chemical drum! When the young man and girl had pulled her away from that sadist dentist and out onto a ramp, she recalled seeing huge drums moving along a conveyor belt far below.

She lay there, thinking, trying to calm herself to rationality. Except for the buzzing of the wasps and her own labored breathing, there weren't any other sounds but those. Going step by step back to the rescue, she remembered being pulled here and there by the tall girl and nice-smelling guy. Up a hill and then someone pushed her into some trees, and lay down next to her.

The last thing she remembered was a dog licking her face. A very large ugly dog with a maternal streak, except it had bad breath. When she told it to go away, it barked like ten dogs.

"Old Lucky's found her," a man yelled. "Good girl! You get steak tonight, baby."

Her next thought was of Willy, her cat. Who would feed Willy? *I've got to get out of here!* Rationality zipped out of her mind, chased by wasps.

Bringing back her feet to the near side of the crate, she began to thump on it, making frantic grunts through her gag. Finally, she had to stop, exhausted. There was no one to hear her, she thought desperately. Even if they do, they'd just ignore it, on orders from that slimy creep Sutton.

Help me, Daddy! Help me!

Something was trying to make itself heard through her complete panic. A thump. Ugly thoughts skittered around like roaches. It was the crazy dentist come to finish off the job. It was Sutton or one of his thugs coming to make sure she was dead. Her heart rattled so loudly, she almost missed the second thump. They were breaking into the crate. Then a new thought replaced all the rest. Maybe it was the police finally starting to hunt for her.

On the other hand, the thumps seemed to be measured, and since she didn't feel any vibrations, not on this crate. In desperation, she hazarded a stomp on the side of her crate. There was immediately an answering thump. Then another and another. Bump, bump, bump, stop. Bump, bump, bump, stop. One, two, three, stop. One, two, three, stop.

SOS?

Murray breathed in, held it, and started again. One, two, three, stop.

The thumps answered in the same order. It was a code.

She tried it, spelling out her name in thumps.

It came back with four thumps. Following those, then five.

Her thoughts began to spin like a squirrel on a treadmill. *Could it possibly be 8995?*

She thumped five times. Five thumps came back. *HolyBejeezuz, it was Jonesy it the other crate!*

�����

Alex had figured Perry Perez for anything else than Poseidon's man. Now, Alex was trying to figure out how he, the smart lawyer, had missed pegging the oilfield worker for a plant. Sure, Perez had worked in the Valley plant. Of course, he knew his way around Sutton's operation. He could get his hands on a real ID badge, an orange jumpsuit, hardhat with the Triton logo. He was one of them!

Dalton managed to get to his chair and fold up again, like a stork settling on a nest. "Oh, come in and sit down, son. But get me another one before you do. And make that a round. You look like you could use it."

"It appears you have been firefighting again, Jimmy." Harris, impeccable in navy blazer and open-necked shirt, held up his empty glass as well.

"Something like that." Alex headed to be bar and began to wash up at the sink, still furious with himself for not fleeing when he had the chance. "You know very well the Prius is hooked up to your Eye system. I found the button."

The colonel was unmoved. "Yeah, but that view is only from your perspective. There are others."

"How about whoever was driving the Jeep that pushed Parker off the road? Did you get a clear enough view of that? Crittenden damn near burned to death. He was so busted up, I doubt if he'll pull through."

A grunt came from Dalton's chair along with a puff of smoke. "You think I'm a real bastard, don't you? Syd and I are a real pair in your book of bastards, right?"

Perez was simply looking from the colonel back to Alex behind the bar, listening. Then he said in a stern tone Alex had never heard him use, "It could have been you, Jimmy. They just saved your damn life and I'm doing my best to help him, okay? I saw the look you gave me when you saw me here, with them. It was me gave Rudolfo the fake ID and beat-up truck. And it was me right out there in the field when we got sprayed. So lighten up and listen, man. You might learn something."

"Couldn't have put it better myself," Harris said with a grunt of satisfaction.

"Yeah, I can see how successful you guys are at it." Alex found himself actually shaking with fury. "Two people dead and two damn near about to make it four. How many more before your game, as you say, is over?"

Dalton waved the criticism away like a fly. "Sit down and cool off, boy. I've got something you got to see." He picked up the remote always by his side in the big chair.

Alex brought the tray over and set it on the coffee table. "Thanks, I've seen enough. Here's your drinks. I'm out of here."

The three exchanged glances and sipped their drinks. As usual, Ed Dalton didn't varnish the truth. "You won't make it to Bakersfield. And they're got that girl and another cop crated up ready to ship out to Savannah, Georgia's port. They'll die in a couple of days, but it's not the best way to go. Those 1212 barrels leak fumes. The crates are sealed so the fumes don't seep through. That's not going to help the girl, though."

"If they have the girl back, where's Darla?" Where Darla was, so was Rick, but Alex tried to keep his brother's identity secret as long as he could. If Dalton knew Ricky was in town, he might use him as leverage.

"She's with some boy she roped into trying to get the girl out of there. They didn't make it before the guards spotted them." Dalton's shoulders began to shake with strange laughter. Strange, since he had lost the capacity long ago. "They sure shook Freddy Wu and his hoochi bar girl assistant the hell up, though." He broke out in to a hearty laugh. "Damn kids locked them up in the closet and took off with the girl. He was maddern' a wet hen."

Alex couldn't share the joke. "Then how did the girl get left behind?" He pictured tall, blonde Silk tortured, in terrific pain, even bleeding. He felt as if he were being torn apart himself. And where was Rick? If Sutton sent his thugs after Darla, he'd find Rick as well.

The colonel was still laughing, so Perez helped him out. "I guess Wu had done a number on her with drugs and they hid her in the bushes to come back later and get her out. But one of the guard dogs found her. Sutton got the cop at the Branding Iron. I guess he was some detective trying to follow up on the girl."

"So far, I'm told, they just beat him silly. Probably, our Freddie did a number on him as well." Sydney Harris tasted his drink. "Very nice. No ice, just the way I like it. If you ever lose your day job, Jimmy, you'll make a capitol bartender."

Alex came over and sat down, knees weak. So Darla and

Rick got away. So far. He sipped his own drink, trying to make plans, but his mind grappled with shock. Silk was actually a policewoman.

Dalton had put the VCR on pause and held the remote up as if it were connecting with a missile system. "The offer still stands, Alex. You in or out? 'Cause if you're out, then you better get out now while Roberts is over at the air force base opening the show and Sutton is trying to find Darla and put the lid on this stuff. If you go, I would head for Nogales like a bat out of hell. They're watching San Diego. Like I said before, if you want to know, then you're in, whether you want to be or not."

"Okay, I'm in. What happens?"

"They're going to steal Poseidon's Eye. Today."

Alex blinked, trying to take the words at face value. "I thought you could just give it to them, like the other stuff. Ship it out like an X-Ray machine or something."

Dalton sat forward in his chair as if an electric shock had pulsed through him. "We'd better order up a pizza or something. We got some planning to do before I've got to go. What'cha say, Perry? Pizza okay?"

"I hate pizza. Let me do the ordering from La Taqueria." Perez looked at Alex, his eyes saying everything Alex needed to know. Rick and Darla were all right even if Dalton didn't give a rat's ass.

What Alex saw next simply blew away his concept of all right.

An idealized painting of the ridge above them drew back, revealing a giant screen embedded in the wall. On the theater-sized screen, a dark, sleek aircraft hovered in the air, its nose pointing straight up like a rocket's. At first, it looked as if the aircraft were climbing perpendicular to the earth, but unlike a standard fighter jet, there was no vapor trail coming from its afterburners.

"This is Dragonfire One. At present, the only successful vertically landing aircraft in the world. Makes runways a thing of the past. Has thermonuclear engines making jet fuel obsolete. Uses thermonuclear heat as weaponry so it has one hundred percent accuracy. People would kill to get hold of this baby. But the really special thing about it, it operates the Eye system, at least within the earth's biosphere. Without that, this baby is just a very pretty and very expensive piece of hardware."

Syd Harris nodded. "Needless to say, people already have killed for it. Witness the attempt on poor Parker's life—God bless him. If I could elaborate, Eddie." He sounded remarkably sober and more like the international trade lawyer he had been before going native. "I really don't agree with you that the Eye merely decorates another pretty face, pardon the pun. You see, fellows, the Eye system needs a booster component to accurately direct its weaponry. The Dragonfire acts as a sort of booster for the satellite signal. But you didn't mention that it has all the capabilities of the old U-Two spy plane with all the updates since the '50s. Its cameras can penetrate brick walls, and sensors that can hear a pin drop from 300 miles. To say nothing of radiowave and radar interference. I think it's an absolute aeronautical engineering marvel."

Again, Dalton stopped the film, leaving the large sweptwing aircraft sitting in space above the ground like a winged harbinger of doom. "You don't need to know all that stuff to appreciate a nice piece of hardware," he said. "In the interests of time, we've got to move on. What you need to know is why we're trying to stop Roberts from getting his hands on the damn bird. If he gets re-elected to the senate, Robert's becomes Chairman of the Arms Committee again. He's been trying to get the Committee to fund the Dragonfire One since it came off the line."

Perry stared at the image on the screen. "You mean that's the only one there is?"

"The prototype," Harris put in again. "The Brits broke ground with the Hawker Harrier years ago. But the poor beggars kept crashing. The Germans gave it a shot, but even they lost so many test pilots, they gave it up. Everyone said it couldn't be done. Flameouts and all that. With the war in the Middle East and the military hardware budget cut, the Committee doesn't have the funds allocated for this baby."

"So he's just going to steal it anyway, right? I get the picture. The only one there is in the world and for sale to the highest bidder. That's where you guys come in." Perry shook his head and sipped his drink. "I don't know. That's a pretty tall order."

The colonel shifted in his seat. "Can we get on with this dog-and-pony show? I got to be out there in less than an hour."

He pushed the remote and the camera moved slowly down to reveal the ground below where people and service vehicles moved around an airstrip. The aircraft was literally suspended in mid-air. Then it descended slowly and vertically to earth, lowering its landing gear until it was parked standing straight up. A truck with a crane resembling a cherry picker came out on to the tarmac, extended a bridge to the aircraft, and the pilot climbed out on the ramp. He waved with a grin, pulled off his helmet, revealing a tousled, blond head.

"Meet Scot Mason," Dalton said. "Shelby's lover boy."

"He's a nice looking boy, isn't he?" Harris sat forward but his large gut interfered and fell back. "Such a young hot shot. Naughty, too. Or so I hear."

"One more little clip from this demo, gentlemen. I'm not much for home videos."

This time the Dragonfire I rose straight up, leveled out, and launched as if it had been fired out of a cannon. The scene switched somewhat jerkily to an airfield where a stack of barrels were stacked up on what appeared to be some kind of platform.

"Watch this," Dalton said.

There was a flash like distant lightening and the piled barrels exploded almost simultaneously.

"What the hell was that?" Alex couldn't help bursting out with the question.

"Thermonuclear-accelerated light, basically. Acts just like a laser, except doesn't leave any sign of burning. Don't ask me any more than that because it's way over my head."

They drank whiskey with Corona chasers, told dirty jokes and stories, and did bad imitations of Fulton Roberts. Although they had pretended, withheld, and deceived him, Alex found himself trusting Perez and Dalton like no other men before him, outside his own family. Perez, disenfranchised, helpless to hold his father's land against a conglomerate worth millions. Dalton wounded and disillusioned by the very government he had sworn to serve. The third and most valid reason was because his life was in their hands. Pierre Bighand was the only element missing to make their fellowship of losers complete. Until the doorbell rang. Perez and Alex were headed for the hall before Colonel Dalton stopped them.

"Is one of you idiots going to answer the door? It's the food, dammit. And I'm starving."

Alex and Perez followed Dalton's eyes to a security camera which had emerged from behind a picture on the wall. They grinned at each other in the dark hall.

"Man, Dalton don't miss a trick," Perry whispered. "You go. I don't have enough cash for a tip."

On his way to the door, Alex grabbed a quasi-Mediterrean style candlestick that could have dropped a charging bull in his tracks.

Behind him, deep in his chair, Dalton was still laughing. "You're learning, Carreras."

Alex opened the door, hiding the candlestick behind him, prepared for the delivery boy to pull an AK-47 out of the food warmer. Instead, Rick mirrored Alex's own shock, disbelief, and finally, joy.

"Thank you for calling the Taqueria, sir. You owe me one great big tip."

Rick filled them in on the failed rescue attempt while the three ate.

The colonel, in spite of his claims to be starving, ate little. Instead, he listened. When Rick was finished, he asked, "Where's Darla?" as if he could care less where Silk had ended up.

"After she dropped me back off, she said since Marisa wasn't home she was going to take her little girl up to stay with Pappy Pierre, whoever that is." He looked around and found them all staring back at him. "What's the matter? Who is this Pappy guy?"

No one answered, but Dalton sat forward, knobby elbows on knobby knees. "How long ago was that?"

Ricky shrugged. "About an hour, I guess. Did I do something wrong?"

"No, kid. You're as brave as your brother and neither one of you have good sense." The colonel grabbed his phone and pushed a button. "Damn it, she's not answering."

Ricky threw a questioning glance at his brother. Alex, however, just shook his head with a warning look. He would explain later. "Call her," he said. "Maybe she'll pick up for you." With a strange expression on his gaunt face, Dalton nodded his consent.

They watched as Ricky consulted his contact list. True to form, he never missed a chance to get a pretty girl's number. His face lit up when she answered. Then he frowned. "Calm down, I can't hear you. He what? Who's dead? What? Okay, okay, stop yelling. Where are you? Just wait there, I'll be there in five. Stay in your car. No, take it around to the alley behind the Taqueria. Wait there. Is who here?" His eyes lifted to Dalton's, then Rick looked away. "Yeah, he's here. Okay." He snapped the phone closed. "I've got to go. She's blasted. Apparently, she found this Pappy guy hanging from the rafter in his barn. And the little girl was with her. It's been one great morning for her. Nice to meet you guys. It won't happen again."

Alex followed his brother to the door, silently pleading for his brother to meet his eyes. "Wait, you forgot your tip, buddy."

"Go to hell. The whole damn bunch of you." Rick slammed the door in his face.

Behind him, the colonel and Perez were in fierce consultation. Alex stood staring at the door, feeling as if he were going to be sick. He had never known such an overwhelming feeling of grief. Even though he had only known him for a day, losing Pierre was what it must be like to lose a parent.

"Come on and sit down, Alex. I've known the man half my life. Never met a better one."

"Can't." Alex went into the bathroom and threw up his dinner. After throwing cold water on his face, the nausea subsided and he made it back into the living room. Perry stuck a drink in front of him and it hit his stomach like a razor. Alex wiped his mouth and nodded.

Machinelike, Dalton never seemed to generate any emotion other than the pain he had displayed when Darla refused his call. "No matter what happens, our eyes have to be on the prize. Hard as that is, sometimes. Figure it's a war. An undeclared war which are the worst kind. People die and disappear and everybody just goes on with their lives like they didn't even exist."

Perez nodded in agreement. "Just like Mexico. People just disappear off the streets and you never see them again 'til what's left of them turns up in some mass grave." He glanced over at Alex. "Even police."

"Whatever happens, our eyes have to be on the prize."

It was all right for Dalton to sit in his recliner, having a drink, and treating life and death as if they were the stakes in a virtual computer game.

Finally, Alex broke his silence. "I have to go in there. Just give me the stuff you brought, Perry. I'll change and get started."

"Just hold on, son. There's a right way and a wrong way to do things. You sending those two kids up there to get that girl was the wrong way. You endangered all of them when you did that."

Dalton's harsh attack wasn't what Alex needed, especially since that very thought had been in his own mind. He had endangered his own brother and Alex felt guilty enough to put his own life on the line, God knows. "Life doesn't mean a damn thing to you, does it? Whatever the prize is, it's not worth one person's life. If somebody doesn't do something now, that girl is going to die up there."

"She might. She might be dead already, in which case you'd be next."

Far below in the hotel driveway, people were laughing, car doors slammed, and good-byes were shouted. Life went on around them as if they were living in the self-contained environment of a fishbowl.

Alex stood up, finding the whiskey had settled his nausea. "What do you care, Dalton? You're safe. For all I know, you've got your getaway all planned. "

"Matter-of-fact, you're right, kid. I'm going to be sitting on the beach on my own private little island I bought for just such occasions. Me and Perez've got it all planned except he wants to bring that bitch of an ex-wife with him."

Perry quickly corrected him. "Just the kids. She can stay in bed with the car salesman, for all I care."

"There's room for you. And Darla and the baby, of course. But you've got to make a choice. Everything in life requires a choice. You spill what you know and you get your freedom, your name cleared, and complete vindication."

Dalton hadn't said whether Alex would be alive or dead when this took place. "Or?"

"Or, like I said, we've got room on our little island for you. Your choice."

In reply, Alex picked up the bundle Perez had given him and, going back to the hall to change, said, "There's a shipment leaving Synotech for Savannah, Georgia at six o'clock tonight. I'm going to hijack it. Get me inside and I'll give your proposition some thought."

Dalton nodded. "It's a deal. Now you two guys are driving me over to the base. As long as you pick up that six o'clock shipment, Carreras, what you do after that is up to you."

CHAPTER 22

The colonel had insisted they take the Prius for reasons neither Alex or Perez could figure out. "Maybe he just wants to be anonymous or something," Perry said as they took the winding highway to the North through the mountain pass.

Whatever Dalton's reason for riding in a vehicle with dual exhausts and an engine as loud as a 747, he sat in the back seat, headphones on, absorbed in his laptop.

"He's really a good man," Perry Perez said, breaking the silence. "He kind of got screwed up in the Middle East when he was a hostage."

"Darla said something like that, too. What do you mean? Is he crazy?"

"Like the fox." Perez lit a cigarette and Alex rolled down the window. "See, he and Roberts were captured together. The warlord had them thrown in a hole in the desert for days. Threw food down there, but just their left over scraps. Sometimes, he'd take them out and beat them for information. Finally, though Roberts makes some kind of deal and gets let out. Dalton, though, he thinks it's his duty to escape. So he tries and they shoot him in the leg and throw him back in the hole. He tried a couple more times and then they broke his legs so he couldn't. One day, a helicopter making a run saw the camp and it was over. Roberts got all the publicity because he said he had negotiated their release with the warlord. But what he did was make a deal with this warlord guy Tiger that, when he got back to the States, they'd send him all these weapons, you know? Roberts told Dalton that, if he didn't go along with it or tried to stop him, he'd tell the Military Intelligence people that it was Dalton who made the deal to get them out and this Tiger would back him up. Dalton spent a long time in VA hospitals. Like you probably noticed, he don't really walk so good. They patched up his legs too late and they had healed wrong. He had been starved and all that. So he was messed up, mentally and physically. Also, he got sprayed with the same kind of stuff they're spraying around all over the hills and you know what it does to people. He never says, but I don't think he's got long."

Since Perez worked for him, Dalton might have simply made up that touching scenario to gain his loyalty. Besides, whatever the colonel had suffered, wasn't worth the pain and suffering of all the other victims of this scheme. "So he's taking out his revenge on everybody around here? I thought he was in charge of the warehouses on the base over there?"

"The military brought back drums of it from the bio-chemical warfare lab of Saddam Hussein back in the late '90s. Tried to find out what it was made of. Then, like a lot of stuff, they just stuck it in a warehouse where Sutton found it and started using it. The colonel says he didn't even know about it until somebody told him. He don't get around much outdoors."

"So is that why Dalton really wants to stop Roberts? Because he hates his guts?"

"Good enough reason, wouldn't you say?"

"I don't know. I don't know what to make of the guy. Are you really going with him to his island?" Alex looked over at Perez, who caught his eye and smiled.

"Sometimes I think, knowing what I know, I'd be a fool not to. But this is my home, Vargas. I'd miss the place and the people. Fools, aren't we? About stuff like that, I mean. Like we say, the heart rules, not the head."

"The heart rules not the head." The song returned as they turned up the access road to the Synotech compound. "There's a young boy that I know…"

"If that's true then Dalton plays a head game for sure."

Perez took a deep breath as if just being inside the compound filled him with fear. "I don't know about that. He loves that girl Darla like his own daughter. And that baby. You've got to remember her own half-brother is Danica's father. When Ed found out, I had to talk him out of killing Sutton. Wanted to go right over and shoot him. I think I talked him out of just getting her and the kid away from here."

"To the island." Alex took his eyes of the road ahead, long enough to glance over at Perez. "You know a lot about him. How long have you been working for him?"

"Since the Middle East campaign. I was a corporal in the One Hundred and First Airborne, doing security escort on the supply trucks. Then got wounded and spent the withdrawal working in the warehouse, shipping stuff back to the States. I was working there when he was put in charge. Man, he was messed up bad, but kept going until everything was out. He's one tough old bird."

Mileage signs for McTigue Air Force Base were coming up, as well as banners announcing the air show the next day on Saturday morning. Alex kept trying to get Rick on the phone and getting the voicemail. Finally, just as they were on the off-ramp, his brother answered.

"Yeah, what d'you want?"

"Look, I didn't know it would turn out this way, Chucho. You've got to believe that."

It came across how angry his brother was, even through the cell phone. "Really? You think I'm some kind of idiot? There you are, up there partying with killers and men who rape their own sisters and you didn't know? My god, you should have been with me when we found that old guy hanging there. Darla and Danica started yelling and crying and I had to send them out of there while I cut him down.

You ever done that, bro? No, you send me to do your dirty work. No thanks. I've got them in my truck and I'm taking them to Marisa, whoever that is. I don't care as long as it's out of here."

Alex took a deep breath. "I know what this looks like and it has to be this way, Chucho."

"Stop calling me that!"

"Okay, Ricky. Listen fast because I have to hang up in a second. There's a truck leaving the Synotech plant at six tonight. I'm going to be driving it. In case—" He paused and looked over at Perez who was talking on his Bluetooth. "—in case something happens, the key to the locker where my stuff is, is in my sneakers in my closet at the Turner place, got it? You know what to do with the stuff I put in there."

There was silence at the other end.

"Hello? You there?"

"Yeah, I'm here. What's the deal with the truck? "

"Nothing you need to know. Just take care of the ladies. You ought to be good at that."

"Alex?"

"I got to go. Bye." Alex shut down the phone and put it back in his jumpsuit pocket.

They followed a line of several limos and other expensive cars up to the guard gate. Perez pulled up to the kiosk and lowered his window as the uniformed MP came up to the driver's side.

"Sorry, sir, the air show's not officially opening to the public until tomorrow."

The back window rolled down and Colonel Dalton called, "It's okay, Mike. I'm disguised as a tank today."

"Oh, Colonel!" The embarrassed soldier snapped to attention and saluted. "Didn't see you back there. Sure, go right on in."

They roared through the gate, turning heads as they passed lines of officers standing at parade. Flags snapped briskly, keeping time with gusts of the fickle desert breeze,

and colorful buntings rippled around the sheltered grandstand. The whole scene had the festive atmosphere of a
county fair.

Sleek cars disgorged men in officer's uniforms, whose
gold braid flashed in the afternoon sun as they shook hands
and cracked jokes about old times. Other invited guests
were dressed more casually in short sleeve shirts and baseball camps with company insignias. As they passed re-
freshment tables, the men grabbed large cups of beer being
handed out by a troop of Boy Scouts.

In the grandstand, Fulton Roberts was introducing one
dignitary after another to a crowd unimpressed by rank.
Dalton got out, dressed in summer khakis and wearing a
VFW baseball cap. Leaning in Perez's window, he looked
as if he might have been handing out programs.

"Carreras, Perry get to the Synotech plant at ten to six
this evening. The rest of the way you're on your own. The
shipment will have the cargo going to Freddie Wu on board.
He worked on the system as a doctoral student at UCLA so
he thinks it should have been credited to him. If he delivers,
he'll get perks back in Beijing. Once his wife gets a look at
Baby Doll, he'll wish he'd stayed in the States. And if he
decides not to hand it over in Macao, and keeps it himself,
he'll be top dog in the surveillance world until word gets
around they need Dragonfire One to operate it. At six
o'clock on the button, the coordinates on the Eye satellite
will do a C-change. The whole system will be focused on
Africa until the engineers figure out how to change it back.
By that time, you'll be home free."

"Home? Where's that?"

Dalton grinned his terrible grin. "Wherever you decide
to make it, Alex, my lad. Wherever you decide to make it.
Good luck."

In his peculiar stork-like gait, Dalton ambled through the
guarded gate, triggering a row of salutes. He waved them
down, grabbing a large cup of beer as he passed.

"Where to now?" Behind the wheel, Perry Perez was

studying the airfield. "Look, those barrels are stacked out there, like in the video."

Alex found himself torn between wanting to catch a glimpse of what he might be giving his life to steal and going back to see if Rick was all right. "You want to stay and take a look, don't you?"

Perez gave him a sheepish glance and then laughed. "You, too? But you want to check on your brother. I know I would. He looked really mad."

"Yeah. It's been a tough morning for a rookie. But when I think about Pierre Bighand, I just don't know..." Alex trailed off, leaving the sentence unfinished.

To his surprise, Perez lowered his head to the steering wheel. "I've known Pappy Pierre since we used to go up to the caves, my dad and brothers and me. We used to sit in there with him and listen to his stories about the Old People."

Hispanic people rarely hid their emotions and Carreras suddenly felt tears stinging his eyes. *They said you would come.*

They were so caught up in grieving, it took a minute before they noticed the truck was vibrating. "Quake," Perez said. Neither of them had to be told, being California natives.

A white-gloved guard directing traffic yelled, "Hey, buddy, move on. Parking's on the left." He waved them forward and then motioned to the car behind them to follow. They had no choice except to follow the line of traffic pulling into the visitors' lot.

"Let's sit here and wait out the tremor, okay? You never know what's going to come down on you out on the road." They were both thinking these little shakes could cause boulder slides that could bury cars beneath tons of rocks and earth. "Then we'll take off."

Taking off became less of an option as the car behind them in line backed into the parking space in front of the Prius, blocking their exit. Perry looked behind them. "I think we can make it out," he said and then turned around, looking up as the vibrations became stronger. "*Dios*," he whispered. "Would you look at that?"

Since Perez was in the seat closest to the runway, Alex didn't have a clear view of the sky. Around him, the guards and guests who hadn't made it to the grandstand stood still, shielded their eyes against the sun just past its zenith. He got out of the truck and saw what had amazed Perez and everyone else.

A massive dark aircraft was descending straight down as if being lowered by an invisible crane slowly to the ground. Unlike the video Dalton had showed them, however, the swept-wing Dragonfire I was horizontal and its landing gear was down, much like a conventional aircraft. Unlike other aircraft, it wasn't taxiing in, but simply dropping from the sky after hovering above the airfield.

As gently as a nesting hawk, it settled down on the tarmac and a concerted roar went up from the crowd of spectators. In the grandstand, Fulton Roberts was trying to make himself heard above the noise and as the cheering finally died down, he shouted, "And the pilot of Dragonfire One, ladies and gentlemen, is none other than our own Scot Mason. Give him a round of applause for that splendid landing. I agree. Ain't she a beauty?"

Perez had also gotten out of the car and stood beside him, staring at the aircraft as if he couldn't get enough of the sight. "Harris was right. People would kill for that baby. It's hard to believe they won't build more of them."

"Won't or can't. One of those must cost as much as ten fighter jets."

"With one like that, they wouldn't need ten fighter jets."

Meanwhile, Roberts was pontificating on the merits of the Dragonfire aircraft, describing the advantages of thermonuclear technology which he humbly admitted still had a few glitches to iron out. However, to illustrate how far this type of "cold but hot" nuclear power had advanced, they were about to see what other wonders Dragonfire could perform. Such as striking the stack of barrels out of the runway. "Not to worry, friends, they're only filled with water and if you get wet, the wind will dry you in a jiffy. We provide a full service car wash here."

He waited for the crowed to appreciate the joke and then said, "Dragonfire, are you ready?"

In answer, the plane played the opening bars of Dixie, and audience laughed even harder. "Get in the car," Alex said to Perez. "I've got a bad feeling about this."

Without leaving the ground, the Dragonfire began to raise up, folding its landing gear until, once again, it was elevated above the tarmac. Slowly, it rose almost magically like a puppet on invisible strings until it was nearly four-to-five hundred feet in the air, hovering like a giant vulture. Then there was a crack as if a bolt of lightning had struck nearby and the top barrel in the pyramid flew upward, exploding in a ball of fire. It hurled flaming liquid in every direction along with pieces of metal like flaming shrapnel. One fragment must have torn through another container and it too exploded, raining fire and metal high in the air. What followed was a holocaust of screaming people fleeing the grandstand which had caught fire and begun to collapse in flames. Drenched in flaming liquid, the very buntings became lethal weapons, dropping fragments of fiery cloth on the panicking spectators. Everyone ran for cover as fire trucks waiting far down the runway raced to the scene.

A piece of flaming metal pierced through the hood of the car in front of them and immediately smoke began to pour from the engine. "We've got to get out of here," Perez said. "That car's going to blow up and take us with it. I can make it if I hit the fence." He indicated the chain link fence a few feet away.

"Pull up and wait for me where you can. I'll find you, but first I've got to check on the colonel. He must've been right up in front." Alex jumped out and sprinted toward the grandstand, dodging shrieking women, some with smoldering clothes. In military tradition, the soldiers stayed behind, generals and top brass among them, working to pull the injured from the wreckage. But as he got there, someone yelled at everyone to get out and then the roof collapsed, front side first.

A graying officer passing him grabbed his arm with an iron grip. "No use, son. Don't go in there. One of those barrels dropped right down in front. Nobody could've made it out. Damn shame. I never thought the thing would work right. This just proves it. Too bad Roberts wouldn't listen." Across the road in the parking lot, the smoking car blew up in flames. "Geezuz, what a mess! Hope you didn't lose anybody in front." The officer gripped his shoulder and moved on. "I'm sorry if you did."

Not knowing whether to feel relieved or grieved, he ran back to find Perez waiting with the Prius's motor running. "No use," he said, climbing in, repeating the officer's words. Perez didn't ask him any more questions. They left the airbase just as a line of wailing police cars was coming the other way.

As they pulled over to let the police pass, Perez said, "We got company. Don't turn around. Check the side view."

Alex did. Behind them in the long line for the highway was the black SUV that had run Crittenden off the road. ""Let's take the long way home. They wouldn't be leaving Fulton Roberts there. They'd be waiting around to drive him to the airport."

They looked at each other, reading the answer in each other's faces. "He must have bought it," Perez said. "Then he must not have known there was anything but water in those barrels."

"Or Dalton either. He was up there, too."

They were on the highway to Diamondback, but Perez took the first exit off to a county road. After a couple of miles of checking the road behind them for the SUV, they relaxed a little and lit up cigarettes.

"It was Wu, then." Perez finally spoke as they turned off

on another dirt road and started up the ridge. "He switched the barrels. That way he gets the Eye system for himself, kills Roberts and Dalton, and puts Sutton out of business. The generals won't want it and the Arms Committee won't fund it. What'd Dalton say? Wu worked on it at UCLA so he thinks it belongs to him."

Alex studied the man he had met picking crops with Rudolfo's crew. "You'd make one helluva a good lawyer, Perry. That makes sense. They wouldn't have been up there in front if they'd known about the switch. But then Dalton gave me the impression he'd do just about anything to stop Roberts being re-elected. No problem now."

"If the colonel wanted to stop Fulton Roberts that bad, he wouldn't do it like that. That was messy and it'll attract attention. No, man. That's not his style. Now, somebody like say Freddie Wu or the Tiger, they could care less about some American generals. In fact, they'd probably get whatever passes for a Medal of Honor over there."

They were climbing up a narrow switchback road which ended when the pavement ran out. "Do you mind telling me where we're going?"

"This is the back road to Pierre's place. I just wanted to pay my respects." Again, the two traded glances. "I expect you do, too."

They pulled up some distance from Bighand's barn where several police vehicles were parked. "We've got to walk the rest of the way." Perry jumped out and strolled over to the nearest officer while Alex stayed by the car, afraid they'd ask for his ID. But Perez seemed to know everybody and, if he didn't, met them immediately. Several of the men went back into the barn, but one stood talking to Perez. Finally, they nodded, shook hands the Hispanic way, and Perry returned.

"Any leads?" Alex couldn't wait to ask him until they got back in the car.

"Took two guys to get him up there, naturally. Sheriff thinks it happened last night or early this morning. They're fingerprinting everything, doing the DNA thing, all that. I told him I'd ask my uncles to come over to get the horses and he said okay." They leaned on the hood of the car, looking down at the valley below where the burned strip of Turner land ran like a zipper across the earth. "Man, he loved this place. Now, I feel like he's still here, but up there with them." Perez nodded at the Devil's ladder outcrop with its nests of caves.

There wasn't anything to say except a prayer. Both of them did just that in the way men do, keeping it to themselves.

CHAPTER 23

She lay in total darkness, trying to breathe shallow breaths. Jonesy must be conserving air because the thumps had stopped since what she guessed was a half hour. At least, Murray hoped that was the reason. By rubbing her head against the surface of the crate she had managed to slip the gag down to her neck and free the upper part of her mouth. That helped her to gulp in some air and kept dizziness at bay. She concentrated on working her hands free of their bonds. It was agonizingly slow work and sapped her waning strength. Pausing to rest frequently, she had almost freed three of her fingers. What would she do then? She was in some kind of a box with metal barrels in one corner. *God help her and Jonesy if those barrels slid over on them.*

Murray gave one more thump and then fell asleep after hearing a tremendous answering thump. Jonesy wasn't about to give up, she could tell. He was just saving his strength for the right moment.

When she woke up, the crate was shuddering as if the floor were moving. She heard the sound of a powerful engine and felt a slight jerk. Then mercifully, through some tiny aperture in the crate, she felt air. They were in a truck and the truck was moving!

Wildly with hope, all thought of conserving energy gone, she began to kick the side of the crate. At once, she heard Jonesy's even more powerful stomps. They took turns, if not able to attract the driver's attention, at least to damage the crates, even find a weak spot that would give way. In her all-out effort, one of Murray's hands slipped loose from the rope that bound them together. Immediately jerking the gag down, she lay back breathing the foul-smelling but cool air. She was going to live.

℮ᗭ℮ᗭ

Perez had driven Alex up to Synotech in the Prius, arriving at ten to six as Dalton had planned. Neither of them talked much, both occupied with their own thoughts. On his pocket flap, Alex had the photo I.D. badge of Perry's cousin, who looked remarkable like him, grizzly beard and all.

They pulled up to the gate and when the guard saw it was Perez, they had what seemed like an agonizingly long conversation through the window about baseball. Then he waved them through.

"Don't tell me he's your gringo cousin."

"No, just went to high school with him. Used to fight him regular. Okay, just listen up." They had gone through the routine twice on the ride over, but Alex listened again. "Go up to the office, clock in. The clock machine's just outside the office door so don't go in, just wave. You've got the time card. Next to the time card machine is a rack with clipboards. Yours is the first one at the top of the row. It'll have the code letter printed real big at the top."

"I know. SAVGA515."

"You know better than me. Yours is the first truck in the bay. The card key unlocks it. But, before you climb in, walk around your rig like you're checking it out. Keep your head down. Check the tires, undercarriage, you know the routine. Then, just climb in. The dispatcher starts the rig with a code from the office exactly at six o'clock." They both looked at the dashboard clock. He had ten minutes.

"How the hell do you turn it off then?"

"It's built to run either way, in case of an accident or hijackers. But the standard keys are in a standard ignition just like a regular truck. But they can disable the key system from office computer."

"Through the Eye system. Got it." According to Dalton, the Eye system would be diverted to Africa at six pm. What if it weren't? In spite of Perez's testimony to his character and suffering, the man had remained an enigma to the end. At least, from the looks of the grandstand where the dignitaries had been sitting, there was no way the colonel could have lived to escape. On the way to see what could be done for Pierre Bighand, Alex and Perez had heard that the bodies of five people had been tentatively identified. One of them was Senator Fulton Roberts who was hit by flying debris. Specifically, a flaming barrel.

Alex and Perez had traded glances. "Destiny's a funny thing, right?"

Perez had a knack for saying the right thing at the right time and saying just enough.

The police were already there at Pierre's place when they arrived. When they left there, they turned around, they went to the Taqueria where the surly manager said Rick had taken the afternoon off. Something about a death in his girl's family. Leave it to Rick to get a girlfriend on the first date.

"Okay, go now. Mitch the dispatcher just got on the phone. He stays on it for ten-fifteen minutes a pop." Perez had held out his hand for a quick shake. "Go for it, *hombre. Vaya con Dios!*"

Alex went, sprinting across the yard to the office, doing the clocking in, waving at Mitch. The dispatcher merely acknowledged him with a thumbs up and turned back to his computer as if there were a problem.

It was all going like a dream, until a mechanic in the yard had hailed him. "Hey, Rojas!" At first, like the name

Vargas, it hadn't registered. Then he remembered, Rojas was Perry's cousin.

He had continued squatting, looking engrossed in studying the undercarriage, making check marks. "Yeah?"

"Mitch says the computer is weirding out, showing pictures of camels or some damn thing. Could be solar spots or something. So use the ignition key. Just check in on the computer log in for messages, okay?"

Log in? The password! Perry either had forgotten to tell him the password or he didn't know. "Log in might be screwed up, too. I'll be in contact on the radio, though, if that happens."

"That'll work. See ya."

It had worked. The truck started when Mitch the dispatcher punched in the code and the bay door opened. Alex had driven Uncle Miguel's old eighteen-wheeler during the summer, bringing truckloads of oranges to market, so he knew the basics of driving a semi. This baby, however, looked like the console of something from *Star Trek*. It even had a video camera which gave a continuous set of views: front, sides, and back of the vehicle. At any point in time, the driver had a view of what surrounded it on the road. One of the views was the interior of the cargo hold. A glance told him it was full of crates and in one of those, was the Eye System.

He switched on the radio only to find out it worked by voice command. The radio came on and, as he pulled out on the access road, the announcer was saying something about the air show disaster. Apparently, the experimental jet had flown back to Washington, DC where the pilot, Captain Benjamin Mason, had to issue a statement.

As the late Senator Roberts had said in a speech minutes before his death, the barrels were supposed to be filled with water. Instead, they had been filled with a toxic, flammable liquid and the FBI was suspecting it might have been a terrorist attack. Nothing was said about the identity of the other victims. Probably because they were having a hard time with identification.

As Alex turned the rig out on to the county highway, Dalton's beat-up Prius came from the side road and followed him. Perez hadn't said he would come along, but then they had become friends instead of acquaintances over the course of a harrowing afternoon. From the safety of the driver's seat high above the road, Alex watched the Western sun turn the sky into a palette of colors a master would envy—gold pools over deep blue melted into shades of rose. He glanced up at the ridge where yesterday, he and Pierre Bighand had stood looking at the valley below. Pierre mourning Shelby and now Alex was mourning Pierre.

'People around will drop like flies but no one can touch you. You're protected by the living and the dead. Listen.'

Alex told the radio to turn off and it obeyed efficiently. Above the rumble of the engine and rush of the air system, something snagged his attention. A sound. An irregular sound something mechanical wouldn't make, but something alive would. He watched the views of the camera—nothing, but Perez in the Prius. He gave the command for the computer to turn on and it obeyed, a log in screen appearing first. *Better not give it the wrong command or it might have a nervous breakdown*, he thought. He shut it off and glanced at the camera again, waiting for the view of the cargo hold to come up again. The sound seemed to be coming from back there.

As it roamed the corners of the hold like a human eye, unlike its prototype, the camera didn't blink as a slat popped out of the forward most crate. Unheeding of anomalies, it simply moved on to the next view of the Prius trailing behind him.

There was no place to stop, no shoulder wide enough for a big rig. Alex continued, flicking glances upward as if in the throes of a seizure. The county highway fed into the downhill slalom passing through the canyon walls, the road where Parker Crittenden had been run off the road. It was then he noticed the Prius pulling around him, playing Russian Roulette with the oncoming traffic.

"Hell, what's got into Perez?"

He forgot speaking aloud would set off the computer. "What's the problem?" the well-modulated woman's voice said. Like the GPS system, he knew they offered the customer a choice of guide's voices and Rojas had chosen a kind of sexy lady's voice to be at his command.

Aware he might be monitored, Alex played the game. "There's a couple of them right now. Some nut case is trying to cut me off and I'm in danger of jackknifing."

"Again, please. You're breaking up."

"That's about the size of it, miss."

"If you are breaking up, then please follow these instructions." As the guide yammered away, Alex geared down and hit the power brakes. A glance at the cargo hold told him that was a bad move. The crates shifted and then two feet, tied together, stuck out of the broken crate.

"Geeezuz! What was that?"

The sexy lady returned. "If you have a problem, please—"

"Oh, shut the hell off!"

The Prius was cutting the space between their bumpers short, hitting its brakes continuously as they rounded each curve. The light came on the console, indicating the cargo hold was out of alignment with the cab. Alex knew that meant there was a danger of jackknifing and took the next runoff ramp. The Prius was forced to continue down the highway to the end where it forked onto the Interstate. He pulled to a halt and got out, ignoring the droning computer which informed him of the dangers of being mugged. The shifted cargo light was on and he could only imagine what that meant for whoever belonged to the feet sticking out of the broken crate.

Going around to the back, he slid back the lynchpin holding the cargo hold doors shut and looked inside. He was met by a virtual sea of large crates nearly his height and large enough to house a tank, if not more. Alex vaulted up to the truck bed and edged along the shifted crates until he reached the feet sticking out of the crate.

"Hey," he said.

"Hey, yourself," a cavernous voice replied. "Get me the hell out of here."

It wasn't as simple as commanding the sexy lady to turn things on and off. He pulled on the feet without much success. Then Alex found a crowbar attached to the wall and used it to pry the crate further open. The smell was a mixture of human odor and kerosene and might have become a weapon on its own. The feet connected to a very large, golden-skinned man who inch-wormed his way through the aperture.

"We've got to get her out quick," he said while Alex worked at the ropes around his arms and feet. "Get your pocket knife on these things." He was a man accustomed to giving orders by the way he shouted in frustration.

"Sorry, flunked out of Boy Scouts. You said she. Are we talking about a woman?"

"That's usually the case. Now, use your keys. Works in the Hood."

It worked and they began opening the next crate where the thumping sound told them the occupant was still alive. She was still kicking after they pried open enough slates to pull Murray out.

She lay there on the truck floor like a captured mermaid, long light hair spread out in all directions, wide blue eyes trying to make sense of it all. Alex felt as if he had never seen anyone as beautiful as this sea-eyed girl. It was the girl from last night, Silk.

"It's you," she said, looking as if she couldn't believe what she was seeing. "I kept hoping you'd find me."

"Next time you go undercover, remind me to wear my cleats," the man said. "Detective Ronnie Jones," he said, extending his hand. "And I've never been so glad to meet somebody in my life." As they shook hands, Jonesy added, "Or have I?"

"Sorry, Detective." As the detective stared at him, Alex turned away quickly. "But I've got a schedule to stick to. Let's get the lady out and on her feet."

They lifted Murray down from the truck, sitting her on a nearby boulder while they worked the ropes loose around her ankles. When she tried to stand up, she sat down abruptly. "My feet feel like they're made of wood," she said. "Like they're asleep."

"If I was wearing those shoes, no telling what mine would feel like. But without those crazy heels, I wouldn't have heard you in that box. I just tore a brand new pair of Calvin Klein loafers in that crate." Jones began to rub her feet to bring the circulation back.

"If you ride up in the cab with me to the next exit, I'll drop you off so you can call somebody to come get you. Hate to rush you, but I've got to get back on the road." At any minute, Alex expected trouble in the forms of Rivera and Burnside or Perez and Springer. The list was growing and getting more dangerous by the second.

"Okay by us, right, Schmitzy? By the way, let me introduce you to the lady here."

Murray held on to Jonesy as she got to her feet. "It's fine," she practically shouted in his ear. "We've met. Hi, Jimmy." Then she glanced at his name tag. "That's not you. And it says Rojas."

"Hello, Miss Silk. We meet in strange ways. I'll explain later, but right now—" He glanced over his shoulder at the busy highway at the bottom of the run-off ramp. The black Jeep was in the slow lane and then, it abruptly pulled over. They had spotted the truck. "We have to get out of here. Close up the doors, will you, Detective?"

Without a word, he swept Murray up in his arms, and carried her to the passenger side. Jonesy was closing the doors when the SUV started up the ramp. A bullet whistled past him and bounced off the corner of the truck. "Here comes trouble," he yelled, dodging to the side of the truck for cover.

Alex got behind the wheel. "Get in!"

The engine was still running and as Jones jumped in beside the girl, Alex began backing down the ramp. The gunman in the SUV was still firing from the passenger side window, but when the semi began to roll down on them, he stopped.

In the side view mirror, Detective Jones watched the Jeep begin to back down. "This outfit you work for needs to work on their employee relations bad. Unfortunately, they took away my gun. That's probably it they're using on us right now, just to be nasty."

When they reached the bottom of the ramp, the SUV was waiting for them on the emergency shoulder. "I don't work for them, that's the problem. Look, I'm sorry, but you're going to have to ride with me the rest of the way. These guys mean business and if I stopped to let you out, you could get hurt and I could get killed."

"Two good reasons why we're riding with you. I know this is a dumb question, but if you don't work for these guys, what are you doing driving their truck?"

Alex was watching the surround camera as the rear view showed two men jumping from the SUV and running toward the truck. One was Angel Rivera, the other Burnside. So he had thrown in with Roberts, instead of his boss, Ed Dalton. With Roberts dead, would he jump ship again?

"If I weren't, you'd be on your way to China by way of Savannah, Georgia." Finding a space to merge on to the highway, Alex pulled the semi into the downhill traffic.

"I take your point," Jonesy replied. "We'll ride as far as you're going and then, I'm taking you in, Carreras. Correction, you're taking us in."

Sitting between them, Murray looked from one of them to the other. "Carreras? But he's not Alex Carreras, he's—" She turned to stare at the man behind the wheel. He was smiling that smile she'd seen in his photograph. "Oh, no! Yes, you are!"

Jones began to laugh, ranging from ho-ho to hee-hee-hee with annoying repetition.

"Oh, just shut up, Jonesy! You don't have to rub it in."

"Just enjoying the moment. You can't blame me."

The SUV was in the lane beside them now. "Better get down. The real bad guys are back."

"In other words, you hijacked their truck."

"To put a fine point on it, yes."

Jones stopped laughing. "Oh, swell. That kind of makes my day."

Alex was watching the SUV moving sharply ahead, the bumper nearly touching the truck's. "He's going to push us over and cut us off."

"To put an even finer point on it, you're the big dog. Slam him."

"That'll endanger the oncoming traffic." Murray sat up, speaking in crisp syllables. "We've got a problem!"

The computer lit up again. "Can I help?" the sexy voice asked. "What's the problem?"

"Oh, you've got one of these! I love these talking computers!"

"That makes me feel very good," the voice said. "Now how can I help you?"

"Well, there are some men shooting at us and trying to run us off the road. That's the problem." A video game nerd from the second grade, Murray addressed the computer like a girlfriend.

"Give me a minute to parse your question. Be right with you."

"In the meantime, we could get killed." Beside her, Jonesy moaned. "No wonder kids don't use their brains anymore."

The computer voice returned, registering neither fear nor urgency in its pleasant tones. "There is no problem. The exterior of the entire vehicle you are driving is bullet-proof up to an including a Sherman tank artillery shell. Any sort of ammunition will merely bounce off the hull. This includes the windows with the exception of the artillery shell. In the instance of being cut off by traffic, merely coast to the emergency shoulder, lights flashing and come to a full stop. You will be safe within the vehicle. Do not emerge from the vehicle. Help will arrive. Do you have any other commands?"

"Yes. Shut up!" Jonesy yelled. The computer acknowledged by going dark. "Carreras, where the hell are you taking this thing?"

Alex was braking, allowing the SUV to cut sharply in front of him to the inside lane. "Hold on," he said, cutting the wheel left to put the truck in the spot just vacated. Then, with the SUV nearest the rocky wall, he began to move over slowly, knowing from Crittenden's accident in the morning, there was no shoulder.

"Gotcha." Jonesy slipped the seatbelt around Murray and locked his arms around her. "Slam 'em, baby."

As they approached the tight curve, Alex edged the truck over to close in on the SUV. Tires smoking, it burned rubber in an effort to avoid hitting a rock slide just at the edge of the road. Their last glimpse of it as they rounded the curve was the smoking front end perched up on a large boulder. "Now, that's what I call LA driving, baby," Jonesy said. "Man, I like that move."

Alex breathed again, realizing he'd been holding in his breath. "That won't be the last of them, but it'll buy us some time."

"Time to do what?" She looked over at Jones. "I'm okay now, Jonesy. You can buy me a car seat when we get back."

He took his arms from around her waist. "But Schmitzy, I thought we were working on our teamwork."

"We're just not joined at the hip, thanks. But thanks for coming to look for me. Without you, they never would have found us. And thank you, Jimmy. Um, Mr. Carreras."

"You've got the jump on me, Miss. Is your name really Silk?"

Jonesy started in again with the ho-ho, hee-hee again and she jabbed him in the ribs. "Sorry, but I just love the whole scene. Silk in the four-inch heels. You, the Century City hot-shot lawyer hijacking a truck. And me, Jonesy, riding with a hijacker. Is this role-reversal or what?"

"My real name is Murray," she said, ignoring the chortling Jones. "Murray Schmitz. My parents were expecting a boy."

"I think I like Silk better. Sort of suits you."

Detective Jones rolled his eyes. "Oh, brother. So what's in the truck, besides us, that is? They can't want us this bad."

"Company." Alex looked at the monitor. There was a helicopter approaching fast, lowering as if it were going to land on the roof. Unbidden, the computer came on, this time using a man's authoritarian voice. "Driver, you are to stop immediately. Repeat, stop immediately by order of Synotech Director of Headquarters. In ten minutes, your engine will be shut off. Find a safe exit from the road and remain there until further notice."

Ten minutes. Would he make it to the safety of the water in time?

"Computer," Jones yelled. "Tell the Director of Headquarters this is the FBI and we're confiscating this whole damn truck, you got that?"

The computer lit up again. "How can I help you? What's the problem?"

"Oh, never mind. Go back to your tea, or whatever. So what's up, Carreras? I imagine you didn't just start driving this liability-on-wheels without a plan." The two detectives looked at Alex and then up at the monitor where the helicopter hovered. "Uh-oh, I don't think that's the CHP boys up there."

"I think this cab is also monitored for sound as well as for picture," Alex said. "So I'll keep my plan to myself and, yes, I have one. By now, you realize, they can't let any of us live, and they have no qualms about killing people, believe me. And I've got plenty of proof on that score."

Jones nodded. "I'll bet. Keep us alive and you'll have even more proof. Okay, we're in your hands. You got us out of that hellhole back there. You're the man. I just wish we could return the favor."

In spite of the situation, Alex smiled again, noticing that was happening a lot lately. "Just testify for me if this goes to court. But I think, when the DA hears the evidence, he'll exonerate me of all charges." He glanced out the window where a red pickup had come up beside him in the passing lane. The driver blew his horn in three short blasts and flashed his lights. "Ricky! What the hell?"

"Rick's your kid brother, right? Going into the police academy, I hear. Man, I got to say you two guys are awesome."

They watched as the pickup stayed in the lane beside them in spite of the SUV riding its bumper.

"He's going to get killed before he goes anywhere." Alex pressed the semi's foghorn and waved. In the side view mirror, the SUV, damaged bumper aslant, was inches away from Rick's light pickup. There was another semi in the lane directly behind the Synotech truck. The SUV was locked in! He got the picture and started laughing. "That damn kid! He's blocking the SUV!"

Like racehorses on the inside rail, the vehicles stayed in a tight group—Rick blocking the outside lane, the helicopter keeping pace, and Alex's rig leading the pack. Eight minutes to go and they were nearly to the Interstate. From there, he guessed it would be another five to the first beach and the safety of water.

"When I slow down, you guys are going to jump and roll, okay?" He looked over at the girl who looked like she rode a semi into the Pacific Ocean every day. "Can you do that?"

"You're planning to dump us on the freeway like unwanted pets?" Her eyes seemed to change shades of blue, as if clouds were passing over the ocean. In the warm glow of the sunset, she appeared to be made of sea and sunlight.

"No, I'll be humane." After stealing another glance at her, Alex reluctantly kept his eyes on the road. There was a deep calm about her, as if jumping out of a moving vehicle were as routine as brushing her teeth. "I'll let you out where it's a lot softer."

"What'd he say?" Above the roar of the chopper, Jones cupped his ear.

"He said he isn't going to dump us out in the traffic."

"That's decent of you, Carreras. Can we get a heads-up when is this happening?"

"In about six minutes. Get ready. Looks like my brother'll be giving you a ride." They heard two gunshots and Rick's right rear tire blew out. The red truck fishtailed on the smoking tire, but Ricky got it back under control. "Maybe not."

Jones swallowed hard. "It's okay. We'll hitchhike home. I count on our Miss Silk here to get us a ride."

"Funny. I'm sticking with you," she said to Alex. "After all, strictly speaking, you are my prisoner."

"I saw him first, Schmitzy. He's mine, all mine," Jonesy replied in a falsetto voice.

Alex was keeping an eye on Rick's slowing truck and smiled as the traffic began to bottle up behind him. "Looks like there's more than a tire smoking out there. There's no way that SUV's going to get a chance to move over unless some nice guy lets them in line. Fat chance on this road. Either way, they'll be way back there. That buys us some time."

They hit the 101 doing seventy, and drivers moved over as the huge purple truck with flashing lights merged. Even more impressive was the helicopter above it which the drivers mistook for the CHP patrol and immediately slowed down. Five and a half minutes to go to the first beach access road. He had surfed the entire coast for years and knew every unofficial entry from Monterrey to Mexico. That way, as penniless high school kids, they wouldn't have to pay for parking.

He saw the unmarked road coming up but there was a chain across it. A sign said No Trespassing. *Nothing stays the same.* Slowing to make the turn, he put the big rig into low gear. If the engine shut down, he wouldn't have enough momentum to get down to the water. Completely faked by the move, the helicopter shot on ahead before banking to turn around. A voice was still blaring orders as it faded away.

"What the hell are you doing?" Jones sat up, putting his hands on the dash. "Don't you see the chain across that road? You got to stop, man!"

"Sorry, just add trespassing to my rap sheet." The rig not only took out the chain, it brought the two posts along with it. "Now, open the door and jump and roll. The sand will cushion the fall."

"Do as the man says, Schmitzy. I can't swim."

"No, I'm staying with him until we stop. Besides, I'd rather jump in the water. I need a bath in the worst way."

Jones opened the door and balanced on the running board. "Suit yourself. Drowning ain't in my job description. Bonsai!" With a yell, he jumped and rolled head over heels in the sand.

The beach had changed over the years. Instead of the deserted white-sand strip it had been, there were signs it had changed hands. Several fancy sailboats and a catamaran were pulled up on the sand in front of them. Beach umbrellas and lounge chairs littered the pristine beach.

Seeing a sailboat directly in their path, Murray said, "Oh, no, you're not going to—you are going to."

"Hope they send the bill to Synotech. You can still jump, you know." He looked over at her and caught her staring at him.

"No," she said. "You've done okay so far. I'll stick with you."

He rolled both windows down just as the engine cut off and, silently, they rolled over the sailboat and into the sea. Clouds of steam rose up around them as the hot undercarriage hit the cold water. The huge purple cab hissed and rumbled as water hit the engine. It roared like some mythical sea monster returning to its lair in the depths.

They looked at each other and then he took her hand and kissed it. "Thanks," he said.

"For what?"

"For believing in me."

She made a concerted effort to appear in charge. "Mr. Carreras, I'm arresting you for…for saving my life. Now get the hell out of this truck and never let me set eyes on you again. No, forget I said that." The water was seeping into the cab over the floorboards.

"No, Silk, my friend. You'll set eyes on me in court, and I hope we're both real people by then. Now, can you slide out through that window and just ease on into the water? It's about up to your waist here." He watched her lithe body do just that, ease out holding on to the door strap and put a leg over the side of the truck.

"'Bye, Alex," she said before she dropped to the running board and from there, into the water. Seeing her safely out, he slid out of the window, pulled his long legs over the side, and dove into the water. When he came up for air, he saw the SUV pull on to the beach, bouncing almost down to the waterline.

Rivera and Burnside jumped out, firing at him and the girl as they ran into the shallow water. Alex dove down, as bullets sped by him. He knew the beach well and that it deepened farther away from shore where the shelf dropped down abruptly. Swimming in that direction, he also remembered the riptide ran offshore, with its treacherous undertow. Coming to the surface for air, he looked around to see if the girl was nearby. The shoreline was now farther away and the gunmen were running along the beach, away from the direction Silk had gone. If he led them far enough along the beach, they would encounter a rocky point next to impossible to cross.

Swimming underwater, he finally felt the chill of deeper water and surfaced. In the distance, Rick's truck bounced down to the sand, followed by three police cars. The girl was wading toward shore where her detective partner waited for her, arms open wide.

Alex made it around the point and started fighting the strong current to come ashore. It carried him farther than he had anticipated, and just as his strength was fading, it released him from its grip. He half floated, half crawled to shore and lay on the sand with waves lapping his lower body.

"Well, look at Superman just lying there like a dead fish," a voice said above him. He straightened up to see Angel Rivera standing on the rocky point, with a pleased smirk on his face. He was holding a gun. "I got to hand it to you, though, Carreras. For a man with a price on your head, you ain't been no easy target, I'll say that. See, your woman Chelsea, is it? She and her new man gave me a real nice bonus to get rid of you, and I hate to disappoint such a good looking lady. I say bonus because the senator set me up for life in my own car operation. Besides that, I owe you for seven years hard time in the pen. So it was a deal I couldn't refuse. Get rid of Carreras and you get out on parole plus all that money. So I took it."

Alex got to his feet, presenting an even better target. "You killed the girl, then, didn't you, Rivera?"

Rivera was savoring the moment, allowing the pistol to stray off target as he shrugged. "So? She was a snitch. That kid was going to pull the plug on the big boys' operation. Forget her! She wasn't nothing special, man. Besides, your very own homies set you up. You are one real unpopular guy, Carreras. Seems like nobody but Mama'll miss you."

A rock tumbled down from the point behind Rivera. The sound distracted his attention for a millisecond, and Alex charged across the sand, ready to kill him with his bare hands.

But Rivera caught the movement and fired. The bullet caught Alex in the side, spinning him around and he sprawled on the sand. A second shot rang out, then a third, and a fourth.

"The first one was for Shelby," a familiar laconic voice said, "the next one was for Pierre, and that last one was for Carreras."

Rivera's lifeless body rolled down the rocks to the sand.

"Anger can be fatal, Alex. Next time, remember that." Ed Dalton's voice rang out from the rocky point. "I can see from here you're not hit in a bad place so I'd better get going. The chopper's waiting for me and Syd. The cops are running this way and that girl with them is a looker, by the way. Perez won't be going with us. We found him by the plant gate. Rivera and Burnside must've coldcocked him and then taken the Prius. You'll both be okay and you've got all the stuff you need to win your freedom. And you never know when I might need a good lawyer, so stay in touch."

Dalton turned to go and then had another thought. "And. by the way, I'm taking Darla and the baby with me to the island, after I spring Darlene out of jail for the twentieth time. I'm even taking Darlene along to dry out so she can babysit her granddaughter. Hell, it's been a rough afternoon. I could use some R and R. Never thought dropping a cup of beer would save my life. I was getting a refill when all hell broke loose."

The helicopter was back, settling in shallow water at the edge of the beach, blaring orders as it landed. "Damn! Forgot that's a prerecorded voice left over from its old days in the CHP," Dalton said as he went by. "I'd give you a lift but the paramedics are on the way and I'm out of practice."

Something landed in the sand beside Alex as Dalton's long shadow fell over him. He was too weak to pick up what look like a microchip. "That's Rivera's confession, in case you need it. Don't think you will, but it'll sure put a kink in Chelsea's and Hardaway's plans. Take it from Syd, nobody wants to hire a jailbird except people like me. Remember me."

As the light was slipping away, she was there bending over him. It was the girl with the sea-blue eyes, her wet hair smelled of flowers drifting over him as she cradled his head. "You can't leave me now that I've found you, Alex Carreras. Stay with me. You have to stay with me."

❧❧❧

He drifted away and followed a long winding procession up the ridge below the Devil's Ladder. Ahead of him, Pierre's body, wrapped in buckskin, was being carried to the burial cave by people all in white. With rattles and drums, spirit voices sang the old chief to eternal sleep. At the top of the ridge, he saw a young girl dressed in white. She looked familiar, but he couldn't recall her name. Then she smiled and he knew who she was, except this time, she was alive and her wounds all healed.

"It's not time," she said in a voice softer than falling snow. "You have to go back. Go back."

He woke up in a white room looking at another girl. This one had hair like sunshine and eyes like the sea.

"It's you," Silk said, with a smile and he realized she was holding his hand. "I've been waiting for you to come back."

About the Author

Even as a child, Trisha O'Keefe was impressed by the inherent power of alternative medicines. Indigenous healing practices are an ongoing theme in her novels. As a native Southerner, O'Keefe claims to have "a lot of red dirt" flowing in her veins. Growing up, she spent summers on her uncle's farm in South Georgia, "mainly getting into trouble." That trend has continued throughout her life.

After traveling abroad for fourteen years, running into revolutions or governmental coups nearly everywhere she went—even Britain was in the midst of a labor strike when she moved there—she returned to the States. She is the daughter of Jimmy Jones, a well-known journalist for the Atlanta Constitution under Editor Ralph Magill. One of her earliest memories was the sound of a typewriter rattling away in the middle of the night. You would think that would have cured her from ever putting two words together, let alone a book. Still, at age six, she co-wrote *Spot, The Dog* with her sister, followed a long time later by *Hanahatchee*, *Poseidon's Eye*, *Love Song of the Chinaberry Man*, *The Magi's Well*, *The Mama Tree*, and *Of Unknown Origin*. "I guess some things you can't cure," O'Keefe says. "You just have to go where they take you."

www.ingramcontent.com/pod-product-compliance
Lightning Source LLC
Chambersburg PA
CBHW070742120726
47910CB00001B/143